Tales from
the moe.Republic

or

(The Chronicles of brother John of the House of moe.)

by
John Derhak

John Derhak
383

Featuring Original Cover Art
by
Chuck Garvey

back channel press
portsmouth new hampshire
www.backchannelpress.com

Tales from the moe.Republic

or

(The Chronicles of brother John of the House of moe.)

Copyright © 2006 John Derhak

ISBN: 978-0-9789546-7-3

BACK CHANNEL PRESS

170 Mechanic Street

Portsmouth, NH 03801

www.backchannelpress.com

Printed in the United States of America

Cover layout by Becca Childs Derhak

Design and layout by Nancy Grossman

Library of Congress PCN 2007926833

A note to the reader:

moe. is an award-winning rock and roll band. They are Al Schnier, Jim Loughlin, Vinnie Amico, Chuck Garvey, and, as you'll soon meet, my brother Rob. Reluctant pranksters or not, I want to thank moe. for allowing me to bring them along, to journey to the Lost Kingdom of Moose Harbor with me, and vice-versa. The foundation for the moe.Republic Hotel rests upon their shoulders and I'm very grateful. All of the moe.tunes mentioned herein are compositions from their widely available discography. They've been on the road to destiny for over fifteen years now, honing their artistic skills, and spreading their brand of music throughout the hinterland and beyond. I can only hope the following tales give you, dear reader, half as much pleasure as I have had listening to moe.'s music over the years.

If music be the food of love…
…play on!

– William Shakespeare

For Wendy...
...the story of my life

Contents

The moe.Republic Hotel
in the Heart of the Lost Kingdom

The moe.Microbrewery
Off the Liberty Ballroom
March 23, 2:21 a.m.

Dear Reader: the following letters and emails stem from a volume of correspondence over the past decade or so from me, your humble publican, brother John, to my brother Rob, your friendly bass player for moe. and my co-conspirator and investor in our little hotel, the moe.Republic.

Long-time moe. fans may be familiar with some of these letters. A few, in abbreviated form, appeared in the old moe.newsletter from the mid-1990s, under the column entitled, "feedin' at the trough." That column ran for five years, when, with the advent of the web, the moe.newsletter, and thusly, the column, followed the path of the dodo.

Until now! Poor old Rob's been asked so many times by so many people whatever happened to me or how things were going at the hotel, that he finally caved and decided to go public with our correspondence and clue you in.

These letters and emails are more than a "howdy do." I promised Rob when I hooked him in the gills that I'd keep him apprised of everything happening here—compiling the daily comings and goings, extraordinary events, and all the ups and downs of family, friends, fans, and philistines far and wide. Though by no means are these the complete letters, they should give one and all a good idea of what we've been up to from the humble beginnings to where we are today. In total, the correspondence here represents a chronicle of sorts for life at the moe.Republic Hotel, organized and presented in acts, over varying periods of time.

I might add that these are the true, unedited, unexpurgated communiqués. My word is my own, as are all errors in style, punctuation, etcetera. That said, enjoy the read, and,

Viva la moe.Republic!

As for me, I'll be "feedin' at the trough,"

brother John

Act I

The Old Mountain by the Sea:
A Mighty Pitch is Thrown

Bullwinkle Lodge & Cabins
Upper Bean's Point
on Moose Harbor

Somewhere in the Lost Kingdom
Tuesday, 9:17 p.m.

Dear Rob,

Father always said it would come to this. Not that I'd end up a basket case, but that my days of wandering would eventually come to an end. "Sooner or later even the last tumbleweed rolls no more, boy," he'd tell me. "One day it bounces into town, the next day the wind dies down, and that old weed takes to root and rolls no more. That's just how it goes."

I've heard that more than once over the years. And I heard it again last week when the two of us took to the road with a fistful of cigars and a battered road map to guide us. Me and the prairie dog's Confucius, cruising in a '58 Rambler, in search of prize real estate for our hotel-country inn project. We've been on the move, too, making time—up and down the coast, over the mountains, along winding roads, and across the plains. A host of carnies and hucksters posing as real estate agents have paraded us through ramshackle dumps, pretentious palaces, and desolate swamplands. Too much driving, really, in such little time. I was set to cave when father received a tip on a happening spot up the Maine coast. A trucker filled him in at a rest stop. The guy had a payload of wood flour, which got the best of father's curiosity.

"Wood flour?" father asked. "For what?"

"It's a filler," he replied, except 'filler' sounded closer to 'phillah.' "For toilet seats and doughnuts. We got both ends of the market covered!" He smiled and gave a shrug. "Think of it as sifted gold!" It was pretty much all he had to say. Father being the consummate businessman, they struck up a conversation. The next thing I knew we were off to the low mountains on the eastern frontier, a place the trucker called the Lost Kingdom.

I was spent and in no mood to drive for hours into the wilderness. "Just a little farther, boy," father pushed me on, "and the tumbleweed rolls no more." He chuckled at his own wit. Up and down rugged hills we traversed. On and on, climbing higher and higher past windswept terrain. We nearly drove the Rambler into the ground on that last mountain pass. The valves were tapping Morse code. Father was cursing and swearing like he had hives. At me, the car, or the trucker? I did not ask and did not want to know. Once we cleared the pass I could see the ocean. I threw the beast in neutral to cool her down, thinking it would be a good thing to coast. Which it was until we hit G-force resistance about a third of the way down the mountainside. I'm not sure if it was the brakes that were smoking on that final turn or if it was father's death grip on his St. Christopher's medal. I have to admit that I was relieved when we rolled into this secluded town. The big, old road sign read: "Welcome to Downeast Way—the Last Sanctuary and Hope for Western Civilization and Your Investment Dollar."

It's been one heck of a road trip, but I think it was worth it. I think we've finally found the perfect spread. Our harrowing journey and everlasting search hath ended.

Quite frankly, when I consider all the miles we put behind us this week, I have to give you credit. How do you do it? Being on the road that is, playing all those concerts, week after week. How do you get any sleep for starters? Especially if Chuck snores as loud as you say he does. Cause I couldn't take another night of the old man's. After a while it sounded like a tuba stuck up a goat's ass. To top it off, those Super Deluxe Econo-Motels we stayed in had vibrating beds. One quarter, thirty seconds later, father was in purgatory, and the band played on. The last night on the road he snored so loud that the windows rattled. At least I think it was his snoring that caused the rattling. Might have been that preacher fellow and his twenty-something year old daughter in the next room. A night's stop, the preacher told me, on their way to a nice Baptist retreat up the coast. That guy must have had a pocket full of change because I could hear that bed humming through the wall for hours. Every now and then I'd hear a shout or a shush, too. It was embarrassing. Father snored so loud that that poor fellow and his daughter couldn't sleep, either.

Anyway, I'm writing this from Downeast Way, at the heart of the Lost Kingdom of Moose Harbor. The property we've honed in on is an old mansion, an expansive estate known as Huxley Manor. Father and I think it's a swell place for the hotel. The mighty Atlantic beckons at our door. That mountain which nearly bagged the Rambler, Mount Agamenticus, shoots up behind the property and over the town. There's sort of an aura about this place—the whole region—an energy that draws you in. It's hard to explain. Everybody's friendly and everyone has a story. We arrived Saturday, but I feel right at home.

The first morning in town we chanced upon Kinghorn's Diner for breakfast before going to the realtor's. I should say we chanced upon this cop,
Mickey McO'Fayle. He was sitting in his squad car, a '71 Jeep Commando,
with headphones on listening to music. "Gentlemen!" he shouted from across
the street, waving us over. Father and I were pounding the pavement, aimlessly, searching for a coffee shop or something. I thought the copper was
going to give us the once over. "'Panama Red,'" he said, holding his hand up,
pausing, continuing to listen to the music barely audible through the headset.

"Huh?" father mumbled, confused. "Panama? Who's Red? What Commie?"

"Apologies," he grinned, pulling the headset off. "I got carried away for
a moment. That's the name of the song, mister."

"'Panama Red,'" I said, relieved. "Jesus, you had me there for a second.
Thought it might be a sting."

"Nah, just an old favorite," he replied, grinning. "There's something
about waking up and listening to a good tune here, first thing in the morning,
especially on a beautiful day like this." He swept his hand over the wide
square. Rows of old brownstones surrounded half the square in a semicircle.
The buildings overlooked an oversized common with intersecting cobble-
stone walkways, lined neatly with well-manicured shrubbery, lampposts, a
few pine trees, and numerous benches. Trawlers, in the distant harbor beyond, navigated in and out of a wispy, light fog. There was an old fort, too, on
the far point, and a lighthouse even farther. "I lift the top off the Commando,"
he continued, "do my thing, and take it all in."

"It's nice," I said. "The view *and* the song. Takes me back." That was
enough for the old man. I caught the calculated cadence of father's eyes as they
rolled in syncopation deeply into his sockets. His stomach rumbled. "We go
back a long way, me and that song." I was feeling bold. "But I never met a cop
who listened to the New Riders, let alone drive one of these old Commandos."

"Most cops drive a Crown Vic," father added. "They got punch and
plenty of room."

"Most cops don't have to drive cross-country in an ice storm, ford a
mountain stream, or plow through a nor'easter—and that's just in one day."
He patted the dash board affectionately. "They also don't take their own car
to work."

"This baby's yours?" I asked, quite surprised. He nodded yes. "That's
insane!"

"Tell me. Would you rather drive around in a big-ass, rear-wheel drive, gas guzzling, piece-of-crap-Ford sedan or take the top off this beauty and cruise the scene?" He looked at us both. "Yeah! I thought so."

"You're going to drive this classic into the ground," father told him with concern. There's an affinity the old man has for classic cars. When our dear sister Liza blew the engine in the Rambler years back he could have put her down for good. He would have, I suppose, except mother wouldn't let him get near Liza for six weeks. So instead, he rebuilt the engine. After all these years, the Rambler rolls on and our dear sister lives blissfully for it.

"Such is the fate of us all," Mickey shrugged. "We're not going to last forever. Besides, the town pays me a good nut to keep it tip top. I got a hundred eighty-seven thousand miles on her now. I think it's good for at least another one-hundred fifty thousand before she's ready for the big sleep," he spoke confidently. "By then I'll have located another one."

"Could we talk after breakfast?" father implored.

"Ah! So that's what you two young bucks were up and about for, aye?" he said. "I should have known."

"Sort of," I replied. "We are, but we're also checking out the town."

"Hop in," he said enthusiastically. "I'll give you a lift over to Kinghorn's Diner and you can fill me in."

"On what?" asked Father.

"Whatever it is you're looking for?"

"How do you know we're looking for something, not just out for a stroll?" I asked him.

"Well for starters, you looked lost. You had that look." He said it like such a thing was common knowledge. "I'll tell you, about half a dozen times a year a moose or two will come wandering right here through town. Right in the middle of Market Square! It never fails, and each and every one of them has the same lost, out-of-sorts, 'where the fuck am I?' look that you two had." He laughed and we did too. He was picking up some speed and the cool morning air stung our faces. We rushed by a number of townhouses and storefronts—a bookshop, cigar store, apothecary, liquor store—in a blur.

"Secondly," he continued, "I was out behind the welcome sign yesterday afternoon doing the radar when I saw this Rambler approaching at mach one. I was thinking, his brakes probably went about a mile back, at about the 7% grade. That the old mountain's launched another one." He gave us a knowing look, while shifting the jeep into fourth. "Out-of-towners for sure. Uninitiated in the ways the 'old man' eases you into town. I saw the look of holy terror on your faces begin to ease up when you coasted by. I'd have pulled you over except I just had lunch. I didn't want to chance inhaling a carload of shit. Probably'd made me hurl."

Well, father laughed so hard I thought *he* was going to right then and there. But we hadn't had breakfast yet and disaster was averted. We told him who we were and all about our enterprise. He thought it was a great idea and wished us all the best. Turns out that Mickey McO'Fayle is the Chief of Police. I learned that when he dropped us off. "Hope you find what you're looking for," he said sincerely, stopping in front of the diner. "Best breakfast in town," he boasted. "Better have those brakes checked out, too," he added. "Bring the car to Buck's Garage. It's over on Grove Street. Tell Buck that the Chief sent you. He's a bit loquacious, but entertaining and honest."

"What more could you want from a mechanic?" said father. We thanked the Chief for the lift and went in. Within a few minutes father was through his second helping of the 99¢ special—one over easy, with a side of baked beans, cornbread, and coffee—when we got to talking to one of the diner's owners, Alexander Bigwood, about what we're doing and the whole project. Thought I'd put it out there. The place was hopping and I figured a little networking would help our cause. The guy was receptive and gave us the inside scoop on the Huxley place. "Right on the edge of town," he said. "Beautiful spread. Wedged in between Crowe's Farm and Moose Harbor." Bigwood, along with his partner, Dr. Jack Kinghorn, apparently wear many hats around town, because they also have a law practice and dabble in real estate among a few other things. Bigwood's also an attorney who used to be a big city cop. Kinghorn's also a realtor who used to be sociologist. I found that out from some waitress in the diner. Anyway, as it turns out, they represent the owners of the Huxley place, a couple of sisters who live on the adjacent property. Seems that they're getting too old to keep the estate up. The last heir, a great-nephew, died years ago. Nobody's lived in the manor house for I don't know how long and the sisters are ready to sell.

After we finished breakfast Bigwood took us up to the property for a walk through. The place needs a bit of work and renovating. It's kind of spooky looking, but overall it's impressive. We drove between a set of brick gateposts, up a long driveway, under a canopy of maple trees. The car rolled to a stop in front of a massive four-pillared portico, which covers the main entrance and a broad, three-step marble stoop. The doors open into a cavernous front hallway. There's wide, dual, winding staircases that spiral up four floors. The balconies have ornately hand-carved railings. When you walk in, off to the left is a set of French doors that lead into an expansive parlor with a large brick fireplace on the back wall. It's incredible! I can see a bar running the length of the room. There's six rooms on the second floor and four rooms on the third and fourth floors, and plenty of room for an addition. There's a carriage house, too, sitting out back, that's a third the size of the manor house. The view is to die for and we're under budget.

Well, I've got to go. Bigwood's coming by and taking us back out to the house for another good, hard look. Enclosed are a bunch of photos. I'll shoot off an update next week, or call me when you get an extra dime. In any event, remember, when you're 'feedin' at the trough,' hogs get fat, pigs get slaughtered.

Till then,
brother John

Bullwinkle Lodge & Cabins
Upper Bean's Point
on Moose Harbor

That day at Buck's Garage
Saturday,
11:19 p.m.

Dearest Robért,

What do you mean it's too far out in the boondocks? It's an old fashioned country inn and hotel. Where's it suppose to be? On 42nd and Broadway? This place is cool and ripe for tourist dollars. People want to get *away*. Times are fucking crazy. I'm telling you this is the place to get away *to*! We're talking vacation land, baby. Think of the spin we have here. The potential's as enormous as the old mountain by the sea, Mount Agamenticus. Rising above the town and harbor like a lone sentry, the mountain guards the entrance to the Lost Kingdom. That trucker was right about this place. Though not really lost, nor really a kingdom, local folks take pride in calling the region such because they know more than most that the mountain, if anything, has kept their small slice of terra firma isolated and alone throughout the centuries. The community is nestled in between steep rocky ledges on either side of the bay. Think of the town as a babe resting in its mother's arms. Ridges rise gradually from the sea. They run perpendicular from the coast, melding into the base of Agamenticus, which tops out at fifteen-hundred feet.

And it's not just scenic, there's also the scene. Serious mojo. Positive karma. One with nature. Cosmic confluence. You catch my drift? Father and I got the scoop yesterday at Buck's Garage. We took the Chief's advice. The harrowing sojourn here necessitated triage on the Rambler. We drove the old beauty over to Grove Street and made a grand entrance. Pulling in, as if on cue, the car backfired and came to a squeaky halt. The guy at the front counter looked as though he'd won the lottery. Who could blame him? He turned out to be the owner, Buck Jones. Father had him buttonholed in minutes. Lean and wiry, you wouldn't have thought Buck could keep up with the old man's gift of gab. He greeted us with a handshake and a smile. Before you knew it, he and father were smoking cigars and getting into it. Buck was a marine biologist who gave it up years ago when he happened upon the town one summer. Sailed right into the harbor on an expedition and never looked back. The man's been here ever since. "There's an attraction about this place that pulls you in," he told us. "The past is alive and walks into the present." I asked him what he meant. "It's a long story," he replied. "Not for the faint-hearted nor dull-witted." I told him I'd been to hell and back more than once and he laughed. I was glad that I passed the first test. On any other day I could have gone for the Cliff Notes version, but we had nothing *but* time. One of Buck's boys was all over the Rambler. The diagnosis was a valve job and new brakes. No surprise on this end, all things considered. We got comfortable in a set of Adirondack chairs, which were lined up in front of the garage. Father lit the cigars, and we found ourselves immersed in the way of the Lost Kingdom.

I didn't have a Zen experience out in front of that gas station, if that's what you're thinking. But old Buck did dance with his words—enough that it made for good theater. "Everything's about the mountain," he started. "A natural landmark, it guided English fishermen here as early as the1580s. Each June and July they'd arrive, set up weirs on the outer islands, and hunker down for the summer. The first European to put it on the map was Captain John Smith, who'd run into trouble farther south in a settlement called Jamestown, and as legend has it, was spared by a young woman named Pocahontas. That was years before the summer of 1614 when he explored the rugged coastline of all parts Down East, Moose Harbor, and Cape Cod—the very same region hailed just a few years later by the great party-crashers of all-time, those indomitable flatlanders, who gave meaning to the concept of pilgrim, the Puritans," he said sharply. "As a man of inestimable vision and endless imagination, Captain John called the region he mapped that summer *New* England, then promptly returned to *Olde* England where he remained till his dying day, wanting nothing more but one last opportunity to gaze upon the old mountain by the sea. But such as dreams are made of, it was not to be."

Buck stopped abruptly when a car with Massachusetts plates pulled in tight beside us. The driver, a bit disheveled and haggard, shouted out, "Hey buddy! Is this the road to Dover-Foxcroft?" The wife was at his side. A cigarette dangled from her meticulously painted lips. There were a couple of really young kids in back whining loudly.

"No sah," Buck replied in a sharp Maine accent he hadn't flushed before. "You can't get there from here. You gotta go back that way," he pointed toward the mountain.

"Okay," the guy said obediently, and took off.

"I always wanted to say that," I said.

"Say what?" answered Buck innocently, still floating the accent. "Now? Where was I?" he asked, speaking as he had before, blinking innocently.

"You were telling us about Captain John," father replied rolling his cigar between his teeth, grinning at the scene.

"That's right," Buck continued. "Even if Captain John had returned to Moose Harbor he would have found more than he had imagined. Long before the coming of the Europeans, the indigenous tribes *summered* along the shores, fishing and feasting on lobster, which was so abundant that the giant, hard-shelled bugs could be gathered by the hundreds along the rocky shoreline at low tide."

"The missus would've liked it here back then," father interrupted him. "She's a lobster nut."

"When you move here you can bring her over to Lizard's Lobster Pound," Buck suggested. "It's right next to an old Indian ceremonial site."

"A ceremonial site?" Father's curiosity was aroused. "What kind of ceremony?"

"Well," Buck hesitated, "let's just say it was kind of a baptism. At night the natives built huge bonfires. They smoked the pipe and dropped mushrooms. Then danced with their ancestors or howled in unison with the wolves perched atop the high ridges; or maybe rode with the magical bursts of light— the aurora borealis— streaming from the heavens into the nether regions of *matter gray* between their ears. At the full moon commenced the great orgies, building to sensual heights beyond the pale scope of the crackers who were gradually drifting toward their shores."

Forget mother, I thought, my imagination drifting. Oh Pan, take *me* back to the Garden of earthly delight.

"The Indians were uninhibited and unashamed," Buck continued. "The meanings had no concepts. Most of the Europeans who witnessed the midsummer evening rituals—bonfires, psilocybic episodes, and sex—were stunned. The Puritans were appalled. A few white men joined in, however, and that was the beginning of the end for the natives."

Buck paused for a moment. "You boys still with me?" he asked respectfully, puffing a few times on the cigar. Ashes flicked incidentally down the front of his shirt. The smoke wrapped around his head like a turban.

"We're not against you," father said. "If that's what you mean."

A car pulled up to the pump. "What'll it be?" Buck shouted and stood up, placing his cigar on the edge of the chair's arm.

"Fill her up, Buck," an attractive brunette called out.

"I'd love to, Sandy!" he said, turning on the pump and winking our way. They chatted while the car gassed up. The woman giggled intermittently. Buck's hands gestured wildly. For a moment I wondered if she was getting the same story, but then the pump clicked off. "That'll be $17.26, Sandy," he said.

"Thank you Buck," she said, handing him a twenty. "Close enough." She raised her eye brow seductively. "I'll see you soon."

"Just as soon as heavenly possible," he mumbled under his breath. "Thanks, Sandy!" he said, waving as she spun off.

"I can see you know your business," father commented. "You treat your customers well."

"Nothing but the best," Buck replied. "Just ask the ladies—down at Buck's, we pump harder!" he said with a big grin.

"You inspire me, Buck," I added.

"There's no secret, you know. In this business the harder you pump, the further you go!" he said, and laughed.

"Good one," father said, chuckling himself.

"I'm afraid I've wandered a bit from my story," Buck said as he grabbed his cigar and sat down. "Now then," he shifted his attention back to us. "We were talking about the natives frolicking in a state of nature. Right?"

"Sounded like the Garden of Eden to me," I responded. "But from what I've read about the Puritans they probably viewed it as Sodom and Gomorrah."

"Close enough," Buck shrugged. "It doesn't matter really, which story from the Book of Genesis you pick or what biblical prophesy they believed. Before the Puritans could impose the full fury of their wrath the skank got the Indians. The Europeans were immune to it, had been for centuries. These were virgin epidemics. The natives were doomed. The Puritans would say that God was punishing them for their debauchery. In some ways they were right. God *was* punishing them, *and* us, by unloading on Western civilization a legacy of narrow-minded hypocrites that continue to hinder progress to this very day." His voice rose intently, as though *Buck* were on a pulpit delivering a sermon. "Like with Job, *He's* testing the limits of our faith in a grueling endurance test with the reason-challenged, intolerant, non-thinking, control-freak fundamentalist rabble. Rolling the dice with Mephistopheles in a grand game of craps. *He* leaves us staring at snake eyes. To laugh time and again at the nation of lovers and fighters, artists and artisans, authors and book burners, the intellectual and the ignorant, the clued and the clueless, the hopeful and the hopeless, the wolves and the sheep—all running amuck amidst mayhem through the streets of that shining city on the hill, the last bastion of civilization and its begotten seed. It begs to leave *me* thinking once again that ultimately, and quite predictably, that we could be standing in the Garden of Eden, but it would make no fucking difference—and I'll tell you why! 'You can take a cow around the world, but it's still a cow!'"

"Ah! You impress me, Buck," I interrupted him. "Gary Larsen. One of my favorite philosopher-kings."

"Indeed!" Buck remarked. "You're tuned in? A fellow traveler? Man of letters?"

"A traveler, yes," father answered before I could. "But a man of letters? He once worked in a mailroom."

"Buck doesn't need to hear that, dad!" I jumped in to no avail.

"Now *that* was a brilliant career move, boy." Father rolled his eyes.

Buck simply laughed. Knowingly, I supposed. We all have fathers until that day, at the turn of the tide, when we turn into one ourselves.

"Gentlemen," Buck said demurely. "If I may continue." He gazed as if asking for permission. Nodding, I was only too grateful to comply. Father puffed his stogie contentedly and popped his thumb up. "Very well, then," said Buck. "The tribes here knew that their time was at hand, and they accepted it without judgment. They came to the region not only for the natural resources, but because it was also considered hallowed ground. They believed that there was a portal here to the other time of their fathers' fathers and their children's children, and the children's children of the other men who they knew not of as they were yet to be. But their coming was well known through the portal. Those who left, did, and went to a time and place of plenty. Those who stayed, did, waiting and watching, guarding to the end the portal which, to this day, has yet to be located." He paused, glancing at us. "*That* remains fixed in the local folklore." Buck paused again. He seemed to be gauging us, waiting for one of us to respond. Neither of us did. I have to admit that he had my attention.

"When they did come, the *other* men, it was for the abundance of fish and the other natural resources that the English fishmongers and Captain John had outlined. It drew them like bums to a soup kitchen on Thanksgiving Day—verily a base simile, yes?" He raised an eyebrow when he said it. "But the Europeans, principally the English and the French, dueled for control of the region. As the explorers came, so did the settlers and the saints, the pirates and privateers. All competed for the prize. Who would control the most land, grab the most riches, and build the greatest empire? It went on and on and on for centuries. Fishermen and farmers, fights and skirmishes, drunken sailors, Indian uprisings, and pirate raids from Captain Kidd to One-Eyed Red Beard. Though the Dutch, Spanish, and particularly the French, attempted to colonize, they were overmatched in this region of the *New* World by the followers of Captain John. Downeast Way was settled permanently by Englishmen in 1624." He settled back in the Adirondack and took a breath.

"1624?" father said, ruminating over the date. "Makes a man think?"

"It should," Buck responded, puffing on his cigar. "When you think about it there's a lot to think about when you think about it." The old man looked like he was about to say something, but stopped short. He left that one to ponder.

"These men," Buck continued, "the English principals, they were merchants by trade, Anglican by sect, who successfully kept the Puritans at bay for half a century. I'll give 'em credit for that," he added. "The King's Inn & Silent Woman Tavern was the first public building erected in 1632. The Queen's Chapel was erected in 1634. This gave the codfish aristocracy and their fine Anglican stock a place to play and a place to pray. Both buildings still stand. The tavern, with its famous swinging placard—a saucy headless woman holding a pint in one hand with the other on her hip in defiance—still greets all those who dare to enter, and still dispenses libations on the south side of Market Square. The chapel, a few blocks north on the Glebe Lane, still redeems souls, dispensing spiritual guidance, and providing a haven for meditation."

"So we could scoot on over to the Silent Woman Tavern today and get liquored up?" I interrupted him. "Or head to the chapel and ponder the fate of the twelve tribes of Israel?"

"I don't see why not," Buck answered. "It hasn't failed the wild or willing in almost four centuries."

"Amazing!" said father, impressed.

"Indeed. It truly is," said Buck. "I guess that's why the sailors and the lost souls, the explorers and the adventurers, the fishermen and the transient tribes all found solace and abundance here, under the shadow of Mount

Agamenticus. The great protector of all things wonderful in these parts." He paused, nodding reverentially in its direction. I looked up, studied the mountain. Its slopes heavily forested—birch and maple, white pine, spruce and cedar—on all but the open ledges on its northerly side. "That old rock has kept the developer crowd at bay," said Buck, "the population in check, and the land much as it's been for centuries."

"Buck, if this is Shangri-La, how the hell do people find us?" father weighed in, taking a puff of cigar and blowing a cloud of smoke over the conversation. "We *are* here to start a business. It would be nice if people could find the place."

"I could say 'build it and they will come,' but that would be a cliché, my friend," said Buck, sincerely. "I don't mean the mountain's a deterrent, it's actually a draw. This place is hopping. People sail into Moose Harbor throughout the spring, summer and fall, or drive in through one of the two access roads—the northeast pass and the northwest pass—year round. We need another inn or hotel here. I think you'll do great."

Father seemed to mull it over, pondered all that Buck had to say, for a minute or so. "We know all about the northwest pass," he finally said. "That was the one that spanked the Rambler."

"It's happened on more than one occasion," Buck sympathized. "The passes can be brutal, especially in winter during a storm. There are a few older tote roads that the loggers and trappers made eons ago, too. A couple lead up to the top of the mountain and around it. They're still in use but not mapped. The only other way in is via the harbor, like I said, which has a heck of a view with the four main islands, several smaller rocky outcrops, Saint Mary's Lighthouse and the old colonial redoubt, Fort Norumbega." He turned, looking directly at father, puffing on his cigar, the rich aroma of the Cubano in the air. "It's nice here. Though isolated, we're never alone. Business is always booming. You'll do fine, gentlemen. When one wanders onto these shores or through these woods, he comes not into exile but into his own." Buck relaxed in the chair. Cigar ashes were scattered up and down his shirt and lap.

"Good as new!" The mechanic stuck his head out from the garage door. "You've got another hundred-thousand miles for sure," he said proudly.

I'm confident that he was right, and was happy to hear it, for us and the Rambler. I'm sure that Buck Jones could have kept going for hours, too. There were still three centuries to cover, but the job was finished and we had to motor.

"Just remember one thing," Buck said as we were leaving.

"You pump harder!" Father answered in stride, which drew a laugh from Buck.

"Ayuh!" He slipped into his accent. "It's what separates the men from the boys. Just like that mountain separates us from the rest of the planet!"

Yes, I thought, that and the mojo. There's plenty flowing along with a lot of other bull, which is why I think we'll fit right in. For me, I can tell you that here, the tumbleweed rolls no more, if you catch my drift. And to you brother, I say it's time to bring the party *home*.

Till then,

brother John

```
From:    brother.john@moe.org
To:      rob@moe.org
Date:    April 9, 9:04 p.m.
Subject: Operation "feedin' at the trough"
```

Hola Rob: I knew that once you came here and checked this place out there'd be no question in your mind that we'd found nirvana. A jackpot awaits. Okay, so neither one of us has ever owned a hotel let alone run one, but what could go wrong? It all comes down to logistics, micro-management of the details, and the subsequent anal-compulsive neurosis that compounds with each passing day. Who knows when it will hit—the realization that you've made a commitment that could influence you and yours and the life of the community for generations to come. So why worry? You may be on tour the rest of your life to fund this thing, but it beats working at the Piggly-Wiggly.

Enclosed are a bunch of papers. The banksters and lawyers await your Hancock. Please sign them at the X's in blood and send them back to me, not to the attorney. The notary said I need to co-sign them in front of Kinghorn and Bigwood to make it official. Kinghorn and Bigwood are the notaries. Once that's done we're ready to roll.

I've lined up a few bids for the renovation project like you said. Deadline is July 15, which, if we're lucky, means an August 1 opening. Who am I trying to kid? We're dealing with contractors and code enforcement types. Quite a few résumés for the masterbrewer position have started to flow in, too (no pun intended). The microbrewery was a great idea and we should have that position filled soon.

I see that we've received a good response from the moe.rons for the 'name the hotel' contest. I'm pleased with the choice of the moe.Republic Hotel. Being the independent type that I am, it's above such contenders as Buster's House or Spine of the Dawg Inn. So if you're okay with the name, I'm okay with the name. *Viva la moe.Republic!* We shall greet ceaseless waves of tourists, down east bound, who flock to Vacationland and beyond, season after season. Those seeking a rendezvous with time, or an adventure, or a refuge from the daily grind shall find it here. It's like father said that first day in town: "There's something about this place that cleanses the spirit." Then again, now that I think of it, that could have been the 99¢ special kicking in, too.

Call me sometime next week,
brother John

```
From: brother.john@moe.republic.org
To:   rob@moe.org
Date: May 22, 11:16 a.m.
Subject: "Habitually feedin' at the trough"
```

dear Rob: Greetings from the friendly environs of the great moe.Republic Hotel. Buying this old mansion and fixing it up was a great idea. I'm glad I thought of it. And I'm even happier that I did it with your money. Here it is late May, and we're in the midst of an unusually, early heat wave, the first of the season. But that isn't getting me down because all I have to do is step on the porch and let the mighty breeze off the Atlantic take me away.

The renovation is going well and the work crews are buzzing along. They're pouring concrete around the deck of the pool today. The building inspector is also the head contractor. A fellow by the name of Sweeney. He told me he was a plumber by trade, which I found puzzling. "I thought a person could make a good living out of plumbing?" I asked him a couple days ago. "Is it really that tough to make a go of it around here in a specific trade?"

"Nah," he said. "I simply got tired of the grunt work."

"Really?" I said, intrigued. "You mean the same old same old?"

"Actually," he replied in earnest, "it was the customers. I just couldn't take their shit anymore."

Fortunately for us he morphed into general contracting instead, landed the building inspector's position, and now every job he has is backed up. I told him and the crew that if the job's finished on time and under budget it's all the beer they can drink Friday happy hour for six months. Nothing like a Pavlovian stimulus to get the most for your hard-borrowed dollars. That said, having not factored in Memorial Day weekend nor the Fourth of July, which is on a Thursday this year, I figure the 'Open' shingle will hang no later than Labor Day weekend, for sure. Hey? Maybe you guys can organize a rock festival and hold it here. You could make it an annual thing and do it every Labor Day weekend! And it would be a great way to roll out the red carpet and open the hotel. You could call it the 'moe. Get Down!'

Moving on, the moe.Microbrewery is up and going, too. The first vat of the precious elixir is stewing and near ready. You can thank Fergus McBain for that, the new brewer. A genuine Irish brewmeister from Cork, father hired him on the spot the day they met. He had to. There were a half-dozen finalists sitting there in the waiting area when McBain first walked into the room. He was the only candidate who had a tie on, let alone a suit. The guy hadn't even applied for the job, but he took one look around the room at the competition and spoke up like he owned the place. "If I may have your attention please," he announced. His Irish brogue gave an air of authority. "Thank you very much for applying for the position as brew master for the hotel, but we've made our decision and you can all go. If any of you need a recommendation, please, don't call us," he said, deadpan. That's when father said he nearly keeled. "Just kidding!" McBain quickly added, brightly, disarming the dejected crowd. "We'd be happy to put a good word in for you. You're all very gifted brewers." Well, father was so stunned his jaw locked up. True! Couldn't say anything until the room had cleared and he was left standing face-to-face with McBain. "Crazy son of a bitch," I said to father when I found out. "How could you hire him?" "I had to," father replied. "There's only one other person I've ever heard or seen do that in all my life and it was me." With that, I'm happy to report that we not only have a brewmeister on the payroll, but two con artists, as well.

On the domestic front, we're starting to find our way around the area. A couple of Sundays ago we all went up to Farkleberry Farm, a petting zoo off Mountain Road. I met the owner, Casey McNugent, one night over at Goatlips Saloon. The missus and I were there mingling with the local citizenry when we got to talking with McNugent and his wife, Shelly. We hit it off and had a great time. McNugent's quite the character and his bride's pretty sharp, too. She's a professor of something over at Bowdoin. Anyway, they invited the whole family up to the farm. The place is awesome. We can definitely steer guests there as a "thing to do." You have your typical farm animals—cows, donkeys, ponies, goats—but there's quite a few exotic types up there, too. A half-dozen or so zebras, four giraffes, a bull moose, a couple of black bears, dozens of llamas, a small heard of bison, a couple of camels, and a young bull elephant by the name of Rafiki. I can tell you with authority that that pachyderm is hung like an elephant. Casey said that Rafiki was begot to butter his bread—that beast's massive tool is going to make him a small fortune the day he reaches his majority. Maybe it's me and my imagination. I don't know, but I decided, seeing as I barely knew the guy, not to pursue the particulars of his business plan. At least not in front of the children.

Mother's made friends with the Huxley sisters, Emma and Edith, who live next door, or more specifically, across the grounds, in the other manor house. A bit daft, and sometimes rude—they act like they still own the place—but friendly enough. They are eighty or ninety something, the last descendents of the fabled Huxley line. They say that the Huxleys once ruled this town. If this old manor house and the one they occupy next door are anything, it's a testament to that. Anyway, the sisters took a liking to mother right away. They were happy to have neighbors again. It's secluded out here on the point, and I'm sure they were lonely. But now we're setting up shop. They've got more people bopping around than during the Roaring Twenties. Those days, the workers tell me, during Prohibition, the rumrunners used to land, or sometimes wash ashore down on the point. They say the Walker and the Kennedy clans fought it out on more than one occasion here. Wild gangs of new world Protestants against old world Catholics. Kind of sorry I missed out on the fun. And they're other stories, too, murder and mayhem, spooks and spirits, more than I have time for. These guys *are* on our dime, and I'm doing my best to keep them moving.

I also hooked up with a guy named Fred Bergmeister yesterday. Goes by the name of Bullethead. Fred has a big-ass boat, the *Jolly Mr. Johnson,* and runs a harbor cruise business down on Hancock Wharf. Father thought it would be good to make a connection. As I mentioned, people are always looking for stuff to do when they go on vacation. After a couple of days around the pool or on the beach they get the itch. They need diversions—a day at the zoo, a booze cruise, a trip to Buck's Garage, et cetera.

One last thing—that dry rot you were worried about on the back side of the porch turned out only to be a small irritant. Sort of like the rash you and brother Kevin got that time mud-wrestling with those fat women in Tijuana. That was a crazy road trip, huh? Talk about a morning after? I never knew the meaning of "fire in the hole" until that dawn. Tequila can do that to you. But hey, we can reminisce about that later. There's a guy named Fonebone coming by to give this place a once over. He's an entomologist, trained in the way of preventive pest-free living. A Zen master of the trade I'm told, and I hear the door bell ringing now…

Ciao! Or is it chow?

bro J

Act II

The First Fall

The moe.Republic Hotel
in the heart of the Lost Kingdom

Hey Rob,

Greetings from the moe.Republic Hotel mi hermano. Today's a bit hot and humid. Perfect weather for that frozen mango, rum concoction the moe.Republic is famous for. Or soon will be. We're hanging poolside catching the rays on this wonderful end-of-summer day, puffing on one of those Cuban cigars you brought back from Canada a couple of months ago, and listening to the music of the Louis Jordan on the radio. In fact, they're playing "Five Guys Named Moe," the song that inspired it all!

The view of the islands across the bay is quite spectacular this afternoon. The smell of brine wafts endlessly and is quite intoxicating; it reaches up and snaps at your olfactory bulb, then slaps you 'side the head with each breath you take. The surf is rather rough, though. I think from the spate of hurricanes and tropical storms to the far south. But the weather has been awesome and I'm not complaining. I saw a wind surfer dude go bouncing by about an hour ago and he hasn't come back. My guess is that he is either half way to Nova Scotia or lobster fodder by now.

Anyway, the grand opening was great, and tell the boys in the band kudos from all of us. The hotel business is fine, and so is the new set of teeth that you bought mother. It's the first time in years we haven't heard the blender crank up at suppertime. The renovation job on the Liberty Ballroom is now complete for the fall and winter tour schedule. We have a kinky Reggae band here tonight, which promises to fill the place.

Now that moe.'s established itself as a big record company, and you guys are formally cogs in the wheel of the decadent bourgeois capitalist recording industry machine, I was wondering if we could hire a janitor, or at least a cleaning service for the bar. It never occurred to me when we agreed to this that I'd have to clean the shithouse, too. I finally had enough and purchased a decontamination suit and gas mask on eBay last week. Things are that gross. Really! How can a woman *miss*? Do guys really *do* that to their toilet seats at home? In *their* bathroom sinks? And then walk away? I'm not even going to tell you what I found in the driveway last Sunday morning.

Be that as it may, don't mention that to any of the boys in the band. Especially Al—we know how particular *he* is! I figure it's going to be tough enough to get the moe.entourage back here anytime soon. I know you're only the bass player, but maybe you could convince the band to come back and play here one weekend? Things have changed. I promise that this time we will not headline you for Sunday midnight. You know I had nothing to do with that at the grand opening, but Sunday night *is* talent night. What the hey? The guys did get a free meal out of it (we really didn't mean to put that seared animal flesh in Al's burrito). We did put you up in the Buena Vista Suite (and I do apologize again about the plumbing debacle—please let Chuck know that we've since downgraded the turbo nozzles in the Turkish Hot Tub), and I bet that Vinnie and Jim would enjoy the harbor cruise this time (I will not forget to bring the Dramamine). Let me know what you think. It would be really good for the family business.

And what was that Rock the Vote mini-tour all about? That was kind of cool. In these crazy days of hedonism, cynicism, and dysfunctional families, it's important to encourage people to get off their duffs come November, join the franchise, register to vote, and stand up and be counted!

Wow!!! You're not going to believe this, but there's a gigantic bull moose coming down the path heading towards the back of the house. He's looking mighty excited about something. Must be in the air by the size of him (they say they're in rut this time of year), and… Holy shit! The bride just went out there to weed the garden! Gotta go!

brother John

The moe.Republic Hotel
in the heart of the Lost Kingdom

Hey Rob!

...and hola to all your moe.amigos out there! Things are quite hectic since the last time I wrote. It's leaf peeping season and the tourists are stopping to feed, water, and rest in great numbers. Down east, we tell them, everyone has his own moose story, and now the moe.Republic has one, too.

I imagine that, given the intense pressure of a being a recording star, your life has been quite hectic, also. I recall your remark about how hard you have worked to this point in your life to not have to work. It offered a unique insiders perspective on the struggle to succeed in an industry governed by high powered corporate executives motivated in kind, sort of. Let me add that the bride and I thoroughly enjoyed the visit down your way for the CD-release gig in the Big Apple. The venue was awesome. I half expected to see Ginger Rogers and Fred Astaire waltz into the ballroom rather than five-thousand stoned moe.rons stumble in. And the show? That wasn't too shab-by, either.

Too bad that you missed father's birthday party last month. He did comment on your alternate career path occasionally. There was talk of six years of college, gas money, and a steady supply of Camel no-filters all going up in smoke. I gently reminded him that you have since quit smoking. I also reminded him that the reason you were not around was because you had gone to Japan. "I thought he said he was in one of those rock and roll bands?" he asked me, quite puzzled. "He doesn't have time to go on vacation."

Oh well, you didn't miss too much. One of the Huxley sisters, I think it was Edith, got liquored up and started jabbering about the hole in the wall in the Liberty Ballroom. She went on and on about how her great-nephew James would never have let the place fall into such disrepair. It wasn't like the guy didn't have a choice, I wanted to remind her. Why in God's name would he up and join the army when he could have lived here next to you and Emma?

That's what I should have said, but passed. Never reason with a drunk or an idiot. Why waste the oxygen?

She was bitching at me because we were still under renovation and repair from "el incidente de bull moose." Do not fear! The insurance covered the damage and your investment is still as sound as the first day you gave in. The moe.Republic is open to the public once again and business is booming. In some ways that big fella's mad run straight through the lobby, into the Liberty Ballroom, and out through the picture window at the end of the bar was a blessing in disguise. I've never seen the bride run so fast, and that includes our wedding night! Unbeknownst to her, she must have been emitting some high frequency pheromone blast which wafted in the breeze. Whatever she emitted it sent that poor creature's sensory gland into seventh heaven.

When those big fellas go in the rut anything can happen. No holes barred, if you know what I mean! Usually moose are quite docile ungulates, which make them exceptionally vulnerable during the autumnal hunt. A sport, if I may digress, which takes all the guile and cunning of walking up to a herded, grazing, bovine and blowing its brains out. I do not wish to trample on anybody's cherished Second Amendment rights, but could we level the playing field? Maybe three bullets a piece, plus we release a pack of timber wolves come opening day?

Anyway, we got the copy of the CD that Topper sent us, and by the tone of some of the reviews going around, it looks like it's going to make a run for the roses. "She Sends Me" has become a happy hour favorite, here. We are offering free pitchers of Pumpkin Ale from the moe.Microbrewery this month to any patron who can quaff a beer and say "Rebubula" three times in rapid succession without spraying the bar.

We are also quite enchanted by the release of the hit single "Meat." The art work and design is visionary and reflective, an eclectic compendium of the savage, primordial beast within. The powerful and mystifying lyric, juxtaposed against the grinding, pulsating rhythm, seems to embrace all that is right and wrong with post-industrial society. Hats-off to Al, who has done it once again. Somehow he manages to express a deeply moving, heart felt, symbiotic angst between the carnivore and the herbivore in a word anathema to his very being. Some would say that he has captured the zeitgeist of a generation… others may contemplate a Sunday afternoon barbecue. I for one have enough moose venison in the freezer for the Upper East Side.

Which reminds me. What are you and the guys doing for Thanksgiving weekend? It's been a long time since you've been home and we're looking for a band to fill that weekend's slot. Just think, moe. could light the fire under the trophy of a moose in heat, mounted there on the wall with a wry, giddy-yup like smile, forever frozen on its hairy, brown face. You don't have to answer me right away. Think about it. Well, the building repair guys are here again. They're looking for some hard currency before they finish off that new entrance from the bar to the patio.

Till then, just feedin' at the trough,
brother John

The Haunting at Huxley Manor
In the office by the vat room
Thursday, 11:04 p.m.

Rob dearest,

Hope all is well and life is grand. A rather brisk late autumn chill is in the air, which is quite apropos, the chill that is, after what has gone down here in the past week. I can say that we were a bit unhinged with all the talk of the place being haunted—Halloween can do that to you! We're back on track now, and have a near full house. Fonebone declared the place clean a few hours ago and left with a check in hand. Sparky took a liking to him, though I think the pooch was disappointed that he missed out on the "exorcism."

The beauty of it is, with all that went down, the guests thought it was part of some kind of living theater—the type of thing that even *I* couldn't have concocted. And we had coverage in the *Downeast Way Times*, too, which, considering the advertising rates of that rag, was a major coup. Mother may never be the same after what happened, but for now those little pink pills seem to be doing the job. At least she doesn't speak of wanting to go stay with sister Liza anymore, or brother Casimere.

The whole affair began early one morning a week ago Thursday. I was upstairs in the head when I heard a primordial scream from downstairs. It was louder than that time in the moe.van when you screamed "Holy shit a deeeeer..." just before we bored into that six-point buck, except this scream was a shriek of sheer terror rather than shit-your-pants surprise. I had just finished shaving—the third leg of the morning triumvirate complete—when I was distracted from the never-ending count of gray hairs and their continuing assault on my head. I ran downstairs fearing the worst. The commotion was in the kitchen. When I burst in I found the bride comforting mother. A few guests had wandered in. Father was standing there, too, mumbling something about those idiot, imbecile, senile Huxley sisters, and telling mother to get off the floor and finish with the bacon. All mother kept saying, in a half whisper, was "I heard *it!* I heard *him*, scratching, right there in the wall.

He's real—Edith and Emma were right!" At that moment, staring at them all, amidst the pandemonium, I realized I was still in my boxers.

Now there's nothing to worry about. Let me assure you, firstly, that the turtle's *head* was still in his shell. Secondly, your investment is as safe and sound as the day you made it. Our neighbors, Edith and Emma Huxley, the grand dames of Downeast Way, as I've mentioned before, are the last in the line of Colonel Huxley, the hero of the Battle of Fredericksburg and the guy who actually built this place. I don't know how leading your men uphill into a wall of cannon fire can be construed as heroic just because somebody told you to do it—even if he did lead the charge. Anyway, as you know, these Huxley sisters have bonded with mother, and have her believing that things are amiss here in the hotel. They've been telling her about the arm of Colonel Huxley. I don't want to get too deep, but this place is supposed to be haunted by him, or it, or whatever. I'm not really sure. And everyone in town knows about it. They'll tell you that the moe.Republic is haunted by the ghost of Colonel Josiah Huxley. Seems it was a minor detail that Kinghorn and Bigwood neglected to mention. It came up after we began to renovate. A few crew members mentioned that the place was spooked, but I just shrugged.

No need to alarm you with any tales from the crypt—you know I've got plenty of skeletons in my closet without being haunted by Colonel Huxley, too. There have been a few unusual things, I suppose, but nothing worth writing about or too odd for a place this old. It's kind of creepy when a few boards creak, a door slams shut, or things disappear from one place and turn up a few days later in another part of the hotel. Father keeps complaining that he can't find his keys, but then again, I told the bride to hide them every chance she could. I'm beginning to wonder if he should even be behind the wheel of the John Deere mower.

And then there is the occasional weird stuff, too. I've overheard guests talk of similar nightmares—the sensation of a heavy pressure or weight holding them down, feeling an icy grip around them, unable to speak or move, waking suddenly in a cold sweat—it all sounds like a bad hangover in Vegas if you ask me. But what do I know? You can't get sucked into the drama and paranoia. I sure the hell don't want to scare off the masses before they show up! I guess *we* should have asked Kinghorn and Bigwood why no one had lived in this place for the past twenty years before *we* walked off the boat and bought it. All I was thinking was location! location! location! And you know how I feel about the view.

Before you think that your dollars would have been better placed in dot.com futures, there's no need to worry. Until mother's scream that morning, it had been smooth sailing. That being the week before Halloween we were able to quiet the concerns of our hallowed guests. I can't say that screams coming from the kitchen is that reassuring, particularly during breakfast, or any meal for that matter. Even though I was standing there in my underwear, I calmed down the curious with a wink and nod. Thus began the theater of the absurd.

Later that morning, after all had settled down, including mother, and the kitchen was cleaned up, I set off to visit those Huxley sisters. Now, we're all confronted with that dreaded four-letter word—time. It can be for you and it can be against you. You can be out of it or it can be in the nick of. You can catch it or it can happen to you again and again. You can have it or lose track of it. But when you start running out of it, when it is at hand, then funny things happen to your mind—cognitive breakdown, momentary episodes of premature senility—the common denominator takes flight. A conversation with Edith and Emma is as trying as watching Alice chase the white rabbit down the hole. It doesn't make sense and all time seems to meld together.

I entered the grounds of the last remnants of the Huxley estate inhabited by Huxleys, an old Victorian mansion where the sisters had lived their entire lives. And by the funk that wafted through the hallways of the place I'd say it was close to a century or more. Against my better judgement I found myself sitting in a musty parlor waiting for tea and "chatting." Idle banter. The women were nervous and uneasy. They finally told me I was the first man to have tea with them there since Porter Gibson Digit. "Come again?" I blurted out. "Porter Gibson Digit? You mean the writer? *The* Bird Man?" I found their association with him unbelievable. How could the guy who invented the finger have had anything to do with the Huxley sisters other than flicking *them* the bird? They told me that this was where Porter's from, Downeast Way. According to the Huxleys he and another guy named Jeff worked off and on for their father and grandfather during the depression. I couldn't imagine why the Bird Man would had ever stepped into this room, even if that visit was 1930-something. Yet, he was the last man not named Huxley who had been in this room. Why was I *not* surprised?

"What about him?" I remarked, purging the thought of any man with either of these two from my head. There was a portrait on the side table of a young man in military uniform. Too recent to be this Colonel Huxley fellow. "Who's that?" I asked casually.

"That's our great-nephew James Huxley," Emma volunteered. The man who would be Lord of Huxley Manor. How could I forget? "Our dear, departed niece Ann's only son."

"Ah! So they're the ones who lived in the house before us?" I said out loud to myself.

"No," Edith said. "Our sister Enid was. Ann was her only child."

"Oh?" I wondered, sensing a *faux pas* on my part.

"It's no secret," Emma spoke up. "Ann ran away. *Had* to. She and the boy lived over on Bean's Point—on the *other* side of the harbor." Bean's Point might as well have been a hamlet on the Arctic Circle rather than a fifteen minute drive to the next town over. Inhabited by the spawn of Irish, then Canadian, immigrants, her conviction bespoke the pomp and pageantry of class and the great divide.

"He was all honors at Orono," said Edith, "despite that."

"And a lieutenant in the army," Emma added. "I think, in time, the house would have been his."

"Handsome lad," I said respectfully, guessing his fate was the same as their great-grandfather, Colonel Huxley.

"Lost in the line of duty," Edith sighed. "A helicopter, down in Columbia."

"No dear," Emma said to Edith. "I believe it was Panama. That invasion. Wasn't it? Right after Ann died?" How could they not know, I thought. Who wouldn't know the where and the when of that?

"Oh yes," replied Edith casually. "You're quite right. How silly of me." I imagined mother, who had formed an alliance with these two, sitting here day after day, inhaling the fumes of decaying minds and timber. I began to imagine how easy it could be for these old babes to sit here and pound down shots of tea, their breath reeking of Earl Grey and their teeth hued the color of sandpaper. As you can tell, I was in my element.

When the tea arrived I made the fatal mistake of asking them point blank the story of the "old man," as Colonel Huxley was fondly called by his wilted offspring. If anything, to change the subject. "Such an impatient lad," Emma whispered to Edith. I said nothing, but smiled weakly. I sipped Lord Grey's finest, which I was certain, by my third cup, had a medicinal edge that set it a part from ordinary tea. We then chatted about how the hotel was going, which was followed by an awkward moment of silence. I had already heard way more than I wanted on this visit. My thoughts were to leave, to say goodbye and try another day. Then Edith let out a sigh and said, "Colonel Huxley was a good man!" It caught me by surprise. At first, I thought that was it, all she was going to say. That it was my cue to leave, till she took a deep breath and began to crank out the family story of their great-grandfather. And other than Emma's occasional nod or supporting "Ayuh," between topping off the cups, Edith was in her glory.

"He was handsome," she began, "wealthy, endowed with a charming wit, and was particularly adept with the ladies. There was something about him they found irresistible." The two women looked at each other and giggled at the remark, the thought of which made me want to gag. "He was fortunate and lucky his whole life. Though he would say that the day he married Mary was the most fortunate and luckiest day of his life. They met on holiday at the Cape, and it was love at first sight. She bore him two beautiful sons and a daughter. Life was about as peaceful and prosperous as it could be for any man. By the time he was in his early forties, he ruled over a small industrial empire, was married to the most beautiful woman in all Downeast Way, and had those wonderful children to dote over. Colonel Huxley would have agreed with you when it was said that he was fortunate and lucky.

"At least until that awful war finally broke out. It was only a matter of time. It had been percolating for decades. The election of Lincoln began a chain reaction of secession among the southern states that led to firing on Fort Sumter, and the great Apocalypse we call the Civil War.

"Because of his stature in the community Colonel Huxley did not have to go. He could have easily paid for his replacement as so many of the wealthy families did when the lottery came up. But Huxley was fortunate and lucky, he said, and also a patriot. He believed in the morality of the cause—the abolition of slavery and the preservation of the Union. His was a righteous crusade. Despite the pleas of his beautiful Mary and the arguments of his colleagues that the war was to be won as much on the home front as on the battlefield, he volunteered, organized, and fitted a company of men, and led them off to battle in the late winter of 1862." She paused for a moment, sipping her tea. I had to admit I was mildly surprised by how tuned in she was. Dare I say lucid?

"And battles they found," Edith went on, "Shiloh in April, the Peninsular Campaign in June, the Second Battle of Bull Run in August, and Antietam in September. The carnage was horrific. By December when they had reached Fredericksburg, Huxley was beginning to wonder what the cause actually meant. This was revealed in the letters home. To his wife he kept his spirits up and wrote long letters of love lost. To his brother, to whom he had left the managing of the textile mill, he wrote of his doubts, the strain of having to lead men to their deaths, and the meaningless destruction of life itself. Man and beast shattered in cannonades, literally obliterated in a red mist before his eyes. He became more disillusioned and distant from the cause. Deeper into the abyss he slipped, more reckless, taking unnecessary risks, placing himself and his men in the line of fire.

"He was, after all, fortunate and lucky. With each battle he passed through he came to believe that there was an invincible aura about him. Surviving the hand-to-hand frenzied combat unheard of on the gentle shores of Moose Harbor—the battlefields were an abattoir of human savagery. He witnessed half-naked men slashing and hacking each other to their deaths amid the whizzing of bullets and cannonballs. Limbs exploded, legs shattered, bayonets efficiently and mercilessly disemboweling man after man. And at day's end he stood once again to carry on the good fight and lead his men into battle."

For love of God, I thought, thankfully I wasn't hearing this over a meal. Because what was left of my breakfast was churning hard.

"He yearned for rest," Edith explained, "the journey home, the loving embrace of his sweet Mary. He wanted to show and teach his sons this game of baseball he had watched and learned from a company of men from New York. It was a grand game, and his letters home spoke of that. He had decided that after Fredericksburg he would take leave and rest. He had been too long without furlough and it was time to go home."

There was a pause. Edith had to take a breather. The story was doing me in—I can't imagine what it was like for her considering that this must have been the tenth-zillionth time she'd recited it. I had had about enough, and the lapse was my chance for a graceful exit. "Time to rotate the filters on the vats," I told them, sounding technical enough. But these old buggers were a persistent pair. I don't think they get much company these days. Though I don't know why? Other than the mausoleum-esque type atmosphere and the overbearing scent of mothballs and mildew, it was kind of cozy. Anyway, Emma filled up my teacup and pushed a plate of brownies in front of me. I sat back, defeated, once again, in a Pavlovian lull, induced by my "sensitivity indoctrination" at the hands of mother, and her endless serenade of "mind your manners, boy," followed by a whack side the head or a slap on the hand. Even then as I sat there I controlled an involuntary urge to flinch as their story continued.

"So it was on Christmas Eve 1862," Edith went on, "he found himself walking up the old North Road toward Huxley Manor. He couldn't quite remember the circumstance, nor was he sure how he arrived there. A bone chilling cold filled the Maine December air. Vaguely he recalled the long train ride home—but his association with that journey seemed remote and distant. It was a release when the train finally came to rest under the shadow of Mount Agamenticus. He had not written to his beautiful Mary in a couple of weeks. He wanted to surprise her for Christmas, to walk up the manor road to the portico, into the great hall, sweep her off her feet, and retire to their chamber. He would then recite the grand poem of Saint Nicholas by Clement Moore to his children, smoke a cigar, and enjoy a brandy before the fire roaring in the hearth.

"He was at peace with himself as he had never been before. He gazed at the winter-scape around him in wonder. Seeing, as though for the first time, the stark beauty of the barren maple and birch trees amidst the tall stands of white pine that rolled up the side of the snow covered hills to his left. On the right were stone walls, carefully laid out and stacked neatly—the refuse of two centuries of clearing the rocky land to till the soil or make pasture.

"His memory was playing tricks on him because the last thing he vividly recalled was that charge across the bridge at Fredericksburg. He didn't care, really, because now he was on his native soil, removed from the blood and toil, the endless explosions, the screams of agony, and the desperate cries of boys, mere children, seeking the comfort of their mother's caring arms. None of that mattered to him now. It was a distant place, a nightmarish glance into the depths of hell. Here was heaven; the rugged beauty of Downeast Way buried beneath the heavy blanket of a virgin snowfall. He was battered and bruised as he trudged along, but ironically was upbeat, too, and felt no pain. He was one with the natural world around him. At times it was though he was sleep walking. He walked through town seemingly unnoticed. He had an urge to stop by the factory to surprise his brother and the rest of the men but decided against it—the urgency of his reunion with his sweet bride was too compelling. The lust overwhelmed him.

"He walked on and saw the great manor in the distance rising upon the low hill. He kept a steady pace, which quickened as he drew near. It was less than a mile when he heard a carriage approach from behind. Tired and weary he waved for it to pull over to carry him along for the last leg of the journey. The driver slowed when suddenly the horses reared, the man screamed in fright, and the carriage bolted by him. Startled, he looked around and saw nothing. It gave him a chill that he had not felt since Fredericksburg.

"As he approached the gate he saw several children coming toward him. He recognized one as his own. He held out his arms to greet them but suddenly they too screamed out and ran away. His head was suddenly aching and he felt a searing pain shooting through his side and into his left arm. The walkway and the front door were now ahead of him. He glanced off and noticed a flag was flying at half-mast. He now realized that something terrible had happened. He wondered if his brother had been killed at the factory, or his dear Mary stricken ill, or one of the children! He ran up the walkway to his front door. The pain overwhelmed his senses, again.

"He stumbled in through the doorway in a panic. All was silent. He looked down the wide corridor. The doors to the inner rooms were open and he could see the mourning drapery in the front rooms. There on the side table in the hallway he noticed a letter. It lay on a silver platter. He rushed over and looked down intently, slowly reading the words:

'Dear Mrs. Huxley, I regret to inform you of the death of your husband Colonel Josiah Huxley at an engagement at Fredericksburg, Maryland, 13 December. Details forthcoming but let it be said that he died in the line of duty, valiantly and heroically, in defense of God and country, and the preservation of the Union. Your obedient and humble servant, Col. Joshua Lawrence Chamberlain, 20th Maine.'

"Angered and shocked, Colonel Huxley reached down to pick-up the letter and tear it to shreds. And that's when he saw himself for the first time. All that motioned to that letter was the shattered stump of a phantom limb. Stumbling back he turned and looked into the study and saw a long, smooth pine box, its lid shut tight. There at its side sat his beloved Mary, clad in black, staring blankly at the walls, as the nothingness was fast consuming him. 'My arm,' he shouted, the pain burning in his side. 'Where is my arm?' Then he remembered the bridge, the explosions, the slaughter before him, and a sudden flash like lightning followed by a calm, a stillness, a drowsiness, darkness and sleep. 'Where is my arm?' All he knew before came and went in an instant. He gazed upon his Mary and sighed. Drowsiness was upon him. And all the world went dark… again!"

A moment or two went by. I sat there in silence waiting. It was though a séance had ended. The still was broken when Emma asked me if I'd care for more tea. "More tea?" I replied incredulously. "That's the story you told my mother?"

"Yes, dear! Many times we've discussed the fate of Colonel Huxley with her," she said. "I can see you're confused." I was about to weigh in on who the hell was confused when Edith blurted out, "but it's all quite elemental you see!"

"What is?" I asked.

"It's like I told your mother, dear," she said. "*He* has never found rest. *His* search continues, and will continue, I suppose, until *he* finds *it.*"

It was one of those Rod Serling-esque moments that tend to forever crystallize in some hidden recess of the mind. I was thinking that the sisters had missed the Age of Reason by about two centuries, having just sat through one of the more morbid tales I'd heard in a while. On the other hand, I didn't want to be too fresh, too curt. I knew that I had to deal with this in the right way or the demented duo could put the monkey on the hotel. They are old family and somewhat of an institution here in town, even if they are daft. So I ask you, bro? What would you have said to the "whack pack" if you were standing in my shoes? To keep the peace and my temper? A diplomatic solution was needed. I settled for a feint and said, "I'm not following you ladies. What is *he* searching for?"

Emma raised her eyebrows. Edith smiled and giggled a bit too deviously. "Why *he's* looking for his arm! What else do you think he'd be looking for?" said Edith like I was a dumb ass. "What do you think we've been talking about?"

"You're telling me that old man Huxley walks the grounds and buildings of the moe.Republic Hotel looking for his arm that was blown off at the Battle of Fredericksburg in December of 1862?" I asked in disbelief.

"That's what this is all about," said Emma. "Haven't you listened *boy*?" She spoke to me like an indentured servant. Is this how they treated everyone who came into their lives?

It was all I could do not to walk out and torch the place. I did, however, say my good-byes and leave. I came to the conclusion, walking back to the hotel, that whether or not you or I believe the story is irrelevant. Mother and the Huxley Sisters—sounds like some kind of retro-sixties Motown pop-diva group—sure as hell do! This was their reality but *I* had to deal with it or it would go on and on.

I can't say what kind of influence the rumors of the hotel being haunted have had on business other than the coming of Halloween. I suppose with a couple of well-placed ads we could make a run on the haunted house angle—

exploit it for all its worth—go Hollywood with special effects, a bit of gothic revival, the whole works. We could pack this old hotel tighter than father's post-operative hemorrhoidectomy. Of course there are eleven other months in the year, which runs the risk, come All Saints' Day, that we could scare off the vacationing hordes till next October. There is also that credibility issue and the prospect of attracting every fringe cult "Dungeons and Dragons" yahoo this side of New York and beyond.

But I digress. I left the Huxley sisters and the ambience of their late-Victorian padded cell determined to get to the bottom of this little mystery once and for all. My plan was to wait it out in the kitchen, even if I had to sit there all night. What I needed was a canary in the cave or mine—wherever the heck they put them—to alert me to any *unseen* presence that may enter the room. That canary was none other than Sparky the wonder dog.

The perfect opportunity. We were dog-sitting brother Kevin's pooch last week while he went to meditation camp. You know and I know that the only meditating Kevin could really hone in on is a couple of quarter-pounders. But when I said that out loud mother was quick to respond with a whack side the head, "He's not heavy. He's big boned and retains water!" Yeah, like Lake Ontario. But that Sparky's a heck of a dog—quite docile. Though a mellow pooch, even the bride had mentioned to me that once or twice he'd become agitated in the kitchen—right near the spot where Mother *heard* Colonel Huxley's arm scratch on the wall. It's unusual to see a dog go through mood swings. Granted Sparky isn't what you'd call the pick of the litter, but he also doesn't usually curl his tail up under his butt, or his hair stand on end along his neck and down his spine when he walks into a room, not unless he's aroused by *something*.

That night I grabbed a pint of brew from the moe.Microbrewery, lit a couple of candles, settled in with a Stephen King novel, and waited for the action. In ten minutes I was out cold. The bride said I was snoring so loud that Sparky began to howl, which pretty much killed that night. So the next night I did a shot of espresso and waited and watched. Fifteen minutes later I was out cold again, and didn't wake up until dawn, which if anything, meant that the espresso had cured the snoring. So it was that on the third night I was determined to stay awake at all costs to solve the mystery of the moe.Republic Hotel. With a roaring fire in the kitchen hearth, a double-espresso, and Sparky at my side I watched and waited for an appearance of the good Colonel. I had asked mother to dig out the Ouiji board thinking I could induce the Colonel to come hither at his own risk, except all she had was a Trivial Pursuit board and a piece from a Monopoly game.

I gave it a shot anyway, and I'll have you know that the longest river in the world is not the Nile! Two hours into Trivial Pursuit, a double-espresso with Sambuca chasers, and I was spent and bored. I was ready to head to the bar for a nightcap, but instead I picked up Mr. King and thought I'd buzz through a couple of more chapters of *The Shining*. I'm not sure if it was the book, the 'buca, or the joe, but after a few minutes of reading I felt my ears pop, like the sudden shift in cabin pressure when you're flying. There was a chill in the room, and as I read, I began to feel narcotized. I was ready to fight it, but I finally succumbed to the drift and dozed. I must have been sawing lumber because I suddenly awoke. I thought I heard distant music, but unrecognizable. Sparky was standing there staring at me. His hair on end. The fire had died out and I saw a mixture of bright lights and shadows dance across the white painted walls above the hearth. It reminded me of that time we went camping for your sixteenth birthday and watched the aurora borealis shoot across the northern sky all night. Or maybe I'm confusing that with that Dead concert at Red Rocks an eon ago.

A distinct chill filled the room, too. I was shivering and it made my nose itch. But when I went to scratch it I couldn't freaking *move!* It was like a weight had descended on me and pinned me down to the chair. I was paralyzed. I closed my eyes to think what the hell was going on, and when I did I felt my nose being scratched! Nearly shit my pants then and there, and I could have fainted. For all I know I probably did …faint, that is. I was hesitant to open my eyes fearing a bloody stump of an arm would be dangling in front of me like a macabre dancing puppet bouncing on some sinewy stringy tendons.

But I opened my eyes quickly and, of course, nothing was there. I relaxed and shut my eyes again. The weight on me was intense, but, with my eyes shut, I found that I could maneuver ever so slightly. I kept telling myself that I was having a nightmare, that I shouldn't panic, that it was in my head, that I would come to just like I did last New Year's Day.

The paralysis was not like I thought it would be, the loss of all neuro-sensation. I slowly realized I could feel my limbs. It was my torso that was encompassed by the weight as though constricted by a boa, or maybe it was Colonel Huxley's death grip on me? Whenever I tried to move I couldn't. The more I moved the tighter the grip. My eyes were slits now, I could see the flashes, the dancing lights and shadows. I could feel the pressure of the boa, compressing, squeezing, gripping whenever I moved. My only thought was to escape. I shut my eyes tight to gain leverage from this thing. I envisioned myself moving my right arm to the side of the chair, grasp the armrest, and pull as hard as I could.

At this point you could say that I was moving closer to the edge of sanity. I could feel beads of perspiration well up and slither down the side of my face. Sticky and dense. The weight of the boa fell on my chest. It spit on my face. It scratched my nose. The warmth of its skanky breath fell on my face. With all my will I pulled on the armrest and fell to the floor. I kept my eyes closed wanting only to slither away to the door across the cold, bare, hardwood floor. I tried to move, but the Colonel had me. I could feel the icy floor against my face. Ready to give in, I opened my eyes suddenly only to find myself sitting back in the chair, immobile again.

I don't know how many times I would shut my eyes and make the same futile effort to escape—fall to the floor, unable to move, then thrown back in the chair by Colonel Huxley each time I opened my eyes. I knew it was a dream. It sucked.

My eyes were open. I could see light and shadow dance. As hard as I concentrated to break the spell gripping me the weaker my resistance became.

The music had faded. I could barely hear it. I shut my eyes tight. I started thinking about the book I had been reading, about the bride, the children, the hotel—and this was the hard part—how right the Huxley sisters had been all along. It was a matter of keeping my composure, or at least my will, intact. There was only one other alternative—yell for help! I heard myself scream but my voice was no more than above a whisper. Again and again I yelled for help and I all I heard was barely a whisper. I couldn't move and I couldn't talk. I imagined myself being found this way. I could hear them now: "He looked like he'd seen a ghost—shit his pants and everything!" Just when I was thinking what else could possibly go wrong I heard the trudging of footsteps ascend the staircase to the threshold of the doorway. I heard a clawing, scratching sound at the door. I shut my eyes as hard as I could. If that door opened I didn't want to see what was on the other side of it. I was sure it was Colonel Huxley—and I damn well didn't want to be a part of the reunion of him and his arm, especially since the arm had me pinned down and he'd be coming right at me. As the latch gave way and the creak of the hinges sounded, I distinctly heard the first footfall upon the floor, and then another. I didn't know what to do or what was about to happen.

I was preparing to soil myself when I heard a bowl shatter on the floor. It startled me and broke the trance. I could move! I could move freely! My body felt contorted and numb. I opened my eyes. I was laying on the floor looking at the ceiling. *The Shining* was laid out next to me. And good old Sparky lay sprawled out across my chest. My legs and arms were tingly. I raised my head and Sparky licked my face. He was drooling and slobbering on me, too. The hair on the back of my neck bristled, but I had to laugh. I rolled over and he fell off with a thud.

Just as I was thinking thank God there was no icy hand gripping my neck the first sound I heard came from the wall—a slow, steady scratch—as though long sinewy fingers with pointed nails were gnawing from *inside* the wall. The scratching was near the cupboard where the bowl had fallen and shattered moments before. I was sitting up, bug-eyed. This was the capstone event of the whole week. I was awake. This was real. At any moment old Colonel Huxley was going to step through the wall in full military dress, all in fine order, except for the bloodied stump of his arm. What he would do next I did not know. In fact I could not imagine what he would do next, but I certainly knew what I would do. My bowels were already quaking from the nightmare. But good old Sparky was holding his ground. He went over to the wall and began to growl. The louder the scratching sound grew, the louder he growled. He followed the sound as it moved down the wall to the lower sideboards, and then under the floorboards. He stopped and pawed at the floorboards.

The vision of stumpy old Huxley walking through the wall and sitting on my chest choking me to an inch of my last breath gave way to sense of relief. Or should I say a realization, an epiphany, that rather than an ethereal specter we were dealing with a terrestrial invasion. I stood up and walked quietly to the basement door. I grabbed a flashlight, and with Sparky at my side, we went down the stairs. You remember when we renovated we had to install all new plumbing and those guys had to punch a new hole through the outer foundation? Not only did they leave some of the old pipes hanging there, apparently our crack team of plumbers failed to patch up the old hole that well. When I flicked on the flashlight, there running across the pipes, in and out of a small hole through the foundation, was the biggest, fattest, bunch of rats I'd ever seen. There were four of them busting butt, going back and forth across the pipes like it was some kind of highway. They'd stop, reach up on their haunches, and gnaw and scratch at the bottom of the floorboards.

It was enough to get old Sparky barking and growling. He actually jumped up attempting to get at them, teeth snapping, drool spraying everywhere. The ballsy little pricks didn't even run. They stopped gnawing, sat there on their haunches, and simply looked at me and the dog. I could have sworn that the little shits were smiling. After a minute they started gnawing again. I reached for the closest piece of free artillery I could get my hands on. A baseball bat would have been ideal, or even a fishnet, then I could have taken the little shits and microwaved them one at a time. Probably would have been tough to explain away to the Board of Health, though. Anyway, I settled for a badminton racket. I swatted at the vermin and missed. I swear they were laughing now, which only pissed me off further. I came with a backhand and connected. One fell to the floor with a smack and Sparky went nuts. Not a pretty sight. Made me change my mind about the microwave thing, too. This got the rest of them to retreat in a hurry. My business was done, except for the mess on the floor.

We baited and trapped the cellar, and father had the rest of them in the frying pan within a couple of days. He wore his old army helmet and said it reminded him of tracking down the last Nazi SOBs in Sicily in '44. That's when we brought in Gil 'Bugs' Fonebone as an added measure. He patched up the hole in the foundation. As I said, we're *clean* now. Fonebone told me that father, Sparky, and I had been very thorough and saved him a lot of work. I can't imagine what his fee would have been if we hadn't been thorough. But hey! It's a write-off! And though the thrill of the hunt has passed, the *mystery* laid to rest, I can't stop thinking of that night, the blast of cold air, the grip of an icy hand. I think of Colonel Huxley and the thought of him still dropping in from time to time. Was it real or all a dream? And then I think: oh, rats!

Till then,
brother John

Act III

Further Seasons, Farther Travels

```
From:    brother.john@moe.republic.org
To:      rob@moe.org
Date:    January 4, 19:57
Subject: Winter Solstice, Christmas Time, into the
         New Year
```

Cher frère Robért: Greetings from the Lost Kingdom. Happy belated winter solstice, and Merry Christmas and Happy New Year to you and the whole moe.entourage, too. I hear that another moe.tour is about to get underway very soon. We're still looking for a band to play the Winter Carnival next month if you can fit us in. You won't regret it this time. I promise.

Weather wise, the carnival should be a slam dunk. The snow is quite heavy again today. The third major storm in the past couple of weeks. The islands across the bay appear as barely visible amorphous blobs against the pale, expressionless, gray landscape. Sort of what your eyes looked like last New Year's Eve. Which reminds me—how did the gig at that club go this year? Sorry we couldn't make it, but we were snowed in. The day before the storm father was out playing with the snowblower you and Becca bought him for Christmas. He left it outside somewhere the night the nor'easter hit. We've been digging around the grounds for a week now, but I think we've seen the last of it until April. It was a heck of a gift, though! Great idea.

Unfortunately the moe.sleigh was down, too. One of the runners collapsed the night we had the Greater Penobscot Bay Weight Minders Society holiday sleigh ride party. So we missed moe. again this New Year's. Hey! Maybe next year you guys could play here? Think it over. You don't have to answer right away. We've got plenty of time to sort out a no frills package for you and the gang.

I wrote this tardy holiday missive from a barstool in the moe.Microbrewery. We are on the last keg of our holiday special, Santa Claus Stout—an exceptionally mellow, yet surprisingly robust, nutty brew. If business doesn't rebound soon I may quaff the whole damn thing myself...

Not to worry! After word of the Halloween *haunting* got around, business really picked up. We had a very busy holiday season here, from a capitalist, bourgeois bent. The Liberty Ballroom was booked solid for the entire month of December, and so were the sleigh ride parties till that fated weekend before Christmas. Everything was going well until New Year's Eve and the big blizzard.

Yet, in some ways the lull over the past few days has been relaxing, because the winter season creeps upon us. Come February we will be getting the spillover from the Bullwinkle Ski Lodge up the road. We are also holding the bi-weekly meetings of the Penobscot Valley Icefishing Club. I think it's the only time all winter these guys use real plumbing. Next weekend is the Great Downeast Dogsled Winter Festival, sure to be insanely chaotic. Having all those huskies around here is quite a trip, especially come the spring thaw. It will certainly add another dimension to mud season. We're looking forward to Saint Patrick's Day, too, the biggest party day of the year after New Year's Eve. I know what you're thinking. What could possibly go wrong? Really! We've got Valentine's Day to deal with yet, and then there's Presidents' Day weekend and winter vacation.

Well, I gotta go. I see the lawyer coming up the walkway. Bigwood's here to discuss a minor litigation problem we're having with regard to one slightly inebriated patron on New Year's Eve. This guy decided it was entirely appropriate to take the moosehead off the wall and place it on his head. The idiot then stumbled blindly off the Liberty Ballroom balcony, rolling head first down the hill and into the bay. Now the guy's suing us for not stopping him. Bigwood's done some sleuthing on the guy—one more thing he and King-horn are in to—professional snooping. I'm hoping Bigwood's gonna tell me he's firmly grasped the guy by the balls and is ready to squeeze on my word. Okay it's crude, but a good hard yank and I guarantee his heart and mind will follow, and we'll be done with it. Like father always says, "better a pain in your balls than a pain in my ass." Well, not much else to say. Nope. That's it for now.

Forever and ever,
brother John

The moe.Republic Hotel
in the heart of the Lost Kingdom

The Saint Patrick's Day Contact
By the fireplace
Tuesday, 8:17 p.m.

Hey Rob,

A big hello to you and the moe.incorporated from the great boreal domains of the moe.Republic Hotel. The bride and I are sitting by the fireplace, basking in the warm, amber glow of a fading Downeast winterscape, at least as seen through the lens of this brew we're quaffing. It was pretty cold this morning. After the snow we had yesterday, the mercury is still heading south with no north in sight. Lest I forget to mention it, there's a G-man sitting across the room staring at me. At least I think he is staring at me behind the dark shades he's wearing. It's been a heck of a week, and I've got a lot to tell you, though I don't know where to begin.

While you and the moe.entourage have been marching toward destiny, trekking across the continent, up the left coast and back, things have been a little bizarro around these parts. It's to the point where I think that Buck Jones wasn't bullshitting me that day at the gas station when he told me all about this place and the lost portal. Okay, maybe it makes for good press, but things have been crazy.

I'm not talking about the drunk who fell off the balcony and ended up in the bay on New Year's Eve. His family decided to settle out of court. That's what Bigwood was stopping by to tell me. They paid for the legal fees and repaired the moosehead. I think there was a general consensus that he put the bottle to his head and pulled the trigger. In this day and age when most folks abhor taking responsibility for their own actions, it's reassuring to hear someone admit when they've screwed up. I don't know how the guy survived the fall, let alone the water, though I'm told he could lose a couple of digits to frostbite.

That's a minor episode compared to the UFO sightings! Verily I speaketh: No shit! U-Freaking-Ohs! Unidentified Flying Objects! The story of what is now being called 'the Saint Patrick's Day contact' is being suppressed.

There is a complete media blackout. The truth will be told. Somehow. Even now as I write this missive father is repairing the sleigh so he may blast off to spread the news (We have to. We still haven't located the snowblower).

From what I know now the commotion began when an *object* crashed into Mount Agamenticus during a not too uncommon late winter blizzard yesterday. The storm was bad enough that the local Hibernian Guard had to call off the annual parade, which ought to tell you something right there. When Chief Mickey McO'Fayle and the clan have to call off the parade you know it must have been a hell of a weather event.

The first reports of the crash went out on WMOE. They announced that a B-52 had slammed into the side of the mountain. Later, the station countered with a report that the Air Force had announced that a satellite had gone down. Quite honestly, it quickly became an item of intense gossip as to what actually had crashed up there. From Kinghorn's Diner to Bagwell's Bookstore to Buck's Garage, the sociology of rumor was in full throttle. People had seen strange lights in the sky. Lights that hovered hither and thither like a humming bird moving around a feeder. Soon, a slew of dark Suburbans with government issued license plates were rolling through town. Curiously enough, only a few of them headed up the mountain to the reported crash site. Most of them were seen zipping along the back roads and side streets. The Chief would later say that it was though they were searching for someone or something, rather than a crash site.

At the time, I really didn't give it much thought. We still had a party to attend to. It *was* Saint Patrick's Day and things were hopping. The hotel was full of revelers. The moe.Microbrewery had just won the blue ribbon for our batch of Shamrock Ale at the annual Saint Patrick's Day Brew-a-thon Derby. We beat Goatlips Saloon, the Silent Woman Tavern, and the rest of them. Unlike that homemade batch you made last year, which, if you recall, gave poor Chuck, Al, and a host of other poorly constituted individuals the green skitters something fierce, this batch had a rejuvenating kick, but without any reverberating gastro-intestinal side effects.

News of the crash soon melted away in the excitement of the 'holiday.' That, and the fact that out of the blue Kevin showed up! Yes, that's right! Our brother Kevin actually came to visit with his black lab Sparky. Thought it might be a swell idea to get out of town and stretch his legs, go on a little trip. I hadn't seen either since the holidays, and before that, Halloween. As a burgeoning actor his time is limited, especially since he landed that gig as a professional mannequin. I guess you can relate being the 'other' entertainer in the family.

"Cripes!" I said to him after greetings and salutations were extended throughout the house. "You know you're lucky you got here alive in this blizzard." He shook the cold off himself as we made our way to the lounge. "The mountain's usually not that forgiving."

"I know," he replied shivering. "I can't stand being on the road in this weather. That's why I let Sparky do the driving. Best damn dog I ever had."

"He's a pretty good hunter, too," I laughed. "Especially pestilent-type rodentia. Aren't you Sparky?" The dog had already made his way to the warmth of the fireplace, sprawling out under the moosehead. At the sound of his name his tail fluttered momentarily.

"I told you it was a rough drive," Kevin grinned.

"You're looking a bit road-weary yourself," I said to him, which was no exaggeration. The guy did look a little drawn and burned out.

"Must you torment me?" he sighed. "It's been what? Five minutes?"

"Hey, relax Mr. World Traveler—performing in department stores in Paris, London, and Montreal! All I meant was that you looked a little tired."

"Yeah, you're right. I don't mean to be so sensitive." His demeanor shifted slightly. "I am burned. This gig as a mannequin is taking its toll on me. You know it's not easy, eight hours a day, five days a week—believe me when I tell you—I feel like my life is standing still!" He was quite emphatic in his irony. "How about an Irish coffee, then, except use Crown."

"That I can do."

"Thank you," he replied. "Now that we have that straightened out, let me say it's nice to be here."

"I'm glad you came," I said. "You picked a good day, too. It's the one day of the year when manly men can write their name in green in any snowbank without lifting a pen."

"Well, here's to you," I handed him his coffee. "And to Saint Paddy's Day. May it be a memorable one!"

It would have been nice to have a few more pops and catch up, but the crowds were rolling in. Instead, we recruited Kevin, and he, father, McBain, myself, and the rest of the crew worked the bar in a frenzy. There's no time to think when you're in the trenches during happy hour, let alone just about all of Saint Patrick's Day. The choreography is not the same as a free-flowing Martha Graham dance production, but there is a synchronicity to the act when wetting the monkeys' heads. Amidst the sweat and booze, as wave after wave of revelers crash the bar, you lose track of time. The evening was upon us in no time. The festivities were going full bore. My only distraction was when these short guys in green face and bowler hats arrived. Man could they drink. "You know you're doing something right," McBain shouted out over the din, "when even the leprechauns show up for your Saint Paddy's Day." I soon lost sight of them and the time. All of a sudden it was around midnight. The Liberty Ballroom was still cranking out the Irish jigs. The storm had come to an end and the stars were shining bright. A frigid arctic blast was beginning to descend upon us. Chief McO'Fayle and the ex-patriots were doing a conga line that snaked right along the bar. They'd shout out an order for a shot. Then in one motion, as the line swung by the bar, they'd pick it up and down it.

That proved to be enough for Kevin, who was haggard and needed to have some 'space.' At least that's what he told me at the time. I was ready to join him on the back porch, but was still needed inside. As it turned out, it proved to be a life-altering decision for both of us. Kevin went outside wearing one of those jester ski hats, the kind with all those multiple pointy ends. He had a matching hat tied to the head of Sparky, who was in tow. I guess he tired of waiting for me and decided to go cross-country skiing. About thirty minutes later I see him and the dog atop one of hills that overlook the hotel and town. By that time I was cooling down myself. I was with the bride on the deck off the ballroom when we heard him yell. You could tell it was him by his and Sparky's pointy-headed silhouettes against the evening sky. He looked like he was jumping and waving his hands frantically so we waved back. Then a weird whirring, humming sound came from his direction. It grew louder. That's when the blackout happened. The deck was quickly overrun by the conga line. Somebody shouted, "look on top the hill!" Before I could say it was only my brother and his dog we saw a shadow, obelisk-like, with a pair of disc shaped orbs at the base rise behind him on the hill. The obscenely monstrous Steely Dan enveloped the darkness. Suddenly, there was a series of strobe-like flashes. There were dots every-where. Like a flick of a switch, the blackout lifted. Nobody said anything. There was absolute quietude. It was hypnotic. It was eerily calm. It was a bowel-quaking episode that will endure in the mythology of the moe.Republic for generations. And that was the whole thing. We couldn't hear *them* anymore! Sparky and Kevin, their pointy-headed silhouettes up on the hill, had vanished!

You know the bride and I would have been perfectly content to file the experience under the "if a tree fell in the forest and nobody's around does it make a sound?" archive. But no! It was bad enough that mother and father were freaking out about Kevin, but half the town was freaked out, too. We organized a search party but came up empty—no tracks, no signs, nothing but this pair of gigantic oval imprints, side by side, laid out in the snow behind the hill. Some crash! Folks are saying that whatever it was had 'waited' out the storm to take off or was completing a recovery mission of its own. I just don't know. Other than that brief instant when that shadow passed, it's too crazy to even contemplate.

All those Suburbans which had been cruising through town for hours converged on the hotel within minutes after the blackout lifted. An Air Force colonel stepped out of the lead SUV and introduced himself. He told me that he and his men would be checking in for a while. And he said it like we didn't have much choice in the matter. Now the Air Force guys have hunkered in with a cadre of G-men, all of whom have been combing the far side of the hill since. They've called for a psuedo-townmeeting here day after tomorrow, apparently to hold court with the eye-witnesses. Meanwhile, the hotel has turned into "contact central," which is not too bad for business. On the other hand, I've got an uptight staff-sergeant giving me a hard time and that G-man is still watching me from across the room. He follows me everywhere. I recall now the dire words of Jorge Ortega, the sage of Weehawken, a scholar and friend, who, despite his many years on the lam, or perhaps because of them, oft warned me to "free yourself of paranoia. Trust no one." In times like these his words ring true. As I sit before the fire writing this bizarre missive, quaffing a pop (or two), it all seems too damn odd. We are still wondering what happened here. On second thought, do me a favor. Don't tell anyone about this just yet. I think they are on to me and I think that they know about you, too. In the mean time, if all goes well, I will see you and the guys at the Orpheum Theater with further intelligence reports. Till then, I will furtively feed the trough...

brother John

```
From:     brother.john@moe.republic.org
To:       rob@moe.org
Date:     March 23, 9:06 a.m.
Subject: thanks for your support!
```

dear Rob: received your reply about last week.

no I have not come unhinged!

I have not had a flashback in two decades!

yes the winters are too long!

who doesn't need a vacation?

I am not drinking away the profits!

and when you say committed, I take it you're inferring to running the family business! otherwise, I'm going to tell mom and dad!

j

-p.s. next time don't hold back—tell me what you really think!

The moe.Republic Hotel
in the heart of the Lost Kingdom

A Fine Web we Weave
In the Parlor
Thursday, 2:22 a.m.

Buon Giorno Roberto,

I'm not one to hold grudges and I accept your apology. And sorry about the sphincter comment, too. It just slipped out, so to speak. I guess I got carried away when I arrived at the Orpheum show and my pass was stamped *persona non grata*. Now that the story's broke over the newswires and I'm no longer certifiable, it's time to bring you up to speed. Spring has cometh for most folks out there in moe.land. Soon the moe.pool will be opened, the moe.beach will be filled with sunbathers, who once again will thirst for the finest ambers and largers that the infinite fount of the moe.Microbrewery can offer.

Alas, spring is but a concept here, a state of mind, somewhere between the deep freeze of winter and the warm rays of summer. The time when folks downeast deal with two of nature's fiercest predators: mud and bugs. There is sort of a symbiotic link between the two. The mud bogs beget the black fly and the black fly begets you—the fodder before the legions. There is nothing quite comparable to the black fly in its predatory capabilities. It will land just about anywhere on you. It will crawl into any orifice it deems fit. It will not bite you until it has gotten to the one spot on your body that you can't scratch—at least not in public. The black fly doesn't just sting. It tears and devours your flesh, leaving its victims with epidermal cankers akin to some distant strain of smallpox. During the spring one often observes perfectly normal people walking about who suddenly convulse and smack themselves beside the head or across their ass for no apparent reason. We have been told that it is not uncommon for moose to run insanely out of the woods and throw themselves in front of logging trucks to escape the swarming ravages of the dreaded black fly. Without a specific proper cultural indoctrination what would one think?

The black flies should be no problem for you and your betrothed's big day, though. That is, if you and the boys ever decide to stop touring for ten minutes. I'm surprised the moe.bus is still chugging after the grueling punishment it has withstood the past five months—down the Chesapeake, back to New England, across Appalachia, up to the Great Lakes, down below the Blue Ridge Mountains, across the plains and prairies, over the Rockies, up the left coast, and snaking back along a similarly inverse, direct route, and onward still. Mush! Is it true that your manager Topper left a career in logistics with Triple A to plot tours for moe.? Just wondering?

The lavender chiffon tuxes you ordered for yourself and the guys have arrived, as have the bone white, patent leather shoes. We have also finalized the arrangement with Big Eddie Munch's Expressionist Polka Band. The cake is still a problem, though. Seems the bakery is having trouble getting its hands on a full-bodied, light-sabered, Darth Vader mold. Tell Becca not to worry. We haven't given up yet. Father is all over it. But just in case, the bakers want to know if you would settle for an ice sculpture of a goose and a layer cake?

As I mentioned last week over the phone, the search for Kevin and Sparky continues. What I didn't tell you in full was how that meeting went when the Air Force guys "debriefed" the community. I'll tell you what, the Liberty Ballroom was packed. Before the meeting got going we had a happy hour run on the last of the Shamrock Ale and made a bundle. Mother made some of her whoopee pies, too, which were a hit. She was high on ceremony that night, wearing a blue plaid tam, with a matching kilt and a white blouse. An accordion rested gently over her shoulder. She serenaded the crowd with a mournful rendition of "Amazing Grace," the first song she ever learned.

In the mean time the Air Force guys prepped to rationalize the affair. It would be the only secret they didn't hold that night. I found myself sucked into the energy of a staff sergeant. He had a large melon-like head, crew cut, and a neck like an English bulldog that melded to his rounded shoulders. The runners on his wire rim glasses burrowed into the sides of his fleshy temples. A laptop was in front of him and even as he spoke to me he continued to type. Every word was accomplished with a pathological fury. His thick, stubby fingers moved with an ungodly, satanic precision across the micro-keyboard. The blur of movement was hypnotic; actually, unnerving.

My trance was broken when he began to lecture me about the correct spelling of the place. "A small m-o-e period, capital R—Republic?" He kept asking me over and over, typing and typing, faster and faster. I didn't know if he was reading what he was speaking or speaking what he was spelling. "The proper spelling should capitalize the M, you know," and before he said *that* he had typed a capital M. "That's an improper usage of a period, too!"

First thing I thought, was this guy for real? Then it struck me. It was all a distraction. The whole pomp and pageantry of the affair was a dog and pony show. Should I tell him off? Should I comment on his robotic ape-like qualities. Then I thought, hey, they *were* paying customers. Besides, what if the guy had stormed the beachheads of Grenada or had been in the Gulf War? This guy was no clerk. By his build he was a gorilla surely prone to psychotic episodes. I didn't want to rile him up and trigger a Manchurian response— could be bad for business. So I toned it down. I smiled. "Yes," I said with a pat on his back which was like striking a concrete slab, "it's a small m-o-e, but it's not a period it's a *dot*. The moe-*dot*-Republic Hotel with a capital R and H! The beer you quaff is from the moe-dot-Microbrewery! The moe-*dot* is an icon, not an act of subversion against the mother tongue."

As we talked people had filed into the room. It was near filled when our friend the colonel entered and sat at the conference table up front, just to the right of where the anal retentive staff sergeant and myself had jousted over the lexicon. At the colonel's left was a G-man, dark glasses and all, who, I surmised, had been keenly listening to our exchange. I moved to the rear and looked out at the masses. Before them sat a ballroom full of plaid-shirted, down-parka'd, ruddy-cheeked, green-tongued, exceptionally anxious townies. My thoughts were that they took us for a bunch of rubes and could and would tell us just about anything.

Then the full bird began to speak. "There were a great many calls and confusion after the blackout. We apologize," he said. "A satellite did crash. We are cleaning up the debris. You did not see anything extraordinary... blah, blah, blah. ...and therefore, a residual electromagnetic impulse caused a brief interruption to the power grid." Point by point he rationalized the whole experience, except of course the Kevin and Sparky part. Then again, he said he didn't have much to say about that, other than he was concerned and sorry about them being lost in the woods, especially with it being so cold out.

He was done talking. Basically he had explained nothing for thirty minutes. I thought it would be prudent to remind him that Kevin and Sparky had literally vanished before a hotel full of people. But did it really matter to them? They were sent here to rationalize and contain the pandemonium. It was done. It had worked. People retreated to the bar, a bit perplexed, but ready to accept the reality as defined, which was a bit easier to take. The full bird walked up to me and thanked us for our *hospitality* and *cooperation*. "Do let us know when your brother and his dog turn up. We're very concerned," the colonel said on the sly. "I'm sure that he'll come in from the cold soon enough. Let's hope he didn't get carried *too* far away." He smiled and winked, and then led the whole crew away. After the townmeeting the "incident" quickly passed into local folklore. The "Saint Patrick's Day contact" was now passé.

We did get a call the other day from someone, somewhere. I soon recognized the voice of the staff sergeant. He said that "section" was seeking closure and wanted to clarify a few things. Then he began to lecture me again about the spelling of the place. "A small m-o-e period, capital R—Republic?" he kept asking me over and over amid the rapid muted staccato of a keyboard. "You really should capitalize the 'm', you know, and the usage of that period is despicable!" So was this conversation, I thought. And I wanted to say as much. But hey, on the other hand, like I said, they *had* been paying customers. If the boy and his dog ever show up again they probably would, too. In all practicality I didn't need to alienate myself from a psychotic, either. Especially one that could drop in the neighborhood at any time. He had my name, number, and the ability to complicate my life at will, with extreme prejudice. Calmly I spoke, "it's not a period it's a *dot*," I reminded him. "We call it the moe-*dot*-Republic Hotel with a capital R and H!" And we laughed.

And now we wait. I've included the article about the "contact" and cover up that reporter, Jackson Grant, wrote for the *Downeast Way Times*. Jackson's a good egg—wrote a couple of choice stories early on when we first opened. Did a nice piece on the grand opening and a dandy on the moose fiasco. Since then he's made a fine addition to the motley crew of regulars who haunt the bar. Always good to have the press on your side—good to have anyone on your side these days. Even Dr. Kinghorn and Mr. Bigwood have offered to do some *pro bono* work on the case. If anything, they can keep the G-men honest, and help to separate the fact from fiction. We're going to need it. The rumors from the underground say that the Air Force has picked up a guy in ski boots with a black lab—both of whom were wearing jester hats—in the middle of the Nevada desert, at a place called Area 51. But we really don't know anything about that…

Till then,

brother John

The moe.Republic Hotel
in the heart of the Lost Kingdom

Dear Rob,

Greetings to you and all the moe.faithful. Spring has cometh and gone, and the warm rays of the sultry summer sunshine have finally arrived. The moe.Republic is filled with happy turistas today. The moe.pool is overflowing and the beach is crowded. It's been one good summer season, filled with endless travelers and revelers. I am sitting here on the moe.veranda sipping some frozen strawberry concoction McBain has blended up.

I see on the moe web site that the summer tour is going full bore, pedal to the metal, across the continent. After pounding away on the road all winter you guys must be having the time of your lives. In fact, by the time you get this letter I imagine the tour will be winding down and you'll be heading off on another adventure. I got to admit that the Great Woods show was fantastic. That was an awesome jam on "Bring You Down." I think it was the first time in years that I hadn't been witness to some kind of pyrotechnic-negative-karma-equipment breakdown at one of your Boston area shows. Even father commented on the turn in fortune, though quite cryptically. He mentioned offhandedly about it being a really good omen, though as a sign of the times, never forget that any omen is still just one letter shy of women, and thusly, you'd best beware!

Speaking of which, the wedding photos have arrived and your bride does look beautiful. But I must say that you and the guys sure do look handsome in your lavender chiffon tuxes. I told you that the bone white, patent leather shoes would add a special touch to your outfit. Also, everyone around here is still in the groove over Big Eddie Munch's Expressionist Polka Band. I know what you're thinking, but you don't have to thank me. Mother always said that she wanted one of her children to play the accordion, and Big Eddie is the next best thing.

The wedding cake blues never really materialized like we thought it would. Seems the bakery had no trouble getting its hands on a full-bodied, light-saber, Darth Vader mold. I told Becca not to worry. And thanks for letting us keep the mold. As I write, I can see some kids on the beach building sand-Vaders again.

Time to wrap this up. Here comes Jackson Grant and his uncle, Porter Gibson Digit. Well, he's sort of his uncle. Porter was Jackson's grandfather Jeffrey's best friend and his dad's godfather. Technically speaking, he's Jackson's god-grandfather, which seems to suit each of them just dandy. That's the same Jeffrey the Huxley sisters told me about the one and only time I went to their house. I guess he and Porter really did work for old man Huxley during the depression. That was a long time ago, which was why, personally, I thought that Porter had kicked it—especially the way people talked about him in the past tense—and said as much to him when Jackson first introduced me. Talk about a major *faux pas*. There I stood, eye-to-eye with the legendary Bird Man—the dude who invented the finger. It was bad enough that I spaced out and was taken aback, but the first thing I started to say was, "I thought you were…" before I caught myself. Porter laughed it off, but not before he busted my balls some. He tells everyone right up front that he's come home to die. I guess it puts them at ease, let's them relax or open up. It put me at ease. I mean, there I was standing across from one of the great personalities of the twentieth century. And what do I do? I inhaled my size 12W Chuck Taylor's to the tip top of the high top the first time I meet him.

The way Jackson tells it, Porter's been using that "coming home to die" line for thirty years. Chicks dig it. I think Jackson does too, because he's putting it in the book. The one he's writing about Porter, his biography. The two of them come here a few days a week to work on it. That doesn't slow Porter down. The old-timer's become quite the regular of late, watching the ball games in the evenings and hitting on the babes between innings. Baseball's his love—once upon a time he played for the Dodgers—and women are his passion. The first time he saw the bride striding through the bar he asked her if she wanted to get digitized and flicked her the bird. She jumped, as all do in the presence of that mighty obelisk and veritable switchblade, but held her ground. "First of all," she said tartly, "you better have a license to carry that thing or I'm calling the Chief. And secondly," she gave a nod toward me, "why would any girl settle for a carrot on a stick when she's got a cucumber on the vine!"

"Hot damn, Sally!" he wheezed out a laugh. "Boy," he shouted at me. "You got yourself a keeper!" She'd passed the first test. Not too many do when the Bird Man flicks you the finger.

Porter's been at it since he left town back in the teens. His claim to fame, his *nom de plume*, came from those early days, back when any kind of protest was a matter of life and death. "Ah, the finger!" He'll spout up from time to time. "The great pacifistic, anarchist symbol of our age. Never meant it to be much more than a hardy *fuck you* to the man." (He always emphasizes the "fuck you" like he's about to go to war.) "But the power of history is such, after that day in Washington Square, it took on a force of its own." Now that's a story I'll have to tell you sometime, or maybe the next time you're in town you can hear it first hand. The guy's here all the time. Him and father have hit it off well. When they start in on the stories, particularly the war stories, they go toe-to-toe. Not sure how deep it gets between the two of them, but it makes for pretty good theater at the bar.

Whoa! Porter just flicked Jackson his trademark invention. He's making eye contact with me. Bang! I just got the bird, too. That's my cue for a Scotch on the rocks—and anything else for that matter.

Time to feed the trough,
brother John

The moe.Republic Hotel
in the heart of the Lost Kingdom

Dear Rob,

Hey dude! Things are grooving here in the blissful wilds of the Lost Kingdom. We held the first annual Halloween Storytellers festival last weekend—did the whole spooky mansion routine—and the turnout was unbelievable. I don't know if it was because of last year's haunted happenings or what. But there's something about a good ghost story that can reel them in. I have to hand it to the old man, too. Father came up with the idea after visiting Key West last summer. He went there to bonefish and rode into town during Hemingway Days. He had no idea the festival was going on when he went. How he even got a room is beyond me because it's one of the biggest festivals in Florida each summer. Hundreds of Hemingway clones and group-ies converge on the town. Father had a two week growth and blended in nicely. On his second day there he walked into Captain Tony's Saloon for a beer and won third place in a Hemingway look-a-like contest.

Amidst the babes, booze, and ballyhoo is the fabled storytellers competi-tion. Prospective writers of all ages read terse stories of lost hope and despair before a solemn panel of judges. Not just any judges. These are hardened scholars who have deciphered and argued for decades the influence and meaning of such Hemingway minutiae as why he hated his mother for dressing him as a girl.

When father returned it got me thinking: why not a festival here? Why not a theme-based gig? Why not Halloween? But something different than a "haunted house" to scare-the-living-shit-out-of-you-type thing. I already did that to myself. Why not a few good stories? So we ran a few ads here and there, and next thing you know we had some of the best storytellers from all over the continent. Okay, well maybe the county. It was a tough choice, but below are the top two entries as voted by the judges—Jackson Grant of the *Downeast Way Times*, Phillip Turner of the *Phoenix*, and Shelly McNugent, who, when she's not helping Casey out at Farkleberry Farm, teaches over at

Bowdoin. There's a brief biography of each writer that's included before their story. The grand prize winner received two front row seats for moe.'s New Year's Eve gig this year. I didn't think you'd care. Oh yeah, and the people get to have dinner with you, too. Mother said that wouldn't be a problem either— it was her idea. The runner-up got three-nights, two-days, here at the hotel. There was some serious bartering going on between the two after it was over, but not to worry. You should know who you'll be spending NYE with by next Wednesday. Just as soon as the auction for those tickets ends on eBay. The bidding is hanging tough at $15.39, but there's a still a few days to go. See if you can guess which one was voted top story. I'll let you know later.

Hauntingly yours,
brother John

The Old Church
By Conrad Dixon

A Downeast Way man on the brink of fame and fortune, internationally acclaimed author Conrad Dixon, gave up the good life and recently retired under the gentle slopes of Mount Agamenticus. Mr. Dixon's third novel, *Ringling's Bulge*, about the coming of age of an innocent trapeze artist and sword-swallower being raised by circus freaks in turn-of the-century Vienna, received mixed reviews. One critic wrote that "the inner cravings of the flesh are aroused ever so slightly." Another stated, "When one thinks of *Fin-de-Siecle* Vienna, one thinks of the art of Gustav Klimt and Oscar Kokoschka, the music of Arnold Schoenberg, Freud and the interpretation of a dream, the architectural symbolism of the Ringstrasse —and now the ensuing decadence of an overly endowed dandy in tights. Be real!" Mr. Dixon seems unperturbed with the assessment, and denied that the reviews sent him to seek refuge in his bungalow under the 'Old Mountain by the Sea.' This is Mr. Dixon's first submission in the genre. "The Old Church" provides us with a chilling tale based upon a true event that shook the Lost Kingdom one Halloween many years ago.

The Old Church

There was an old Catholic church under the shadow of an ancient oak tree. Built in 1853, it lay in a hollow on the east side of Mount Agamenticus. Serving first the Irish, and later the French Canadian communities, which had migrated to the Lost Kingdom, as all eventually do, in search of a higher plane of existence. The church was a holy place of worship that had a spiritual bond over its parishioners. That was, until they found Father Remy Durrell that Sunday out behind the rectory.

All Saints' Day 1932, was cool and crisp. An occasional gust carried in off the bay. The old oak, which stood tall in the backyard of the rectory next to the church, barely swayed in the wind. Its barren branches, sprawled wildly, reaching out like gnarled witch's fingers. That late autumn morning you could hear the dead leaves whooshing and rustling at its base with each gust of wind. That, and the creaking body of Father Durrell. He was hanging by his neck, swinging and twisting in a hooded vestment five feet off the ground. It was a ghastly sight to behold — as though he had been picked up and tossed into the tree. His robes, entangled in the gnarly branches above, flapped eerily as he swayed. But he was bruised and beaten, too. It looked as though he had fought his assailant or assailants. His wrists were burned raw like they had been bound by an invisible rope, which only contributed further to the great mystery surrounding his death. A mystery made more so by the imprint on the ground below his body. For directly beneath his dangling corpse an inverted crucifix as large as the man lay smoldering on the barren grass.

No one really knew what had happened or why. There seemed no worldly explanation for the priest's demise. Rumors circulated in hushed tones. People swallowed hard to even breath it above a whisper lest *he* might overhear and come forth again. Years passed, and many priests came and went. None stayed on that long, and the diocese refused to comment on why that was. As children we would rush by the church with a sense of foreboding about the grounds. Was it our imaginations? They say children can feel and see things unto realms that most adults can't grasp or have simply lost touch with. Perhaps that was why the children always found it particularly difficult to pass by each October 31. When the sun went down, it became a very sinister place.

Allhallows Eve was when the shadows rose up in and around the old church. The children could see them plainly like jack-o-lanterns flickering in the dark. The adults chided them for their imagination, but held their breath nonetheless, remembering faintly a nightmarish residue that lingered from their own youths. The presence of evil radiated out of the walls to the backyard under the tree. They say that a battle raged there — screams and cries, curses and damnation — could be heard. That was why, after many years had passed since the mysterious death of Father Durrell, three devout young men were sent by the diocese to spend the evening of October 31 in the church.

They arrived there unassumingly and entered unnoticed. The darkness fell and the hours passed. The three sat contemplatively in the pews, praying and meditating. By 11:45 they had come to the conclusion that they could rightfully and honestly report to the Bishop that all was well in the old church under the shadow of the oak tree. That was just about the time the furnace kicked on. At least that's what they thought it was initially, for the sound rumbled from the basement. Quickly it welled up into a dire, whispering desperate moan. A subtle descent of frigid air followed, enveloping the room.

The men looked at each other and murmured "did you hear that?" and "I can see my breath!" The faint, yet distinct moans, continued to emanate from below. The sound was rising, coming forth, welling up through the vents. It was then that the ancient radiator near the altar burst, piping steam heavily. Shapes gradually took form within the mist. Incorporeal apparitions, that of a woman, the other a young child, perhaps four or five years old. There were now two distinct cries and moans coming from the area of the altar, which grew louder as the minutes passed. Without warning, all went silent. The lights fluctuated brightly and fizzed out in a power surge. A rack of prayer candles, which were lit near the front altar, glimmered in the icy silence of the hall. A fetid ripe odor filled the room. An odor all too familiar from their years as missionaries in war-ravaged villages in distant lands. They gasped now to catch their breath amidst the overwhelming raw stench of decaying flesh.

A rustling sound from the rear of the church distracted the men, who turned slowly with apprehension and dread. Behind them, only a few rows back, a lone figure sat motionless in a dark, cloaked hood. That was enough. The men stood up quickly to make their escape, but they could not move. Perhaps fear gripped them or an unseen hand, or maybe it was much more fundamental, a true testament to their mortality. Ultimately, like the many before and the many to come, when finally confronted by the demon why does the faith of our mothers and fathers collapse? Why do we fall to temptation? Paralyzed, all they could do was gaze. Deep within the coal pit darkness of the hood a pair of reddened eyes glared at them. In the dimness of the church hall they burned like fiery cinders. The cloaked figure abruptly rose and lunged toward the terrified men. That instant the radiator exploded, steam engulfed the room in an icy fog. Through the swirling vapor apparitions, a woman and a child, formed and dissolved, whispering, barely audibly, "beneath the tree."

A piercing yell of pain broke the trance of one of the men. Whether by luck or the power of will he stumbled blindly outside. Following his instincts, running madly to the tree, he saw what no other had in all the years since the hanging. A swath of burning embers at its base glowed white-hot. He snapped a low branch off and began to gnaw and dig frantically into the glowing embers. He wasn't down far when lights appeared behind him. A police car flashed its blues wildly. Fire trucks rolled in skidding to a halt, their red domes swirling madly. He held his breath as he looked down into the earth. There in the musty soil he saw the old bones cast side by side in rotting linen and sheets of newspaper. It was then he noticed the flames rising from the church. He thought it all a bad dream. Exhausted or overwhelmed, he collapsed and fell into darkness.

The next day the newspaper said that the old church and the adjacent rectory had nearly burned to the ground. The rectory was a charred shell. And the old church? All but the vestibule of the altar was consumed by the flames. A boiler exploded in the church basement, the paper claimed. The fire so intense and savage jumped the building. Two deacons perished. A third, they wrote, escaped unharmed. It reported the bodies unearthed beneath the tree, the bones of a woman and a young child, wrapped in linen and old newspapers from the autumn of '32. What the paper didn't say was that no one knew what kind of deal Father Durrell made with the devil to rid the world of his concubine and bastard offspring. And the paper didn't say how the men were found dead, splayed across the altar, each with an inverted cross seared on his chest. Their orbs sunken, hollow pits.

Let me say, I've always been a skeptic. I've always looked for the logical answers to the unexplained. And this story could easily be passed off to the imagination, I know. However, this story, I can say, has no true explanation. Because I was the one who escaped that church by the grace of God.

That *Winged* Thing: The Strange
Halloween Odyssey of Malcolm Glover
By Timothy Tucker

Timothy Tucker comes to us from a long line of geeks. Originally from Exeter, after serving a stint in the army and working as a doorman in a Tijuana brothel, he relocated to Downeast Way, whereupon Mr. Tucker established himself as the premier guide and outdoorsman in the Lost Kingdom. He is the proprietor of Timmy Tucker's Moose Safaris. He also volunteers at the local adolescent center counseling teens on the dangers of throwing rocks and other such projectiles. His curriculum on preventive methods for putting someone's eye out has been adopted by the State Council on Teenage Nervous Breakdowns. His true love is the great outdoors. He has written for *Nature's Way, In the Buff,* and recently published his first novel, *Ungulates Gone Wild,* one man's harrowing sojourn through the north woods at the height of the autumnal rut of the bull moose. In "That *Winged* Thing," Mr. Tucker continues his fascination with the creatures of the north woods by resurrecting one of the more haunting legends ever told in the Lost Kingdom.

That *Winged* Thing: The Strange
Halloween Odyssey of Malcolm Glover

It's hard to believe that two years have passed since the town's strange encounter with that large winged creature. It was Halloween, late in the evening of October 31, when the reports started filtering in throughout town...

Two couples in a minivan were coming from the moe.Republic Hotel's Halloween bash when they drove past the old Pratt Sawmill, its phantom shell illuminated in the pale moonlight. The driver, Sheila Quigley, glanced at the old works as she sped past, bewitched by its eerie, cold emptiness. Her lapse was momentary, broken by the sudden shouts of her companions. There in the middle of the road was a shadowy figure, standing on two legs, at least seven or eight feet high. At first they thought it was a prank. It had huge feathered wings folded across its back and two very large eyes, brilliant as emeralds, made more so by the illumination in the van's headlights. In its arms it held what appeared to be a good-sized dog. Sheila slammed the brakes, causing the van to do a three-sixty, and was about to plow into the creature when it rose up, actually flew away into the night. The passengers jumped out of the van and watched it fly away, but lost sight of it after a few minutes.

What they didn't know was that old Malcolm Glover had called the Downeast Way Police Department an hour earlier, around 9:30. Glover, a widower, lived up in an old farmhouse off Mountain Road, nestled in under Uriel's Ledge. He had been watching a hockey game on television when he said he lost control of his set. The volume went haywire, he would say. First, white sound filled the room, followed by a low, distinct voice. Barely audible, but oh so clear, "leee-ave," it breathed in a deep, airy baritone. All at once, he found himself watching the hockey game again. At first he thought he had fallen asleep and was awakened by the old hoot owl that perched nightly on the high ledge. But he was awake and that was no owl. For his dog, Nutcracker, a border collie mix, who was on the front porch, began to bark when something thrashed loudly in the barnyard. Glover went outside without caution, thinking he, too, as the van load of revelers would assume, was a victim of an elaborate Halloween prank.

He saw Nutcracker, with her familiar red bandana tied around her neck, facing the barn, which lay across the wide yard. She was now growling ferociously. The dark, thick hair along her spine stood on edge. It made Glover smile, thinking that the prank was about to turn on the prankster. He turned his flashlight on and scanned the barnyard. He moved the beam across the yard slowly and stopped when he spotted two large greenish eyes, luminescent and blinking, peering out from over a row of bushes near the barn door. Malcolm stands a good six feet high. The bushes, he realized, about a dozen mature sea roses, peaked above *his* eyes. Malcolm gawked at the phosphorous-like orbs, which overwhelmed its featureless face. Its head rested on broad shoulders, which were graced by, or what looked like… wings?

That was all the dog could take. Highly protective, Nutcracker bolted toward the barn. Glover called for the dog to stop, but it sprinted into the darkness. Turning into the house for his shotgun, the old man heard the dog screech loudly, painfully. That's when he called the police, then nervously went outside with his gun and flashlight. He scanned the yard with the light. The green eyes were gone and Nutcracker had disappeared. He lowered his flashlight and gazed above, up near the jagged ledge. In a fleeting instance he saw a flash, two green dots, like a pair of fireflies hovering over a meadow. And then a silhouette resting on the ledge… No—could that be possible? he thought.

A few minutes after Malcolm Glover stood terrified on his porch Margaret Connor and a few girlfriends had just left a screening of *The War of the Worlds* at Bud's Bijou Theater. There were dozens of people filtering in and out of the movie house when they spotted a "funny greenish light" that hovered high in the sky above Market Square. They stood watching as it turned down Brighton Lane towards the theater. "It wasn't an airplane," Margaret recalled. "No one could figure out what it was, but then, no one gave it much thought." It flew out of sight quickly, sinking behind the row of low buildings.

A couple of minutes later the women arrived at the lot behind the theater and piled in to an Oldsmobile. They started the car. The music was blaring so loudly on the radio it startled them all. Then the radio tuner moved across the dial on its own, stations faded in and out evenly, before stopping at the end of the spectrum. White sound filled the car. Deafening at first, then spelled by an airy, deep vibration that seemed to pulsate through the car's speakers. At that instant, before their eyes, a tall, winged figure rose up in front of the automobile. "It was though it had been crouching there hiding," Margaret would tell the police. "It came up slowly from the hood of the car. It was huge, wider and taller than a man, sinewy and muscular, with haunting, pale green eyes. It kept rising, too, right above the car. It held out a dog with a red bandana, which lay limp under its left arm, like it was trying to give it to us." The women were scared and began to scream. Margaret, who was driving, quickly hit the door locks. When she put the big old GM in gear it stalled. They were trapped and, were certain, facing their doom. The creature peered into the windows of the car looking at them closely, as though examining them under a microscope. The strange pulsing vibration increased to a high pitch. Each woman could hear it plainly through the radio.

There were at least a dozen people who were in the vicinity of the lot watching in stunned disbelief, amazement, and horror at the spectacle. The thing turned at them when the wail of police sirens alerted it. The creature rose quickly and ascended into the night, heading out towards the harbor, still clutching the dog. If this was a prank it was well staged. It defied the law of gravity and all known order of species in this and any ecosystem on the planet. By the time the authorities arrived the thing had vanished. Chief McO'Fayle heard the same story he had heard from Malcolm Glover, who was sitting in the front seat of his Commando. Was he really supposed to believe a *winged thing* was on the loose?

By now the news of a strange winged creature was spreading all over town. Everywhere it seemed but the moe.Republic Hotel, which was in the throes of its annual Halloween ball. The crowd was dressed in wild, outra-geous, and frightful costumes, and was so big it had spilled out onto the side porch overlooking Moose Harbor. When the lights went out and the music stopped abruptly, at first the party-goers thought it was part of the evening's festivities. The flicker of candles in a dozen or so jack-o-lanterns and the silvery moonlight cast ghostly shadows across the faces of the revelers and grounds.

Then, above the murmuring and growing confusion there rose a low, but distinct, sound. A vibration pulsated in the air, coming from the lawn off the side porch. The throng startled, reeled in horror simultaneously, when from nowhere, across the yard, a tall man-like figure with broad wings could be seen aloft. Its eyes flashed green in the dim light, "like reflectors on a mailbox," one witness would say, and it was gliding in right at them. The creature alighted softly at the end of the porch. There was something in its arms, limp and unmoving, what they soon recognized as a dog. The thing shuffled towards them slowly. People retreated in fear and apprehension. Just as it placed the object down, there was a booming thunderclap from up on the mountain akin to a sonic blast. It shook the grounds around them. The winged thing then lifted and glided away into the night. The power returned. Lights flooded the porch. That was the last sighting of the creature.

Whatever it was or may have been, it seems clear, by the number of witnesses, that it was very real. But was it something of this world? Everybody had their own explanation—a parasailing hooligan, a jet packed maniac, a large bird-like creature, even an alien visitor—but none more so than Malcolm Glover. He arrived at the moe.Republic Hotel with Chief McO'Fayle moments after the creature's departure. He had been with the Chief chasing the reported sightings all over town. They ran up to the porch where the guests, in stunned silence, had huddled around the dog, which lay still. Malcolm knew that it was Nutcracker. He recognized his border collie with the red bandana immediately.

Just about everyone knows old Malcolm, and Nutcracker, too. That's why everyone was baffled and bewildered at what they saw, and then heard. Because at that moment the Chief's two-way radio went off breaking the silence. The dispatch screamed loudly, excitedly, that Uriel's Ledge had collapsed above the farmhouse off Mountain Road right after that thunderclap. Malcolm Glover's house had just been obliterated under tons of granite. The ledge had simply cracked, a fissure, the state geologist would later report. She made no mention of *what* was left on that ledge. What did that have to do with the fact that the old house was flattened instantly? Other than the old man and his dog would have been crushed if… it hadn't been for that… winged thing.

Malcolm looked down at the dog, which all at once became alert and began to lick its master's face. People stood in wonder, some in doubt. Yet, incredible as it seems it's all true. True as the color of Nutcracker's coat, which from that day forward was an oddly, pale shade of gray. The queer thing was, come each full moon, the fur took on a starry, silvery hue that radiated in the night. People would say she'd been touched by moonbeams on that flight. Enchanted by that winged thing. Malcolm would only laugh. There were no further explanations necessary. Not about the creature, anyway. Or why it came. He knew what it was. Those who were there would agree. They'd seen it with their own eyes. The two of them, man and dog, had been saved on that Halloween night, not by *a* winged thing.

What then you say? Just look up on the ledge. It's there, your answer, high above, jutting out, to this very day. For all to see. Just as plain as the first time Malcolm had seen it. A silhouette which appeared before him in that instant. How else would you explain it? That when the wall of granite collapsed all that remained above was that formation. Eerily precise. Clinging to the precipice. Forever watching over the Lost Kingdom. Its wings expanded. A fiery sword in its hand. Out of the rock a perfect sculpture of the archangel himself. Uriel, the guardian of the ledge.

The moe.Republic Hotel
in the heart of the Lost Kingdom

Winter Cometh Again
At the bar
Friday, 2:06 a.m.

Dear Rob,

Hi-di-ho from the ice encrusted environs of the moe.Republic Hotel! Another New Year is upon us, and we certainly hope that it's the big one for you and the moe.horde. Now that the another CD is in the hopper we're already planning a special "gold" brew for the occasion. I don't know how much pull you have with the band, you being just the bass player, but maybe you could pull a few strings, as it were, lean on Al or Chuck, to come back this way again. It's been a long time since the animated, robust melody of "Head" has rocked this old house. Hell of a song. I can't seem to get enough of it, either. Don't get me wrong. I do understand your limitations over the schedule. Just rest assured, the door's always open for you and the boys to rock the moe.Republic, whenever that day may be.

For now, the big news downeast way has been the weather. We were able to help out the locals after that ice storm a few weeks back. We put up about twenty families who were hardest hit by the deep freeze. It proved to be a strategic move for business. Not only did we have quite a run on the winter's brew of the month, the Aurora BoreAle-us, the Down East Regional Chamber of Commerce cited us for their monthly Good Doobie Award.

Thanks for sending us the recording of the New Year's Eve gig at the Great American Music Hall, too. Though it's been quite awhile since we last saw moe. perform, that tape was the next best thing to being there. It's already become a regular happy hour favorite. A transcontinental moe.venture to see the concert live would have been dandy, but between father passing a gallstone, and the fact that it was New Year's Eve, one of the two busiest days of the year for us publicans (Saint Patrick's Day being the other), we just couldn't afford to leave. Business is good, but not that good, yet.

Oh yeah, I almost forgot—hope the winner of the great Halloween Storytellers festival wasn't too much trouble. I know it took a lot for Timmy Tucker to come out of hibernation and leave the Lost Kingdom for a few days.

He was hesitant to go, but he did so well auctioning that other ticket on eBay it paid for his flight. Nobody knew what was going on until the auction was over. The bid was holding steady at $18.22 with two minutes left. Timmy was pretty frantic. But there was some intense bidding in the closing seconds and the hammer fell at a whopping $423. We were all blown away. The winner, as you know now, bustercrabcakes2, turned out to be Timmy's Uncle Funkle, who'd set up a shill bid to buy the ticket as a Christmas gift for Timmy. He just kept bidding it up and up until he'd paid for Timmy's flight and then some.

Uncle Funkle's quite the prankster and quite loaded. They all laughed when he gave up the family horseshoe business back east and moved out to Montana on a wing and a prayer. The year was 1969. That spring, Funkle Tucker planted his first crop of dental floss, and he's never looked back. Timmy says he's got a ten-thousand acre spread now. Has diversified his crops, too, grows polyester and ranches earth worms. I met him last summer. A gregarious, burly fellow, big as the front end of an SUV and just as loud. Wild bushy hair and beard, topped off with a Stetson and cowboy boots. The guy must have drunk twenty pints of blond ale that first night in town. When he's had a few he tends to come at you like a freight train and stop on a dime two inches from your face. And that's just to ask for another round. Who'd dare say no? Heck, I'd have rather carried him out to the back of Timmy's truck than suffer the consequences of shutting him down.

That's why I can't say I was surprised when I heard about the pre-concert festivities. Timmy told me things were pretty dicey at the Japanese restaurant you brought them to. That everything went to hell when Uncle Funkle re-fused to remove his lizard-skinned cowboy boots, as is the custom. I told mother she owed you and the boys a batch of whoopee pies for talking you into doing that pre-concert dinner. It's the least she could do considering the Sumo wrestling contest Uncle Funkle got into with the maitre d', who, I understand, was a waif of a man newly arrived from Osaka and the brother-in-law of the owner. I can imagine the look on your face when you discovered the restaurant's owner was the son of the Japanese Consul, who happened to be there with the rest of the family for NYE. It's funny how far a few rounds of sake, a few laughs, and a big wad of cash will take you in this world. I suppose it didn't hurt that the Consul's daughter was a big-time moe.ron. Springing a pass for her and the rest of the clan was a diplomatic coup. Nicely played. Virtually guaranteed a lift in the Consul's limousine, too. Good thing. Other-wise, I don't know how you, Timmy, Uncle Funkle, the Consul, his daughter, the mother, and the maitre d' would have made it to the performance! Let alone moe. ever touring in Japan again. Now, every time I hear that NYE recording it's hard to believe just an hour earlier you treaded the razor's edge—a tick-tock from the slammer—and somehow averted an international incident. But hey, that's show business and a typical night on the town with Uncle Funkle.

Fortunately for me I won't have to deal with the big guy from Montana for a while. Good thing, because our winter agenda is coming together. We've set up the usual series of different theme-based weekends. Winter Carnival will be here soon enough. If it's anything like last year people will be lining up to quaff from the glacier carved fount of the moe.Microbrewery. I'm not too sure if we will be inviting back the group from the annual Great Downeast Dogsled race, though. As I anticipated that spring cleanup was a bear, even though the back lawn was looking pretty green last summer. We're booked solid for Valentine's Day weekend and Presidents' Day weekend, too. Just yesterday Chief Mickey McO'Fayle called to book the hotel for the Greater Downeast Chapter of the Hibernian Guard for all of Saint Patrick's Day week! Seems that after last year's debacle, between the conga lines and the close encounter, the Guard decided to hold their annual convention here, again. Said it was one of the best light shows they'd ever seen. More of a disappearing act if you ask me, but who's to argue?

All I know is that as we enter week 43 of the Kevin and Sparky watch, there's no sign of them. I got another call a couple of weeks ago from that bureaucrat—had to be that staff sergeant, but the guy never gives me his name. He said that "section" wanted closure. I asked, "Why do you keep calling back if you want closure?" There was an awkward moment of silence before the line went dead. He hasn't called back since. Truth be told, I'm beginning to doubt everything—what I did or did not see. Kevin's probably gone off on another self-imposed journey in search of himself. I expect that someday he'll come walking over that hill again wondering when the party broke up.

Till then, stare as I might at that yonder hill, we'll feed at the trough, and wait for that day to come…

brother John

Act IV

On the Far Side of the Mountain

About that Hedge Fund
A year or so on
Thursday, 4:10 p.m.

Hola mi hermano,

Thought I'd put down a line or two while I have a chance. I've been busy of late. The routine of a humble publican is consuming me. But I'm not complaining. Spring is finally here, for the most part. The cold snaps are getting fewer and the days are getting longer. People are beginning to amble out and reclaim the great outdoors—at least as long as they can tolerate the black flies, which have arrived a little early this year.

Yesterday the whole family went up to Farkleberry Farm just to air it out. It was kind of neat to see all the animals. Zebras bolting. Giraffes galloping. Bison stampeding. Seems that the animals were showing their restlessness, too, after being cooped up all winter. The six of us were in front of the elephant pen when Casey McNugent walked by. We'd already been there a couple of hours and were set to leave when he bumped into us. By then the child units were running around in circles so fast and tight that they were making mother dizzy as she tried to calm them down. Father couldn't have cared less. Too tired, he sat on a nearby bench smoking a cigar. The bride was indifferent to it all, mesmerized by Rafiki. McNugent's overly-endowed pachyderm was hanging near the front of the pen, trumpeting. His harem was cornered in the back, apparently exhausted from a night on the town.

"He's magnificent isn't he?" said McNugent as he approached me, nodding toward Rafiki. "I have a half-dozen zoos around the country waiting for that big boy's sperm. And that's just the first round," he said. "We'll know if he's reached his majority in about a month. He was with Clara there in the back over the last couple of days," he added, pointing to one of the females. "If we're luckly, that's $10k a pop for Farkleberry Farm!" he breathed excitedly. "Let's hope that buck's sperm count is off the chart! Then the grand experiment, Operation Overflow, shall commence." That's his code name for you know what, the *how* was a mystery to me, and I didn't want to know. He probably should have called it Operation Big-O or even Operation Cash Flow. It would have been apropos, as it were. "I'm going to need some help extracting," McNugent said to me casually. "Why don't you help me out? It'll be the experience of a lifetime and I'll pay top dollar." I wanted to tell him that genital contact with this or any elephant is not my gig. I really did. But, cornered as I was, I said I'd think about it. McNugent was a bit giddy for sure. I would be giddy over a sixty-grand payday, too, even if it meant jerking off an elephant. To wit: me thinketh the line between bestiality and free enterprise hath grown finer.

As I was conceptualizing the inconceivable, McNugent's attention began to drift. He seemed to be preoccupied and growing impatient. At first I thought it was us, considering the kids were going bonkers. Not so. It turned out that he was concerned over the belated arrival of a new addition to his animal kingdom. McNugent had hedged elephant sperm for a small flock of emus. "There's a truck load of them past due," he told me and father, anxiously, when we finally pressed him. I suppose that's why, as a distraction from himself, he turned to the children, who were preoccupied with a passing llama.

"Have you ever heard of an emu?" he asked them. They stared blankly at him. Struck by the sudden attention brought upon them. "An emu is a large flightless bird from Australia," he said, distractedly. "Related to the ostrich, they're as tall as a man and run as fast as the wind." The boys looked at him like *he* was from Australia, wondering whether it was a place or a state of mind. They were quite surprised that an adult other than a parent or teacher took notice of them, let alone addressed them without anger, an order, or instruction—even if it was about a silly bird that had to run because it could not fly. They ran off pronto, in confusion over the breach in adult-child protocol, clucking like chickens, "We're emus! We're emus!" I guess that was our cue to leave. The bride and I quickly rounded them up. It was getting late, anyway. McNugent, by now ashen, waved goodbye, staring down the driveway past us.

We soon found out he had good reason for his concern. The truck transporting them had overturned less than a mile from the farm. We happened upon the accident minutes after we left, down near the junction of Crowe's Farm, Falmouth Road, and Mountain Road. The driver swerved to avoid a moose that had darted out across the highway. By incredible coincidence, the guy turned out to be the same trucker that steered father and I here those oh-so-many years ago.

"I can't believe what happened," I heard him say to the Chief, who had arrived on the scene quickly in the Jeep Commando. The trucker seemed a bit shaken, like he'd lost his wits. "I saw movement out of the corner of my eye. Then all of a sudden the beast dashed out of the woods. The moose was so damn big I swear I could have driven the front end under its belly." He caught his breath. The adrenaline still pumping hard. "It's head was completely enveloped in a swarm of black flies. I swerved at the last possible second and just missed him." The guy must have cut too hard to the right and jackknifed the trailer. He wasn't hurt and neither were the birds. That was the good news.

Buck Jones and his tow truck arrived on the scene in no time. The birds were squawking crazy-like. That's about the time that McNugent showed up, too. The man went in a tizzy. Cussing and swearing and walking back and forth. We were watching Buck set the chains around the flipped truck—the Chief, the trucker, father, the family, McNugent, myself, and the few others who had happened upon the scene. Buck began an insightful oratory on the free roaming habits of ungulates and how something like moose running across the roads should not be unexpected. Somehow, just as he was righting the overturned truck, the lock on the cage popped. Jolted on impact we later conjectured. The flock of emus sprang. Stunned and disoriented, the birds, which actually *are* as big as small refrigerators, charged Buck, who froze in the face of the onslaught. It was over in a flash. Our buddy took a good beating—multiple lacerations and an indentation pecked on his forehead. That was the bad news.

The herd quickly scattered and have been on the lam since. Residents have reported seeing them along the back roadways, sprinting through neighborhoods, and there was one wild chase through Market Square. The Chief brought in the pest man, Gil Fonebone, to help out. Or it could be that McNugent asked the Chief to bring him in. In either case, he's spearheading the efforts to round up the herd. I believe he's got half of them already, which would still leave four or five at large. I don't know what the bird's diet consists of, but if they take a hankering to black flies or mosquitoes, they may never be lured out of the woods—at least not until the first frost. Well, I gotta go. I promised McNugent I'd take a ride with him up around the back roads of Mount Agamenticus to track emus, and that's him honking the horn now.

Just a routine day at the trough,
brother John

The moe.Republic Hotel
in the heart of the Lost Kingdom

Dear Roberto,

A quick hello is in order. I remembered that you were getting ready to go on tour, so I thought I'd drop you a quick missive and bring you up to speed. I'm managing to keep myself busy enough. The daily ho-hum is injected with just enough craziness to keep me sane. Yesterday was no exception. I rolled out of bed at dawn to the sound of the bride sawing lumber like she owned stock in Great Northern Paper. Not that it mattered. I had to get up anyway. My event calendar was booked. I had a rendezvous with Farmer McNugent up at Farkleberry Farm—him and a bull elephant named Rafiki. The day had arrived for man and beast to make deposits in their respective banks. Yes, I finally caved. I told McNugent I'd help him after the umpteenth time he asked me.

When I arrived at the farm the sun was shooting through the pine branches. Farmer McNugent was up and about. Had been, he mentioned later, for over an hour. I thought that was pretty amazing considering the number of shots of Crown Royal he put down the night before. The ongoing emu debacle has gotten the better of him. I suggested a boys night out to level off the angst. We went on a full bore pub crawl through Market Square. Somewhere between Goatlips Saloon, Lizard's Lobster Pound and the Silent Woman Tavern the talk turned to Rafiki and Operation Overflow. Good old McNugent has staked his claim to young Master Rafiki's hose as long as I've known him. Waiting like a trust fund baby for Rafiki to reach his majority, the bull apparently did that weekend we visited. Clara, his paramour, is now a rose in bloom. On top of that, Rafiki has something going for him that zoos place at great value and demand—a high sperm count. There's simply not enough healthy, hung, and able male elephants to sustain zoo populations around the continent. McNugent claims he can corner the market given enough time, some cooperation, and a little help from his friends. "There's one catch, as it were," he said sometime after God knows what shot of the prize Canadian whiskey. "I need a bag man."

Maybe it was the timing. Maybe it was the booze. When he put the monkey on me to help him the very next morning I couldn't say no. In a moment of weakness I collapsed. "You know what?" he belched loudly. "And I'll even throw in a free pass for life."

So it was I found myself nursing a fog between my ears anticipating with apprehension an encounter with the aforementioned overly endowed, exceptionally fertile bull elephant. Standing there, I burped sour Royal and swallowed it hard, watching McNugent bandy about the yard taking care of the animals. Looking him up and down he was dressed in khakis and a battered old Red Sox cap. His rubber boots had shit all over them. I had on my shorts, my old Red Sox cap and sandals. You're not considered a native unless you wear a Red Sox cap. Not that I'd have it any other way. But it's considered a great affront to one's sensibility and character otherwise. That aside, it occurred to me that I was woefully underdressed for the occasion.

He was walking across the grounds when I hailed him. "I was beginning to wonder if you actually were going to come," he said, glad to see me, though too perky for this time of day. "I really needed a good bag man and I knew I could depend on you!"

"Well here I am." I smiled back nervously, still wondering why I showed up. Wondering if this job were better suited for a lower order of primates. I could have easily blown it off as a drunken promise. But no. I decided to stick with my guns. "I wouldn't miss this for the world." I lied. What the hey?

"That's the trick isn't it?"

"What is?" I asked.

"Not to miss!" he chuckled a little. "Want a coffee?"

"Yeah. I could go for a cup of joe right about now," I replied wearily. Sour Royal clung to my palate and I really wanted to get the taste out of my mouth before the flies set in.

"Good, 'cause I need my bag man to be sharp and alert when we get going," said McNugent. I followed him into a small out building. The words "EMPLOYEES ONLY" were tattooed on the door. There was a fresh pot of coffee on the side bar under a long, wide bay window. Through it, across the yard, I looked out into a newly built stall. There was Rafiki—10,000 pounds of bull elephant ass looking straight at me.

"Stunning view." I stared ahead.

"Yeah," he said pouring the coffee. "I wanted a panoramic effect."

"I'd say you captured a Kodak moment. The big picture. Nice."

"Well, you should probably slip into a pair of those boots over there," motioning with his head to a row of rubber boots hanging on the far wall.

"Unless you want to take off the sandals and walk through the stalls barefoot, which is cool. It's good for bunions."

I went with the boots and we drank our coffee. My head was pounding from the night before. "Okay McNugent," I said. "What's next?"

"A man of action. I like that," he said. "No wonder that inn of yours is taking off. I was hoping after today you'd give it all up and get a real job. Right here, maybe."

"We'll see how it goes," I said. "I always like to keep my options open. Make it worth it."

"You mean a genuine career move?" he replied. "That kind?"

"Well, before I even would consider a move, could you explain to me what I have to do that you couldn't train a monkey to do?"

"Ah! The parable of the monkey and elephant. You need not worry about that. This is not an experiment. You *do* have to be a special kind of breed to be a professional elephant ejaculator, though," he smiled broadly at me. "What you're gotta do is, after I chain his back legs to the side boards, is reach under his ass, caress his balls and slowly jerk him off into this plastic bag." He pulled a clear plastic bag from his coat pocket. It could easily have fit into a waste basket. "No monkey could do that."

"Like hell!" I answered, shuddering repulsively. "What the fuck are you gonna do?"

"Shit, somebody's got to work the video camera. Otherwise no one will ever believe me!" He liked that one and laughed hard. "Honestly, old Rafiki here is young, hung, and full of cum. This young buck was born to perpetuate the species. All you have to do is put this bag on the end of an extension rod that I'm going to give you. When the time *comes*, as it were, you capture the effluvium when he releases. And whatever you do don't spill it. Do *not* spill it! There's a stool out there. You're going be nice and comfortable and I'm going to be doing all the *coaxing*," he laughed again at himself.

"Sounds more like it," I said, taking a good, long hit of java.

"Right, now let's get this over and I'll treat you to breakfast." We started walking towards the door when McNugent stopped short. "Whoa man! There's just one more thing." He reached on the top shelf by the door and pulled down a pair of elongated rubber gloves. With the precision of a surgeon he snapped them on all the way up to his biceps. "Okay, I'm nearly ready to operate." He held up his hands, palms out. "One more thing, amigo. Grab the duct tape," he said holding his arms out. "I want you to wrap my gloves off—seal them tight right up around the end by my shoulders. You don't want them to slip off in the heat of battle. Could get messy."

"Messy?" I asked, confused.

"Relatively speaking," he replied. I wrapped the gloves off snug-like and opened the door for him. "Excellent! Now just grab that gallon jug of K-Y jelly please," he added. "Oh, and grab the ponchos, too, and let's get to it."

"Anything else?" I asked him, my arms full. "Mukluks? An umbrella?" He shook his head no.

As we walked across the compound I noticed McNugent's look of determination. His mood had shifted. He had his game face on. When I saw that I started asking myself again—what am I doing here? I had no game. I was not determined. I was here on a drunken whim. Note to self: make no commitments when liquored up. Before us was the stall. I dropped all the crap in a pile and stepped in. The great beast seemed to yawn.

"You ever do this before?" I asked him.

"Nah! But I read the manual," he added, laughing happily.

We were standing directly behind Rafiki now, and old man McNugent was face-to-face with his ass. His head was so close that, mathematically speaking, at the right angle his melon could easily been mistaken for an elephant grape—one really bad hemorrhoid.

"You know in the old days we would have packed the big fella up and carted him around the country," McNugent said, interrupting my train of thought. "Going from zoo to zoo, putting Rafiki up for stud for a buck or two. But not today. We've got the technology to deliver elephant seed around the country, or planet for that matter, as fast as any jet can get there. It has a shelf life of thirty-six hours. You can't beat the overhead."

"Sounds like that'd have been quite a fun adventure," I thought out loud. "An old-time journey through the heartland."

"When you think about it you can see the possibilities, I suppose." He stopped for a moment, looking around. "Get ready with the bag, amigo," McNugent said, dipping his arm into the jug of lubricant. "I don't mean to cut you off, but I'm about to dive." At that McNugent did what most men would think unthinkable. Could not conceive or even imagine. Who would? He lifted Rafiki's tail and slowly worked his hand into the beast's mammoth anal cavity. Rafiki squirmed and trumpeted at the intrusion. McNugent, undeterred, gently pushed to his wrist, his forearm, elbow, bicep and up to his shoulder.

"Damn, Casey," I said. "Be careful you don't fall in!" The game was on. The plan was to tickle Rafiki's prostate to induce ejaculation. Now it was up to me, the bag man. I sat down trepidly on my stool right under McNugent. Opening the enormous zip-lock bag, I fastened the pouch securely to the extension rod. Things were happening quickly.

"You sure he's not going to kick?" I asked.

"How the hell do I know?" he said bluntly. "I think it would have happened already, and he's chained up pretty tight." His nose was upturned, his voice had a nasal pitch to it. "Besides, right now that's the least of *my* problems!" I think I understood. He really did look like he was about to fall in. The stink was getting pretty heavy, too. "Next time we should wear nose plugs, or one of those gauze painter masks."

"Yeah, next time," I said, catching my breath.

The gigantic tool of Rafiki sprang to life. Thoughts of Frank Howard's baseball bat came to mind. It had to. I had nothing else to compare it with in my vast reservoir of experience. "I got it," McNugent shouted excitedly. "I'm tickling his prostrate." Rafiki suddenly went turgid and trumpeted loudly. The bag began to fill rapidly with staccato bursts of jizz. McNugent had turned the faucet on full bore.

"We're gonna need a bigger bag," I shouted helplessly.

"Too fucking late for that!" McNugent yelled.

"Men overboard! All hands on deck!" I belted out, laughing gleefully at the rapidly filling bag. This wasn't so bad. I'd forgotten about my hangover. What's more, it wasn't *my* arm stuck in an elephant's ass.

"Keep her steady, man," McNugent implored. "That's all you have to do. You're holding liquid gold!" He was sweating profusely, concentrating. "Okay, I'm going to release him!" And he did. Too quickly in retrospect. Young Master Rafiki's trumpet of exultation morphed quietly into waves of satisfaction. Then, like a greased monkey fired from a cannon, the elephant blasted a voluminous fart that enveloped us like a mushroom cloud. I choked. The stench gagged me. My hangover came back in a fury. The gas was outrageous. He farted again, loudly. On its heels, a projectile-like fusion of mass erupted savagely from his butt, spraying us with heaps of dung. "That wasn't in the manual," McNugent coughed, spitting and choking.

As for me? I held my ground through it all, even when the second wave followed. McNugent, noble warrior that he was, ducked. "How about those ponchos?" he asked, with a glance outside the stall. They lay, within our reach, where I had dropped them, in an unassuming heap on the ground.

There, right next to where I left my humanity minutes before. Back in that ancient time when the world was young and innocent, and grace and dignity flowed over me like a summer breeze. I held the extension rod away from me, careful not to expose the sea of squirming Rafikis to the pool of pachyderm pooh in which I wallowed! I had gone this far, I thought. The perpetuation of the species was within my grasp, as it were. I'd earned my merit badge and a lifetime pass. Besides, there was no way I was gonna do *this* again.

"Did I ever mention Rafiki is Swahili for friend?" McNugent asked me later while he was preparing to hose me down.

"Well, I guess that makes us best buddies," I said. "What's a good friend for if you can't shit on him from time to time." I glared at McNugent, but he only laughed harder. I was all contorted. Hunched over. Teeth clenched. Breathing cautiously through my mouth. Grunting. Avoiding inhalation at all cost while swatting at the swarm of carrion flies buzzing around my head.

I took heart in knowing that within the next day little Rafikis were planted in fertile wombs in zoos far and wide. St. Louis, San Diego, Syracuse; D.C., Denver, and Disney—all would have a slew of Dumbos in the oven, induced by a God-like act. And like Him, so often in the deliverance of divine providence, we were meted out a just reward. At that moment of inner peace and hideous stink, I didn't care. My head didn't hurt anymore. I'd found the perfect cure for a hangover. Later, I reflected, drawn to the old parable of the monkey and the elephant. After all these years, I now knew what happened when the poor little monkey pulled that massive cork from the elephant's ass—at least to the monkey—and why you couldn't train the little buggers to do it more than once!

I shall not feed at the trough again today,
brother John

The moe.Republic Hotel
in the heart of the Lost Kingdom

From the far side
June something,
8:08 a.m.

Mon frère,

There's nothing better than a down east summer breeze, especially to shake a residual elephantine funk from the furthest recesses of my brain. I keep the windows open throughout the hotel. Let the scent of brine waft in the warm air. In the distance I hear the sound of waves crashing on the shore and a Greyhound pulling into the yard. Another busload of tourists have arrived, wanting to kiss the sacred ground of where it all began. Exactly what began here I do not know. But the consensus from the moe.ron tourheads is that something did, so I'm not asking. And I'm sure as hell not going to tell any of them about that dogsled convention we had here and that hideous spring cleanup.

That was a good idea selling those midweek two-for-one vouchers on tour last winter. It gives the ever widening circle of the faithful a connection of sorts. Mother and father seem a bit perplexed by it all, though, witnessing the eccentric dance rituals that take place in the Liberty Ballroom whenever a particular tune, say "Tin Cans and Car Tires" or, one of my personal favorites, "Crab Eyes," pops up on the CD player.

Talk about good tunes, we're all getting psyched to go hear moe. at this year's moe.down. And what about the big autumn tour? Keep in mind we do have a spot open for the third weekend in October if you can convince the guys to make a beeline for the eastern frontier. The Pumpkin Ale will be running high and flowing fast by then, and I guarantee without any unusual side effects this year. Rumors of a psilocybic lag still abound. I don't know what happened or what got into that batch. Mother and her friend, Irma Hoarywell, were tending bar that day, and neither of them knew what happened. You remember Irma. She's the one who's been sharing a few of her recipes with mother and helping her in the kitchen from time to time.

They met one Sunday at a Saint Alphonzo pancake breakfast. Irma's the resident organist for the church. Tickles the ivories pretty good, too. She was playing the piano at the breakfast that morning, entertaining the crowd. For some reason mother connected with the music. She walked right up to Irma and whispered something in her ear. Irma nodded silently and mother bolted. Fifteen minutes late she returned with her accordion, and they proceeded to jam the rest of the breakfast. Since then they've become good friends and play together all the time. Father O'Neill regularly asks them to perform at church recitals and weddings.

In fact, the two of them played at the wedding ceremony we held here last Saturday. Now we're not going Vegas in the way of nuptials. More of a one-time experiment. See if it could work *and* be worth the effort. The ceremony was outside overlooking the harbor. The problem, I soon found out, is you never know what's going to happen on one of those hot summer days. Sometimes it's the weather. Sometimes it's mother nature. Last weekend it turned out to be a little bit of both.

The day was particularly hot and humid. One of the best things about our location is the steady breeze off the Atlantic, but there was next to nothing on Saturday. I was sure we were going to get nailed with a thunderhead or two by midday. I told the father of the bride as much, but, as an old merchant marine, he insisted that we "stay the course." I'm happy to report that the weather did hold through the ceremony. Unfortunately, just as the groom was about to kiss the bride three emus came sprinting out of the woods and ran right into the throng. Yes, incredibly, there are still birds on the lam since their escape in the aftermath of that fateful accident on the way to Farkleberry Farm. The three of them appeared out of the brush and rushed down the makeshift aisle straight toward the bride and groom. A quick thinking photographer jumped in front of the birds at the last moment and used his strobe flash to divert them. It did. And, as the ensuing photographs revealed, it diverted them right into the father of the bride, who was pecked at when he either attempted to shoo away the birds, or simply reeled back in fright, depending on which interpretation of the chain of events one accepts.

Not that it mattered in the ensuing chaos. The birds broke free of the crowd and ran for their lives. They passed the veranda and went through a crowd of moe.rons playing Frisbee golf. They were on the golfers so fast that one bird actually caught a Frisbee with its beak while it sprinted by. The buzzard kept right on running with it, too, around and around in circles until he and rest of them were out of sight. Later in the day, while looking out her kitchen window, a stunned Emma Huxley would report a UFO had landed on her back lawn. I know. I was standing next to the Chief's Commando when the report came in over the radio. He was here with McNugent and Fonebone, tracking emus.

I called McNugent pronto, but he seemed to move on it at the pace of an iceberg. The prick was probably jerking Rafiki off again. By the time he, Fonebone, and the Chief arrived, the uninvited guests had eluded capture once again. McNugent came barreling up the driveway, horn honking, with the Chief in hot pursuit. "What took you?" I asked him. "You been popping off the pachyderm?"

"No, but I'm diving in tomorrow if you want to come by and *plop* yourself down, again," said McNugent, smiling widely. "We couldn't get here any quicker. The Chief received a call earlier. Someone reported sighting three emus over near Crowe's Farm. We swung by, but by the time we got there they were long gone."

"Well, three of them sprinted through here twenty minutes ago," I said. "Right through a wedding ceremony."

"You've got to be kidding me," he replied, dejectedly. "Man, I'm sorry. This is getting out of control. We went to old man Crowe's, but that SOB is so mean he wouldn't even open the door. Just shouted for us to leave." I'm surprised they even got that far on Jacob Crowe's property. A real old buck with a bad temper, the guy only lives out on the far side of us. Yet, in all the years we've been here I think I've seen him maybe twice. He's that much of a recluse. Porter Gibson Digit says he's loaded, told me that his family made their money in banking during the depression. It's his farm that's out under Uriel's Ledge. The one that inspired Timmy Tucker when he wrote "That *Winged* Thing." "He said he wouldn't open the door without a warrant," McNugent went on. "Can you believe it? We just wanted to ask a single fucking question!"

"We saw his man Miles Winslow and asked him," the Chief said. "Or I would have gotten a warrant. Winslow's the one who called it in, anyway. Said he saw the birds meandering behind the barn, but they took off the second they saw him."

"It's a bummer," added Fonebone, "we've caught all but those three. Well, at least we know they're still alive." Fonebone and McNugent went off to track the birds, but came back in a short time, frustrated once again. Meanwhile, the Chief spoke with a few of the guests. Reassured the father of the bride while the EMT's patched him up. The guy was fuming, something about a bunch of amateurs. Hand it to the Chief. He took the brunt of it from the old salt and calmed him down. "Mister," I heard him say, patiently, "you're on the far side of the mountain, now. There are no guarantees. We don't just live day-to-day around here. Sometimes, it's moment-to-moment! Smile, you just had one of 'em."

Other than that, it was a grand experiment. The wedding thing. The subsequent thunderstorm cleared the air, so to speak, and the photographer promised the father of the bride he'd air brush out the lacerations from the wedding pictures. After today, I can't see much of a future in weddings. Best to do what you know. If not that, then the next best thing. In which case, I think I'll have another.

For now, from the trough,
brother John

The moe.Republic Hotel
in the heart of the Lost Kingdom

Dear Rob,

It's that time of summer when I could kick back and do nothing. Let the dog days carry me away. Once upon a time, come August, the bride and I would pack up the old VW bus and head up the country. Do a little camping, maybe a little fishing, watch the Perseid meteor shower. That would be nice. We could use a break, but things are too hectic around here to even begin to contemplate a few days off. Put another way—you play the hand that's dealt you, as father always says. These days, I'm happy to report, we're quite flush, which makes it hard to give up this hand. Because, as father always likes to add, on the next deal, a pair of jokers might land belly up on the table and take you down.

Such is the prevailing wisdom of our fathers that when the Huxley sisters showed up the other day I knew it was time to fold. They had come to speak with mother and Irma. Don't get me wrong. I didn't see it as hurting business in any way. I just figured something was up. Since the wedding season came to a merciful end that fateful June day, mother and Irma have been kind of lost with regard to their music. I guess the church recital circuit isn't what it use to be. The Saint Alphonzo season doesn't kick in until All Saints' Day. Besides, according to the bride, mother and Irma got the itch, want to branch out, expand their repertoire from hymns, carols, and psalms to a few standards. That can mean anything from a Polka dance number to a Lawrence Welk sing-along.

This is where the Huxley sisters come in. Mother and Irma asked Edith and Emma to join them. Apparently the dynamic duo are accomplished with the strings when they're not in an Earl Grey induced stupor. The four of them practice over at the Huxley's mausoleum, daily, right there in the living room parlor. Just far enough away so you can't hear them. Mother keeps pressing me to let them play a Sunday night or two here. She said they need the practice in front of a live audience. I told her we needed the customers alive, too. That's the best way I know of to ensure repeats. She didn't like that joke so I made a deal with her. If the four horsemen could learn "Captain America" and a few other rock and roll numbers we'd fit them in a Sunday ten o'clock slot. Considering they're usually in bed by nine I thought I had one-upped them. Damned if they didn't take me seriously, though, cause they're practicing to beat the band. I don't know how the heck I'm gonna weasel out of this one, either, short of closing the place up at nine-thirty.

I suppose I could hook them up at the astral blast Timmy Tucker's organizing. He wants to do something cosmic for the upcoming Perseid meteor shower. The problem is, he hasn't found a location for it yet. I know because he's been at me for weeks to have the party up on the back hill. He wants beer and live music to set the mood right for the evening. I have to admit, it's as good of an excuse as any to throw a shindig, but I'm not too psyched about going up that hill. Haven't been since the whole Kevin and Sparky episode a few years back. The place has the feel of an Indian burial ground to me. You can even hear the coyotes up there some nights, howling and shrieking. Gives me the willies just to think about it. When Timmy pressed me, I suggested that we go up even higher, maybe up on the side of Mount Agamenticus somewhere. He probably knows that mountain better than anyone. For the better part of the year he leads sojourning turistas up there on moose safaris. That's why this summer we jumped into the fray and started working with Timmy. I figured, why not? Since you chronicled his early life exploits in song he's passed into legendary status in these parts and yon. There's a symbiotic connection between him and us. So we put together a moose safari vacation package. Should have thought of it a while back, because it's been a big success. I bet a quarter of the busloads that pull in are here on moose safari. The moe.rons love it. Each day he comes by early in the morning to pick them up then drops them off around nine or ten a.m. Timmy says they ask him a lot of questions, especially if he really is a one-eyed geek. He simply laughs and plays along.

His thing about an astral blast has got me a bit perplexed, though. Not too sure of his angle at first—was it business, pleasure, or both—nor what it had to do with the moe.Republic Hotel. Maybe it's because we're doing business together, or maybe it's because the hill *would* be a good spot to watch the Perseids from. For whatever reason, once he got it in his head to celebrate the meteor shower, he began a slow, steady campaign that had me guessing.

"If you haven't seen the Perseid Meteor Shower," he began one morning in early July. "You're missing out on one of the great natural light shows of the Northern Hemisphere."

Two days later he asks me, "Did you know that each August earth's orbit carries it through the ancient cosmic roughage from the comet Swift-Tuttle?"

The day after that he says, "You know dude, over the centuries, the comet's battered remains have expanded across the heavens. It's spread so far it's like a veritable moving river of debris a ka-zillion miles wide and a ba-zillion miles long." He swept his hand in a broad stroke across the blue sky as though the debris was right above us. "Our small planet is carried through this river every August on its whirlwind tour of the solar system."

"Now that's a trip, dude!" I said to him, beginning to wonder what his obsession was with the Perseids.

By mid-July he was all over me. "Did you know that tiny little Perseid particles, no larger than a pea, shed long ago by the comet, burst into oblivion when they enter the earth's atmosphere?" he paused, looked up at the sky, like it was about to rain pea-sized particles. That morning he stood outside his van waiting for the last moe.ron to amble out of the moose mobile. "Or is earth's atmosphere colliding with them?" he asked, rhetorically, struck by a wave of infinite contemplation. I wanted to tell him once again I knew all about it. Not about which celestial object struck what, but about the Perseids. You were born on a night at the height of the shower. One could say that was a cosmic event! And least we forget the time you, Kevin, and I hiked into the backcountry for your sixteenth birthday? Good thing, because as I recall, between the three of us, the aurora borealis, the meteor shower, and the mushroom stew, we had a pretty good light show on that camping trip. "I've been thinking," Timmy said, hopping into his van. "So what do you think about a gig—an astral blast? Celebrate the Perseids. We could throw a bash up there on the hill." Finally, I thought, it only took him about two weeks to spit it out.

Never really did give him an answer that morning, though I was open to the idea. It didn't take me long to realize the work involved. Too much for a couple of hours. Now, here we are with a week to go and he's still pushing for the hilltop over the mountain. In fact, I can hear a horn honking in the distance. It's probably the famed moose mobile, now, which means I must bid adieu. We're going to hammer out this astral blast thing today even if I have to dangle the four horsemen in front of him.

Giddy-yup!

brother John

From: brother.john@moe.republic.org
To: rob@moe.org
Date: September 2, 11:16 p.m.
Subject: when you wish upon a star

Dude—Received your message last night. Relax will you? For the umpteenth time mother and the girls are not going to play Sunday nights. That's passé. Though she did mention the possibility of opening at moe.down next year. Now *you* can keep your fingers crossed—it may be the only way I'll ever get to the festival. What can I say? I missed moe.down again. We've been too busy. Labor Day weekend and all. In my naivete, when I said we'd come, I thought there'd be enough coverage, but we're stretched. Can't seem to make anytime to do anything but manage this place. I've had one day "off" since I last wrote, if you want to call it that. That was for the astral blast, which turned out to be a struggle of and in itself.

Talk about the heights of absurdity. I really don't know how I get myself into these situations. Okay, I'm easily seduced. A sucker for a good time. A huckster's wet dream. When my life story appears in print, they're going to call it *Gullible's Travels.* Should be a bestseller, even make it to the big screen. A dark comedy. The hit of the season. Much like the astral blast, which was as dark as it gets.

Don't get me wrong. For the most part it was a good night. Though, one strangely detached from reality. There was *one* minor triumph. After much deliberation we held the bash up on the mountain side. I finally convinced Timmy that if we had it here we'd have to be *on,* like *work.* There'd be no way I could hold a private party up on the hill with the number of guests around. "Bottom line, Timmy," I laid it out for him. "Do you want this to be a money-making affair or a keg party? Do you want to watch the best natural light show this side of the equator or watch other people watch it? Because I'm not flying solo and there's not enough staff to help." He thought about that for a minute. "Also, as for the live music, at this juncture, the only group available would be the four horsemen," I added with a chuckle. "A little Guy Lombardo, a little Pat Boone, we'll be cookin'!"

That was my trump card. Timmy knew that the old ladies wanted to play in front of an audience, but he didn't know they'd passed on any night gigs. Edith's arthritis tends to flare up after six o'clock. Makes her a bit spastic unless she takes the cure, and she takes the cure most evenings. Hits the tea hard until the fairies come and tuck her in. I overheard mother telling sister Liza, Irma, and the bride the full scoop. Not that the Huxleys would ever come clean with me. Instead, they see me, pack my bags and send me on a guilt trip. As usual, I got the old 'if our great-nephew James were alive you wouldn't take advantage. We'd play every Sunday night and headline the show.' Yeah, I thought, P.T. Barnum's freak show. I know it sounds harsh, but the thing that gets me is their attitude. They sold this place to us. We didn't take it from them. Yet, every time I see them I'm beset with a conspiratorial angst served up with the right amount of indignity. Just enough to set the veins in my temples bulging with a subdued rage.

On a brighter note, I shouldn't complain. I didn't have to weasel out of anything. I was off the hook. Not only for Sunday nights, but the astral blast, too. Timmy, ever the shrewd business man, cut a deal with me. If we had the blast up on the mountain, I'd bring a keg and he'd take care of the rest. Fine by me. That's what I'd been leaning towards for weeks. It was though everything fell into place like I'd scripted it. Which was cool, until the night of the party, when the Perseids were peaking, and I nearly spaced it out. When I think about it, in a night of many omens, that was my first. A portent to back off and stay on the porch. Not to go anywhere. But hey? This was the night of the cosmos. It only happens once a year. The grand parade across the northern hemisphere. The night a thousand falling stars land on your lap. How many wishes do you have in you? How many dreams will come true?

That evening I was sitting on the back veranda, near dusk, gazing up at Mount Agamenticus. A few bats were flapping about close to the porch when a coyote howled in the far distance, starting me. That was creepy enough, then, suddenly, there was a flash of light, one after the other, moving along a line through the trees. Too freaky. The scene momentarily befuddled me before I realized they were cars. The glow of headlights cast an eerie serpentine pattern as the caravan slithered up the mountainside. "Whoa honey!" I shouted, calling out to the bride. "The astral blast!" I lugged a keg of moe.Ale out to the Rambler and we jumped in, but it wouldn't start. The Rambler was due for another triage. Had been for a while, but I'd put it off because we'd been too busy.

There was only one thing to do. I gave Buck Jones a quick call. He told me he couldn't do much right then, but he'd get one of his boys on it first thing in the morning. He was, however, on his way to the astral blast, and would be more than happy to pick me and the bride and the keg up. I was surprised Buck was even going. I thought he was still in recovery mode from the emu attack. He still wore a big circular patch in the middle of his forehead from the plastic surgery, and was prone to headaches. "I'll be right over, baby," he said, excitedly. "Been waiting for this for weeks!"

Fifteen minutes later we were off, heading up the mountain. Not surprisingly, our destination was Uriel's Ledge. Timmy's happy place. Where he goes to catch a vibe. One of the few places on the mountain that's open faced, the ground's also fairly level there, which makes it an ideal spot for a pow-wow. The ledge looks out to the northeast, away from the town lights. There really is a rock formation that looks like an angel. It's beautiful, too, but way out on a precipice. Too narrow a walk and too much of a drop off for me to go out there. I prefer to look up at it from below, on *terra firma,* than risk vertigo and a swan dive. Timmy will actually climb the ledge sometimes. There's lot of crevices, deep fissures, and cracks all the way up to and under the precipice. "It's a bit of a challenge," he'd told me. "The climb?" I'd presumed. "No," he'd replied. "The footing's pretty easy. The challenge's not to grab a snake instead of a rock when you reach up to pull yourself, or to step in bat shit and slip and fall. There's a ton of bats that dwell in the cliff and the guano tends to pile up thick and gooey. Other than that, the climb's no sweat." He asked me to climb it with him once, but I passed. Scaling an open rock face hundreds of feet vertically to sit out on a ledge is not my bag. I'd rather get there the old fashioned way, in the seat of a car.

Buck knew exactly where we were going. Made good time bouncing along the old tote roads, climbing steadily on the long switchbacks. "These roads were made by the lumber barons," he said, "from the paths the natives used to traverse the mountain."

"You ever been up here before?" the bride asked him.

"To Uriel's Ledge?" he replied. "Damn straight. You know it was a mystical place, quite sacred to the Indians, especially this time of the year."

"We didn't think you were going to make it," the bride said to him, indifferent to his comment.

"It's not as bad as it looks," he answered. "My headaches have subsided. The bandage comes off in another couple weeks. Besides, I wouldn't miss this for anything."

"What do you mean mystical?" I asked, not liking the tone of it.

"I'll tell yah," he said. "I've been here a few times, but only during daylight, which was hard enough. Believe me you! I'd never go there at night alone. No way!"

The bride and I looked at each other and laughed nervously. "What in God's name are you talking about, Buck?" she said to him, but he fell silent as we approached the turnoff to the ledge. Drove past it a few feet and came to an abrupt halt. For a split second I thought he was going to tell us to get out. But he put the Subaru in reverse and backed in, all the way down the road, till the caravan and astral blast rolled up before us, or should I say behind us.

"I think Hamlet said it best," he finally answered, shutting the car off, "when he spoke about the confines of human knowledge. So I'll say the same to you tonight, so you'll know where I'm coming from. 'There are more things in heaven and earth... than are dreamt of in your philosophy.'"

"What!" I exclaimed, exasperated. But he was already outside the car, already waving at someone. A dozen or so people were milling around. Lawn chairs were laid out in a semi-circle. A little jukebox was set on a cooler. Tiki torch lamps were set around the parameter and lit. In the dim light I made out a few familiar faces, mostly from the ever-widening circle of the moe.Republic faithful. I noticed the Chief, Fonebone, Bullethead Bergmeister, and Jake the Lizard stacking logs for a fire. Their better halves were at hand, talking to another woman I couldn't make out. Buck went over to join them. Aha, I reasoned, Buck had himself a blind date.

Porter Gibson Digit was sitting in a lawn chair next to this forty-ish, hot-looking blonde who'd checked into the hotel yesterday. He was holding a bottle of Scotch. When he spied me staring at him he winked and flicked me the bird. Damn he was good!

"Where's Jackson?" I called out to him.

"I tucked him in bed an hour ago," he replied, and turned his attention back to the blonde. Then I remembered that he and Kinghorn and Bigwood were up in Bangor on some business deal.

I saw Timmy and waved. He had been talking to his buddy Conrad Dixon, who he'd befriended at the Halloween Storytellers contest a couple years ago. At first, Conrad had been sore about losing the contest. I told him he'd probably have won if he hadn't scared the shit out of the judges. One of whom, Philip Turner from the *Phoenix*, turned out to be his soul mate. Conrad waved back at me, but Timmy was bobbing around with the nervous energy of a kid.

"About time!" he shouted at me.

"I forgot," I pleaded innocently. "Then the Rambler wouldn't turn over!"

"How could you *forget*?" he asked incredulously. "Did you at least remember the *beer*?" he added, sarcastically.

"*Yes*," I snapped back, "and this was *your* idea."

"How could *I* forget!" he responded sharply.

"If you're done *yapping* I could use some help with this keg," I said, determined to get the last word.

"I'm not *yapping*," he said. "I'm *venting*."

Just then I heard the bride clear her throat. Through it all she had stood there and watched us banter like two kids in a schoolyard arguing over marbles. I presumed that was my cue to get on with it. "What are you so uptight about, Tucker?" I softened. "I think it's safe to say that we've all done this before, had a keg party or two."

"They say there's a chance of a thunderstorm later tonight," he said. "I thought maybe you heard the weather and you weren't coming. It put me on edge."

"Well, we're here. I don't know anything about the weather. So, until then, I say, enjoy the ride." That seemed to cheer him up. He got all perky while we handled the keg, moved it over in the vicinity of the pending bonfire and the rest of the crew.

It was unusual to see the Chief in civilian attire. Even when he came by the lounge for a pop or two he normally wore his khaki cop shirt. Tonight he was in plaid. He and Fonebone and Bullethead looked like lumberjacks engaged in a heady philosophical debate on the physics of a bonfire. Jake the Lizard was waiting impatiently, listening to them. He had brought a cooler filled with lobster tails from his pound to shish kebob and they weren't getting any closer to the flame while they talked.

"Evening all," I shouted, placing the keg down.

"Evening moe.Republicans," said the Chief to me and the bride. "And I mean that in a strict Jeffersonian way."

"We couldn't possibly conceive otherwise," I remarked. The bride smiled and we said our hellos. "Thomas Jefferson set a standard which his modern incarnates long ago abandoned."

"Actually I was talking about *the* Jeffersons, George and Louise, and *'Moving on up!'*" he sang, snapping his fingers and breaking into a few refrains, "*'to the East Side...'*"

"That was a helluva TV show, wasn't it?" said Bullethead, humming along.

"Certainly ahead of its time," Fonebone added, laughing.

"Be careful you don't burn yourself there, guys," I said. "That would be a damn shame."

"You need not fear my friend," the Chief replied, confidently. "Bonfire prep is the most subtle of art forms. It's a calculated nuance dating from the time prehistoric man first captured a spark and transformed his environment. Each log must be laid just so."

"Jesus Christ, Mickey!" Jake laid into him. "You're not having sex with those logs. Just pile the damn things in there, throw some charcoal fluid on, and torch them!" Jake was one of the few people who called the Chief by his name. They went way back together, "Burt and Ernie" types, who weren't too shy about giving each other advice.

"Hey Jake! Who's fucking this horse, anyway?" the Chief countered.

"As long as you're playing with the fire, I'd say the horse is fucking us," Jake snapped back. "We were all hoping there'd be an outside chance of having the lobster kabobs before dawn."

The Chief growled.

"Jesus guys, here," I interrupted them, tapping the keg. "Relax, have a beer." I filled a few cups and passed them around.

"All I need is that stack of newspapers you're standing next to," said the Chief, pointing to me. "Could you hand them to me, please? They'll do fine for an extra bit of kindling."

"I'm sure that old Crog sat around the cave reading the *Globe*, Chief," said Jake. "Dining on fried mammoth, Pterodactyl eggs, drinking his coffee, and reading the morning edition."

"Hold it," said Fonebone as I placed the pile of newspapers down. "Save the sports page."

"Why? You gonna need it later?" Bullethead asked him with a chuckle.

"Holy snapping assholes!" Jake said disgustedly. "I don't even want to think about that. I don't even want to have to visualize it. Just alluding to it is making me ill."

"Hey, everyday a wild bear shits in the woods," said Fonebone. "Yet, when posed as a question it serves as the prime metaphor for one of life's great riddles wrapped in an enigma."

"Not in the winter," Buck interjected as he walked into the firing line to get a couple of beers. The mystery woman, who turned out to be Conrad's sister, Debra, was next to him. "They're corked up for six months in hibernation."

"Corked?" Bullethead said incredulously. "No way!"

"Yeah! It's true," said Timmy, at which point the bride and Buck's "date" walked away in disgust, meandering over towards the other women. Looked like Buck had struck out before he even got the bat off his shoulder.

"You ever try to shit in a snowbank in the dead of winter?" Buck asked.

"Not without the sports page," I added.

"Which is why you should always keep one handy," said Fonebone triumphantly. "To the sports page!" We raised our cups to the starry cosmos.

"Okay, baby, come on light my fire," said the Chief, striking a match. He flung it into the midst of the logs. A flame rose under the kindling and spread progressively throughout the timber. Then went out. He did it again and *it* went out. After several more futile attempts the Chief gave up. Bullethead and Fonebone stared in frustration.

"Hey, Moe, Larry, Curly!" said Jake, looking at the Chief, Bullethead, and Fonebone. "You ready for the charcoal fluid yet?" he asked. "Get over it. You're still manly men. Nobody ever complains about the aesthetics of charcoal fluid when it's a backyard barbecue!"

Dejectedly, the three of them relented. In no time a steady blaze was snapping and cracking in front of us. A few more people showed up, too, including McNugent and his wife, Shelly. They arrived in the new Land Rover the 'Bank of Rafiki' had just financed for Farkleberry Farm. McNugent had been antsy to take it off the road and tonight he'd gotten his wish.

"What took you?" Buck asked them.

"I had my last seminar this afternoon," said Shelly, who teaches philosophy over at Bowdoin. "Existentialism and the material world. Didn't get out of class until five."

"Ah, how's my cycloptic friend doing these days?" McNugent asked Buck when he saw him.

"The all seeing eye sees everything, Casey," he replied. "And it sees you getting my medical bill soon enough."

"Hey, Buckaroo—I am but a victim, too! Speaking of which," McNugent turned to me, grinning. "Rafiki wants to know when you're *coming* again."

"That's privileged information," I said loudly, and gave a nod toward the wife. "You can give the big fella my regards, though. Be sure to tell him from me—when the opportunity *does* arise I don't need someone's arm stuck in my ass to do it."

That loosened all of them up. Set the mood. As the fire slowly turned to warm glowing embers, we hunkered down for the light show. Between the lobster kebobs, moe.Ale, snacks, and sundry organic accoutrements, soft music, all and all, up to that point, the experience was a celestial success. Through a steady chorus of oohs and ahs it was nothing less than ethereal. We were on the verge of a true Zen-like experience when, somewhere between "It's the Time of the Season" and "Fly me to the Moon," a coyote howled up on the adjacent ridge. The wail was lonesome and desperate, and trailed off into a high pitched shriek. Timmy quickly shut the music off. Seconds later the call was answered by another howl from the ridge above us.

"What the hell, Tucker!" Jake shouted out, bug-eyed.

"Hey," he responded. "I'm not the one who wanted to have the party up on the mountain."

"Whoa," I replied. "You might have mentioned the possibility of being coyote bait, Timmy. That minor detail may have carried the day!"

"Calm down! Everyone," said Timmy. "Coyotes don't attack people. There's nothing to worry about. We're safe here, anyway."

"Yeah," Fonebone said. "The fire's burning hot, the tiki torches are lit, and I got a Ford Exploder, if the transmission doesn't blow again, that can outrun any wild dog."

"There's also that twelve gauge in the back of the Commando," the Chief added. "If it gets down to it."

"You're not going to need any of it," Buck spoke up.

"And why's that?" Timmy asked.

"Because the coyotes were telling each other to move on," he said, "and they were also speaking to us. They were trying to warn us."

"Warn us about what?" the bride asked him, which, I'm certain, related to our peculiar conversation on the ride here.

"That we should move on, too," he said. "Leave Uriel while we can. On our own two feet."

"Buck," I said. "You were talking like this on the way here. What in God's name do you mean?"

"Uriel's Ledge." He drew a deep breath, contemplating the question. "It's been a while since I've been up here. Never at night, and those coyotes just let me know why."

"I come up here all the time," said Timmy. "Sit for hours. Take it in. Enjoy the peace and quiet. There's nothing here."

"Exactly," Buck replied. "Don't you think that's kind of odd?"

"Odd?" he asked, perplexed. "To get in touch with nature?"

"That when you sit here, after a while, the only thing you *do* hear is the wind rustling—*and nothing else!*" That stirred us all up. Everyone quieted down. Listened intently. No crickets chirped. No owls hooted. No insects buzzed. No coyotes. Nothing but a light wind, whooshing and rustling around us. The realization made me uneasy, and I could see it in the faces of the others, too. "When have you ever been in a forest, night or day, and not heard it speak to you?"

"All right, Buck," said Shelly. "I have a feeling you're about to go metaphysical on us with one of your stories."

"Shelly dear," he replied, "you're perceptive. Enough that I think you know the story about this place already."

"Oh, I have a few stories about this place," she giggled and elbowed McNugent. "But I think I know which one you mean."

"We'll have none of that Shelly," the Chief piped up. "This is a family affair."

"Yeah, Mickey," Jake interrupted. "I don't know about you, but I always bring my kids out drinking and parking with me. That way, when I'm sitting around the camp fire getting liquored up and start cussing, I don't have to worry where they are at two o'clock in the morning."

"Well, that doesn't surprise me Jake," replied the Chief, "considering how many times I've arrested them since Girl Scouts."

"Whoa-ho!" shouted out Porter amongst the hoots and whistles. "I didn't think you had it in you Chief."

"A rare moment of clarity," he answered.

"Very rare," said Jake. "Mark the time and date. The Chief hath humbled me."

When the laughter died down, the last giggle subsided, we sat there, seemingly lulled into silence. Hypnotized by the glowing embers, no one spoke for several minutes. In those moments it seemed as though we each became aware of just what Buck had been talking about. There was no sound about us, yet there was a feeling, at least for me, that there was *something* about us.

"It's deafening, isn't it?" Buck finally broke the silence. "When you realize that you're truly alone, yet you *feel* you're in the presence of something." A trail of meteors burst on the horizon. Followed shortly by another meteor, several degrees higher, which left a fiery tail miles long across the sky. "Let me ask you, Timmy. What did you know about this place when you wrote that story of yours?"

"What do you mean—about *this* place?" he answered guardedly. "What is there beyond the rock formation and the view? That's all I know. That and my imagination."

"I thought so," Buck replied coolly.

"Hey, that was a good story," said Bullethead, defending Timmy. A few more of us piped up and jumped on Buck, too.

"I'm not putting down Timmy's story," Buck responded over the hubbub. "I liked it, too. All I meant was if Timmy knew about, or was inspired by, the Abnaki version."

"I don't know anything about the Abnaki version," said Timmy, sincerely. "Didn't know there *was* another version of 'That *Winged* Thing.'"

"Don't any of you know what this place meant to the native Americans?" asked Buck loudly. "What it was called before the white man came along and named it after a kick-ass archangel?"

"Buck, why are you the only one who ever seems to know about this kind of stuff?" I asked him.

"What stuff?" he replied.

"All this campfire-bogeyman stuff," I answered, looking at the campfire.

"I know," Shelly volunteered, reluctantly.

"Me, too," said Porter, which was followed by a few other grumbles of acknowledgement.

"Are me and the bride and Timmy the only ones in the dark here?" I asked incredulously.

"I don't know anything," the blonde on Porter's arm spoke out for the first time, which drew more than one laugh. "What?" she said with a blank expression. "I *don't* know anything!"

Porter gave her a quick hug and a reassuring smile. "You're the only one whoever thinks about it, Buck," said Porter. "I've forgotten about it more times than I can remember. And it's just a fucking legend, anyway."

"Legend or not, I found it interesting that Timmy would write *that* story while he was here on Uriel's Ledge," Buck responded. "Here in *this* spot—the place the Abnakis called hockamock. Roughly translated, we're sitting in a place filled with 'evil spirits,' a 'hellish place!'" When he said it there was just a hint of a collective gasp—barley audible. A marked shift in the mood of us all. A wave of nervous energy.

"Nope," Timmy perked up, "I definitely didn't hear that one."

"From my research of Abnaki mythology," Buck continued, "and its place in the local legends, I believe that somewhere in this very vicinity is the lost portal. The place where the natives came to transfer to the other side and back again. The portal to the other time of their father's fathers and their children's children, and the children's children of the other men who were yet to be. Namely, us!"

"Come on, Buck," said Shelly. "No need to get *that* metaphysical on us."

"I'm not getting heavy, Shelly," he replied. "I just think it's queer that Timmy here would write a story about a winged creature up on Uriel's Ledge—and he didn't even know anything about the ancient legends."

"You're talking like there's some kind of coincidence or plagiarism, Buck," Shelly said with an edge. "I hope it's not the latter."

"Now you're the one who's getting heavy, Shelly," replied Buck, "when you, of all people, should be getting metaphysical. I think it's amazing that

Timmy would write that story here. That's all. Because the Indians believed there was a presence here, too. Winged creatures imprisoned on the other side of the portal, barred from entering the *other* world, and always trying to escape into this one. I think that it's remarkable. That Timmy could be so dead on centuries later, with no knowledge of what this place truly symbolized."

"Thank you," said Timmy, awkwardly. "I thought it would be nice to have something good come of this place. Because I like it here so much."

"Well, the Abnakis didn't quite see it that way, Timmy," replied Buck. "The winged creatures, and there were many of 'em, were considered evil. Known as the Askweeda'eed. Bearers of misfortune and death. Monsters that rise like will-o'-the-wisps and take flight. Incredibly, they could secure their release into this dimension only once a year, each summer, at the passing of meteors."

"You're freaking me out, man!" Timmy burst out. "This was supposed to be a keg party."

"No Timmy, you're freaking *me* out," Buck replied. "You wrote the story. You chose the place. You picked the night. I had to ask myself, when you invited me, why? Is this cosmic or what? You got inside *my* head. I had to come."

"Are you making this up?" asked Conrad, who'd been quiet up to this point. "Just say so if you are."

"You're missing my whole point," said Buck. "It's Timmy here who's somehow, blindly, connected with the old legends. The only difference was that his 'winged thing' was benevolent. The Askweeda'eed is not. On top of that, he chose *the* night, when, according to the Abnakis, the meteors would open the portal, allowing the monsters to cross over, and take flight into our world. That's why the Abnaki elders and the keepers of the portal came here each year, as we have tonight, at the height of the Perseids. They entered this hockamock, made huge bonfires and smoked the pipe or dropped the wild herbs. They ran with the wolves and coyotes across the mountain. Jumped the tails of passing meteors and took a mystical ride through the aurora borealis. It was the only way to capture the Askweeda'eed. Return them to their purgatory, and keep vigilance. For the elders and keepers knew that those creatures must not be allowed to take flight into this world or we'd all be doomed!" There was a timely pause on Buck's part. Enough to allow all he'd said to sink in. "So, I thought I'd come and see for myself what this was all about," he said, composed, "and take that mystical ride." Just as he finished a dozen meteors burst into the atmosphere simultaneously, arcing across the sky brightly.

"And I thought I was going to pound down a few beers and watch a light show," said McNugent, who took a deep breath and exhaled slowly.

"It's like we're in some Twilight Zone reality show," said Conrad. "The Reality Mind-Fuck Hour."

"Well, Buck," said Jake. "You really know how to liven up a party."

"Hey, hey! Don't mind me, folks," said Buck, cheerfully. "I'm merely conducting a crypto-anthropological study."

"Well, you've wigged me out," said Timmy. "Cause I sure as hell am not coming back here again."

"Damned if it wouldn't take much for me to leave, now," said the bride.

"Ah, there's nothing to worry about," Shelly reassured her. "It's all a bunch of myths. Buck's just messing with our heads."

"Speaking of which," the Chief stood up. "I have to go shake mine." He picked up his flashlight and went off into the bushes toward the ledge.

"Well, at least he didn't ask for the sports page," Bullethead said, with a nervous chuckle.

"I have it right here," said Fonebone, holding it up, "and if Buck keeps up with these stories, I'm gonna be forced to use it real quick."

"People! That's what they are—*stories*!" Buck exclaimed. "Like Shelly said—myths! If the portal were opening, the winds would howl and the earth would shake." When he said it, he kind of laughed, like he was just trying to keep us off balance. He didn't have to try too hard. We all were, by then, anyway. Yet, I think even Buck was surprised about what happened next. When he got a taste of what he was looking for. The stuff legends are made of. Cosmic enlightenment. Because when that blast of wind came, it came with a fury. It rolled up out of the valley, up the side of the mountain, and struck us blind. Hot and voluminous. As though a fire breathing dragon was expelling its gaseous lungs right on us. The look on Buck's face went from poker to panic in a real hurry. That would be the last time I'd see it that night. And let me tell you, that look said it all. This wasn't in any books he'd read. In the next instant, in one mighty breath, each of the tiki torch lamps were extinguished, as was the fire. If that wasn't strange enough, a sudden, ear-splitting thunderbolt cracked over our heads. And then all went silent. It could have been five or ten seconds, or minutes. I don't know. I was too disoriented. The bride had a death grip on my arm, which probably kept me from collapsing. Especially when a beam of light appeared from out of no where and we heard the Chief begin to scream madly.

"Ahhh-yeee! No! Get them off me." He came running out of the bushes blindly. "Run!" he shouted. But it was too late for us all. All but Timmy Tucker, who was sitting behind the wheel of the moose mobile. He'd made a dash when the wind kicked up and got there just in time. He turned the headlights on and caught the Chief, a flashlight in one hand swung wildly through the air. He groped futilely with the other—to no avail. A wave of bats enveloped him and then struck into us with the force of a biblical flood. There had to be ten thousand of them.

"The Askweeda'eed!" screamed Buck insanely, and he ran off towards his car. The rest of us hit the ground. Later, Fonebone would correctly identify the critters as the little brown bat, the famed *myotis lucifugus*. Everyone there that night thought it was short for Lucifer, but actually is Latin for "to flee or runaway from light." Though, I don't think you could ever convince the Chief of that. That flashlight of his didn't repel a single one. Those little flying monkeys picked him up and tossed him in the trees like the Scarecrow of Oz. By Fonebone's reckoning, the bats were roosting in the caves and hollows on the ledge and under the precipice. When that first thunderbolt cracked into the side of the mountain it must have short-circuited their little sonars, sent them fleeing for their lives, and right into us.

Within moments after the attack the rains came. A grand thunderstorm it was, too. We were happy to ride back with the McNugents, especially as we sloshed our way down the mountain. Not that there was much choice. Buck had split pronto, like he'd been flung out of the bat cave, at the moment of attack. But hey—we all survived. I sat placidly in the middle of the back seat of the Land Rover. Holding the bride in one arm and the keg in the other.

What did I care that we were all covered in guano? Another first for me in a summer of firsts. Though, I found the bat shit to have a more piquant, overly pungent, funky odor. Not even close to, nor in the same league as, the repulsive stink bombs Rafiki dropped on me. To think: I never thought I'd look back with fondness on those times when I merely *stepped* in dog shit? Those were the days!

As for Buck, everyone's been sore at him for the past couple weeks. I have to admit, it's kind of funny now. He did humbly apologize for abandoning me and the bride. He felt really bad leaving us behind to be devoured by the Askweeda'eed. Very bad form. "There really was such a monster in Abnaki mythology," he defended himself a happy hour or two ago. "I guess I got carried away that night—psyched myself out something fierce when that storm came out of nowhere!"

"I'd say that's an understatement," I replied, "when you had twenty adults screaming and running for their lives along the edge of the abyss." He started to chuckle, but thought twice about it and cringed.

The Perseids were over, thankfully. A fleeting night of omens had passed. The Lost Kingdom had thrown another challenge my way, and I'd made it through without going too batty. Though, next year, I told Timmy, we'll have the astral blast out back, up on the hill. Not that the guy will ever go back up on that ledge. I figure, for me, 'tis better to deal with my own demons than conjure up the ancient ones.

As the trough turns,
brother John

The moe.Republic Hotel
in the heart of the Lost Kingdom

The Turkey Bowl
In the Sauna
Sunday, 1:06 p.m.

Dear Rob:

Sorry you couldn't make it here for Thanksgiving, but I know the day after gig in the City is always one of the most happening of the year. I don't know what it is about that Friday. What spurs the orgiastic free-fall into the depth of materialistic depravity. I guess it's the thrill of the hunt. But when the day's fight is over, the party begins, and that's where moe. comes in (not a bad jingle, aye?). Frayed nerves need to be satiated by the soothing sounds of "New York City" or a restful retreat into the nether regions of "Recreational Chemistry." Believe me I understand.

Up here in the Lost Kingdom we had a good day. Though things did get backed up in the men's room. Reports of a new life form surfaced in shitter number two late Wednesday night, which precipitated an evacuation of the stall. Early the next day, I donned my contamination suit, but quickly retreated. It wasn't like someone had simply lit a bum cigar, dropped a deuce in the hole, or punched a grumper. I needed a professional head hunter. I was forced to call upon Sweeney, our old contractor and erstwhile plumber. After listening to his diagnosis I was more concerned about what, not who, did the deed. He wanted to know what we had been feeding the guests. Here's a man who's plumbed the depths of depravity, burrowed into the lowest bowels of hell, and he claimed he'd never seen anything like *it*. I asked him, for the sake of humanity, could he slay the beast? "Did Saint George slay the dragon?" was his reply. "He did," I answered him, "but only after he made an offer the people couldn't refuse." In my case, I didn't have to go through any conversion. The price was but a few shekels and all the moe.Ale he can swill Friday happy hour until his dying day or liver gives out, whichever comes first. Believe me, that was a deal. Music to my ears. A symphony. Bigger than Beethoven's last movement, or whatever was down in that hole. Finally relieved that morning, I said my good-byes to Sweeney, at least till the following afternoon.

|105|

I caught up with everyone at the annual Thanksgiving Day high school football game. One of the more popular local holiday traditions. The Downeast Way HS Woodchucks and the Moose Harbor Regional HS Black Flies squared off in the famed Turkey Bowl. A grudge match like no other, it's normally played under the guise of a charity event for the National Rice Foundation, but this year's funds were earmarked for the families of the September attacks.

The weather was frigid and blustery. By halftime my pudendum was as cold as the balls on an arctic seal. The boys had long retreated into the inner sanctum of the shell. I didn't care. We were there, amidst the cold and all, to root for Downeast Way High and our very own Wilson Butwell. The star offensive lineman, third team all-state, and dishwasher extraordinaire for the moe.Microbrewery.

The game was a nail biter. The old-timers say it will go down in the annals as one of the more thrilling. I say that it will undoubtedly go down as the most memorable. With less than a minute to go in the game, the score's 17-16, Downeast Way. Moose Harbor had the ball on the Downeast Way 15 yard-line. It was fourth and two, no timeouts, and the clock ticking. The Black Flies rushed their field goal unit on the field. They lined up to score what was sure to be the winning field goal behind the sure-footed Nick Millette. He had already kicked field goals of 33, 26, and 17 yards, and the wind was at his back. The ball was snapped. I was watching Wilson, who was on special teams, rush the line. He broke through. I was on the edge of my seat. Everyone was. The kid looked like he was going to block it. Then, with the clock winding down, an emu sprinted onto the field from out of the Woodchucks end zone.

The bird had eluded capture for months. The last one that had escaped after the trailer jackknifed on the way to Farkleberry Farm last spring. I think that everyone had thought it was 86'd by now. But no. Suddenly it was the twelfth man on the pivotal play of the most exciting game in recent memory of the Turkey Bowl. Just as the hammer-toed, young Millette, who has committed to play football at U Maine O next year, went to kick the ball he slipped on the frozen turf. The kick nicked Wilson's fingers, shanked low and wide-left. The Woodchucks were already opening the cider, when the ball ricocheted off the charging emu's head and arced skyward. As the clock ticked to zero the stunned crowd watched the biggest turkey ever bagged in these parts hit the tundra, at about the same instant that the ball bounced off the left upright inches above the cross bar and trickled feebly through scoring the winning goal.

Final score: Black Flies 19, Woodchucks 17, Big Bird 1.

Some would say it's all stranger than fiction. I suppose. No need to be too sad, nor alarmed, though. That bird has one tough nugget. It only sustained a slight concussion and has since been reunited with the rest of its flock. Up at Farkleberry Farm they're celebrating the end of a long, strange trip. And the rest of us? Well, it was a short walk from the field, but we'd seen a heck of a game, and we had a turkey-tale for the ages.

What can I say? Feedin' as we do, here, on the far side of the mountain.

brother John

From: brother.john@moerepublic.org
To: rob@moe.org
Date: the cusp of a winter's solstice, 8:01 p.m.
Subject: holiday wraps

dear rob: A quick hi-di-ho to you and the moe.faithful is in order as we approach one more winter solstice, ebbing further into the millennium. These Saturday night gigs at the hotel are draining—especially around the holidays. Tonight we're hosting the Downeast Polish-American Society's annual Christmas Party. Right now Big Eddie Munch's Expressionist Polka band is playing their version of "Happy Hour Hero"—and the crowd is going wild! Father is jamming with them as we speak. When they asked him to play he whipped out his harmonica faster than his teeth at bedtime. The Santa Claus Stout is flowing freely. The holiday revelers are clinging to every refrain like it was their last plate of kielbasa.

Did you guys ever think of doing a holiday CD? "Royalties in perpetuity!" father declared. Then again, he thinks that you should use your weighty influence with the band to go polka. Mother said you'd have to learn to play the accordion. She was so excited about the thought that she already set out a course of instruction for you. Not to worry! Before they went overboard I quickly reminded them that you were only the bass player.

What's this with New Jersey on New Year's Eve? You told me after Thanksgiving you were possibly thinking about considering playing here? Why would you want to play in Jersey in front of all those screaming fans when you and the boys could relax in the solitude of the Lost Kingdom for a few kicks and giggles, and all the beer you can drink? No hard feelings. We'll have a full house, anyway. Pistol Packing Pedro and the Latino Swing Orchestra is prepping and ready to play in your stead. The final gig of another chapter, another year, in the moe.Republic Hotel.

What a year it's been. When I think back I really can't complain. There were a few highs, a few lows, and a few survivors. Conrad Dixon surfaced among the latter, and won this year's Halloween Storytellers festival. Wrote a fantastic tale about a native American monster of legend, rising from the depths of hell on the night of the Perseid meteor shower. Put a nice spin on it, too. We all fell into the abyss and woke up naked, stranded in some kind of purgatory. A shadowy, dank world infested with ancient, bat-like creatures, who carry away the fallen, one-by-one, through a distant archway. The remaining survivors are left to guess what fate will befall them when their turn comes, all the while confessing their darkest sins and deepest regrets. Until the last soul, standing naked and alone, waits and ponders his fate, staring at the archway, fearful of the universe beyond. Even when he realizes he's been forgotten, when it dawns on him that he could leave, he chooses to remain forever in the hell he has landed in rather than take a chance and step into the unknown. I'd say Conrad summed it all up nicely. A good story. All about lifting the veil and confronting your demons; to take that chance in life when it presents itself, rather than living your life cowering in fear and regret.

Buck Jones is on my list, too, of highs and lows. I saw him the other day when I brought the Rambler in for another check-up. Just hasn't been running right since the Perseids. You'll be happy to know that his plastic surgery went well, though. You wouldn't know the guy had a dent in the middle of his forehead just a few months ago. He was happy and talkative as ever. Cheerfully rendered a discourse on the cell biology of the emu testis, and how its structure and function may have played a part in defining the aggression we witnessed last spring. What could I say? Unlike the emus I had no where to run. He had me by the balls. And such is the wisdom of our fathers, my heart and mind followed.

I ran into Buck again days later at the Farkleberry Farm Christmas party and he had the whole table going with the emu story. Casey McNugent, bless him, held the bash here. He invited Buck, that trucker, whose insurance ponied up for the birds, and me, along with the whole Farkleberry clan. Naturally I told McNugent I couldn't attend, seeing as I had to work the gig. He's *overflowing* in cash these days. Elephant futures have been good to him. "Rafiki really misses you," he told me over his fifth eggnog. I wanted to tell him that that was the whole problem. Rafiki *didn't* miss me. But like that pachyderm, I simply let it pass. "You're the best bag man I ever saw, and I want you to know you gotta a job down on the farm anytime you want," he continued. "We got a 401k and medical." Comforting, I thought. I can't imagine the transition from bartender to animal husbandry could be that different. Nothing more than shooting the shit one day, and shoveling it the next.

Say hi to the bride and the child units, and I'll be seeing you at Christmas. Oh, and one more thing. Thanks for adding that link to the moe.Republic Hotel on the moe. web page. Father thinks we should start hocking our moe.Republic tee-shirts on the web before someone else thinks of the idea! You know how it is, here on the eastern frontier...

Happy holidays,
brother John

Act V

Routines of a Wayward Publican

The moe.Republic Hotel
in the heart of the Lost Kingdom

The Fourth and Beans Incident
Several years hence
June 24

Dear Rob,

How goes the mighty trek among the moe.nation these days? It's summer time and that can only mean one thing—the end of black fly season. Just in time for the Fourth of July, too. That time of year when the warm Atlantic breeze kicks in, the pace picks up, the crowds surge like a lunar tide, and fireworks explode. A veritable coup for business.

Speaking of which, it's a done deal. The Downeast Way 5th Annual International Hot Air Balloon Races will be held here on the Fourth. I have to hand it to you. That was a brilliant suggestion to make a pitch to host it. We'll have dozens of those balloons tethered throughout the weekend. Talk about hot air, we got plenty of free coverage in the *Downeast Way Times.* Jackson Grant laid it on thick and heavy.

The new gazebo is finished, too. Father's been on it for some time. It would have been done sooner except the black flies were ferocious this spring. You can only smoke so many cigars so fast in one day to keep the swarming savages at bay. He put the last coat of paint on it yesterday. A commanding shade of lime green with a peach flavored trim. You have to give him credit. He may be colorblind, but he got the job done for the Fourth. He'll have a place for all those picnic tables he's rented. We're going to need the room. The hotel's booked solid. As in we're at capacity. Balloon teams from a half-dozen states, Canada, Ireland, England, Sweden, and Latvia will be here. There's also a gaggle of moe.rons who made reservations months ago. Pistol Packing Pedro's Latino Swing Orchestra will be jamming throughout the afternoon, and Big Eddie Munch's Expressionist Polka Band will be in for the evening show. Believe me, you haven't lived until you've heard the *1812 Overture* on the electric accordion.

The impending onslaught has had everyone on edge. Mother, the bride, father, myself, and sister Liza have been discussing, negotiating, and deliberating over the menu for the past week or two. A delicate dance of shifting alliances in the kitchen has formed and dissolved repeatedly. The menu, however, has not changed, only who's going to do what task. We'll be having an authentic baked bean supper, a pig roast, and broiled lobster courtesy of Lizard's Lobster Pound.

I wanted to cater it all, especially after I got stuck digging a fire pit, plus building a fireplace, but was voted down four to one. I was lamenting, nay, actually bitching over it, down at Kinghorn's Diner the other morning to anyone who would listen. Don't get me wrong. I'm not trying to break the karma. I am psyched about the balloon races. It's a major coup for business. The event's the talk of the town and we're right in the middle of it. But my days of manual labor are reserved for sixteen ounce curls and that's it. I've dug ditches, cleared land, loaded and unloaded semi's, and a lot more. I've pounded my last nail. These feats of engineering tend to sap me of my energy and ache my bones. At least that's what I was yapping about to the tides of humanity who rose and fell within earshot.

Actually, I was crammed into a booth with my usual social circle of mad dogs and derelicts—Gil Fonebone, Chief Mickey McO'Fayle, Fred 'the Bullet-head' Bergmeister, Jake 'the Lizard' Hutchinson and Buck Jones. They were attentive and talkative, except for Fonebone. The guy's been straight out of late. Over the past few weeks a major pest invasion's struck town—bears, skunks, and other critters. By the looks of him the "Bug Man" must have worked another all-nighter. At any moment his face and the bowl of oatmeal before him could become one.

I think what kept him going was the continuous banter between the Chief, Bullethead, and Jake. The Fourth is a pretty busy day for the Chief and Bullethead. They're in charge of the town's fireworks, at least the Chief is, and he *hires* Bullethead and the *Jolly Mr. Johnson* to tow the barge of fireworks out on Moose Harbor for the annual orgy of pyrotechnics.

"I landed the fireworks gig a few years back," the Chief boasted proudly. "They'll never take it from me," he said as though he were carrying the secrets to the atomic bomb. A singular obsession for him and Bullethead—fire and all things 451 degrees-plus Fahrenheit. It makes you wonder if both of them were Hindu priests in a previous incarnation. It would make sense, grand pooh-bahs of the funeral pyre. Sacred torch men.

"For Christ's sake Mickey, tell him!" Jake, who was busily spreading jam on a bagel, unloaded on him. His elbow jabbed steadily into the Chief's rib with each layer of jam. "You got the job because you told 'em you'd do it for nothing."

"Cut the shit with your elbow, Jake," the Chief swore. "I'm trying to drink my coffee."

"You do that for nothing?" I asked, even more puzzled. The Chief shrugged like it was nothing.

"The only nut the town has to crack is for the fireworks," said Bullethead. "That and a free boat ride."

"Easy sailor," the Chief frowned slightly as he looked at Bullethead. "Loose lips sink ships. You could easily lose your commission."

"A case of beer?" Bullethead scoffed.

"With the best seat in town and everything that goes with it!" the Chief winked and both men laughed fiendishly.

"It's true," Bullethead smiled. "Every man has his price. For me, my hearty constitution demands the amber elixir." Both of them laughed that fiendish laugh again.

"What's with the laugh?" I pumped them. "You guys sound like Dr. Frankenstein and Igor at the moment of creation."

"They kind of look like them, too," said Fonebone, yawning. "Don't you think?" That roused him and got a good laugh at the table.

"They just like to dangle their angle," Jake added. "It's their stellar hour. The one time each year they get away playing with fire."

"Playing with fire ain't so bad," I said. "Digging a fire pit and building a fireplace to play with fire, now that's a bitch." The Chief went bug-eyed and Bullethead choked on his coffee.

"When were you planning on telling us about the fire?" asked the Chief, surprised.

"I was bitching about it when I came in," I replied incredulously. "Christ, I just told you. I got stuck with the project yesterday."

"It's kind of vague, what you were saying when you came in," he replied. "You know how self-absorbed I am. But now that you mention it…"

"Of course, we'd love to help," Bullethead pitched in. "You don't have to go it alone."

"What kind of wood are you planning on burning?" Mickey asked me. I was on my third coffee and had to take a leak, but it wasn't going to happen. I was jammed in against the window. Buck wolfed at a plate load of scrambled eggs and oysters next to me, seemingly indifferent to the conversation. Fonebone yawned again, fighting off the sleep. Jake rolled his eyes in anticipation of another dissertation. The diner was packed. A good sign we're closing in on the holiday and peak turista season.

"Should go with a high-heat yield hardwood," Bullethead contemplated. "Don't you think?" He looked at me eagerly.

"I was going to use charcoal," I said, not thinking that much about it.

"Sacrilege!" the Chief bellowed.

"No, no, no!" Bullethead added in a huff. "You're really out of your element, man."

"Yeah, but Jake here's going to be there too, roasting lobster, or whatever he does to it," I said, deflecting my incompetence on Jake. "You know how pissed he gets over the fire. I got the beans to bake, the pig to roast..."

"Don't bring me into this," Jake responded defensively. "You may as well give a drunk a bottle as give these two an excuse to light a fire and expect nothing to come of it."

"Pork and beans? Lobster and beer?" Buck raised his head from his plate abruptly. "Christ you're not going to actually light a match, let alone start a fire?"

"Strike a match!" I was irked. "You're shoveling mollusks and protein down your throat. Damn good thing you own a gas station. You can hide behind the fumes."

"Hey, I'm just looking out for you," Buck said, sipping on his coffee. "You don't have to get riled. I'm just saying, you're not careful there, you're liable to immolate the hotel."

"Could be bad for business," said Bullethead, matter-of-fact like.

"You also can't facilitate illicit gas emissions," said the Chief with authority. "Hasn't been legal since the great Grange Hall methane asphyxiation."

"Come on guys," I laughed. "That's a bunch of crap!"

"Not quite, gas. You can't release in public." He was serious. "It's a blue law." I stared in disbelief. "It was that bean supper. Happened in the dead of winter. The Grange Hall was shut tighter than a bank vault. The furnace was going full bore. Simply no ventilation. Five people were hospitalized."

Fonebone laughed suddenly, roused from his dormancy. "It's funny because you know it's true."

"Don't laugh. Old Irma Hoarywell was in the kitchen," said Bullethead sympathetically. "Seventy-seven years young, she's had respiratory problems ever since."

"She's had respiratory problems because the woman smokes dope all day," said Mickey.

"Irma gets high!?" I was in disbelief. "She's the one who gave mother the whoopee pie recipe. Christ! They play in the church orchestra together."

"Enough said?" the Chief replied. "It's a sad thing when you have to bring in someone your grandmother's age. I keep telling her 'out of sight, out of mind,' but she just keeps pushing all the wrong buttons. I had to bring her in for questioning about the Grange Hall after she was released from the hospital. Couldn't prove anything, though." He added with a shrug.

"Good old Irma," I muttered. "*Incroyable!*"

"Doris!" the Chief shouted out above the crowd. A short middle-aged woman with a pot of coffee in each hand turned and glared at him. "You know you're beautiful when you're totally overwhelmed and on the verge of a psychotic episode."

"Mickey!" She snapped. "State your case before I accidentally spill this coffee in *someone's* lap!" She stared down at him intently. "I was going to ask for a half-caf, half-decaf, low-fat latte, but I guess I'll have whatever is in your right hand." He placed his cup down on the table carefully, and gently edged it away from him.

"Thank you, Doris," he said as she topped him and us all off and moved on in a tizzy.

"Menopausal," Bullethead whispered. "My old lady's showing the signs, too."

"What did you say, Fred?" Doris trumpeted from across a row of tables.

Bullethead stared at her, more stunned than anything. For me it was a moment of relief. I had been about to weigh in on being on the front lines. Standing daily amidst the vicissitudes of the feminine mystique in all its glory. I was prepared to give a thesis. That was the moment Doris picked him up on her subatomic radar. He should have known better. Loquacious and affable, she's widely known for her intense gift of gab. More remarkable is her auricular deftness. She has a Promethean ability to pick-up conversations at exceedingly distant intervals. In the world of busybody-dom, gathering and distributing calculated rumor and innuendo is fiercely competitive. Doris can pick up the scent of a scurrilous or scandalous conversation as easily as a hound dog can mark a raccoon a mile away. Bullethead was at her mercy—the entire diner had honed in with her for the kill.

"Men are pigs, ah, Doris," He said awkwardly in cadence to 'men-o-pau-sal.' "Pigs I tell you."

"I thought so. Next time speak up so everyone can hear you!" she said loudly and triumphantly so everyone *could* hear her. There was a momentary pause among the vacationing plebes, long enough for Bullethead to sink under his ball cap and into his chair.

"Anyway," the Chief jumped in. "If you're done harassing the help, Bullethead..."

"Don't *even!*" Bullethead exhorted, then looked over his shoulder. "Is she gone?" he whispered. We nodded.

"As I was saying," the Chief said calmly, directing his attention my way. "After the Grange Hall debacle the town council passed an ordinance prohibiting the passing of gas in public venues."

"Too bad," Fonebone said. "There is a certain element of fun watching people squirm in public while the methane builds up in their lower tracts."

"Especially the women." Bullethead glanced furtively in a Pavlovian reflex, then grinned. "They tend to get real sneaky, if you know what I mean, ripping silent eddies of high octane swamp gas amidst the crowd."

"You know something's going on when they suddenly stand perfectly still and start to concentrate," Fonebone smiled.

"The key is in their hands. They can stop talking anytime to listen, but when their hands stop moving, too—walk away!" added Buck.

"Okay, okay." I raised my hands in defeat. "I'll have a bowl of Beano on the buffet table," I said, wearily. "Because I'm sure as hell not going to change the menu. I can't. I've already lost that battle. Nor am I going to get busted on the Fourth of July!"

"No one's telling you to change the menu," Bullethead reassured me.

"You just can't use charcoal," the Chief said firmly. "You'll need a good high-heat yield hardwood."

"It'll reduce *emissions*," Buck added, his cheeks crammed with oysters and eggs.

"I think we'll go with a red oak," Bullethead said.

"Red oak will do the trick," the Chief added.

I left the diner under a cloud, as it were, pondering a menu change and wondering if I was being hosed once again. I had gone there to vent and left roused, yet deflated. I had a major project on my hands. The following day, true to their word, Bullethead and the Chief arrived with a pickup filled with red oak. We unloaded a near cord and stacked it neatly.

Having resigned myself to accomplishing an engineering feat akin to the Panama Canal, I've spent the last two days moving earth and laying brick and mortar. Actually, I paid Wilson Butwell and a couple of his fellow linemen to do it. I reserved my strength to instruct them dutifully and deflect their questions about what was for lunch, or the possibility of liquid refreshment. The place looks great and we're near ready to go. I see father coming my way. It's about time. We've decided to go with a traditional Abnaki pig roast. With arrow and bow in hand, we're garbed in deerskin loin cloths, doused in mink oil, and off to hunt wild boar on the backside of Mount Agamenticus.

Till the fireworks explode,

brother John…

```
From:    brother.john@moerepublic.org
To:      rob@moe.org
Date:    July 1; 11:29 p.m.
Subject: Fourth asunder
```

hola bro: Well there's good news and there's bad news. The bad news is that Pistol Packing Pedro has had to cancel on the Fourth. The good news is that we have a slot open now, if you catch my drift. Maybe you and the guys could hop in the moe.bus and make for the eastern frontier. Tell Chuck and Al, and Vinnie and Jim, we pay top dollar—a buck an hour and all you can drink! Let me know, otherwise I have to find another band pronto.

    Love and kisses,

    John

From: brother.john@moe.republic.org
To: rob@moe.org
Date: July 2; 11:02 p.m.
Subject: re: Fourth asunder

Yo! Not that it really matters but isn't the Chicago gig later in the month? Aren't you guys in the studio finishing the new *opus maximus*? It's hard for me to keep track. Just tell me that you're not doing the old 'I'd love to but, I gotta wash my hair' soft shoe. Don't leave me hanging! I'm only bird dogging about a dozen details as we edge closer to the big day. We're already pretty busy. The hotel is full, or as father reflected so eloquently during breakfast today, we're packed tighter than a Christmas goose.

Losing Pistol Packing Pedro at the eleventh hour bites. Maybe if I had got the word out sooner we could have connected. Then again, if I gave you more notice you could come up with a better excuse. Unfortunately, we found out late last night. Fonebone came by, haggard and bent, to give us the scoop. The old man was behind the bar trading war stories with Porter Gibson Digit and anyone who'd listen. Porter had come by to watch the Sox game as he always does. I have to say, the two of them had a small audience in the palms of their hands. Or should I say they had them amidst a long forgotten campaign of espionage and intrigue, somewhere behind the Western front. But I'll save that story for another day. Or the next time you're in town with the bride and wee ones, you can ask either Bigwood, Timmy Tucker, or the Chief, if you happen to bump into them. Because they and a few turistas were front and center listening attentively to the old man and Porter when Fonebone walked in and spoke up.

"Dude, I got some bad news." When he uttered those dreaded words the shift in karma was abrupt. "It's about Pedro and the boys." There was the obligatory pause, accompanied by a sudden hush that befell the crowd. The kind that no one ever wants to hear. You know that Pedro's real name is Wolfgang Peterson but everybody calls him Pedro. He and half his band are working for Fonebone this summer.

"They okay?" asked Father, concerned.

"Nobody got hurt?" Porter added. "Did they get in an accident?"

"No, no. It's nothing like that," Fonebone replied. "Nothing critical, more victim to a work-related hazard, especially this time of year."

"You're not going to make them work on the Fourth?" I pleaded. "Say it ain't so!" I pressed him. "Not on the Fourth?" Granted, Fonebone and his crew have been straight out since Quigley's landfill relocated across town. All those critters that called the old dump their home for generations were dislocated. They wander all over the place like zombies. When darkness falls they rise, perambulate aimlessly, in a quest for new food sources. As Fonebone tells it, preferably manmade, in any backyard, alley, or dumpster redolent with the funky scent of decaying garbage. Sort of a *Night of the Living Dead* thing, except the cast of characters are bears, raccoons, skunks, and unspeakably repulsive species of rodentia.

"They won't be doing anything for the Fourth, I'm afraid, at least not in public," said Fonebone solemnly. "It's not because of me, amigo, either."

"What the heck has happened?" I asked him, stunned.

"We received a report that a herd of skunks were making their way through the back alley near the Silent Woman Tavern," he said. "It was just after dusk. I sent Pedro and his crew to track them. Make a visual and report back."

"You can't be serious?" I was in disbelief.

"I don't have all the details, but Pedro was tracking them when they doubled back on him," said Fonebone. "They'd been gone longer then they should have, when word trickled in. No need for a search party."

"There was a herd of skunks right here in town?" Father was incredulous. "I didn't think skunks traveled in herds. Who ever heard of skunks moving in herds?"

"I remember once in Colorado," interjected Porter, getting our attention. "I was golfing near the Springs, right under Pike's Peak. We were on some hole on the back nine. There were four of us playing. I was out there for a few days scouting a catcher for the Dodgers, and I hooked up with one of my old teammates, 'Coyote Phil' Jenkins. He teed up and drilled the ball two-hundred and fifty yards. We watched it go a mile high then hook off the fairway over a sharp rise. It took us a minute to get there, but as we came to the embankment," Porter quieted down, "the air quality changed drastically." He paused, as he often did when telling a story. The old-timer was a master fisherman in the way of words. Once you took the bait, he gently reeled you in. The eyes and ears of the bar were now fixed on him as he continued. "Let me put it this way. We knew when we stepped over that ridge we weren't walking into a field of posies. Something had died and it had been a while. Sure enough we stood at the crest of that hill and looked down aghast. There was the biggest damned jack-a-lope any of us had ever seen. Dead and bloated, actually. The poor bastard must have been dropped by a mountain lion or grizzly. Something big by the teeth marks on its side. Anyway, the stink of the carcass was bad enough, but there was a shit load of skunks working on it, too. They were ballsy little shits and stunk to hell. And there right in the middle of that mess was Coyote Phil's golf ball, lodged in the jack-a-lope's eye socket. We stared in disbelief choking from the fumes."

"Jesus man! What in God's name did you do?" Bigwood shouted out. I was about to ask the same thing.

"Cripes, Alex! What do you think we did? What would you have done?" Bigwood shook his head unknowingly. "Shit, Coyote Phil took a stroke and we played through. We sure as hell didn't wait for one of them critters to lift its tail and fire, let alone finish eating. Once a skunk sprays you it's a week of loneliness. Just you and a lot of Bloody Mary's. Never did forget that sight, though. A dead jack-a-lope being devoured by a herd of skunks under the Rockies."

"Disgusting," Timmy bellowed with a shiver.

"That's repulsive," Bigwood added.

"Immensely," Porter said as he turned toward father. "But my point is Big Ed," which was what Porter always calls him. "Skunks do indeed travel in herds, particularly when it comes to feeding." We all pondered the gruesome demise of the fabled jack-a-lope. In a macabre, but all too human way, it was visually compelling.

"You know Porter," father said dryly after a moment or two had passed. "When you're long gone, every time I walk by a pasture and inhale the sweet, pungent smell of bullshit I'll be thinking of you."

"The important thing Big Ed," he answered, pausing as a diplomat may as he presents his credentials, "is to make sure you never step in it."

The old man liked that one. Father laughed loud and hard, which got the whole bar laughing with him just as hard.

"Here Fonebone," said father, handing him a beer and wiping a tear from the corner of his eye. "Now son, what the heck happened to Pedro and the boys?"

"Thanks Ed," he said with a nod. "Let me tell you, I spent the better part of the last few nights myself tracking a herd of skunks through a bunch of neighborhoods. I tracked them to Moose Harbor and back through Wentworth Junction. Last night they took me over there," he pointed across the cove in the direction of Crowe's Farm, "and then vanished. The sons of bitches are wily." He took a long swig off the brew and polished it off.

"Still at large?" Bigwood asked.

"Actually, Crowe's Farm's not that far from here," said Timmy. "You'd think if old Jacob Crowe saw anything move near his property you'd of heard plenty of gun fire. The son-a-bitch's crazy enough. But if all those critters are still on the lam…" He paused to think through the logistics.

"I wouldn't be taking any midnight strolls," Porter spoke up, completing his sentence.

"I'd advise against it," Fonebone added. "The skunks are still at large *and* on the lam." He sounded frustrated. The tone of his voice hardened. "But it doesn't matter because if it isn't the skunks one minute than it's raccoons or black bears the next."

"You're still tracking black bears?" Timmy began to sound concerned. "This could be bad for business."

"Whose business?" Father baited him.

"My business! I'm bringing a dozen people or more each day into the back woods on moose safaris," Timmy explained. "I sure as hell don't want to, nor can I afford to, run into a hungry bear!"

"A good businessman," Porter advised, "adapts to an ever changing environment, Timmy."

"You could start giving urban safaris through the back alleys of Downeast Way," the Chief raised his head up from his glass and spoke for the first time in a while. "Hey Fonebone!" he said, surprised. "When did you get here?" He seemed to think about it for a moment, swaying gently in his stool.

"Why fight nature, Timmy," Bigwood laughed, nodding toward the Chief. "When you can make a career out of it?"

"I already have a career in nature," said Timmy, whiffed.

"The way it's going it might be a good career move Timmy," said Fonebone. "There's that much mayhem! Two nights ago a sow and her two cubs strolled right down Market Square. You think that was a chase I could've lived without?" Fonebone shook his head while father pulled him another beer.

"Look at it this way. You'll be able to write another book, Fonebone," said the Chief. "Just as fast as these beers are going down." He popped the rest of his ale in one gulp and just about keeled over, then steadied himself at the last possible moment. "Bartender! Another for my friend, the great white hunter."

"I need to write another book now as much as you need another beer," said Fonebone. "Besides, the way it's going I'll never be able to write the final chapter."

"It's been the warm weather I tell you," Bigwood added. "It's got all these critters moving like weasels in the night."

"How do you know how weasels move in the night, Bigwood?" the Chief asked with a confrontational edge. He cleared his throat as though preparing a cross examination. "Can the honorable gentleman please clarify that statement for the court?" he demanded.

"They're nocturnal ain't they?" Bigwood defended himself. "And carnivores?"

"Recorder, ban that testimony." The Chief belched heartily and slammed his fist on the bar like a gavel. "Next witness, Marlin Perkins! Could Marlin Perkins approach the bench!"

Bigwood rolled his eyes. "Could someone get this man another drink," he said loudly. "He obviously needs one more for the road."

"Weasels or not," Fonebone interrupted them. "There are certain times of the year you expect major outbreaks of pests. You can expect black flies in the spring—you button up your collar, light up a stogie, and stay out of the woods. Raccoons come and go all summer. You know they have thumbs like we do? It's true!" He wiggled his thumb for effect. "It makes it very efficient for removing lids on trash cans and slashing open garbage bags. The little suckers will actually sort the contents evenly across the lawn."

"Yeah. You got that right," the Chief bobbed his head. "I heard some racket in the backyard a week ago, right. I go and look out the porch, from the mud room. And there's the biggest, bad-ass raccoon mauling the lid on my garbage can. I had the top snapped shut and this bandit was working the lid hard. Two more minutes and he'd have it busted open. I open the door and shout at the prick to leave, clap my hands loudly." He slapped his hands hard for effect and nearly lost his balance. "The son-a-bitch stood up on its hind legs, stuck its thumb up its nose and gave me the finger. I was so pissed I looked around for something to throw at it. There's nothing out there in the room but a few coats on the wall, my waders, a pair of boots, the washer-dryer, and the freezer. In a frenzy I open the freezer looking for a can or something. Anything to put my hands on." He paused to take a drink of his beer.

"Well, what did you do?" Bigwood had to ask him.

He shrugged his shoulders. "There was a bag of peas, a few steaks, some ice cubes, and a five pound lake trout I caught last winter."

"You didn't?" I asked unbelievably.

"Did you ever see that movie, *The Last of the Mohicans*? When Daniel Day Lewis throws that tomahawk and the camera does a slow-mo of the axe turning end over end till it whacks that psychotic Indian?"

"Yeah!" I said.

"Yeah, that was a cool movie," Timmy added.

"Well, forget about the tomahawk and picture a five-pound frozen lake trout hurtling on a beeline, end over end, dead on that raccoon, from the comfort and security of my back porch." He took aim and threw the imaginary fish right at Bigwood on the other side of the bar. I watched the phantom trajectory of the lake trout nail Bigwood's skull dead center.

"You actually impaled a raccoon with a frozen lake trout?" asked Bigwood, the phantom fish stuck in the middle of his forehead.

"For Christ's sake it was a raccoon!" Timmy shouted. "How could you!"

"I guess the tail could be pretty sharp if frozen and thrown at the right speed," said Fonebone, contemplating the physics. He picked up an empty glass and moved it end over end in his hand. "But the weight is too forward."

"Calm down!" the Chief yelled, then burped loudly. "The little bugger ducked. I missed by a mile. I was trying to hit the garbage can anyway. It's not like I was trying to harpoon a raccoon. The last thing I wanted to deal with at that time of night was a raccoon impaled with a lake trout in my backyard." He flinched thinking about it. "I just wanted to scare the critter off."

"Too messy." Porter waved his hand at the thought.

"Not only that," Mickey added. "The little bugger jumped to the ground, picked up the lake trout, and sprinted off with it under his arm like a football."

"Well, at least you got rid of him," said Timmy.

"Not so fast," he said holding up his hand as if stopping traffic. "The next night, about the same time, there were three of them out there up on the garbage cans, standing on the hunches with their thumbs up their nose, flicking me the bird.

"Shit, no!" exclaimed Bigwood, his forehead now cleared of the imaginary five-pounder.

"No shit!" the Chief quipped. "My wife started feeding them dry dog food. Thinks that they're cute."

"Probably not a good idea," Fonebone said sharply. "They're not the family cat. They're rabies carrying wild critters."

"I'll tell her that Fonebone said not to," the Chief pontificated. "I'm sure she'll stop immediately. She's a woman after all, docile, dependent, and obedient. Listens to any and all that I may say or suggest. Being the feminine, gentle creature that she is."

"Just tell her this: that I haven't had a decent night's sleep since they moved the dump across town. All those critters running around—bears, skunks, raccoons, and rats—are doing it because their food supply was cut off!"

"Yeah, okay, but they are cute for wildlife, and they don't smell," the Chief said, effeminate-like.

"Seriously!" Fonebone replied with angst. "When the skunks show up for hand outs it won't be cute. You can't have-a-heart trap a skunk without getting sprayed—sooner or later you have to release them. You can't spring trap them in your backyard, either. Their last act of consciousness on this ethereal plain will be to spray!" His voice rose to an emphatic pitch.

"Hey dude!" Father said calmly to Fonebone. "We believe you," he added. "Here, relax, have another beer. If anything it will help you sleep *tonight.*"

"I know. Sorry everyone. Sorry," he said looking around at everyone in earshot. "I don't mean to be a bear myself," said Fonebone apologetically. "Though we've caught and relocated about fifteen of *them.* I've eighty-sixed more rats than I thought existed in these parts or could imagine. And these skunks! They just keep flaring up. It's driving me crazy I tell you. There's a small herd on the lam somewhere in town," he cried. "Tonight, when Pedro and the boys had them down that alley I thought for sure they'd finally got them. Maybe even found their nest."

"But things didn't turn out like you planned, aye?" Porter said. "It never does."

"Not for Pedro, or any of them," replied Fonebone. "They must have walked right past the skunks going into the alley or the critters actually snuck back passed them. It's crazy, but it was like a classic pincer move. They let them come into the alley, blocked off the point of egress, and closed in." He clenched his fist and ground it into his other hand.

"So what the hell happened?" I asked.

"What do you think?" he asked like we all knew the answer, which we did. But that doesn't mean we didn't want to hear every sordid detail. "You wouldn't think an animal that small with its puppy-like eyes and flatfooted waddle could be so fearless. Pedro and company got whacked in a voluminous crossfire.

"Skunk piss!" Father shouted.

"Actually, it's a musky liquid really, as penetrating as ammonia. Butyl mercaptan it's called. One nasty organic sulfur dioxide compound that will blind, burn, and gas anyone or anything within fifteen feet. I got the boys in a make-shift de-tox center out behind the office now." He gestured with his thumb like they were in the next room over. "The four of them are in a tank of Bloody Mary mix. The bad news is they'll be there for the next three days," he shrugged. "The good news is—there's plenty of Smirnoff!"

"Agh!" I shouted.

"Don't worry, man," Fonebone consoled me. "They didn't know what hit them." Like I cared that the dumb asses were stupid enough to get sprayed by a herd of skunks. They couldn't have done it on the fifth of July? "I have enough Bloody Mary mix to neutralize the odor."

"Or maybe they'll have just enough Bloody Mary's in 'em not give a shit about the odor," added Porter.

"To Bloody Mary's then!" shouted the Chief, who raised his glass for the toast, swiftly, and missed everything except his lap. "Shee-it! I piffed myself."

Which, if you think about it, was pretty much how the night should have ended—and only could have ended.

Let me know when you get back from *Chicago* or finish drying your hair.

Till then, whilst I mop up the trough,

brother John

The moe.Republic Hotel
in the heart of the Lost Kingdom

On the Fourth Day
Wednesday
1:03 p.m.

Dear Rob,

Where the heck have you been? We've been trying to get a hold of you for a week. The insurance adjuster should arrive any minute, so I thought I'd spring this missive while I had the chance. Let me assure you. Do not worry. Contrary to published reports, Kinghorn and Bigwood say that they have no case.

Before I get to that, let me say that the balloon races were a big hit. People came from miles around. The event was quite the spectacle. In more ways than one I suppose. Captain Larjs Pfinktör and the Swedish team won, catching a gust of wind in the last minute to beat the Latvians. There was a tense moment when the Latvians appeared to lose control of their balloon. The wind shift which propelled the Swedes to victory nearly sent team Latvia to New Brunswick. Fortunately an easterly picked them up and brought them back to Oz. Good thing. Cause the balloon ride extravaganza was about to get under way. Mother pitched the idea to the team captains the day they arrived. We charged five bucks a head per ride and split the pot fifty-fifty. In return we charged the teams half price for their rooms. The town's folk were lined up around the corner of the mansion all afternoon. Balloon lines dangled over the grounds like Spanish moss in a sleepy bayou. The airships moved up and down, slowly and hypnotically. At one point a group of moe.rons went up in the Swede's balloon singing a 'heady' *a cappella* rendition of "Plane Crash." Things were going okay until they hit an air pocket causing an involuntary discharge of the lobster burritos they'd polished off before the ascent. Fortunately they missed the feast below, but for a few seconds there chunks were popping off like fireworks all over the ground and the roof of the new gazebo. Old lady Huxley, I think it was Emma, took a direct hit in the side of the head. She said something about the seagulls getting pretty big. Father said it must have been a cormorant and we all laughed.

Speaking of the Huxley sisters, the gruesome twosome, mother, and Irma Hoarywell picked up the slot left by Pistol Packing Pedro. Verily I shittesh you naught. The 'four horsemen' took the stage and jammed away for a couple of hours. Mother on her accordion, Irma tickling the ivories, and the sisters Huxley on the viola and violin. I was loping hunks of wild boar next to Lizard, who was personally overseeing the lobster roast. I wouldn't have believed it if I hadn't seen it. The four of them practice together all the time for Saint Alphonzo's church recitals. But I had no idea. When they got a standing 'O,' for "Sympathy for the Devil," it nearly blew me away. I'm beginning to really wonder what exactly is in that tea they've been pounding down all these years.

On the culinary front, I have to hand it to Bullethead and the Chief. The red oak burned hot and blazed brightly. Best of all there were no involuntary "reports" as it were, or serious "side effects" amongst the crowd. Nothing that I could pick up in the wind, anyway. Though I did notice father sitting off by himself on the far end of the gazebo.

Late in the afternoon the Chief and Bullethead took off to rendezvous with the *Jolly Mr. Johnson*. We were sorry to see them go after their efforts. But duty beckoned. The town awaited in anxious anticipation for the fireworks. The Chief and Bullethead awaited anxiously to light them. Their annual rite of passage was at hand.

After they left it got me thinking again, mulling actually, over their little inside joke. I know it sounds petty but it had been on the back of my mind since it came up at the diner. That invidious laugh had me guessing. I still didn't get it, the dangle of the angle as Jake called it. Captain Bergmeister towed the firework's barge out to the middle of Moose Harbor each Fourth of July. Yeah? That the Chief *hires* him? Pays Bullethead for the ride with a case of beer? That's the big joke? Not that I'm keeping score, but hell, I slipped three coolers filled with moe.Ale into the back of the Jeep Commando before they took off. That should be worth a free cruise to Bar Harbor. Standing near the fire pit, dusk had come and the fireworks were set to begin. I was watching Jake tending a few more lobster tails when I mumbled out loud, frustrated, "I just don't get it?"

"What?" Jake asked me. "Don't get what?"

"The Chief and Bullethead," I replied. "Why anyone would want to work on the Fourth? Especially if they don't have to? And for nothing?"

Jake laughed, nay, bellowed, right in my face. "You're still thinking about that?" he said to me, spreading another row of tails across the grill.

"Can't you see? Why are you working today? Why am I working today?" He stared at me waiting for my answer.

"Because if we stop working we die?" It was feeble, I know, but I'd heard it since the day I was born.

"No. Because if we stop so does the cash flow," he said.

"Yeah, that, too," I replied, perking up.

"We're here doing this to keep pumping the money. I've a crew down at the pound today banging out the lobsters as fast as they can—baked, broiled, boiled or take out."

"It's called busting your balls," I said, attempting to sound intelligent.

"Exactly!" he snapped. "Yet, you wonder why those two yahoos go out on such a glorious day rather then stay here and play?"

"Yes," I said, "other than they get to play with matches."

"You don't think that's enough?" he said with a chuckle.

"Well, Captain Bergmeister does have a boatload of tourists."

"Ha!" He clapped his hands. "You were beginning to worry me."

"I thought of that earlier." I really did, but it just seemed too obvious. "Besides, Bullethead could easily have his mate at the helm. And what about the Chief?"

"Easy, easy now," he said calmly. "In the years before your grand entrance into the Lost Kingdom, the fireworks were held out behind Downeast Way High. A nice place, but tough to get into, and the crowd control was a bear. Then Mickey went to the town with his plan—offered to run the whole show for nothing except the town pays for the fireworks. They don't have to pay a company of pyrotechnics because they have one already on the public dole—him! There's no traffic jams coming out of the high school anymore, or backups at the traffic light downtown. The Chief tells everyone he does it for the thrill of it. The joke is that he pays Bullethead with a case of beer every year, that and they're a couple of pyros, which they are. But what Mickey doesn't say is that Bullethead charges double for the fireworks cruise. That he and Bullethead split the proceeds fifty-fifty."

"They split the proceeds?" The fog lifted. "Sons a bitches!" I laughed.

"Boy? Are you even paying attention?" It was father and he was holding another bowl of beans in his hands.

"Eddie!" Mother snapped from behind him, somewhere. "What do you have in the bowl?" she yelled from across a picnic table.

"Nothing woman," he said, waving her off. "Will you quit stalking me," he added, under his breath.

"He's eating more beans," I heard Edith say to mother.

"That's his fourth bowl," said Emma conspiratorially, ratting him out.

"You're sleeping in the Rambler tonight if you're eating what I think you're eating!" she said in a huff. "Don't even think of coming inside!" Father rolled his eyes as mother turned her head. She and the girls laughed, enjoying their new found celebrity, signing autographs for the Saint Alphonzo's faithful.

"So boy," said father, turning his attention back at me. "As I was about to tell you, what Lizard is saying and what you should know by now—follow the money trail and you'll always have your answers—if it means that much to you." He hesitated momentarily. "Hey Jake? Could you throw a couple of those tails in here?" Holding out his bowl, Jake dropped a few in. "See you boys," he said happily. "I'm going back to my perch. You really can't beat that view of the harbor from anywhere."

I thought about what father said and let it go. The fireworks began shortly, anyway. The show went well until the grand finale. What happened then has been a source of debate and contention for the past week. The Sheriff's report was inconclusive. The Coast Guard said it was a close call. The Chief's had to recuse himself from the whole affair. He and Bullethead had loaded up every canister—all ten—with Big Berthas for the grand finale. When Bullethead handed the Chief the next to last Big Bertha it ended up in the canister backwards. Whether or not Mickey loaded it backwards, or Bullethead handed it to him backwards or that the Bertha itself was manufactured backwards, which the Chief and Captain Bergmeister claim, has become the focal point of the investigation. I began to wonder if Bullethead took an advance on his pay before the show, or if they both got their money's worth during that boat ride. It was a hot day in the fire pit, and I imagined that the boys were thirsty. That was of no consequence at the present. We know this much: when that Bertha shot out of its canister she wasn't facing skyward. The subsequent explosion blew a hole through the barge and tipped the last firework canister as it launched. All the previous Berthas had gone polar, right up into the aurora borealis. That last one went horizontal and headed straight for shore. Just like one of those smart missiles from the Gulf War, nobody knew where it was going to land. What a rush! That mother passed the crowd at the harbor landing at mach one, zoomed through Market Square, shot over Goatlips Saloon, and suddenly zoned in on us up here. Let me tell you, bottom line, in 'the twilight's last gleaming,' people scattered everywhere.

In retrospect, thank God that father did not heed mother's warning about those fourth helping of beans, because by the time of the fireworks he was sitting alone in the gazebo, reveling in his repast, when that last Big Bertha honed in. Later he would remark that he hadn't dug in that deep since the beach at Normandy. One minute we're celebrating the Fourth in style, the next I'm trying to take it all in. I watched Jake the Lizard's jaw drop and his eyes bug out of his head. I could see the barge sinking rapidly into the harbor, the spotlight from the *Jolly Mr. Johnson* caught the Chief and Bullethead swimming frantically over to the boat. And our new gazebo? I watched in slow motion as the Big Bertha slammed into the Swedish team's balloon. Plummeting, it crash landed with the force of a cement truck right on the gazebo. Balloon and building burst into a thousand flaming pieces. I lay witness to the spectacle as the final refrain of Tchaikovsky's polka masterpiece—*The 1812 Overture*—fizzled out slowly like a torch buggering a snowbank. That big Swede who owned the balloon was madder than a wildcat being jerked off by a fistful of cockle burrs. By that time he was quite smashed on moe.Ale—to the victors go the spoils. He had handled the moe.ron's hurling in the gondola, but this was too much. A stream of guttural, polysyllabic, Swedish explicatives poured forth from the inner well of his Nordic soul. I couldn't understand a word he was saying but I understood every word. He was ready to punch someone and was running right toward me. His face was covered in soot. A lime green splinter the size of a golf pencil was impaled in his cheek. There are times in my life in which I have contemplated the philosophy of chance versus divine providence. Have you ever been convinced that a higher order in the universe is in place? At that precise moment I came to believe that there was. Amidst the anarchy a herd of skunks suddenly materialized. They had been burrowed in under the gazebo, and were making a mad dash to safety after the explosion. I was frozen. One move and I get sprayed, but if I don't move the big Swede takes me down hard. Later, Fonebone would tell me he believed that the secret lair of the skunks was right under our gazebo all along. "It makes perfect sense," he would say, "why their trail always circled 'round this neighborhood."

Incredibly, in the wake of the destruction and pandemonium, all but one skunk got away. Unfortunately, it was the one that the big Swede stepped on in his blind rage. I can honestly tell you, it didn't make that skunk too happy, either. The little bugger aimed and fired, drilling Captain Pfinktör with a direct hit to the face, blinding him and allowing me to get away. He's threatening to sue us, but nothing's come of it so far, just a lot of posturing. I think it's because he bonded so well with Pedro and company over at Fonebone's de-tox center. Three days on a Bloody Mary bender will do that to you.

All I can say is those T-shirts you sent from the old "No Hard Feelings" tour came in mighty handy that night. Though we thought it prudent to sell them at cost after the gazebo debacle. All things considered, they went briskly. We ended up with all the free publicity that we could handle, too. The fireworks had been simulcast over the local community cable channel. Amazingly, the cable news Mafia quickly picked it up and arrived pronto. The various network crews, MSNBC, CNN, FOX, ended up staying for a few days—in high style. People in Hong Kong, Australia or Athens—Greece and Georgia—were able to watch a gazebo blow up in the Lost Kingdom of Moose Harbor on the Fourth of July every ten minutes for twenty-four hours. Somehow they managed to turn a disaster into entertainment. I asked them how they do it. Father asked them why they do it. The CNN guy said it was simply all about the ratings. The woman from FOX said it all about the money. "A good looking whore always gets top dollar!" she hooted sometime after her fifth martini. I know that all those news people sure liked the moe.Ale, cause it went down faster than that barge did on the Fourth.

Well, I gotta go. I see the claims adjuster walking up the front yard and the crew from Fonebone's Pest Control has arrived, too. Not to worry. Pedro and the boys are back on the job, smelling like roses with a hint of Tabasco. We'll get this thing settled and have that gazebo rebuilt by Labor Day. Meanwhile, we'll have those skunks rounded up in no time—right after we get the raccoons out of the boathouse!

Till then, "no hard feelings!"

Your man on the front,

brother John

Act VI

Requiem for the Bird Man

The moe.Republic Hotel
in the heart of the Lost Kingdom

Dear Rob,

A big hello from the rugged outback along the eastern frontier. It's been a while since I heard from you. Thought I'd drop a line and bring you up to speed. Business has been steady, which is a good thing. We had a group of Franciscan monks on retreat a week ago. They were a spirited bunch, nearly drank a full vat of the moe.Ale while they were here. During the day they played a lot of Frisbee golf. I have to say that they were pretty good at it, too. You wouldn't have thought it possible wearing those big, heavy, woolen robes, that a person could be so nimble and dexterous. But they were as graceful as antelopes frolicking on the lonesome prairie. It was sad to see them go.

I guess because their arrival followed the sudden passing of Porter Gibson Digit, which has left a big void around here. The Bird Man of legend is no more. I find that very hard to write. I'm sure you've picked up his obituary somewhere by now. It's been the talk of the town. Not that a 106 year old man's death can be viewed as sudden, as it were. Though he was in here the day before he died, perched in his usual spot, drinking scotch, watching the Sox game, and ragging on the Huxley sisters. It's still hard to believe, that's all. The man who invented *the* finger—the grand pooh-bah of anarchist symbolism, the last vestige of free-spirited individualism, the gesture of choice on every expressway, parkway, intersection, parking lot and interstate of the American and international highway system—expired in quiet slumber on Monday last. Everyone's been deeply affected by it. More than losing a customer, we've all lost a friend.

But it's bigger than that, too. He was, to say the least, a local legend, a national character, and by all standards an international enigma. That is true. Yet his mark in history will endure throughout the ages. More than the twenty-one books he authored, what Porter Gibson Digit left us transcends time. His passing not only marks the end of an era—the Twentieth century and the post-industrial madness consuming the planet—but it also marks the end of an epoch. No man in the past century had more impact on the counter-culture than he. In terms of self-expression, nobody came close. Porter had huge paw-like hands with a middle finger that extended a good seven inches, plus. When he raised his finger, in its solitary splendor, it stood like a lone obelisk over a vast field. You knew that you had been told to go fuck yourself for real!

In his own right, Mr. Digit was a ship without a port for many years, until he finally found his way back home to the Lost Kingdom. The moe.Republic Hotel was his last watering hole, literally and figuratively, these past few years. Father and I and hosts of other patrons would sit with him for hours listening to his tales. His life was an open book filled with adventure—baseball, protests, gangsters, sex, spies, and war. Though he and father were particularly fond of sharing the World War II stories, day after day the subjects varied. In retrospect, we got to know him as well as anyone could have at this stage of his life. Remarkably, close to a thousand or so people showed up for his funeral. All the cable news networks were there, too. The event was a solemn affair.

We held a memorial for him in the lounge after the service. It was great. Father had a plaque made for his favorite barstool, where he sat, pontificated, flirted, and watched the ball games. The newly christened "Porter Gibson Digit Memorial Drinking Port" was cordoned off for the event. People from all over came. The hotel was filled and so were a lot of eyes and beer mugs. The infinite fount was flowing that day along with the tall tales. Every story was a veritable celebration of his life.

Mine began one lazy afternoon in the bar. A kick-ass rendition of "Head" blared on the sound system. Not sure really when or where you and the boys recorded it, but I think it's from that gig at Lyndon State some years back. I remember going to see that show. That was the time that Fred the Bullethead, the Chief, and I went on that road trip to Montreal to buy some Cuban stogies for father's birthday. We were lost in the old port of the city and wandered into a winsome looking establishment called René's Lost Lumberjack Palace. It took a day to find our way out. I'll say no more about that except you *truly* cannot appreciate being a man until you've witnessed the 'Ooo-La-La" Revue. I guess that's why that particular version of "Head" has always struck me right. The day I met Porter I had it cranking on the sound system pretty good. I usually don't have the volume that loud, but the crowd was thin. That's when this old dude strolled in. He'd been around lately, but I'd only seen him in the evenings and never really had a chance to talk to him. He seemed to always show up to watch the ball games on TV. Either that or to hit on the babes. You know what they say, 'eighteen to eighty—blind, crippled or crazy.' This guy went after them all. I don't know what it is about some older dudes, if they think that they're cute or they simply don't give a fuck what anyone thinks anymore. But he always got away with it. If he got slapped he'd just laugh. I had to admit, I liked his spunk. He was an interesting read. For an old dude, he didn't have that vacant look—the kind I get whenever I ask one of the Huxley sisters a question—nor did he carry that self-entitlement cross-to-bear attitude, either. Better yet, he was a single malt man. Anything with a *Glen* in front of it, be it Garioch, Scotia, Livet or Fiddich, worked for him.

I figured this afternoon he was coming by to watch the Sox play the Dodgers. That year's first round of interleague play. But Jackson Grant strolled in behind him, our buddy from the *Downeast Way Times*. He was calling for him to wait up. I wondered what was going on, if this was a long, lost relation of his. Or maybe this had something to do with the G-men he said were on to him. After Jackson did the exposé on Kevin and Sparky's disappearance, he swore his phone lines were tapped in his office and home. I told him it was more than likely. After all, the Pulitzer nomination for wacko reporting tended to draw the attention of *the man*. He told me I was a bullshitter, if you can believe that. Said he had heard the same clicking sound on his phone as a kid, when the town still had the early single operator system. "The old party lines had enough clicking going on that it sounded like a tap dance recital most of the time," he had whispered to me. "The best way to fuck over your busybody neighbor was spread a secret about her on the phone. Tell 'em that her old man's got one ball shooting blanks and it would be all over town within an hour."

Could that old guy be in some way connected to all of that? I dismissed it. He just didn't fit that G-man *m.o.* I wondered what Jackson was doing with my new happy hour hero when the old buck hit the bar. "I'd ask for a Scotch," he shouted, "if I could hear myself speak."

"What?" I shouted back, taking the hint and turning the volume down. "Scotch you say?" I smiled and he grinned back. I reached up to the top shelf and felt a searing twinge shoot through my spine. "Damn my back!" I grimaced.

"What's the matter, sonny?" the old man asked.

"Nothing," I replied. "Just an experiment in the *Kama Sutra* gone awry. I should have stretched." That got a laugh from him.

"Wait till you get to page sixty-nine!" he said with a look of mischief. "You may want to take a sauna first to get loose." I started to laugh myself but grimaced again as the pain flared.

"I hate getting old," I blurted out.

"Son, when you start counting the years going by in decades, then you can count yourself old," he said in a heavy down east accent, a bit gravelly and slightly worn. "And need I tell you, *old* is a relative concept."

My guess was he had to be in his early eighties—I mean you could tell he was up there in the count, though still tack sharp. "How many decades do I have to count before *I* qualify?" I quipped.

"When you hit double figures," he said, straight-faced.

"Come on!" I laughed. "You're a hundred? Out and about on your own for happy hour?"

"I can tell you have your doubts." He eased in closer to me. "You can see I'm not *on* my own. I'm babysitting Jackson Grant here," he cocked his head at him. "And God knows I'm old enough to drink!"

Jackson looked at me and thumbed the old buck. "He's 101, actually. You know my mother wouldn't trust me with just *anyone!*"

"And still taking care of business, son!" He arched his brow quickly. "Never threw my back out, either. Not while entertaining the ladies, anyway."

I was still staring in disbelief when he added, "You going to pour me a few fingers now or are you waiting for my wake?"

I poured a shot. Filled the glass, actually. "This one's on me!" I said, still unsure if I was being hosed.

"Age does have its entitlement," he raised his glass and downed the shot. It was then that I noticed the size of his hands. The glass disappeared into it and reappeared like a magician's sleight of hand when he set it down. "Put a little ice in the next," he said pushing the glass to me. "I'll be sipping it slow."

"I'll have the same, amigo," Jackson said to me. "Allow me to introduce my sitter, Porter Gibson Digit."

I shook his hand, which completely engulfed mine. "I've seen you in here of late watching the ball games. I've been meaning to say hi, but you always come when it's busy." I pondered the name, though, for a moment. "I've heard mention of you before," I said. "Don't I know you?"

The old man smiled and laughed a little. "Don't think we've ever met. I just got back in town last month. Thought I'd come home to retire, get my house in order before I die."

"Don't listen to him," Jackson interrupted. "He's back in town because of me. You're face-to-face with the Bird Man, and I'm writing his memoirs."

"*The* Bird Man?" I replied knowingly.

"Yes. *The* Bird Man," Jackson repeated proudly.

"But I thought you were…" I caught myself on the verge of a major *faux pas*, "… out of town."

"You thought I'd kissed the reaper." His eyes narrowed menacingly.

"I didn't mean anything by it," I sputtered defensively. 'The slings and arrows of outrageous fortune' be damned! I just insulted the Bird Man.

"Thought I was down for the count?" he growled. "Walked the plank? Rolled a pair of snake eyes?" He stared threateningly. "Nah!" he laughed. "Had you going there didn't I?"

"Yeah," I said relieved, "you had me by the balls!"

"I've slipped the Angel of Death more than once. She's gotten close on a few occasions. The last time I flicked her the bird," he said, amused at himself. "She started laughing so hard I got up and walked away. She's sexy as hell, too—got a rack to die for. Some day I'm going to let her take me away and then I'll introduce her to Mr. Digit." He growled softly and took a long sip of the Fiddich.

"Can I put that in the book?" Jackson mused.

"You'd God-damned better!" he belched.

"I was leaning towards another angle," Jackson added. "How about our great national treasure—walking, living, breathing…"

"Calm down there Sonny Jack!" Porter jumped in. "No bubbling up like that or we're not going get past the introduction, ever," he said firmly.

"I'm going to put your face on Mount Rushmore Uncle Porter," Jackson insisted. Porter looked him down and stared. It was all he *had* to do.

"Just tell the story," Porter said intently. "And the story will speak for itself."

"This is your uncle?" I asked. "Really?"

"Nah," Jackson replied, the wind knocked out of his sails.

"Get over it, kid," Porter said. "His grandfather Jeffrey was my best friend. He was a good man. I'm doing this because of him, in his memory. To Jeffah!" he said affectionately, raising his glass. Porter sipped his scotch and wheezed. "This malt has kick, boy," he looked at me. "Good choice."

"He was my father's godfather," Jackson said. "I've been at him for years to do this book project."

"Ah, ignore him John," he said to me waving his hand. "We use to come to this place together, Jeffrey and I, when old Jonah Huxley lived here. His son Sterling lived next door in the other manor house. He had three daughters,

Enid, Edith, and Emma." He took a good look around, then leaned in, spoke in a low voice. "That was when we were a couple of swinging dicks looking for action. Every hung buck in the Lost Kingdom and beyond was after those sisters." He winked and sat back in the stool. "I haven't been in this place or the other one in over sixty years. Remember them well enough, though. Each house smelled like a mausoleum."

"You should go over to their spread next door, " I added, "if you really want to want to see a mausoleum."

"They're still kicking it?" He seemed stunned, ruminated on it for a second or two. "You did a good job remodeling this place," he said, deflecting his own question. "A very fine job."

The *Huxleys*!? I flushed the thought. Kind of like imaging mother and father at it. Couldn't really see the dowager princesses involved with anyone, or thing, for that matter. This was an interesting turn of events, though. Here was slanderous gossip within my grasp. I remembered that the sisters had mentioned him the one time I was at their place. Probably all I had to do was press the issue. Did I really want to know *le affaire* Huxley? Nah! Not really. It may have the effect of humanizing them. "Thanks," I replied politely. "It's a family venture." Then as an after thought I added, "By the way, Edith and Emma live next door. Enid's been gone a long time from what I know. Long before we arrived on the scene."

"Edith and Emma, huh? Never thought...," he trailed off momentarily. "You know this place was quite a landmark. When I heard it was restored, been turned into a hotel, I thought I'd come and take a look. Back in the twenties and early thirties this was a happening spot. Rumrunners used to land here, came down from Nova Scotia and New Brunswick. Had a nickname, the Whale's Jaw, I think. Not sure if it was a codename for old man Jonah or for the shape of the cove. There was a wharf right on the point. They'd dock their trawlers and unload. The sisters were young then," he said, tapping his forefinger against his head. "Thought they were helping the fisherman and lobstermen. The old man and the son knew—thick in it. The girls didn't have a clue, too naïve." Oh how time does remain constant, I thought, though naïve was not a word I would choose to describe Edith and Emma.

"I've heard rumors of rumrunners," I responded, "adds to the character of the place."

"You've done a good job and it's a comfy place to watch a ball game, too. I like that."

"I like to think this is a good place to watch a game and relax."

"Anywhere is a good place to watch a game, son," he added.

"Porter was a hell of a ball player in his day," Jackson enlightened me. "Bet you didn't know that?"

"High School? College?" Trying to imagine the local baseball scene when Taft was president. All I saw was a bunch of kids in overalls throwing rocks, playing stickball.

"He played for Dartmouth," Jackson said proudly, "then the Brooklyn Dodgers!"

"What!" I stammered incredulously. "Hold it! *The* Dodgers?"

"He faced Babe Ruth in the World Series," Jackson added, smiling broadly. "Not too many people from Downeast Way have done that." Jackson had a way about him that I always admired. Behind the boyish enthusiasm was a strong intellect. He wrote a pretty good story, too.

"The Dodgers," I said again.

"I thought I was the one hard of hearing, boy?" Porter remarked.

"How could the Bird Man have ever played baseball?" I wondered out loud.

"First off, can you really call yourself an American if you've never played a game of baseball? If you've never gone out on a steamy July afternoon and thrown the pill around with your old man? But if I were to tell you that the story was connected, me playing baseball and coming up with the finger, that it was part of a string of events that led me to that fateful day in Washington Square when the bird took off, would you believe me?"

"Maybe," I said, feigning a disinterested reservation. "If it doesn't get too deep and I have to slip into my waders, 'I'll be your huckleberry' and hear what you have to say." I topped off their glasses and poured one for myself.

The old man smiled. "Huckleberry my ass!" He shut his eyes for a moment to fire up the electrolytes, I thought. That or he was in the midst of a narcoleptic episode. In which case I started to count to ten. If he didn't wake by then I'd shake him. "I was a rookie," he said abruptly at the eight count, slightly startling me and Jackson. "A third-string bullpen catcher, really. The Brooklyn ball club picked me up after I graduated from Dartmouth that spring. Chief Meyers was their starter, and they had Otto Miller on the bench. I was their insurance, the bullpen jockey. I never thought I'd play with the likes of Meyers. He was a Dartmouth legend, which was why he took to me, I guess, and became a mentor of sorts. The man was a full-blooded Cahuilla Indian and despised the nickname Chief, but he couldn't shake it. He made his name with the New York Giants—hit well over .300 on three straight pennant winners, 1911, '12 and '13. But old John McGraw ground him out and let him go at the end of 1915. Brooklyn picked him up in January of 1916, which was good for me *and* the club. That year, 1916, we went to the World Series, and it had a lot to do with Meyers's leadership. It was a dream come true for me. Here I am, a rube kid from Downeast Way, fresh out of college, and I land smack in the middle of one of the largest metropolitan centers on the planet playing ball for the Robins, with one of the legends of Dartmouth baseball."

"The Robins?" I wasn't sure if I'd heard him right.

"Yes. The *Brooklyn* Robins. They weren't really called the Dodgers, yet. Ballclubs then didn't really have 'official' names like today. The Robins were nicknamed after their coach, Wilbert Robinson. Before that they were called the Superbas or the Bridegrooms. The Yankees were called the Highlanders. The Red Sox were called the Pilgrims. The Dodgers came later, after 'trolley Dodger.' That's what people in New York called the people in Brooklyn. With as much respect, I might add, as a Brit had when he called an Irishman a Mick or Potato-head. What were we talking about Jackson?"

"The 1916 World Series," he answered, as if on cue.

"Oh yeah! You getting all of this boy?" I hadn't noticed, but Jackson had been quietly taking notes. "I may run out of fuel any minute and keel over. I'm living on borrowed time—a gypsy woman told me that on the outskirts of this very town in 1930 something—just before she got 'Digit-*tized*,' if you know what I mean!" He gently passed the back of his huge paws under his nostril, inhaling deeply. A glow of reflection passed over him with a broad smile.

"Now!" He came back to us in a flurry. "The Fall Classic of 1916 was in our favor. At least that's what the reporters wrote. We won the pennant the last week of the season, and were on a roll. A guy named Zack Wheat made sure of that. One of the finest ballplayers of his generation, he could drill the ball to all fields. The man was a magician, his bat a wand. We also had the arms, a 25 game winner named Jeff Pfeffer, and two other outstanding pitchers, Rube Marquard and Jack Coombs, that the ball club had picked up from the Giants and the A's, respectively. Each were World Series veterans, and Marquard was one of the best southpaws of his generation. He'd won 19 games in a row once. Everyone gives a lot of attention to DiMaggio's streak, but Marquard's record will never be touched—not even by those steroid-jacked freaks on the field today."

"Uncle Porter?" Jackson chimed in. "What about the Series?"

"I'm getting to it boy!" he bellowed in his gravelly centenarian voice. He sipped the scotch and wheezed, again. "I'm simply setting the table."

"Just making sure we're sitting down to the same meal. That's all."

"I'd be happy to watch the game and get liquored up. No qualms at all. I'd rather do that anyway." He looked up at the tube and watched the game, ignoring us both for about half a minute.

"I get the point," Jackson said soothingly. "I'll write, you talk."

"Now you're getting the hang of it," he said, appeased, but kept *us* hanging for another half minute or so, quietly watching the game.

"So," he piped up suddenly, and turned his eyes on us, "we go to Boston to play the first two games of the Series. We're the hands down favorites. But the Sox were not that bad a club. They were the defending World Series Champs, and they didn't take too kindly to being labeled hacks or has-beens. Their team was good—pretty much the nucleus of the team that Harry Frazee would fire sale to the Yankees a few seasons later. Ironically, we did not play the games in the Fens. We played at Braves Field instead of the Park to handle the big crowds and for the owners to get a bigger gate. Robinson's strategy was to send his lefties, Marquard and another standout on the staff, Sherry Smith, to the mound for games one and two. In the first game Rube pitched okay through the first six innings, but gave up a bunch of runs late and we lost that game. 6-5." He paused momentarily as though collecting his thoughts.

"Robinson was pissed," he continued, "and so was Marquard. But neither of them," his voice rose in frustration, "was as pissed as Pfeffer who rightfully thought he had earned the start and should have gotten it. Instead, he went in to finish the game in the eighth. I warmed him up and he was cursing and lashing out like a madman." He raised his left hand, palm out, like he was about to receive the ball. "Almost got the win, but we ran out of outs before they did."

He paused again, and turned to Jackson. "You getting this? Cause I don't think I have it in me to ever tell this story again." Jackson simply nodded, scribbling away on a large pad, head down, concentrating. "It's beginning to bore me," Porter yawned. Jackson slowly placed his pen down and looked up. "Just making sure you were listening, Sonny Jack!"

"I am," Jackson replied. " I write, you talk. Remember?"

"Okay then. For me, game two's the one that stands out. That's when we faced a young lefty named Babe Ruth. A game later dubbed the 'double masterpiece.' Sherry Smith went inning for inning with Ruth. Through thirteen each pitcher had scattered six hits and one run. Ruth had given up an inside-the-park home run to Hy Myers in the first. In the third inning Ruth drove in the game-tying run. And then both pitchers locked in and went into a zone. They achieved a higher state of consciousness that I've only experienced with the peyote buttons old Pepe Hernandez brought back each spring from the Mexican League." He raised his glass. "To Pepe!" We toasted him in honor. "I liked Pepe. He was a lot of fun. Then one spring he didn't returned. The ball club never knew why or what happened to him. I heard he ended up running with Pancho Villa, but that's another story."

"Uncle Porter?" Jackson spoke as though he were asking permission for something.

"Yeah?" he answered with a look of defiance. Jackson sighed deeply, deflated again. "I thought so," was all Porter said.

"In the thirteenth inning I got my shot. The Chief twisted his ankle on a play at the plate in the bottom of that inning for the third out. Miller was nursing a hangover so bad that by the twelfth inning he was spewing bile. Robinson was pissed at him, and probably would have canned him right then and there if he could have proven it was booze. Miller swore he had a hunk of bad cod down on the pier. It didn't matter. I was the last hitter off the bench and the only receiver he had, so I was in. Meyer looked at me and said, 'Do Dartmouth proud.' I looked at his bloodied pulp of an ankle, now swollen the size of a grapefruit. My mouth went dry and my asshole clamped shut. 'Hail to the Chief' was all I could muster, and that was like chewing on sandpaper.

"I came up with two outs and nobody on in the fourteenth. Ruth was still throwing hard—his fastball wobbled and his screwball was dubbed unhittable. He threw one of each in succession at me. I didn't get the bat off my shoulder. How could I? I was too nervous and a bit overwhelmed. I kept telling myself that this was Ruth's first World Series game, too. But it didn't matter. He had thirteen-plus innings under his belt. There were over forty-thousand people watching me. That was about nine or ten times the population of Downeast Way staring at me all at once. Twenty minutes before that I had been a spectator. Watching from my stall in the bullpen. But suddenly I was down 0-2 in the count in the biggest at bat of my life. Ruth's next pitch was a fastball down and away. I almost chased it but I took it for a ball. I figured the next one would be a chaser, too. So I moved in on the plate. It was a buzz saw, high and tight. I felt the wind rush by under my Adam's apple and landed flat on my ass. I heard more than a few laughs and sneers in the stands. Their catcher—Pinch Thomas—gave me a crock of shit about being a rookie and who the hell did I think I was owning his plate. Thomas was acting tough. I guess he could because he'd caught two World Series Champions. He was their primary catcher and, defensively, was regarded as one of the best in the league. But there and then I really didn't know or even care about that. I was pissed about the brush back. Christ! The guy had humbled me on two pitches and now he dared mock me? Did he think I would let him get away with mixing a fractured skull into the pitch count? That's when I commented to Pinch about the prosthetics of a thirty-four inch slab of ash being removed from his rectal cavity along with the post-operative recovery time if he tried that shit again. The ump told both of us to shut up and play ball or he'd run us. I settled down. That was the spark I needed to get rid of the jitters and the cotton mouth. The next pitch was a fastball and I fouled it back. He threw the next pitch in the same spot and I fouled *that* away. The fastballs kept coming and I kept hacking away at 'em. I was more relaxed and comfortable. I had forgotten about the crowd, too. It was just me and Ruth and the ball. I realized I hadn't seen the screwball in a while so I knew that it was coming. When he threw it I just reached my bat out like I was trying to catch it with the wood. I did, too, and dropped a duck fart over the third baseman's head for a hit. Pinch Thomas was cursing and yelping at me right down the line backing up a would-be throw that never came. Smith then came up and went down on three pitches. I didn't care. It was beautiful. I got a hit in my only at bat in the Series." Porter took a sip of scotch and smiled at the memory. I did, too. Smile, that is. It was, after all, pretty cool if you think about it. To actually *be* in the presence of such history.

"In the bottom of the fourteenth," Porter moved on, "Carrigan, the Sox manager, played a little small ball on us. After a lead-off walk to Dick Hoblitzell, and a sac-bunt, he brought in his last left-handed bat, Del Gainor, to pinch hit. The sonna' bitch was only a .250 hitter, but he delivered, and they beat us 2-1. We pulled out game three at home, 4-3, but that was our last victory for the season. Boston took game four, 6-2, and game five, 4-1. The Red Sox had won back-to-back World Series. They simply had too much pitching—Ernie Shore, Ruth, Dutch Leonard, Carl Mays— and were the better team. Our only bright spot was the hitting of Casey Stengel, who batted a Series tops of .364 that year. Robinson didn't like Stengel though, too animated for him, and he traded him off to the Giants.

"As for my immediate future my choices were limited. Go back to Downeast Way or continue my education. I decided to go to graduate school and headed over to Columbia. That's when I was introduced to another world. My horizons broadened. My eyes opened. As a catcher I had learned to judge the playing field on every pitch, with each batter. It was level. Success or failure was determined by talent based upon fixed rules. At Columbia I found it wasn't so. I was appalled by the Machiavellian machinations of our 'enlightened' leadership—so much so I entered the world of dissent. It was a life altering experience for me, in many ways. And I finally discovered a use for these hands other then catching and throwing a ball." He studied the palms of his hands, reading them. His fingers were gnarled and bony, but even so I could see the lengthy, spidery phalanges, and the mighty obelisk on center. "I gotta take a leak," he squirmed out of his seat. "My bladder's 'bout the size of a walnut these days."

"Don't forget to zip up," Jackson said.

"What? You worried? Had a bad experience with a babysitter once?" He gingerly walked off down the hall.

"That was an incredible story," I said to Jackson.

"Yeah, that was," Jackson said, writing a few more notations on his pad. "I don't think I've ever heard it in such detail. You're lucky, amigo. He's been dictating for weeks. That's the most complete telling of that story, yet."

"It's the scotch. It works the mind and tongue in funny ways."

"Could be."

"I've seen it bag three-hundred pound men or melt one-hundred ten pound ice queens—splay their legs open like porn stars on holiday."

"It doesn't seem to have an effect on Porter no matter how much he drinks," Jackson murmured, still writing. "There are times I wonder if he's human?"

"That's your *God*-grandfather you're talking about, man!"

"Whoa baby! I'm not putting him down. He's family. I'm just saying it's scary how the guy barely ages. It's like his metabolism is going half the speed as a normal man's. You know I never met him until the summer of 1976. He had been in self-imposed exile or on the lam, depending on which way you read the story, since he and Papa Jeff got in that trouble smuggling. Everyone in Downeast Way *knew* who Porter Gibson Digit was—an old time counter-culture radical of sorts—a free spirit more than anything, and a successful author."

"Yes!" I interrupted in an epiphany. "I had to read two of his books in college. I remember them both, *Escape From Industrial Time* and *The Theory of the Deferential Continuum.* The first was a thriller, the other dryer than a bag of bones."

"That about covers them," said Jackson. "Porter's experienced more than you or I can in ten lifetimes. He dabbled in Socialism with Eugene Debs and the Anarchist movement with Emma Goldman. He did that while in graduate school. But he hated fascists and communists. The man fought in Spain and went to fight in Bucharest years later. In between he hooked up with the OSS and served in Europe. He did what he could to undermine the spread of both during the war," he said proudly.

"It seems almost incredible, doesn't it?" I asked rhetorically. "That a person could experience so much in one lifetime? I can't imagine it in these crazy times. That it could ever happen again. I think it's a good idea to write this book. I'm glad his story's being told and that you're doing it. I can't think of anyone more qualified."

"I've always wanted to do it. Ever since I first met him," said Jackson. "That's a story in and of itself. I caught up with him at the end of my first year of college. I was on an internship with the *Times* as a cub reporter. Miraculously, I convinced the old editor, Charlie Logan, to let me do a series about the bicentennial on the road. Later I found out that Logan was happy to let me go—didn't want the long hair and hot air filling up the news bureau all summer long. Didn't care really, I went on a tour of America writing weekly features from such exotic places as Atlantic City, Cleveland, Dayton, the Badlands, Mt. Rushmore, Sacramento, the Grand Canyon—you get the picture?

"Crazy as it sounds," he said like he was thinking out loud, "it was by complete chance that I bumped into Porter in Ludlow, Colorado. Even then he looked pretty much the same as today. I bet you thought the guy was in his late-seventies or early eighties didn't you?"

Nodding, I had to admit that I had.

"When I ran into him Porter was organizing a protest to mark the sixty-second anniversary of the Ludlow Massacre. I mean *the sixty-second* anniversary! Who the hell was going to show up? But he was there and thought he'd tell the world. He was handing out white t-shirts emblazoned with the famous seven-inch digit fully extended. 'This is for the man!' he stated emphatically in that same gravelly, voice, shoving a T-shirt in my hands. 'Slip into this and stand there. When the man comes don't move.' In my naiveté and eagerness to please I put the shirt on and stood there waiting for an ambush. Then, in a moment of youth, blurted out, 'You know my dad said you're getting to be too old to be running around the country giving people the finger.' I thought he was going to explode, but instead he laughed out loud and said, 'You *are* Jeffah's grandson!' That afternoon I got jumped by a bunch of redneck cowboys for giving them the finger. Of course I was just standing there and they weren't going to pound on an old man. But Porter and I've been in touch ever since. Though I haven't seen him more than a few times in twenty-odd years, he never looks *older*."

"So you think Porter's a ghost?" I asked, off-handedly.

"I often wonder," he responded seriously, "how he got out and Papa Jeff didn't. I've been trying to get him to tell me, but we never quite get there."

"What do you mean? I thought he was your grandfather's best friend?"

"He was—back in those early days. They were inseparable until Porter went off to college and baseball and back to college. My grandfather did what most people did back then and still do—he fished—but he also struck a vein of liquid gold. He ran the rum from Nova Scotia. Had himself a little smuggling empire."

Now this was juicy, slanderous gossip, I thought. My ears perked. "So the stories *are* true?"

"Jesus yes, man! Prohibition was a Godsend for these coastal fishing villages, believe me. My grandfather would dock right out there." He pointed toward the harbor. "Jonah Huxley took his cut and old man Walker's people or old man Kennedy's people would send in their trucks. Such are the sins of our fathers—and how fortunes and presidents are made."

"Hey, I'm not judging you or anyone, Jackson."

"I know. But I still have to remind *myself* from time to time. Papa Jeff would hook up with the Canadian trawlers. They'd sail out of Yarmouth or there abouts under the blind eye of customs, rendezvous with one of Papa Jeff's boats off one of the outer islands, and make their exchange."

"Booze for a bag of gold!" Porter added, shuffling up behind Jackson and me.

"Yes!" Jackson answered, both of us surprised at the old man's spook-like stealth. "Booze for gold, and there was plenty of both."

"Too much, but that's how it is with gold. There is never enough!" Porter said.

"So you think Papa Jeff got greedy? Is that what happened?" Jackson asked anxiously.

"Jeffah?" Porter said befuddled. "No way! He was a free spirit. Running the rum was a good living. Bailed a lot of people out of the depression that they had no part of. The rush of the adventure's what lured him in. Prohibition was winding down, the control freaks and Christian nuts had had their day. The Treasury goons saw billions of dollars in revenue lost annually. Pocketed by men like Jeff. Prohibition provided a niche like no other. It was a federal grant for the entrepreneurial minded. In the urban centers the entrepreneurial spirit had a much more ominous undertone among the distributors. At times it was like packs of wild dogs fighting each other to the death to feast on a kill. In rural towns it was different. There was an implied civility of sorts. I suppose because everyone was your neighbor. Your kids went to the same schools and you went to the same churches each Sunday. Yessah!" The old man nodded his head.

"It was all so long ago that at times it holds nothing more than a dream-like aura for me. But I remember your grandfather, well. Being here, brings back a lot of memories. It's like I half expect him to walk in and sit a spell. And when I look at you Jackson, in some ways he is, 'cause you look just like him." Porter leaned back, overcome by contemplation.

For a second or two *I* half expected old Jeff Grant to come walking into the lounge in a ghostly apparition. God knows stranger things have happened since we'd moved here. I heard the crack of the bat on ball and was drawn to the game. The Sox were beating the Dodgers, 6-2. We all were drawn to the game, which served the moment well. The awkward silence we teetered on was covered by another base hit and run. The early evening crowd was beginning to wander in, the shift in energy ever so subtle all around. I was about to slide off my stool and go help somewhere, and let these two work it out, let Jackson hear his story and Porter give his confession.

But Porter slid his glass at me instead. "Well boys, by the looks of this crowd I'd say that the day's still young. You better top me off while I still have your attention," he said to me. I looked at Jackson knowingly. That story would have to wait for another day.

"I always found that you could judge the quality of an establishment by the cleanliness of its crapper after happy hour," Porter pontificated.

"How do you rate it?" I asked him.

"Either thumbs up or the bird—there is no middle ground in the rating system."

"No! I mean how did you rate *this* place?"

"I think you can judge the quality of the *clientele* of an establishment by the cleanliness of its crapper after happy hour," Jackson weighed in.

"Not fair, really, considering the longer the happy hour the broader the aim," Porter countered.

"I'd like to know why a toilet bowl becomes the size of a Dixie cup after a few beers?" I added, "speaking professionally."

"I guess you would know," Porter said.

"I try to make it a habit not to let people drink till they can't piss straight anymore," which was true. "Early in the game I'd let people get away with too much. I'd let them drink as much as they wanted as long as they weren't driving."

"And you had an epiphany?" Porter asked.

"If seeing someone grab the moosehead off the wall," I pointed over at it, "place it on their head and walk off the balcony is an epiphany, then yes!"

"Ah… so you've pressed the flesh with the hand of litigation?" Porter said knowingly.

"More than once!"

"It's happened to me on more than one occasion, too, all because I discovered *this!*" He quickly flicked his hand up like a gunslinger in a B-Western, and fired me *the* bird. The enormity of the moment was not lost on me. I wasn't just told by anyone to go fuck myself. I had just got the finger from the man who invented it. It was like staring down the horn of a rhino, and I don't mean the one on its snout. The people who were around us gasped. He dropped his hand and smiled. Then bang! bang! I got the double finger, this time prodding me like a pair of elephant tusks. It was a veritable safari of similes. Everyone around seemed to be holding their breath like it was high noon and I was the sheriff. I guess in some ways I was, but Jackson burst out laughing and slapped Porter on the back, and he slowly lowered his paws.

"That's how it was done," Porter explained. "Stunned you didn't it? Imagine what it was like in the beginning? Back in the teens?" I did, and thoughts of an obscenely phallic monster flashing a crowd or entertaining an ebullient minx filtered through my mind.

"In those days you couldn't protest," he said, with conviction. "If you did some idiot cop, Treasury goon or Immigration thug would come along and bust you 'side the head with a billy club. It was the Progressive Era. Some progress! Any form of dissent was crushed with extreme prejudice by the state. It wasn't business. It was personal. They'd label you commie or anarchist, then throw you in jail like they did to Eugene Debs, or deport you, like they did to poor old Emma Goldman. They sent her back to the Bolsheviks. I'd of felt sorry for the bitch but she tried to take credit for inventing the finger. She told John Reed and Thorstein Veblen that she had come up with a new symbolic gesture to stand up against the man.

"That was 1918. What she forgot to tell Reed and Veblen was that she had seen me reel it off against some potato-headed cop in the spring of 1917.

We were in the City near Washington Square when my plan to flick the bird went down. Emma was there with me and Alexander Berkman, and about a hundred others protesting the war, and we were ready for them. She can take credit for that. She was there. And she and Berkman can take credit for their sloth-like strides up an alleyway in a futile effort to get away. It was pathetic! They both got thrown into prison for demonstrating against God knows what the charge was. That I'll give her credit for, but not the finger," he said quite satisfied.

"Emma was a firecracker. She used to bring books with her to protests so she'd have something to read in jail. It was just a few weeks after the 1916 Series when I met her, couldn't have been more than a month. My folks wanted me to come back up to Downeast Way for the winter. I had *other* things on my mind. Back then, when a ballplayer finished the season he had to find some other gainful employment to see him through the winter. My father and uncle had the bookshop and antique store here in town—the one that Charlie Bagwell now runs. He married my niece. I didn't want to return—go north for the winter. Too fucking cold. I was afraid that I'd never get out if I went back. It's not that I was against the family business. I was in New York City and I didn't want to leave. That's why I turned to graduate school, decided on a Ph.D. in history from Columbia. I figured I'd like to teach. Contrary to popular belief I always found it enjoyable in the academe. I was on scholarship, too, an assistant with the baseball team until 'spring training.'

"Our professor, a genial, gentle, intellectual soul, by the name of Clark—I can't remember if that was his first or last name—wanted us to hear a lecture series over at a place called Sanford Hall. Thorstein Veblen was a speaker. So was Emma. Eugene Debs was supposed to speak but had been jailed for subversion. He sent a speech that someone read. The lectures weren't sanctioned by the school and the professor was flirting with disaster if caught. For me, if anyone in the Brooklyn organization knew I was there my ass would have been out of baseball for good. These lectures were not just 'enlightening,' as Professor Clark had remarked, innocently. Some of them were out and out subversive by any day's standards. Veblen was more of a rationalist, anthropological in his analysis. One night he spoke on the theory of the leisure class. Another time he warned of the rise of the engineers, and their taking over every aspect of our lives. With every advance in technology would come greater dependence, he predicted, and thus control over our lives. How eerily prescient he was. Debs, his reader that is, spoke out against the war, at least our involvement in it. He was running for President again, this time from jail, and was a few weeks shy of being blown out of the water by the electorate again. For what he advocated and represented, he must have scared a lot of people. Wilson hated him—being a Princeton man—didn't think Debs was up to the task for one thing, but he had all that socialist rhetoric bullshit going, too. Wilson thought that was dangerous and had him locked up after a fiery speech in Canton, Ohio... Wilson. Some idealist!" he scoffed, and took a sip on his Scotch and looked around. There were more people up at the bar now. A few were watching the game. Most were tuning into Porter. He'd got their attention when he gave me the finger, or more aptly, when he demonstrated the power of the finger. There may have been a realization by some of who he was, or it could have been the fascination with the story he was telling. In either case, like a Shakespearean actor on center stage, we hung on his every word.

"After Debs we went to hear Emma. She was a fire and brimstone anarchist all the way. You wouldn't have guessed it if you knew her, because she was a dancer, too. The woman loved to dance. Crazy about it. When those dour-faced anarchists once told her that dance was bourgeois and frivolous she fired back, 'If I can't dance, I don't want to be a part of your revolution.' That shut them up good. When I think about it, it may have been the most profound statement she ever made. Think what could be accomplished if we all learned to dance through the transitions in our lives?" He paused in reflection. "That's the way she was. It captivated me. There was something about her that I couldn't quite forget—couldn't quite understand the feelings I had for her. After a few lectures I went up to her and introduced myself. It was gutsy. She invited me to a dive over in the Village, then up to her apartment. Started drinking wine and talking about the rise of the proletariat and the injustice of the capitalist system of government. Next thing I know she's got me pinned to the floor and riding me like a nor'easter. Crazy, I know. She was twice as old as me and wild out of her mind, just as intense as if she were fighting to free the working classes from their oppressors. Being a rube from Maine, I thought I had died and gone to heaven. Women can do that to you. The smart ones, the aggressive, 'liberated' kind or the conservative control freaks—they know how to manipulate. Before I knew it I was standing on the stage at those lectures. During the day, after classes, I'd go stand outside factories handing out flyers, or go down to the docks and recruit there.

"It was heady stuff for a catcher. I didn't realize it but I had been recruited, too. Before I knew it *I* was pissed off at the man. It was the scene—rallies, demonstrations, organizing—it bred a lot of energy and channeled a lot of anger. People all over were pissed off. There were a few of us helping to organize. I met a lot of people from all over the world. More and more guys like me—young, simple-minded 'intellectuals'—went on stage with her, backing her up each lecture. It took me a while, but I finally figured out why the methods of recruitment were so highly effective among the male 'workers.' I had to laugh. It wasn't like we actually had a *relationship*. Her main squeeze was Berkman, anyway, one of the head honchos of the anarchist crowd. And as far as I was concerned it was more the action than anything else that got me hot and bothered. It all withered, *le affaire* Goldman, with the end of the semester. That, and a good dose or two of socialist-anarchist poon-tang my own age, did wonders for me. Burned out and exhausted, I headed back to Maine for the holidays. It was good to go home." He paused a moment to take another sip. There had to be baker's dozen or more gathered now. I couldn't quite tell where there were two deep. Other than a murmured order for a drink, or the game on the TV, the only sound was the gravelly, down east-accented voice of the Bird Man.

"I went back to New York rested and willing to go. I took up classes again, and began to work with the baseball team. But the old crowd was still around and I couldn't help myself. I missed the energy of the movement, whatever or however it was defined, and I have to say that some of those babes were pretty wild. My oats were being sown all over the city. That's how I found myself in Washington Square. She was there with me, Emma, still pushing me on, challenging me. I still think how fate had cast me there at that moment in time. That if I hadn't played baseball I would not have gone to Dartmouth. I wouldn't have met my roommate, W.O. Tanner, who was also from Maine and played ball there. His father, also a baseball man, had a connection with the Dodgers. He knew Wilbert Robinson. Because of that I would not have been signed by the Robins out of college, would not have gone to Columbia or picked a course taught by some free-thinker who, to this day, I believe had no fucking idea what he was sending us into. Consequently, I would not have cruised the anarchist scene, or banged their leader and a half dozen or more of her vixen disciples. I would not have found myself in the City, near Washington Square, when it all went down.

"Above all I would not have conceived this," he popped the finger at the crowd with menace and authority. There were "oohs" and "ahs" of amaze-ment and astonishment all around the bar. "I had been working on 'the draw,' which is what I first called it, in private for several weeks. I was thinking that we needed some kind of salute of our own, nothing too fancy or aggressive. I tried the thumb and the index finger straight up, but I didn't want some moron, lackey cop blowing someone away for the cause—especially me—because they thought they saw a gun. Then I tried the long-horn, you know the index and pinky, but it didn't feel right. Then I was toying with the index and middle finger spread apart slightly like a V. But that seemed too passive and friendly—if I'd only known," he said rolling his eyes. "I could have bagged that one, too.

"Anyway, it was then, in my frustration, that I swore out loud 'Fuck!' At that same moment I was messing with my finger, dropping my index limp. *It crystallized.* I was standing in front of a mirror and I liked what I saw. So I practiced 'the draw'—whipping out the finger like this." He demonstrated with a quick flash, snapping the wrist forward and bringing the big fella to attention, thrusting his hand up and outward. "It was great. It was so cool—a phallic, obscene gesture mocking the industrial-technological establishment and the class of plutocrats it produced. I worked with the group for a week. We practiced hard, and when we were there in Washington Square and those flat-footed lackeys came at us, in one fell swoop a hundred of us gave them 'the draw' and shouted out 'Fuck You!' at the top of our lungs. The cops were stunned—they stood there for about 30 seconds like they'd lost their woody at a peep show. It was incredible. I think those dumb asses would have stood there all day if I hadn't burst out laughing at them. In fact, we all started laughing so hard that it really pissed them off because they knew that they had just been had—really badly. Berkman gave the order to runaway and we scattered like jack rabbits. I made it out of there, but quite a few, like Berkman and Goldman, were chased down and got the crap beat out of them, some their fingers broken.

"Word spread quickly about the draw. It went far and fast, and became the *nouveau* gesture of choice for the anti-establishment. Man did it ever enrage those coppers, and it still does! I tell you the beauty of it is that you can say what you want and feel what you say without bullets, bombs, and billy-clubs. It's the perfect instrument of non-violent protest this beautiful nation has ever had."

He said this as proudly as I've ever heard someone say anything about any accomplishment he's achieved. I wasn't sure if I believed him that day. I had listened to his story and it was like magic. A few weeks later I found myself at the library, fishing through the microfilm. I came across an article in the old *New York World*. There was a photo of a May Day riot in Washington Square. The image captured a row of protestors with their hands raised high and their middle fingers extended facing the camera. Most of them had smiles, a few were laughing. On center was a familiar face, though many years younger and leaner. And there was the finger. Long, lonesome, and rigid as a flag pole. The caption read: "*Communists attack police with secret Bolshevik hand signal. Detectives work frantically to decipher meaning.*"

That, brother, was the beginning of a friendship. One that endured through last week when Porter Gibson Digit cocked the bird one last time and flew away, I'm sure, to a better place, to finally greet the Angel of his dreams. He left the rest of us wondering if she really *was* to die for. My guess is that her introduction to Mr. Digit went rather well—win, lose, or *draw*.

Till then, feedin' on the memories and the good times...

brother John

Act VII

The Adventures of
One-Eyed Red Beard

From: brother.john@moe.republic.org
To: rob@moe.org
Date: August 16
Subject: the higher stages of the barbarian culture

dear Rob: Sometimes the path of a wayward publican leads in directions you never dream of. Sometimes amidst the daily challenge to keep the party hot, the music playing, and the beer flowing you forget about the life that's out there on the other side of the door. You forget about the bourgeois decadence and hedonistic fury that struck each Friday happy hour like a summer lightning storm. That's when routine actually meant something and was not, simply, routine. You realize what a creature of habit you've become. An insidious monster. All the scarier because the fiend's a bastard offspring of your own stupor. Sometimes one must retool—need I remind you—to seize adventure at the tide before it ebbs away and you're left mired in the shallows, if I may paraphrase my old comrade Bill Shakespeare. Sometimes *it* happens, adventure, and you break out of the routine, one way or the other.

That day has arrived, or I should say it will tomorrow. Though I can't dismiss the last twenty-four hours. They've been anything but routine. Maybe it's an omen, which father is always quick to remind me is one letter short of women, the most dangerous of five letter words. I wasn't thinking about that when earlier this evening our good buddies Dr. Kinghorn and Mr. Bigwood strolled into the moe.Microbrewery looking pretty antsy. I figured something was up because each of them walked like they had a woody undercover. A borderline film noir look, minus the trench coats and fedoras. The two of them are regulars enough. But tonight I had a hunch they showed up for a reason. They had the same game face when they skewered that insurance guy last summer over the gazebo fiasco. So now it was my turn, I thought, to get my rosebud plucked. They were here to drill me about what happened yesterday. I knew it. I could sense it—it was the talk of the town. Juicy, fresh pulp. When that many bales of marijuana wash up in your backyard it usually is.

"Well boys, what's on your mind?" I asked them tentatively, serving up a couple of pints.

"This is highly confidential," said Bigwood in earnest before he even took a swig. "We have a few things we'd like to talk over with you."

"Guys!" I snapped, anticipating the question. "If this is about the dope I had nothing to do with it." I was on the defensive. "I told Chief McO'Fayle and all the other cops everything I knew. Did the Chief put you up to this?"

Mind you, I was sensitive about all the pot that washed in with the tide. The bucolic shores of the moe.Republic may never be the same. Don't be surprised if a couple of Feds come knocking at your door asking questions, either. As a longhaired musician you fit the profile. I didn't mean to imply when I was getting grilled that your long hair or playing the bass in a rock band had anything to do with smoking dope. So I would just avoid the whole "the hotel's a front for smuggling" line of questioning when it comes up.

What happened was a half-dozen bales floated in from Moose Harbor, prompting a massive search for drug smugglers. A guest found the first one while strolling on the beach. Just appeared out of the morning fog, he'd say. I wasn't sure if he meant the weather or himself. The "dude" was a moe.ron from Jersey here on holiday—could that have ever happened to me on vacation? Nearly thought he'd died and gone to heaven. Next, mother and the Huxley sisters found a bale during their morning perambulation along the beach. First, I had to endure a ten-minute berating from mother like it was my own stash I'd hid there. I don't know how many times she shouted, "how could you?" or "when are you going to grow up?" before the Huxley sisters pounced on me. No dope had ever washed ashore at Huxley Manor when their family ruled over the property. Nothing of such sorts would have ever happened if their nephew James had lived. He was a smart boy. Yeah! James Huxley was smart enough to join the army and get the hell away from those two, the spawn of Cruella DeVil. Alas! The gene pool was not deep enough to sustain him during some invasion of some Latin American country some many years before. His was the same fate as his great, great, great grandfather Colonel Josiah Huxley. Except, rather than *la cause noble* of the Battle of Fredericksburg and the preservation of the Union, James was lost forever in the battle to grease the palms of the Americas and the preservation of the banksters. I couldn't endure another "if James were alive" rant. Not then. I've only heard it ten-thousand times since we moved in. When I finally broke free of the three amigos, amicably, mind you, I called the Chief and all hell broke loose. You can't believe how many cops there were. The Feds, state troopers, and local law enforcement elite arrived in force. The weather was crappy and foggy, but they still sent out a helicopter and two boats to scour the coastline. Four more bales wrapped in white burlap sacks were found, but nothing else.

The Chief told me that this was nothing new. According to him Moose Harbor is a hot spot for smugglers, always has been. "My father used to say that during prohibition the rumrunners came across the Bay of Fundy from Nova Scotia." He looked at me, smiling knowingly like I knew something I didn't. I rolled my eyes in frustration. "Barrels of rum and crates of scotch and whiskey were easily smuggled in on fishing trawlers. There was supposed to be an ultra-secret drop-off where they stored the booze, a place they called the Whale's Jaw. No one ever found it, if it ever existed. Mostly because everyone figured it was here, Huxley Manor. Your beach there," he pointed, "the way it curves sharp on this end and that little peninsular on the other end. Well, there's your open Whale's Jaw. Anyway, that's what everyone thought. Another indication was that the Huxleys were said to be in the thick of it, letting the trawlers dock up here rather than down at the town wharf, and unload the booze in waiting trucks. They thought they were doing the fishermen a favor and making a little cash on the side. Had no idea what was going on. Not until that one time, at the height of it all, there was a big gun fight between the Walker and Kennedy gangs." He told me that Jackson Grant's grandfather was wounded in the melee. The guy ended up in jail for a few years. He wouldn't name names. "I can tell you with the rise in the popularity of smoking dope," the Chief added, "it was fairly common during the drug-trafficking decades of the nineteen-sixties, seventies, and eighties for smugglers to bring in a bale or two as the 'catch of the day'— the elusive square flounder."

The Chief asked me to keep an eye out for strangers or unusual looking characters. I wanted to remind him that just about everyone who walks through the door is a stranger, let alone a *character*. Maybe I should have asked him what type of character. At times the place is a rotating door for freaks and merry pranksters. They keep coming here looking for answers. Which I don't have for them and didn't have for the Chief. But considering the alternative, I told him I'd keep an eye out for anyone who looks suspicious, and we left it at that.

I guess I snapped at Kinghorn and Bigwood because I had been through the wringer over the past day. I'm surprised they didn't get up and leave. But they laughed at me. "Dude," Bigwood calmed me. "If we wanted to score this would be the last place we'd come to." Not sure if that was a sign of respect or if I'd just been labeled an L-7, I took a deep breath, exhaled slowly, and asked quite calmly, "What's up?"

"Plenty!" Kinghorn replied. "And it's bigger than any dope bust!" So began a tale of discovery in the offing out at Popham Island, out on the fringe of Moose Harbor. I listened closely to what they had to say. The more they told me, the deeper into the story they went, the mystery unraveling, the more I realized that the tide had just come in. Finally, when I was just about to ask where I fit in they asked me if I wanted to go with them on a boat ride, if I could help. "Where and when?" I pumped up. "Count me in!" After the brush with reefer madness it was just what I needed. If Kinghorn and Bigwood were right, if their research and investigation were accurate, then the end of a near three-hundred year old mystery was at hand. Even now I keep asking myself—have they really located the lost treasure of the pirate One-Eyed Red Beard? The grim reaper himself?

Ha! You say! He's quacked! Before you start counting marbles to send me you can relax. Unlike some of the other episodes I've encountered in the mystical oasis of the Lost Kingdom, I was invited to this one. Dr. Kinghorn and Mr. Bigwood are legitimate, and unlike the Huxley sisters, sane. You'd think that they would be busy enough between the law and real estate practice and the diner. But they got this Holmes and Watson mojo going for them, too. Sleuthing for the cause. Whatever it may be. Which I always thought was kind of cool. Especially after the boys helped out in the post-Kevin and Sparky debacle with the G-men. Still, it did get me thinking, "Why me?"

"We need more hands," replied Bigwood. "We can trust you. First, you got fat lips, but they're not loose lips. And second, it's a well-known occupational necessity that only priests and bartenders can keep a secret."

"First, chicks dig fat lips." I leaned in. "And what do you mean it's an occupational necessity?"

"It's like this," he said with the seriousness of a Zen master. "Do you know any Baptists?" I had to think if I knew any. It's not like I ask people their affiliation when they walk through the door. Then it struck me.

"Well, there was this preacher fellow with his daughter in the motel room next to ours one night," I started to recall.

"Hey, I'd really like to hear that one sometime," Bigwood cut me off, "but what I'm trying to tell you is more on an ecclesiastical plane. The very foundation of all things sacred. You see, when a priest hears confession the first words spoken are 'Father forgive me for I have sinned,' which, if he's a true man of the cloth, that's his cue to hit the on switch of the tape recorder. A Baptist, on the other hand, is much more subtle. He avoids his minister at all costs and his minister avoids him in kind, except on payday. Because each of their first words at confession are 'Hey bartender!'" he laughed out loud at his own joke. "'And never the twain shall meet!'"

That's why I like those guys. They know how to smooth the edges. I remember telling them how pissed off I was over the haunted house debacle. Why the fuck couldn't they have mentioned what we were getting into when we bought the place? The three of us were all sitting together in a booth at Kinghorn's diner one morning. "Getting into what?" Kinghorn replied nonchalantly. "What did you expect us to tell you? That your new landlord's named Casper? Not to worry, though. You've got Scoobie-Doo at your back! Or in your case, Sparky the wonder dog." That abruptly ended that *discussion*. A fool and his errand endeth. It didn't matter that Bigwood laughed as hard then as he did tonight at his own joke.

"All right," I replied. "I'm glad I made the cut. Am I the only one, or is there anyone else on the team?"

"Captain Bergmeister," Bigwood replied. "Popham *is* an island. Besides, he's thrilled to be in on the action. The *Jolly Mr. Johnson* will now sail into pirate folklore." I should have guessed. I can imagine that the thought of adding One-Eyed Red Beard to Bullethead Bergmeister's repertoire had him salivating. The summer was good for him and his business. Hard to believe that sinking a barge laden with fireworks one Fourth of July could add to your reputation as an able seaman, let alone if your business depended on it. But since that fateful day his business has boomed. Good for us! He's tapped into the fount of the moe.Microbrewery. His twilight party cruise, or as they say in the vernacular, "booze cruise," is good for a half-dozen kegs a week. He says that if we ever bottle the stuff we'd make a fortune. Most nights feature a who's who of the local music scene. Such luminaries as Mojo and the Flipside Five, Pistol Packing Pedro, and Bwana Dick and the Hooded Dakotas, have had a boatload of success. I've told Bullethead about you and the boys many times. He said he'd give you guys a weeknight slot if you wanted—just name the date! He owes me. We chauffeur hotel guests to the *Mr. Johnson* for coastal tours and whale watches—part of the whole moe.Republic experience. Father loves the cruises, too. He can't get enough of the salt snapping in the air. Kevin used to always go with us when he was in town, particularly on the Popham Island bingo cruises. A fistful of Dramamine, a pint of Crown, and the boy was ready for anything.

Those bingo nights are something, but the boat ride can be a bear if it's crappy out. Popham Island is about a forty-five minute cruise from Hancock Wharf. A rocky outpost, harsh, and except for the bird life, uninhabited. I've been by it, but never on it. From the hotel, looking out onto Moose Harbor's edge, it's the furthermost of four islands on the outer bay. The other three islands, Clapp, Goat, and Frenchman's *are* inhabited and have been since the 1580s. "Fishermen out of Bristol first came and cashed in each summer on the cod runs," Bigwood enlightened me. "They shared the islands with a few dozen species of semi-exotic seabirds which nested there," he added, reverentially. The man has a thing for birding in case you didn't know. I imagined him envisioning the whole topography of the island as he spoke cause I know he'd gone out there more than a few times. "Most of those early days were spent in constant vigilance," he said stoically. "From the pirates?" I asked eagerly, struck by the possibility. "Nah!" he shook his head. "The men had to protect the catch from ravaging birds and themselves from raining bird shit." That problem was soon solved when the fishermen found a market for the birds, particularly the Atlantic puffin. It wasn't just their plumage that the European haberdashers were after. Nay. When Lord Reginald Shaftpacker made the startling discovery that the puffin's colorful little beak made a scintillating aphrodisiac when grounded into powder, the chunky little auks became the rage of European high society.

I can't imagine that world of cod, birds, and fishermen—living in a state of nature. But the seeds of western civilization, and its advances, at least Downeast Way, were planted on those rocky outcrops, and within a generation had moved ashore. The irony being that a corollary to the *advance* of civilization is the continuous fight to set it back. Real estate and resources— what else do people fight over? Some would say religion? But I don't know. "Religion isn't a want, it's a weapon to get what you want," Porter Gibson Digit once told me. "A cultural artifact. Behind the shroud of religion lies the bane and beauty of humanity," he waxed poetically. "Marx got it wrong. It's the opiate of dumb asses," he'd say, with a laugh. Accept that he'd pronounce dumb asses, 'DAH-masses' like 'DAH-bears.' "If people would accept their religion, whatever their belief, as a spiritual release to free them from the earthly bonds, rather than a cave to crawl into, we'd be in a much better place." Under the gaze of the Old Mountain by the Sea, in the name of the Father, Son, Holy Ghost, for the power and the glory, the advance of civilization took a beating. The English fought the Indians, the French, the French and Indians, and did battle with an occasional wayward Spanish or Dutch ship, too. It's amazing that anything was accomplished on those islands, but it was. "Each had a purpose," said Bigwood. "Each played a part in the Red Beard story."

Goat Island was where most of the livestock was herded. Clapp Island was where most of the women were herded. Frenchman's Island, the island that made a name for itself, was site of the last stand of Pierre de Acadia and his men. Tragic squatters caught raiding puffin nests in an ill-advised attempt to corner the European puffin market, circa 1610. Defiant to the end, when they ran out of ammo Acadia and his merry band of rogue traders were said to hurl stones and insults at the English rather than surrender and abandon the puffin catch. They were served up as cannon fodder by a Franco-phobe English captain who, many years before, as a plucky lad, was initiated into the ways of a hardened seaman one summer evening whilst stranded in the port of Marseilles. Rather then physically remove the Frenchmen in irons, on his order, Pierre, his men, and every bird that didn't fly were blown asunder, their parts used as bait by the English fishermen. As a consequence, the puffin population, devastated, migrated farther down east, never to thrive in these parts again. Bad timing for Pierre, his men, and the birds. The great puffin slaughter on Frenchman's Island was for naught. With the discovery of a superior aphrodisiac in powdered rhino horn, the European puffin market collapsed.

Skirmishes, battles, and puffin intrigue aside, within a century the transformation everywhere along the eastern seaboard was remarkable, by the early eighteenth century, amazing! Commerce, and the great mercantile invasion, had come ashore and was booming. The epic struggle over who was going to control and profit from the abundant natural resources was in full swing, too. It was not just the European nations and their native American allies, but a class of roving banditos, the Mafioso of the high seas—a hardy class of pirates and buccaneers in the hunt for blood and booty.

Which brings me to the crux of this lengthy epistle. There are a long list of stories and tall-tales of the pirates that wandered the high seas at that time. The last one known to frequent these waters was the grim reaper himself, One-Eyed Red Beard. Renowned for his penetrating keenness with women and hair as red and fiery as the setting sun. One-Eyed's real name was Flannery O'Fayle, an Irishman, whose ancestors had survived the great Elizabethan Wars and the resulting famine, plague, and executions exacted by the Crown on County Cork. A shipmaster he became, and took to the sea, enraged and determined, taking his vengeance out on every English vessel he could waylay between Nova Scotia and the West Indies. He was known to hit a Dutchman or Spaniard, too, for practice, but his true passion lay in whacking off the Union Jack.

One daring raid immortalized One-Eyed to the present day. He and his buccaneers attacked, captured, pillaged, buggered and then executed or enlisted the crew of the HMS *Queen Bee* off the coast of Rhode Island. Reports from the day said that he bloodied the water with victims of the attack and waited for the great whites to swarm. Then he slit the wrists of the captain and his officers, and one by one, pushed them to their doom.

A full complement of volunteers was gained that day, enough sailors to terrorize the eastern seaboard for years to come. And he probably would have done so had it not been for the *Queen Bee's* cargo. By accident or design, no one quite knows, that ship, with its letters of marque, had captured a Spanish galleon laden with gold mined by Indian slaves. The galleon carried another prize, also. A treasure of legend. A goblet cast of pure gold and encrusted with gems and jewels from an ancient Aztec city beyond the Sierra Madre. The artifact had been forged by powerful, mystical Aztec priests and shamans centuries before. Cortez himself had coveted it, and he sent an army to track it down. An army which was said to have met an horrific fate when it came into the presence of the goblet. Truly, they believed, it was indeed, El Diablo's Chalice, the antithesis of the Holy Grail.

The Spanish were no match for the *Queen Bee* on that fateful day, which went down off the straits of Florida after a brief, futile chase and exchange. The Spanish captain, his officers, and crew were tied belly-up to the mast, buggered by a complement of merry Englishmen, and thrown into the deep. Broken Catholics with swollen prostates. Wondering how it could have ended like this? A sole survivor was found by One-Eyed a day later. The survivor revealed the fate of the Spanish galleon, its officers, the crew, and most importantly, the bounty on board. The chase was on.

The English captain was on course for Nova Scotia to re-supply before crossing the Atlantic when One-Eyed Red Beard overwhelmed the ship in the pre-dawn.

A few weeks later, bearing south in the Gulf of Maine, not too far from Moose Harbor, One-Eyed and his band of pirates were captured. He and his entire crew were taken to Boston where they were summarily hanged. The Chalice and gold were never found, but much sought after through the centuries.

The tale of One-Eyed Red Beard took another twist. Nine months after the demise of the dreaded pirate, one of his amorous adventures came to fruition in a small fishing village. 'Twas located on a rocky wind-swept island situated under the watchful eye of an old mountain by the sea. A boy was born to Sally Micholson, a minister's daughter and a pirate's mistress. The boy was said to have hair as red and fiery as the setting sun, and in later life, a penetrating keenness for women.

"Thus commenced the celebrated founding of the clan McO'Fayle in the Lost Kingdom!" Kinghorn proclaimed. "Behind the cool, calm demeanor of our beloved Chief of Police lies the heart of a bloodthirsty bandit."

"And here our story really begins," Bigwood added. "The founding of this venerable clan provided the clue we needed." Apparently nine months before the birth of the younger "Mc-O'Fayle" the bodies of two men, sailors, were found floating in a small cove on Popham Island. Church records and a few entries in a long forgotten captain's journal they unearthed over at Bagwell's Bookstore, indicated that the men were covered in "the most foul red blisters and boils" across their arms, neck, chest, and face. "Each had his throat cut," Kinghorn said, lashing his finger across his neck, "an inverted pentagram carved on his forehead, and a hoof print branded into his chest."

"Legend has it that Satan straddled each man," Bigwood added. "Welting, blistering, and slashing them." The horrific find terrified the entire islands and Moose Harbor region for years. Their gruesome deaths were never solved, either. No one ever went near that cove again least they catch the wail of desperate men and the shrill, diabolic laugh of Beelzebub.

The Devil's Cove, since called, is out on the northeast side of the island. Popham is shaped like a kidney bean. The island's good sized for a rock. Nothing but forty-five or fifty acres of granite, high-rising knolls and low-lying dales, and covered with thick vegetation ranging from wild rose bushes to copses of stunted, windswept cedar trees. It's an anomaly compared to the other isles, Clapp, Goat, and Frenchman's. Popham and its birds' nests remains inaccessible. Yet, it serves as a buffer from what the mighty Atlantic churns up.

Over the years the search for One-Eyed's treasure has focused on Clapp Island, where Sally lived. Bars of silver and a few gold doubloons have been found on all three. In one spectacular find after the hurricane of 1938, a box was found exposed in a hollow along a rocky ledge on Clapp Island. The box had 12 bars of silver stamped with a Spanish cross. The find was long held as the final chapter in the search for the lost treasure of One-Eyed Red Beard. Pundits declared that the Spanish gold was a fantasy; and that the lost chalice was a myth—a storybook legend divined by the mortal keepers of mirth and mayhem. That the legend of the treasure had taken on a force and shape of its own over time. The scribes could not weave nor have perpetuated a taller tale.

That was until the day Alexander Bigwood came across a body, or what was left of it. A skull and bones, and bone fragments, bleached white, laying in the sun, scattered on the edge of Devil's Cove. The coroner's report later revealed the deceased was close to three-hundred years old, a victim of a gun shot wound which had entered between the eyes and exited through the back of his skull.

Bigwood was out there birding, of all things, for a glimpse of the enigmatic Atlantic puffin. He's keen on birding, as I mentioned, been a hobby for years. As chair of the local ornithology society he's often out in some swamp or hiking the backside of Agamenticus in search of "prey." When word hit the street that a flock of puffins had descended on Popham he jumped the *Jolly Mr. Johnson* to look for himself. Nearly four-hundred years since the great decimation, he knew that viewing the plump little, doey-eyed buggers out there would be a find. They just didn't come this far down east anymore. Maybe it was that mega-summer nor'easter we had that knocked them off course or drove them south. It's been a stormy month, with a lot of mid-day thunderheads rolling in from nowhere. Bigwood didn't care how they got there. He needed to verify, take a census. The *Return of the Puffin* had the makings of a good paper or book. The news would surely send a tizzy through the birding community. A beginning of an epich cycle of re-population and resettlement equaling the brown pelican and the urban rock pigeon. Thoughts of a significant puffin find filtered through Bigwood's head. Envisioning the corpulent little alcid, solemn and comical as Chaplin's Little Tramp, had found its way "home." These days the only place in the United States that you can see the plump auks in action is to go parts thither east way beyond the Lost Kingdom. That's why Bigwood's curiosity got the better of him that day. That's why he went out to Popham and dared enter the lair of Mephistopheles and the cursed cove to catch a glimpse of the fleeting puffin, as Pierre de Acadia had dared centuries before. That's how he found himself waist deep in a thick patch of poison ivy as he closed in on the nesting grounds. "I was only searching for a good view to observe the exotic ritual billing of the mating puffin," he recalled.

"You went out there to watch puffins have sex?" I asked, interrupting him, taken aback.

"It's a courtship of nuance and subtle positioning of male to female," he replied, as though a common fact. "You have to be sneaky."

"I can't leave here to go out there to watch puffins fuck," I squawked. "The bride will never let me hear the end of it. Let alone anybody else."

"Don't soil yourself man," said Bigwood, looking up and down the bar. "And not so loud. Just listen to the end of the story."

"Like I'm going somewhere?" I said.

Bigwood was following his ears and emerged through a thicket. Puffins were aplenty, and it would have been a pinnacle moment in the career of any seasoned birder. But there was the issue of the skull and bones that lay awash through the eroded soil. Ever the investigator, he knew he had stumbled upon a crime scene—just as the low purring of auk love erupted. The steady pummeling and primordial growling of randy puffins surrounded him. He studied the remains. The lure of that old puffin magic evaporated. The end of courtship and conquest. With a forensic eye Bigwood saw the clue he needed.

Fortune or luck, the coroner knew nothing of the island's racy past. The papers reported that the storm must have washed up an old grave. Bigwood, however, did know of the island's past, and was quick to make a link. He and Kinghorn turned to the early records of births, deaths, and marriages. They went over to old Charlie Bagwell's bookstore. He's got an antiquarian room in the back, what Charlie calls his room of lost secrets. I've been there a few times. It's stacked floor to ceiling with ancient material going back at least four centuries. You'll find anything that's ever been written over time about the Lost Kingdom in there. Charlie showed them the old diaries and they read them all thoroughly, even before the coroner's report was published. "It all made sense you see," whispered Bigwood. And it really did when he and Kinghorn laid out the story to me as I've laid it out to you. "The birth, the mysterious death of the two sailors, Popham Island, Devil's Cove, and especially the body that unearthed itself after the recent storm." Bigwood was beside himself, eager and anxious. "That *had* to be where One-Eyed Red Beard had buried his treasure." He raised his eyebrows in excitement. "The birth of his son proved he was here just before he was captured. The mysterious blisters that covered the two sailors were poison ivy—Popham is the only island of the four where it grows—and only in the vicinity of the cove. The two sailors were fellow-pirates who went ashore with One-Eyed to bury the treasure amidst the ivy. They must have had their shirts off while they were digging for their bodies were covered by the reaction to it. After they buried the treasure old skull and bones, the guy I stumbled on, must have helped One-Eyed murder the two sailors. Imitating a satanic ritual, they dumped their bodies in the sea only to have the tide wash them back in the cove. Old skull and bones pointed the way to the burial site. He was the last one to see One-Eyed's buried treasure and he paid dearly for it. A bullet between the eyes and a quick burial by the sea." Satisfied, he looked at me, waiting for my reaction.

"That's pretty good," I said. "But then what?"

Kinghorn laughed. "Like any hearty scalawag, after weeks of plundering and cold-blooded murder, One-Eyed went over to Clapp Island and initiated the clan McO'Fayle."

I stood there dumbstruck, not knowing what to say. In truth, I didn't know how to respond. The story was fantastic, thrilling, and wild. It was brilliant detective work and an incredible scenario. Now that I think of it, I must have had a goofy look on my face.

"So what do you think?" I heard Bigwood ask me. "Are you in?"

"Are you ready for an adventure?" Kinghorn added.

Oddly, through the buzz of the bar, the conversations and chatter fanning out to the crowded tables, I looked across the lounge and caught the wry grin of the old moosehead mounted on the wall. Even in the wide expanse of the room the big fella was staring me down. High above the mantle the beast looked me dead in the eye, watching every move as though he had been listening in. Maybe it was the beer, the light, or everything that had gone down over the past twenty-four hours. Or quite possibly a psilocybic flashback, or a fleeting gasp of my impending dotage—the ebb and flow of momentary episodes of premature senility. For suddenly I saw myself there. It was my head and shoulders stuffed and mounted up on the wall. It was me who peered down with a confounded grin on my face. I didn't know what to make of it, but I took it as a sign when, with a nod, wink, and shrug I said to myself, "father always said it would come to this."

"What are you thinking about?" I thought I heard myself say, but actually it was Bigwood mouthing the words, snapping me from my flitting trance. And that's when the totality of it all struck me.

"I'm thinking it's time for a toast," I said. "This calls for something... *special*," I added, quickly pouring three shots of the Gran' Marn. "Gentlemen," we raised our glasses, "count me in!"

"We already have," Kinghorn nodded. "Cheers!"

"To the good life!" Bigwood wheezed, inhaling the shot.

Everything's set to go. I'm meeting those guys down at the wharf tomorrow morning. My job's to be the equipment guy. A pack mule to help lug the equipment across the rugged terrain of Popham and carry the goods back. Really, I can't believe that I'm going on a bona fide treasure hunt. Too bad you're in—where the heck are you? Oh well, when you read this we'll be back here with the goods. Swilling moe.Ale from El Diablo's Chalice till pigs fly or the sun rises. I forgot. I'm sworn to secrecy. I'm only telling you in case Beelzebub ambushes me. In which case, "don't forget to throw roses on my grave..."

From the higher stages of the barbarian culture, give my regards to Thorstein!

brother John

The moe.Republic Hotel
in the heart of the Lost Kingdom

On the Adventures of
One-Eyed Red Beard
Monday, 3:23 a.m.
In my solitude at the bar

Dear Rob,

Hola from the sacred terra firma of the moe.Republic. Many thanks to you and the boys for the box of Cohibas. I don't know where you found them, but they were a welcome sight when I finally regained consciousness. Father had managed to pillage only half of them before I came to. I've squirreled the rest of them away. I just stoked one up to fire off this missive. It might take two to get through the full account of what happened on that God-forsaken rock of an island.

You'll be happy to know that I am now well on my way to recovery from one of the wildest twenty-four hour stretches of my life. I can't say that on this side of the day if I'd gone for it. Yet, here I am despite the bumps and bruises, scrapes and scratches, scabs and scars, contemplating the misadventures of One-Eyed Red Beard. An adventure that played like a late-night film down at Bud's Bijou. A true tale of stooge-like cunning and chance. Daft it was! I never really appreciated what Burns meant when he wrote that "the best laid schemes o' mice and men gang aft angly." Mainly because I never did get a handle on archaic Scot in my travels. Trust me, though, when I say, the guy knew what he was talking about.

That day began unassumingly enough. First thing in the morning I buzzed down to Hancock Wharf looking for Fred 'the Bullethead' Bergmeister's harbor cruiser. There was a thin fog and the scent of brine was heavy in the air. I found myself momentarily distracted when I arrived. A couple of dozen locals and a minor throng of tourists mingled on the dock near the newsstand and Java d' Hut. I was gawking at the working seafarers who gawked at the scene on the wharf as they made ready to escape, preparing for another run out in the Gulf of Maine. Soon the horizon would be lined with the silhouettes of their lobster trawlers, fanning out on the bay. I saw Jake the Lizard on one of his boats and I ducked into the Java d' Hut for a joe. I didn't want him to see me. He'd ask me a million questions for sure and I'd end up blowing the cover. Bigwood may have got it right, but I ain't no priest and I'm a lousy bartender. I can drink more than I serve. Fortunately, Jake's boat quickly got under way and I slipped outside. Bigwood happened to glance my way from the deck of the *Jolly Mr. Johnson* and hollered. He stood there, taking it all in, smiling. As I boarded I noticed a guy from the Department of Interior. He and Kinghorn were aft, jawing about something. Jackson Grant of the *Downeast Way Times* was there, too. He had arrived to cover the "breaking news," Bigwood told me, and had worked his way on board. A top-secret affair, how Jackson found out was anybody's guess. I think the guys took him on board to prevent him from "breaking" the news. They were baffled about how he got wind of it, which was probably what Kinghorn was grilling the Interior guy about. Jackson had found his way to the helm, where he and the skipper, Captain Bergmeister, were perched above, joking and laughing. I wondered where Jackson Grant stood. Bigwood said that the Department of Interior guy was here under the pretense of searching for a colonial burial site. "Give those guys a dig," he quipped before he went off to join Kinghorn, "and they've got a cow to milk for years."

I had all that going for me while standing on the deck of the *Jolly Mr. Johnson*. Bullethead was set to go and we were about to embark. I resumed people watching as we moved slowly from the dock, struck by the sight from my vantage point. The custom of easing coffee addictions with doughnuts, all the while reading catastrophic news from the Middle East, Africa, and Miami, the hunt for Osama, weather projections for Kansas, or last night's box scores—it fascinated me. Jackson Grant notwithstanding, the landlubbers were oblivious to our quest. Even though a sense of anticipation gripped us on board.

The spell was broken when a loud horn blew abruptly off the harbor side. I nearly spilled my coffee down my pants. Jake the Lizard was waving at me. He had turned the *Blubber I* around for some reason. "Ahoy, Captain Stubben!" he joked, bellowing over a megaphone, as he waved at us. "Where you headin' to buckos?" I waved back, as did the others. Captain Bergmeister, who'd shut his radio off for just such a reason, revved up the engines. Bullethead eased us out into the harbor pronto and turned about, away from the *Blubber I*. We waved goodbye to our buddy Jake, who seemed at a loss. We were off, finally on our way. The air cooled. I sipped at my coffee, watching the old town's brick and wooden colonial row houses and warehouses grow smaller from the stern. Jackson Grant spied me and waved me over. He was as excited as I was. "So Jackson, level with me." I had to know how he pulled it off. "How did you know?"

"Know what?" he replied innocently.

"Jackson! This is *me* you're talking to remember?" There was a hint of exaggerated exasperation for effect. "Good old brother John—Saint Patrick's Day? 'Uncle' Porter? We've been through a few things together. I'm not going to rat you out."

"Ah," he mumbled something under his breath. "Yeah, I know what you mean." The words rolled out in his heavy Maine dialect, squeezing life out of every syllable. "It was just a hunch." He shrugged his shoulders. "I got lucky. I told Kinghorn flat out that I knew what was up, and I'd like to go."

"You bluffed!" I said impressed. "He just let you aboard? Just like that? I can't believe I'm even here and you bluffed your way on board?"

"Ayuh," he said calmly. "I was tuned in to what was going on."

"The bride thinks I'm searching for a lost graveyard from three centuries ago."

"That's the cover? Pretty good."

"Yeah. I thought it was. The bride saw right through it. She couldn't care less, but made a point of telling me I was packing fudge."

"Call it an educated guess," Jackson said. "I didn't know anything about any cover story. After Bigwood found the body in Devil's Cove it got me thinking. I've lived here my whole life, know all about the One-Eyed legend. When I heard that these guys were on a tear through the early town records and burrowing through that lost secrets room in the back of Charlie Bagwell's bookstore, I put two and two together—made an educated guess. Charlie doesn't allow just anyone to go in the back of his shop, not unless it's important."

"How'd you know it was today?"

"Oh that? I was at the diner yesterday, heard Doris Peck telling someone she was waiting on that the bosses wouldn't be around today—thought something might be up."

"Another guess?"

"No. Well, maybe. I come down to the Java d' Hut most mornings looking for a scoop. I got here early today—saw them guys making their way on board with all this equipment, and decided to go put the monkey on Kinghorn."

"Was Kinghorn pissed? I saw him getting into it with that state guy."

"If he was he wasn't mad at me. A little surprised, but then he got a kick out of it. Said if it was the only way to keep it out of the papers for a few more days, he could use the extra hand."

"Fuckin' aye! That's pretty good," I told him.

"Ayuh. Not bad."

"What's good about it then?" a voice said from behind them. The man from Interior had lumbered up quietly and moved in on the conversation.

"You must be Burt Slocum," I said to him. We shook hands as Jackson smiled and introduced himself. "Bigwood told me you're an archeologist from the state Department of Interior," Jackson said. "I guess he and Kinghorn wanted to cover all the bases."

"Perhaps," he replied smugly, and gave a nod to us. Burt wore black rimmed glasses and sported a crewcut under his ball cap. That look reminded me of that staff-sergeant from Saint Patrick's Day a few years ago. He wore a dark green Department of Interior polo shirt and khakis, and held a jacket bearing the same green and khaki colors. The department's initials, D.I.M., were stitched brazenly across the front of the cap. Apparently someone at Interior had a sense of humor. "It's important that history in the making has as many observers as possible, especially with what we have here," he said officiously. "We need to put the local folklore to rest. Tales of pirates and ghosts and hauntings are for tourists and the superstitious. We can't take that position. The good Lord wouldn't allow it. The only question for us is whether or not it was a single grave or indeed, a graveyard."

I wasn't sure when Burt said 'we' if he meant us on board or him as the embodiment of the state. If he *knew* what we were really going after. If so, the latter was rife with overtones of bureaucratic possession and outright seizure. In which case I would have to loathe him. He continued to talk about the "find" with authority, and how *we* were on the verge of a major archeological *dig*. When he emphasized dig he looked at me and Jackson like we were county gravediggers and he was the boss man. The dude was disrupting the karma flow. He was too chatty, a bit boring, and we'd barely met him. I was beginning to wonder why Kinghorn or Bigwood acquiesced and brought the guy along when he blurted out "Jackson Grant?" It was though a shift in the time-space continuum had knocked him off balance. "Aren't you *that* reporter?"

"I could be," Jackson replied cautiously. "Depending on what usage you mean by *that*?"

"Oh, don't be going Harvard on me man!" He chuckled at himself. "All I mean is that I enjoyed your book on Porter Gibson Digit."

"Thank you," Jackson replied sincerely. "Mr. Digit's a wonderful man—a giant of a man. In his own way he changed the course of history and contributed to the culture on a global scale," he said proudly. "His story needed to be told. I was really flattered he allowed me to tell it."

"Yeah." Burt exhaled slowly as though bored. "Well, what I wanted to know was did he really fuck Emma Goldberg?" he asked, indifferently. "You think he actually banged a communist?"

"Her name was Goldman, Burt," Jackson corrected him with controlled patience.

"Goldman, right," he purred. "Was that bitch hot or was he drunk? I mean how else could you fuck a communist?"

"As I wrote in the book," Jackson bristled icily. "The word he used was 'relationship,' and as Mr. Digit's like an uncle I would find it difficult to describe any of his encounters in such base terms."

"Hey relax man. Don't be so sensitive. I was just wondering." He laughed again at himself, then looked at me. "You know, speaking of uncle, I had one who looked just like you." He pointed a chubby finger right in my face.

"Like me?" he caught me off-guard. "Christ I'm not that old!"

"You look just like him. You do, man! I wanted to tell you earlier." He smiled a toothy grin. "Right when I seen you walk on board, but Kinghorn had me buttonholed."

"I'm sure he was a handsome, vigorous man." I said, lightheartedly.

"Actually he was a drunk. A stinking, toothless, rot-gut drunk. The poor bastard lost his left testicle in a trapping accident and never was quite the same." He paused. We both cringed and gasped. "You're a bartender, right? How's business?"

Before I could say anything to him Kinghorn and Bigwood sidled up from no where. "Where did you find this guy, Kinghorn?" I sputtered out.

"Hey, how's my tool boy and scribe doing?" Kinghorn asked. "You're not letting Burt here bullshit you two, too badly are you? I meant to warn you. He's a pain in the ass."

"I'm being as gentle with them as I was with your sister the first time, Kinghorn!" Slocum defended himself.

"You know Slocum the only reason we're not related is because size *does* matter, and God knows I'm not talking about your IQ or bank account."

"Was it that painful for her, Kinghorn?"

"Don't flatter yourself, Burt. You're where you're at today—a cog in the bureaucratic wheel—because, when it comes down to it, eventually, people end up where they should. Remember that the next time you're bored pushing pencils and you ask yourself, 'why me?'"

"Bigwood—you going to let him talk to me like that?" Slocum implored, affronted.

"Hey Burt, when you throw chum in the water best be ready for the sharks to circle."

"Yeah, yeah, yeah," he paused looking dejected, then let it pass over like a breeze. "You know, it's a great day for a boat ride. You boys ready for adventure?"

At that, the wind shifted from the north and warmed a bit. Shortly, we were approaching the island. Bullethead was turning about to ease us up to a rickety old landing dock. "Don't worry about the dock," Bullethead shouted out over the engines. "It's pretty old, but safe enough." Even as he spoke the pilings wobbled and swayed from the wake of the boat. "It'd take more than five of you to drop it," he added assuredly while the entire structure rocked. "At least in theory," he shouted. It wasn't too bad. The weathered planks creaked and bounced under our weight, but we made it to shore. The distance to get to the other side of the island was not that far, Bigwood told us. The problem was circumventing the massive boulders and vegetation, which would take some time. I really didn't mind the bother. We were trudging along. The weather was fine. Everything was going as planned.

Forty-five minutes later things changed. All around the clouds swirled, ready to descend. Dangerous looking clouds, dark and purplish. Shucking and jiving like a Bourbon Street carny. The sky had grown ominous. The clouds had rolled up suddenly. At first I didn't give it attention. The cumulus mass had already backed in and out a few times. I thought they'd finally passed and nothing would come of it. But the son-of-a-bitches were real. All those feints were just a ploy. They up and merged into an entity, a cognizant being. The thunderheads had encircled us. The whole time we trudged across the island they were in pursuit—through the thick underbrush, up and around granite boulders the size of dump trucks.

"Couldn't that guy, what did you say his name was? Bullethead? Couldn't old Captain Bullethead have let us off on the other side of the island?" Slocum complained nervously. "That storm looks nasty."

"The Devil's Cove? No fucking way!" Kinghorn snapped right back at him. "You're out of your fucking mind as usual Burt!"

"What do you think? Old Lucifer's going to rise up and from the burning depths of hell?" he parried back. "What's he going to do? Throw a blazing pitchfork at your sorry ass?"

"*She!*" Bigwood interpolated. "Lucifer's a she. And the depths of hell are cold—frozen barren. Cold as the harshest Arctic blast on the darkest winter's day."

"Sounds like you've been there and you know *her* well?" Burt quipped sarcastically.

"Indeed I do. I was married to *her*," said Bigwood bluntly while we trucked along. "Sixteen fucking years it was. The icy tentacles of her heart strings gripped my soul, lulled me into a false sense of security and whole-ness, drew me into the frozen, cavernous wasteland of hell. I was there, laid witness to it. She was that cold." He spoke compellingly, unruffled, like he was presiding over a jury or lecturing a class. "Took me years to climb out of that wretched hole. Me and Captain Morgan—he was the only company I had. So when you speak of hell and Lucifer and all things fucked on this planet, as I live and breathe I've seen it and I've been there. And I can tell you, *She* sits on a throne of ice."

"Whoa man! Sorry I brought it up," Burt jeered.

"Should we ask him what happened?" Jackson murmured to me.

"Do we really want to know?" I muttered under my breath.

"You can ask him all you want," Kinghorn volunteered an answer. "That's the most I've ever got out of him."

"Listen!" Bigwood stopped, sniffed at the air. "Duck!" he shouted. The conviction with which he said it sent us down. A thunderhead exploded directly above us. Lightning cracked a cedar tree in half off to the right. Cedar's a tough wood but that sucker looked like a singed banana peel splayed down the middle. This wasn't in the script for today. For a split instant I could feel the hair across my neck and chest stand on end. I was bracing for another strike. A violent crack and flash shook the ground we were standing on. Instantly a seagull crashed in front of us with a violent force. A kamikaze pilot out of the sky, on its mark. It lay there, partially charred and smoldering, a portent from the ice queen. We stayed crouched. The air felt heavy and electrically charged.

"Looks like you pissed *her* off again, Bigwood," Burt shouted out. "Could you apologize to the bitch before we get quick fried!" Another can-nonade of thunder erupted. Lightning flashed in succession. "I told you we should have docked over there!"

"Bullethead couldn't drop us off at Devil's Cove," Kinghorn grunted on his haunches like an ape. We all looked like apes, squatting nervously. I could see the headlines now—a bunch of simian men in a circle jerk, panicked and confused, fried by lightning. "There's no place to dock and he couldn't get close enough." The first pings of rain began to slam into the rocks and off our heads. "Too many rocks, too rough seas on the Atlantic side of the island, Burt. The *Jolly Mr. Johnson* would end a wreck. Even the best maritime insurance doesn't cover stupidity."

"Maybe we should find some cover," Jackson interrupted them.

"We're in the home stretch," Bigwood shouted. "Follow me!" We ran as fast as we could past a boulder and up into a thick grove of cedars. Equipment flapped and bounced. Probably not the safest place I thought, going into a stand of trees on a rise. Bigwood knew the island well, though. We entered a narrow dell in the middle of the stand, which led down near an embankment under the cover of thick bushes. Thunder and lightning crashed and flashed rapidly, but the air was not heavy like above. The rain washed over us. At one point the force of the wind pushed it diagonally. I could hear waves smashing on the not too distant shore—sounded like a sledgehammer splitting granite. The spray was shooting high. Its mist added to the drenching downpour.

The storm lasted another half-hour or more. We squatted anxiously. Burt talked continuously, nervous chatter, as the thunderheads slowly receded. Staring at the DIM cap, listening to banter, was a distraction from the intensity of the storm. I never did like thunder and lightning storms. When we were kids mother used to freak us out, make us hide under the kitchen table during really intense ones. Then there was the time at the picnic when the storm came up out of no where and I dropped you on your head. I was holding you when the thunder struck so loud you soiled yourself. I nearly had a catatonic seizure from the clap and the sight of your skivvies turned an ugly, stain mocha. Mother was screaming at me all the way home. It didn't matter that you got up and instinctively walked under the picnic table to hide. Your head was as hard as a bulldog's and as big as melon.

My reminiscence of family dysfunction dissolved quickly when my ears picked up a queer sound. I wasn't sure what I heard to tell you the truth. The thunder had died off by then, and the rain was light. Besides, what I heard sounded like a laugh, quite diabolical at that. To be honest I thought I was hearing things, a gust of wind. That was until I looked up and the saw the look on Burt's face. We were still in our simian pose and his head tilted at a slight angle. He looked like a confused ape. There was a moment of silence and I heard it again. This time Burt tilted his head the other way. His look changed from confusion to fear.

"Did you hear that," I whispered furtively. We all nodded straining to hear it again. And then we heard it again. High-pitched, shrill, faintly, with a slight echo.

"What the hell?" Bigwood said, confused.

"Nice going Bigwood," said Burt, alarmed. "You've managed to rouse *her* from the icy depths of hell." He sounded nervous.

"Eat me, Burt," Bigwood muttered. He drew a sharp breath, about to utter a few more choice remarks when we heard the laugh, again, from the other side. It had moved behind us. At least it carried from that direction.

"What the fuck do you think it is?" Jackson asked out loud.

Bigwood and Kinghorn looked at each other puzzled. They looked at me. I didn't want to admit it, but I was actually beginning to think Burt could have something. Yet I found it equally disturbing that I could agree with him. "We're all adults here," I volunteered. "Let's not get carried away with our imagination."

"What if it's the ghost of One-Eyed Red Beard?" Burt blurted out. "What if he's the one who kept this place off limits all these years?"

"Get a hold of yourself, man!" Kinghorn exclaimed. "Listen to what you're saying. I shouldn't have told you about that pirate tale."

"You know," Jackson interrupted. "I don't know how much you fellows got into the history of this treasure—I know you've been very thorough—but Burt there isn't that far off from a few stories that have floated around this place."

"What are you suggesting Jackson?" Bigwood asked him. "Are you going to tell me that this island, this place, that cove, *is* haunted?"

"I'm saying that a few tales about this place have dealt with the supernatural," he replied. "I'm not saying I subscribe to them, at least not yet."

"See," Burt chimed in. "What did I tell you."

"You told me and Jackson that those tales were for tourists and the superstitious," I reminded him.

"That was before I got here," he answered.

"You're talking about the Lair of Mephistopheles," said Kinghorn, skeptically. "Come on?"

"People who've been trapped on this rock for any length of time have talked about hearing a wail of desperation, or sometimes a hideous laugh," said Jackson. "There's a good reason that no one lives here."

"Yeah," Bigwood interrupted. "It's covered with bird shit."

That nearly broke the spell we were falling under. Until a second later when I could have sworn I heard another moan rise and fall in the wind. "Did you hear that!" I snapped excitedly, in spite of myself. I didn't want to fuel Burt's imagination or my own. The reality was, at that point, I was moments away from psyching myself out à la Colonel Huxley. I sure could have used Sparky and that nose of his.

"That's exactly the kind of thing I'm talking about," Jackson whispered. "There's a reason this treasure has never been found. El Diablo's Chalice, the Devil's very own goblet, it's guarded by Satan... herself," he added as an affirmation to Bigwood.

"Hold on. What treasure?" said Burt, struck by an epiphany. "I thought we were investigating a colonial burial site?"

"Jackson, you're beginning to sound as daft as Burt here," said Kinghorn. "Burt," he turned towards him. "We *are* here to investigate a colonial burial site. It's a matter of public record. That's why you're here." Kinghorn shifted his gaze, stared right into Jackson's eye when he said the last part. He furrowed his eyebrows tightly, menacingly, as though to tell him to be quiet. "What Jackson is talking about are old pirate tales." He stared at Jackson. "Just like I said to you earlier when you first came on board."

That pretty much answered my thoughts about Burt from earlier. He truly was a clueless dick who had no idea what we were actually here for.

"If you're up to your old games Kinghorn," said Burt, threateningly, "I'll never forgive you for this one."

"At the risk of sounding redundant, Slocum, by all means, eat me, Slocum!" he shot back.

"If I may continue," interrupted Jackson. "I can assure each of you that I can claim no ownership of what I know. It's stuff that was passed to me and material I've come across. They say that the Chalice is cursed," said Jackson uneasily. "When you two were reading up on the Lair of Mephistopheles I bet you didn't come across that?" he said to Kinghorn and Bigwood. "That an Aztec shaman cursed it, swore vengeance on all who possessed the relic."

"Jackson!" said Kinghorn, frustrated. "Please! We came across the shaman bunk. It's nothing."

"Wait," said Burt eagerly. "Let's here what he has to say."

"Yeah," I added, a bit intrigued myself.

"Why not?" said Bigwood, who seemed to have a genuine interest. "There might be something we missed." Kinghorn looked around the simian circle frustrated and wrung his hands. A portent perhaps; knowing Burt for as long as he had, maybe he was trying to protect us. Not that he knew what lay ahead, but because he knew Burt, he shrugged and resigned himself to Jackson's tale.

"It wasn't just any curse," said Jackson. "The Chalice is said to capture the soul of the last person to possess it. To take hold of it, to torment it. The story goes that Hernán Cortés ordered an army into the dense Mexican jungle, up through the valley of the Oaxaca. Accompanied by a half-dozen Jesuit missionaries, they were in search of an ancient village of Indian mystics who, it was said, guarded a temple there. The walls of the temple were reputed to be lined in gold. The chambers filled with jade carvings and ornaments, gold and silver, emeralds, gems, and other jewels. The most sacred object of their worship was an idol, cast of solid gold, that stood over six-feet high. The statue was a representation of the powerful Aztec god Quetzalcoatl—the god of wind and air, civilization and learning. That is, if you consider human sacrifice civilized, if you consider strapping a victim to an altar and carving his beating heart from his chest cavity educational; if your god is depicted as a monster, a coiled, plumed, serpent rising from the earth, shaking the atmosphere, unleashing powerful thunderstorms, sweeping down furiously, purging the wicked and cleansing the pure."

"Where're you going with this?" Burt chirped restlessly. This was Jackson at his best, I thought. When he wrote Porter Gibson Digit's story, more than bringing him to life, you walked through it with him. Hearing Burt teeter on this one, I sensed we were on the same path.

"He's not going anywhere if you keep interrupting, Burt," said Bigwood. "Let him tell us, man."

"Mind you," Jackson continued, "as with most cosmologies, the degrees of wickedness and purity are relative to which altar one's praying before. From the Aztec's cosmology, Quetzalcoatl was a force, and their mystics controlled him. The Spaniards, three-hundred strong, had no idea what they were dealing with. Yes, they easily took the village, overwhelmed the guardians of the temple, and prepared to enter the sacred shrine.

"It was too easy, they boasted, the slaughter of women and children, caretakers and holy men. The temple, a great pyramid rising amidst the jungle, proved much more of a challenge. The commander ordered a captain to take a third of the men and a few Jesuits into the temple. Reluctantly, they entered, and soon came to a great hall, the walls of which were indeed covered in gold. Torches lined the cavernous walls around them. A ghostly amber hue covered the faces of the conquistadors as they stared spellbound, overcome with greed and lust. The captain summoned the commander, who upon entering the cathedral-like hall with his retinue, was astounded by the sight. Curiously, but for the men and torches, the room was vacant. Across the great hall a series of ramps fanned out and up leading to two broad passage ways. The commander divided his men evenly, sending half to the right passage. He led the other half to the left. Truth be told no one knows what transpired in the right passage. Except for the desperate cries and screams which echoed faintly from the depths of the inner sanctum, those men—one-hundred fifty— did not return. Is it an act of bravery or foolhardiness that drive such men to certain death? Is it honor or pride? The commander, who was well into the left passageway when they heard the faint cries, summoned the courage of his men and proceeded.

"On and on they traversed, winding, rising, descending through the dimly lit tunnel. Past ornate walls painted and carved with ferocious creatures and ungodly symbols. How long did they march? It may have been hours or even days! Or could this be? Do the walls shift? The floor move? Had all measure of time and space ceased? The men became fearful, sensing a great evil was upon them. A Jesuit priest conveyed his thoughts to the commander, that they were in the presence of the fallen one. He had marked a small cross under a mural of what surely was evidence enough they were being lured into darkness. For the mural depicted a fantastical feathered serpent rising menacingly, breathing bolts of lightning. The commander only shrugged and laughed apprehensively. 'Do not be swayed by Pagan superstition,' he told the priest. 'There's nothing here that cannot be explained.' The priest, agitated, pointed to the small cross under the serpent. Could the commander explain to him how or why they passed his mark again—for the sixth time! This was not lost on the commander who had spied the Jesuit mark the cross into the wall what seemed like days before. 'I am but a soldier, Padre,' he answered. 'We will not find what we seek standing still and we cannot stand and fight a faceless enemy. As there is no way *back* we move through this timeless abyss until we confront our demon or destiny. Like life itself, I suspect it's very much one and the same. For now, bless us and pray that we move beyond this point once and for all.' And they did, or at least it seemed so. For the air became heavier, oppressive, stifling. Further they went, barely able to withstand the heat, creeping into the inferno..."

"They were walking into hell!" Burt exclaimed.

"Shush," we hushed in a chorus.

"I knew it was hot, Bigwood," he added.

"Not now, Slocum," said Kinghorn, who himself had become entranced by the story, and waved to Jackson to continue.

"Then, what seemed at first a godsend," he said with a look toward Burt, "a numbing chill descended upon the soldiers. Their breaths billowed a hoary vapor, which became denser about them. The men shivered in the cold, frigid air. A thin rime coated their armor. With each breath they exhaled, the hoary vapor expanded until they found themselves engulfed in a thick fog. The walls sweated, coated in a blood-red resin. The fog intensified. Its essence took on the quality of incense, though dewy, with an aroma of burning hemp, except sweeter, more pungent. Unexpectedly and quite suddenly the chill in the air broke and the fog began to dissolve. It was, as they say, the *coup de grace*. The strain upon the men had reached its breaking point. For the very passage in which they stood took on a life of its own, as though breathing, pulsing. The fearsome creatures depicted on the walls took flight. Dancing, sparring, hovering, and lashing right through the soldiers. The men, frightened beyond their wits, went insane. They drew their swords and parried at the phantoms. They flayed savagely and blindly until the specters receded and dissipated into the walls and all was still. Only then did the men regain their senses and gasped in horror. The floors and walls and themselves were splattered in thick crimson. The mad frenzy had not slain the demons. They had slaughtered each other. A hundred and twenty-five men lay hacked and skewered, dead and dying. The Jesuit, who had collapsed in fright, stood up and stared at the carnage. He froze when he saw the commander gazing blankly, disemboweled and quite motionless, leaning against the wall. Instinctively, he said the last rites over him. As he prayed he stared into the commander's eyes. The priest started as he caught the reflection in the dead man's gaze. Turning slowly with dread, he noticed a small cross carved meticulously into the surface on the wall. The priest screamed in anger and desperation. He rushed at the wall in madness. When he struck it, it gave in, opening to an antechamber, filled with treasures that overflowed into another room, which he and the remaining men entered. Across from them, upon a dais, was an altar. There stood an aged Aztec shaman, grinning diabolically. On the floor lay the bones and remains of dozens of sacrificial victims. Through the carnage and gold, the Jesuit's eyes flared at the first sight of a magnificent ornate cup. It's golden aura blinding, the ceremonial chalice of the dead was before the shaman. He cast a spell over it with his hands, then raised the cup to his lips. 'Those who possess the cup and drink from the cup, shall be swallowed by the cup and possessed ever after.' As he drank from the cup a shadow spread forth from him, over him, growing larger around him. The Jesuit and soldiers reeled back, frightened. The treachery of Cortés's men was not lost on the Aztec priest. With his last breath the shaman had transferred the ruthlessness, hate, and deception enacted upon him and his people to the chalice. In a deafening thunderclap he was gone. You may think it the stuff of melodrama or voodoo, but Cortés would never see the chalice. Yes, the few men, led by the Jesuit, ransacked the temple and made their way out. I tell you now that what was left of that army was swallowed in an earthquake when it reached the edge of the village. The cup was reputed lost by the lone survivor. The man who wrote the journal of the Quetzalcoatl Temple, the Jesuit, Padre Flavio Leone, reported on his return that the Chalice was lost. But actually the Jesuit kept it for himself, smuggling it to present day Honduras where it stayed for nearly a century hidden away in the vestry of a chapel in a monastery. The very monastery where Father Leone was found dead one morning, an inverted pentagram branded into his forehead.

"There the cup remained until discovered by a Spanish Viceroy, Hector Fuentes, while preparing to deflower a native girl in the back of the chapel. The girl recoiled in fear at the sight of the cup, knowing full well its cursed legacy. Hector was not so lucky. He died an horrific death shortly thereafter from a gonorrheal infection. The disease that claimed him was such a severe strain, so painful, that the locals reported that his dick rotted off in a blistering foul blackish pus before succumbing to the inevitable."

"Damn," Slocum whispered, looking tense and uneasy.

"There's more, Burt," said Jackson, "and I could go on, but I don't want to get *too* heavy. Let me say this—one tragic story after another continued to befall all who took ownership of the Chalice till that fateful day, when, unbeknownst to its crew, it was brought aboard that fated Spanish galleon. As the Aztec shaman had forewarned, all who possess the cup shall become a victim to its power. Each of the gems encrusted on it—emeralds the size of large stones—is said to house the souls of the possessed in a fiery torment. And it would seem that's been the case. Right up to the fateful day that Red Beard seized it. You all know what happened to him. God only knows if the treasure is indeed buried here along with the damned Chalice, but what we're hearing now, this could be the sign to turn and run." He looked around the circle. "That's the full story." There was an awkward moment of calm.

"Jackson," said Kinghorn, finally. "Are you *sure* you haven't forgotten anything?"

"Where in God's name did you hear that?" said Bigwood. "That was pretty intense."

"That's an understatement," I added.

"I've heard that story my whole life,' said Jackson. "Nearly every camp-fire and cookout. Cripes! Why else do you think I'm here? I wanted to see for myself if there was any truth to it."

"I'm not sure if I want to know the truth," I said.

"You mean there really *is* a pirate treasure?" Burt's voice wavered hesi-tantly. "Gold?"

"Do you see any treasure?" Kinghorn answered, frustrated. I guess he was in a fix because the cover story was all but blown, but I also think that good old Jackson had him by the balls like the rest of us.

"It's part of the legend, Burt," said Jackson. "That's all. A legend that's as old as any in this port. Stories of pirate gold and El Diablo's Chalice, yes. And it's supposed to have been buried over there," he pointed to Clapp Island. "But now we think it's buried here. Anyone who has ever given any thought to it—who's ever been intimate with the details of the legend—knows there's a reason that it's never been found. That reason is, quite simply, because the deal old Red Beard made with his maker was so profound and eternal, that all who ventured near his mark would, too, be forever cursed and haunted by it till their dying day!"

"Yeah?" Burt swallowed hard, looking like he'd been possessed.

"Yes! It's still not too late to run. It may save your immortal soul if you do!" Jackson sang out with an evangelical fervor.

There was a momentary pause. For a second I was thinking of sprinting myself. It's a funny thing. As a kid you never really fear the boogey man until you're left in a room by yourself at night and you have to confront the demon. Sitting in bed in the semi-darkness, staring ferociously, intently, forcefully at the closet door across the room, waiting for the monster to barrel through and devour you. Now, that I'm writing these words is a testament to the fact that that closet door never did open. But at that moment in time, on that hunk of granite, sand, and stunted cedar, after listening to Jackson roll on and on about the curse, surrounded by manly men engaged in manly activities of manliness, I was ready to run. But I was distracted from the thought when old Burt simply stood up and sprinted off. "I'll see you on the other side of this rock," was all he said, running back from where we came.

Confusion abounded on all sides. I didn't know what was going to happen next. The storm had finally died down and it wouldn't surprise me if we all threw in the pitchfork—no pun intended—and blasted off. That was just before two things happened. "That'll teach him to diss my uncle Porter," Jackson laughed. So did we all until we heard the echo from across the way. The hideous laugh and moan rose and fell again.

"What do you say we give Bullethead a call?" Bigwood proposed suddenly. "Just so we know where he's at."

"Good idea," I said, as we all reached for our phones at once.

"I have no reception," Bigwood said. "I specifically checked for that when I got off the boat."

"I don't get it," said Kinghorn. "The cell phones worked fine before the storm."

"I have no service, either" Jackson looked up confused.

"Me either," I added.

"Are you trying to tell me that we're stranded here?" Bigwood asked with frustration.

"Well I wouldn't say we're exactly stranded here, Gilligan," Kinghorn replied.

"I told you that we should have had Bullethead rendezvous at a certain time," said Bigwood. "Now we're going to be here all fucking night."

"We're not going to be here all fucking night," said Kinghorn calmly. "Don't go Burt on me."

"I'm not going Burt on you. All I mean is that it's going to get foggy soon enough. It usually does this time of year. When the fog rolls in there's no way Bullethead will chance bringing the *Jolly Mr. Johnson* near this rock."

"Can we not think about that right now," I said.

"We're just talking shop," said Bigwood. As he did the moaning sound rose and fell again. This time without the wind or storm or whatever it was distorting it. The sound came from the other side of the bushes.

"Didn't you say we were close to the cove, Bigwood?" Jackson asked quietly.

"Yes. The cove is on the other end of the shoreline," he responded quietly. "We're almost there. We follow the shore for about another forty or fifty yards. Down to the point. There's a big boulder. The cove is right around the other side of it."

Jackson stood up, moving behind the shrubs, listening to Bigwood talk. "Guys, you better come see this," he said softly, indicating we should zip up. We all peered through the stunted trees and thick bushes to the shoreline. On the opposite end of the beach were five men. One of them was on the ground.

It was a good ways away, but you could still see that the dude was in obvious pain. His leg looked bloodied and slightly mangled. The other four were standing around cavorting, ignoring the guy on the ground. They were in shorts and combat boots. All looked pretty wet, which meant that they had been caught in the storm, too. Three of them were shirtless and had tattoos over their arms and upper torsos. Most disturbing of all was that each of them had side arms. They looked like a cross between cowboys from the old west and lumberjacks from the north woods.

"This is a most unfortunate development," said Bigwood uneasily.

"Not really what I had in mind when we were planning the expedition," said Kinghorn in a low voice. "By the looks of them they've been here for a day or two."

"So what's your read?" Jackson looked at both of them. "Or need I ask?"

"Who are those hombres?" I asked under my breath. I threw the question out even though the answer was fairly obvious.

"Well, in a nutshell, by the looks of them, smugglers," Bigwood surmised. "Probably dope smugglers."

"What?" I spoke softly. "Whatever happened to those fun loving, dope smoking, stoner, Jimmy Buffet-types in Hawaiian shirts?"

"The fun loving, stoner types smoke the dope and laugh," said Kinghorn. "That hasn't changed—not that I'd know anything about that. But these guys, they move it for a living. They're professionals."

"By the looks of them I'd say they haven't laughed in a long time," said Bigwood as an afterthought. "My guess is that these guys and that dope that washed up in your backyard are connected."

"You think they might be here looking for it?" It was the first thing that came into mind. One of those brief moments of clarity that increasingly elude me with each passing day.

"It's as good a guess as any," Kinghorn answered. "But I think you're probably right about that. I seriously doubt that they're out here bird watching, eh Bigwood?"

"Not the cedar waxwing kind of crowd," replied Bigwood. "Take a good hard look at them."

I did. At first I thought my eyes were deceiving me. Was it the sun or the reflection of light on the water? No. The biggest, bad ass looking one was all too familiar. His shirt was off and he had pistols holstered on each hip. A hunting knife was strapped to his right calf. Jim Bowie would have blushed. The thing was the size of a machete. It could have been the tattoo across his breast, right over his heart. A skull and crossbones. That struck me. Even at this distance I could see it clearly. But that's not what threw me and the others off. It was the thick, bushy hair and beard, long and curly and as fiery red as the setting sun. "My God! Is that One-Eyed Red Beard over there or am I having a psychotic episode?" I spit out.

"This is surreal," Bigwood exhaled slowly.

"Are we talking real-life, fucking pirates here?" whispered Jackson.

"Either that or we just stumbled into hell itself," replied Kinghorn.

"Yeah, maybe the storm conjured up One-Eyed Red Beard himself," said Bigwood, toying with the notion.

"That's real funny," I spoke softly. "Inside I'm laughing. Outside I'm filled with the irony of Burt actually having the last laugh."

We were staring silently at the distant shore. Wondering what the next move would be. The guy on the ground moaned out again. Big Red apparently didn't like it. He turned at him, picked up a nearby duffel bag and heaved it at him, but missed. The other guys all ducked when he threw the bag, like it could have blown. Then he walked over and kicked the injured guy hard in his mangled leg. The guy screeched. Red Beard pulled one of his pistols out threateningly, aiming right between his eyes. The guy, in all of his agony, writhing in pain, shut up.

"Don't make a sound," said Kinghorn under his breath. "Let's just back out of here. If we're lucky, maybe we can get phone reception on the side of the island we came in on."

"That storm probably saved our collective asses," Bigwood reflected. "We were probably a minute or two away from walking right into them."

"Probably why we didn't hear them," Jackson weighed in.

"Probably why they didn't hear us," Bigwood added.

"Looks like *she* was looking out for you today after all, Bigwood," Jackson forced a smile.

"Let me add, as the devil's advocate, that the day isn't over yet," said Bigwood. "If I know her like I think I do, and I know her very well, she's got bigger plans for us than a thunderstorm." He hesitated, looking out through the bushes, down the shoreline. "That storm scare was merely an appetizer."

"Like I said, let's back out of here real quietly," Kinghorn spoke silently. "We get to the dock, we're on the opposite side of the island, and the phones were working there. If not, it's a waiting game. Bullethead's apt to swing back at some point, even if it's out of curiosity."

The plan, in theory, was good enough for me. I wanted to get as far from those dudes as I could. I make no bones about it. I am afraid of people with guns. Call it what you like, cowardice, yellow, chicken—I don't care. Guns make me ill at ease. They always have. I get the heebie-jeebies when I'm around those big city cops with the side arms the size of bazookas. And those are the good guys! I was all for moving out, pronto-like. All we had to do was back out quietly like Kinghorn said. Distance ourselves from the banditos. We were going to do it, too, I swear. But that's about the time that Burt came plodding back through the bushes, stumbling in the gravelly soil and cursing loudly.

"You asshole, Jackson!" he shouted caustically. "What the fuck's your problem?" We all tried to shush him up before he gave us away. It was too late. I glanced quickly down the shore. Red Beard's ears had pricked up and his head turned quickly. We had the cover but they had heard us. All the buccaneers looked in our direction. In unison they reached for their pistols. Mangled-leg guy began to crawl away behind some rocks. He was the least of our problems. The other four crouched slightly. A pack of jackals picking up the first scent of fresh blood. They said nothing. Red Beard motioned with his hand and silently they fanned out towards us. When I saw them break out, let me tell you, it really added another dimension to the concept of the word fucked. "Holy shit!" I mumbled. My mouth went dry, my lower tract quaked, and my asshole clamped shut.

Meanwhile, Burt's summarily ignoring our pleas to shut up. The guy was too busy unloading another salvo of invectives. His yapping was a veritable homing beacon for the psycho-pirate-smugglers, who were moving at us quickly by following the sound. I'm not sure what they could see through the thick bushes and overgrowth. If they could actually see any of us. I took my cue from Kinghorn, always the able organizer, stalwart Rock of Gibraltar, quiet leader. "Run away!" He shouted amidst the growing pandemonium. We dropped the equipment in unison. Burt was still standing there cursing when each of us bolted by him. I swear both feet were off the ground when I launched past him. "Run you dolt!" Kinghorn hollered at him. Yet, for a split second our friend from DIM stood in defiance. Burt wouldn't be fooled again by a carefully executed ploy to make an ass of him. That was the second before the shots rang out. "Blam! Blam! Blam!" The bullets whizzed through the tree limbs above us. That got his attention. All I saw of him was a streak dart by me. As the blur passed I picked up a whiff of bowel in the air stream. I think Bigwood must have, too, because he was ahead of me and Jackson was behind me. When Slocum went past us Bigwood veered off to the right pronto and we followed. The three of us were heading into the interior. Kinghorn and Burt were running back from whence we came.

The next thing I know I'm out of breath laid up in a thicket of bushes and small boulders. Bigwood and Jackson are next to me. We're all trying to catch our breath. My heart's pounding. I don't know if it was luck or instinct that made me follow Bigwood. Though, if I may interject, I learned a long time ago to follow my instincts, even if the gambit *de jour* was against my better interests. When your intuition speaks to you—listen! Why fight it? Some may say it's your guardian angel whispering in your ear. Others, steeped in cosmology, will tell you it's the universe guiding you along. Then there's the school of thought of the divine id—that inner self which exists in a state of absolute clarity. That place of no doubt, no confusion, no hesitation. Maybe it's all three, really. The delineation mere philosophical constructs. Who am I to know such things? Cause when it came right down to it, right then and there, I was playing a hunch. I was happy to follow Bigwood because he knew the island better than any of us.

"What is this place?" Jackson asked, panting. We were burrowed in a near imperceptible nook, like a crow's nest. Completely surrounded by a thick growth of bushes over a bunch of boulders. Bigwood had led us to the perfect hiding spot.

"I have no idea," Bigwood replied, taking a deep breath. "It just looked like good cover."

I didn't know what to make of the place, either. We had been sprinting along a makeshift trail, rising higher as we moved through the interior. Dashing and darting in and around the flora, fauna, and chunks of granite. I couldn't have gone much further at the pace we were moving when we hit the crest of the island. I glanced quickly ahead and viewed the mighty Atlantic in the distance. The breeze in my face. In another time and place it would have been one of those awe inspiring moments that a Thoreau, Longfellow, or Frost would have coveted. Yet, the poetry eluded me and my fellow prey, diluted by fear. Not knowing if the jackals were to or fro, we were running out of steam. Just over the crest, as the trail sloped down, Bigwood spied a copse of bushes above. Without hesitation we scrambled steeply ten feet or so up, and dove blindly over the thicket like lemmings off a cliff. The nook had a feel about it, like it was out of place, or more aptly, placed. You could pretty much see all around the island and beyond, up and down the coast, the mainland, the deep blue sea.

"You couldn't have picked a better spot," I said in a low voice, distracted by the view.

"It's like a lookout or something," Jackson added. We were no more than thirty or forty feet above sea level. But it was a gradual, haphazard, unassuming rise to this height. We were high enough to see the Atlantic. I could hear waves crashing below, too, which meant that somehow, in our mad dash we had looped back. We were not that far from where we intended to be. Unfortunately, the rise was not high enough to see down to the shoreline or the cove. Actually we couldn't even see that far down the trail or anywhere else those freaks could lay in waiting or track us.

"I just happened to look up at the right time," Bigwood whispered, still panting. "When in doubt, I always take the high ground. Metaphorically and practically, it's better to see the forest *and* the trees."

"Yeah." I had a half grin on my face and was still catching my breath. "That's why I followed *you*."

"Did I mention that, besides, if I didn't stop running I was going to keel over," he added.

"What do you suppose happened to Kinghorn and Burt?" Jackson asked. Beads of sweat trailed off his forehead and down his face slowly. "Do you think they got away?"

"The question is did they find a good enough place to hide?" answered Bigwood, rhetorically. We were looking through the heavy wall of underbrush down the trail. "I've never played hide and seek when the stakes were this high. I know that Kinghorn hasn't either, and God knows if Burt's done much of anything."

"So what's with that guy?" said Jackson, irritated. "Where did you dig him *up*?"

"The guy's imbalanced!" I added. "He almost got us killed."

"It's hard to explain," Bigwood replied, breathing a bit easier. "We needed to make this official. You just can't go around digging up public property." We nodded like we knew what he was talking about. "Kinghorn knows Burt. They grew up in the same neighborhood—he really did date his sister when they where teenagers."

"No shit?" I said.

"True. So he told him about the skeleton I found and the prospects for the gravesite. Nothing about the treasure, that it could have been pirates. We wanted to know our options with the state. Honestly, we didn't expect him to come, but he insisted. Said he had to accompany us to protect the integrity of the project." Bigwood rolled his eyes.

"So he's just plain rude and not as numb as I thought," said Jackson.

"I realized that this is all turned upside down," said Bigwood. "We came here on a long shot, to see if there is pirate gold buried on this rock. Imagine if we found it. All the legal expertise in the world will not help you if you don't have the right people on your side. In this case it's Burt."

"All that may be true, Bigwood," answered Jackson. "But the guy's put us in a hell of a jam."

"No offense, Jackson," Bigwood sounded a bit piqued, or maybe it was frustration, or anxiety. "Who was the one that spooked him with that story?"

"First of all, you wanted to hear the story, too, and everything I said is part of the local legend," Jackson replied defensively. "I didn't make it up. And I did say *legend*! People have talked about hearing strange, fleeting cries of desperation around these shores for centuries. And secondly, I was playing with him, man. Okay? I had no idea that the guy would freak out and takeoff. Nobody else ran away."

"Guys," I jumped in. "We don't have time to bicker here. God knows especially not over Burt." Jackson's mouth opened like he was about to respond, but he paused. There was a shift, a presence. We could all feel it. Sort of like when a person comes into a room and you know he's there before you see him, hear him, or before he speaks. It was like that. And it happened quickly.

The rush of footfalls was upon us, treading lightly, imperceptibly. We fell into silence. From our perch in the nook we could see a guy in a knit cap with mangy, dark hair drooling out from under it. He was wearing cut-off fatigues with combat boots, stalking quietly. We were close enough to see a tattoo of a snake coiled around a dagger on the side of his upper calf. Beside him, standing taller, was Red Beard himself. He was a big motherfucker, muscular and menacing. The skull and crossbones on his chest laughed at me. His red hair was flaming, thick, tangled and serpentine; moving in the wind like Medusa's. One look in our direction and I would surely turn to stone. We needed a miracle. What were the prospects? It wasn't like three against two. These guys had guns. They had already fired on us for no reason other than we had seen them, which somehow threatened them. And now they were twenty or so feet away.

Red Beard and mangy-hair stopped at the crest as we had minutes earlier. Mangy-hair began to sniff the air. Red Beard was looking down through the rocks, studying the landscape—searching, seeking, pressing. Mangy-hair was moving his head slowly, continuing to sniff, like he was trying to pick up our scent. Incredible. Could he actually be honing in on us?

I know that neither of them could see into the nook. Yet, I had the feeling that he could actually smell us. Not in a funky B.O. way, but in an out of sorts type way. Picking up the scent that did not belong. Maybe I was reading too much into it. I'm only telling you this because that's what he did. When his head stopped in our direction he looked down, sniffed a bit, and took a few paces right at us.

"They went right through here, Red," mangy-hair grunted, sniffing rapidly about again. "It's fresh, too. The air reeks of them. It reeks of fear!"

Red!!? I thought to myself. Impossible! Surreal! Did I hear right? After everything that had gone down since we landed on the island, this was the balls. Had we slipped into another dimension in the wake of that storm? Broken the time barrier and crossed into the unknown?

"Might you just fucking show me which God-damned direction they went, Tar?" Red Beard snapped. "And I'll show them what fear means!" And I was convinced that he would. As it was the pressure was immense, the intensity overwhelming.

"That's just it, Red," he pondered. "It's all around me, the dread, it stinks of it." He turned toward us again and drew a long, sharp whiff. The guy had a narrow, aquiline nose. The stubble on his chin and neck was greasy. His face was covered in grime. Across his upper torso was scar tissue from old gunshot wounds and knife fights. Oversized pock marks in a mish-mash of connect the dots. "They've gone this way," he said, pointing in our direction.

"Be sure, Tar!" Red Beard demanded of him. "We're wasting time standing here. No man escapes this island."

"You think they know about *it?*" Tar asked, hesitating.

"The gold?" Red Beard replied, bothered. "No one does. We haven't been here that long, but we're running out of time. The boat should be here around five."

"How are we gonna pull it off Red?"

"We'll salvage what we can and hide the rest. It's safe to say no one will find it there."

"What about Wolfman, Lister, and Jimmy? You think it will be safe? You said that about Panama."

"I'd be worried about myself if you bring up Panama again," Red Beard threatened him. "Wolfman and Lister are the least of my concerns. Jimmy isn't gonna make it off this rock. I know that. Sure as I know they'll be no other witnesses when we sail off this rock. We take no prisoners. They've seen too much! We'll tie them all up, throw them in that hole, and blow them all to hell. Just like those others, they'll never be found."

What the hell were they talking about? We hadn't even seen anything but them and a shit load of rock. Tar stepped a few more paces in our direction, his nose skyward. Sniffing intensely, he was coming right at us. The three of us burrowed down in the nook. I could easily hear his foot slip on some gravel. The guy was rising, nearing the thicket with each whiff he took. The crux of it was plain and simple. We were fucked. Fucked beyond the pale. Fucked beyond fucked. We were at sixes and sevens. How did I get here? To actually believe that I could find a lost treasure? Come here on a search for pirate's loot and stumble upon a real-life Beelzebub and his mangy cohort of demons. All this amidst an ongoing dope investigation affiliated with the hotel. In less than an hour I'd gone from nearly quick-fried by lightning bolts to being shot at and hunted down like a wild dog. Just once! Just one time in my life why couldn't a simple little plan go as, well, planned? It wasn't like I needed to find pirate treasure or booty. My life is full enough. I'm a regular guy with a wife and two kids, a dog, a mortgage, a caring family, and just the right dose of insanity to keep the ball rolling. I just went on this gig for a few laughs. Really. It was a diversion from the mundane. Do a little bonding with the boys. And now this. Stuck on an island. Trapped with no where to go or hide but a shallow nook where we were about to be exposed by some freak of nature who had an olfactory bulb akin to the hound of the Baskervilles.

My back leaned into the base of the nook. My hand fell upon a rock. It was loose, about the size of an Aroostook County potato, and I grasped it. If that son of a bitch stuck his nose into our den it would be the last thing he'd ever smell. His sentient being would return to the bowels of the frozen hell from whence he came. Fuck it. What the hell did I have to lose? I noticed that Bigwood had a rock, too, then Jackson grabbed one. Tar was right on us. I could hear him whiff and sniff. Just steps away from being brained and done with. But, at the near moment of discovery, in the far distance below, several shots fired off in succession. That got their attention.

"Tar!" Red Beard shouted. "That's what I've been waiting to here. Sounds like the boys 'ave got 'em on the run."

"But, Red," Tar implored.

"Hear me man!" Red Beard ordered him sharply. "Let's move. We're running out of time!"

Tar said no more and in an instant they were gone. We had a stay of execution. At whose expense, though?

"What a freak!" Bigwood broke the silence with a sense of relief.

"He was like some wolf," said Jackson.

"Really!" I said, throwing my rock to the base of the nook, which made a dull thud. "What was that about the gold? Did you guys hear that?"

"Yeah," Bigwood said. "One-hundred percent Colombian Gold. I told you they were smugglers."

"They're probably here to salvage dope," said Jackson. "There must have been an accident."

"I think you're right Jackson," said Bigwood. "I think these guys are here on a down and dirty clean up operation and waiting for their rendezvous."

"We picked a fine day!" I scoffed.

"What the fuck are we going to do now?" Jackson asked, piqued.

"Hey!" I said. "Why not try to swim ashore, or to one of the other islands?"

I thought it was brilliant myself, but Bigwood looked doubtful. "Even to cross the channel to one of the other islands we'd be in great peril. The currents are too strong here, the water's too cold, and there are blue sharks in these waters."

"Good," I replied. "For a second there I thought you were going to say that we didn't stand a fucking chance."

"Okay. Let's just say if it came down to it," Bigwood added. "I'd rather take my chances with the elements and nature then these guys."

"Till then?" Jackson asked.

"I'm not sure," Bigwood answered, juggling his rock. "I hate to think what those shots mean. This island's not that big and there's only so many hiding places."

"I would say that this is probably the best of them," said Jackson. "Which means there's only so much time..."

"Before what?" I asked apprehensively.

"Before they find one of us and we find out just how serious a game these boys are playing," Bigwood replied. At that he threw his rock sharply, angrily, into the base of the nook. I flinched in anticipation of the ricochet, but incredibly, the earth moved. Not like a quake, but gave in, absorbing the rock. A depression formed. I wasn't really thinking about the consequences or anything like that. In fact, I wasn't really thinking. For some reason I stamped on the ground where the rock landed like I was putting out a brush fire. The last sound I heard was the voice of Bigwood crying out, "No! Wait!" That was just before the cracking and snap of rotted timber, of me crashing through the bottom of the nook, which collapsed, and I... kept right on going.

We all know what happened to Alice when she fell down the hole. In that futile chase for the white rabbit her world was never quite the same. Granted,

I wasn't chasing a white rabbit, more a red herring. And it wasn't into Wonderland I fell, but a skanky chute that deposited me into the base of a pseudo-cave. A spelunker I'm not. There's always been a tendency toward claustrophobia in me I can't explain. The hole had a hideous odor, too. The rot and decay of piss clams, crabs, periwinkles and God knows what filled the air. I mean I could barely take a breath without gagging on the stink. The air was heavy with it and now I was covered in it. The base was wet and the walls were damp. Small shallow puddles of water filled the crannies on the bottom. When my eyes finally adjusted to the dimness I could see that where I was standing was tidal. The cave was more like a gaping crevice. It was asymmetrical in its dimensions, formed by massive chunks of granite tossed atop each other from the Atlantic during the last ice age. The height averaged about seven feet in some places and four or so feet at its widest. Not good for the claustrophobia, but not too bad, either. The footing was slippery. The walls were too, but were narrow enough for me to get some purchase wedging myself with both arms. The hole, or slew, was not natural. It looked like it had been gnawed and chiseled through at an angle up to the nook. Perhaps a spot or two of gunpowder had been used. Undoubtedly, the place above, our nook, must have really been a lookout.

I was staring up the chute when I heard some rumbling above me. You could make out the light seeping down the hole. I don't know how far up it was, though. I was overwhelmed amidst the rush of falling into the unknown. I slid down too fast. "I'm okay," I called up to Bigwood and Jackson. "Just a few scrapes here and there." I was about to scale out, or at least attempt to. But it was too late. One after the other they plopped into the cave beside me. Each of us was now thoroughly covered in the muck of piss clam slime.

"We thought you were hurt," said Bigwood, concerned.

"We called your name as loud as we possibly could," Jackson continued, "but you didn't reply." He paused and inhaled. "Phew! This place smells like the dumpster behind Lizard's Lobster Pound."

"Worse than that," Bigwood gagged. "It's repulsive."

As each of them adjusted to the light and stink, a momentary calm fell over us. We were safe for the time being. Jackson and Bigwood checked things out, getting their bearings.

"This is incredible!" said Bigwood. "You don't suppose this place has anything to do with Red Beard?"

"Do you mean the original or his long-lost incarnate?" I asked.

"Maybe both," Bigwood answered. "Why not? Anything could happen. This day, all this craziness. It's getting more and more surreal by the minute."

"There's only one way to find out if this is the true lair of Mephistopheles and Red Beard," said Jackson. "And it's not by going back up there." He pointed at the chute. "It's that way." Each of us looked down through the narrow crevice. "We can always come back if it dead ends."

"Yes," Bigwood agreed. "Let's follow the fresher air and see where this comes out."

That was true. There was fresher air, relatively speaking, wafting in from that direction. I had no doubt that it led back to daylight. We moved cautiously. We had to. The subterranean footing was much like it was above, minus the cedars, bushes, and stink. Our pace was slow, compounded by the lack of light. After about five minutes of carefully maneuvering through the rocks and slime we came to a halt at a bend. The crevice abruptly narrowed. We'd have to wedge our way through to continue.

"Wait a second," I said anxiously. Waves of claustrophobia, followed by dread, struck me suddenly. "What if this really was or is Red Beard's hideout? It could have traps! Sort of like Indiana Jones or something." That made them think for a moment or two.

"I don't know," Bigwood pondered. "That's a big 'what if.'"

"Well there's been no sign of him yet," said Jackson. "Nothing to raise concern."

"What about that nook we hid in?" I replied. "What about that hole we fell through? Somebody made them!"

"What I mean is that I'd expect to see more than that," Jackson responded. "Some markings or findings. Even in this shithole, through the ages, you'd think that there'd be some physical evidence, some remains that show a human presence or alteration of the environment. Check out this granite!" He slapped the walls with a whack. "Did you get a look at the hole we slid through. Not what you'd call an engineering marvel. They were lucky they had enough powder or found enough earth to dig their way through. That's all they could do. I can't see how they could do much more than that." Jackson seemed satisfied with his summation of the lack of evidence at hand. "Look, I say let's go forward and just keep an eye out for anything unnaturally placed, unusual, or contrived."

At that, he turned sideways and jimmied himself through. I swallowed hard, took a deep breath and followed. What was I thinking? I felt like I was trying to fit into a coffin a size too small by sliding into it sideways. I know it sounds wimpy, but I actually felt the first pangs of a panic attack coming over me. The slow, crushing weight of thousand pound slabs of granite sucking the life from my lungs.

"You going to go or what?" Bigwood asked me from behind.

"I can't," I answered reluctantly. My heart was pounding hard.

"Yes you can," he reassured me. "Or I'm going to push your ass through." He smiled, but put his hands on my shoulder firmly. I'm really not sure if he would have gone through with it to tell you the truth. He probably would have. I was suddenly flush with sweat, clammy and sticky. My legs and arms were in irons. I was shackled to where I stood by the grip of my own neurotic fear. I took a deep breath again. "Ready, set..." Then, in an instant, my anxiety was diverted by a terrifying, startling gasp.

"Jackson!" both Bigwood and I yelled out. No this can't be happening. Without another thought I plunged through the coffin, slipped through the narrow passage, forward into the unknown darkness ahead. Bigwood's hand was on the nape of my neck. I suddenly realized, at the moment I broke free of the grip of the wall, that we, too, could be harpooned, lanced, or disemboweled by some archaic, technologically retarded Elmer Fudd-like contraption. In a split second it would be over. Bigwood pushed me and we fell forward onto the floor of a broad natural chamber.

Jackson stood there aghast. That was a relief. He held a pocket lighter above his head, barely transcending the dimness of the room. Yet it was enough to see that Bigwood and I, as had Jackson before us, were rolling through a heap of skulls and bones. The skeletal remains of a mass murder, centuries old, but starkly frightening. I would have screamed, too, if I hadn't lost my breath when I stood up quickly and was face to face with a skeleton, dangling from a wall like a marionette. The poor bastard had been impaled into the granite wall with a steel spike right through the center of his forehead. The savagery of the scene still makes me queasy.

With extreme irony, there, amidst the ruthless execution of a dozen or so men, we viewed in a shallow carved well, through a mound of bones and skulls, a large, flat metal chest. Though long rusted and fully oxidized, you could still make out a broad Spanish cross that had been forged across the top. Red Beard had found the perfect hiding spot for his plunder on the far flung fringe of civilization. But he could not bore through solid granite. No. In its stead he buried it under the blood and flesh of his own crew. His own men served as earth. Or perhaps these men were prisoners from the HMS *Queen Bee* who were forced into brief indenture. That was more likely. The man nailed to the wall had the long tattered remains of what appeared to be some naval uniform.

"Fucking gruesome, man!" said Bigwood, disgusted.

"We thought you'd been booby-trapped," I said to Jackson. "Scared the shit out of us."

"I landed right where you guys did." He pointed at the scattered bones. "Make no mistake. That'll cure your constipation."

"I've seen a lot in my day," Bigwood reflected. "You witness some horrible things as a city cop. But this, this is an atrocity. I've never witnessed an atrocity." He looked sadly at the remains. "May they finally rest in peace." We nodded and paid silent homage. What else were we supposed to do? We did not knowingly disturb the site, and it's not like you could call this conse-crated ground. There was no protocol for such a thing.

"Well?" Jackson asked as though reading my mind. "You can't really say we'd be disturbing a proper gravesite, could you?"

"Not really," I said. "There's nothing proper about what happened here."

"I think we can agree on that," Bigwood added, studying the scene. "Could you help me with this?" He looked at me while glancing at the chest.

"You mean touch the bones?" I asked, repulsed. "Dead people's bones!?" Pathetic, I know.

"This is the culmination of three centuries of searching," said Bigwood. "The stuff legends are made of."

"There before us," added Jackson, solemnly. "It's what men have sought for hundreds of years. El Diablo's Chalice! The embodiment of the anti-Grail. Drink from its cup and enjoy your ride to hell. All that was and would be of the New World is in that box. No greater symbol of greed, avarice, and betrayal in the name of progress and the holy cross. How many men, how many people have died because of it? Trying to find it? Been cursed, crucified, and exterminated for it? Shall it be in vain? Over a few bones? Or are we going to lift the lid and take a look. See if it's been worth it. The suffering, the sacrifice, and the advance of Western Civilization!"

What was I supposed to say? What would you have said? Bigwood and I looked at each other. We reached into the bones. He had one side and I the other. I can't recall if we even bothered to move aside the piles of bones. I think we simply lifted the box gently, carefully, and let the bones fall where they may. All I can remember is watching Bigwood, there on his knees, the ancient chest before him, his eyes fixed intently on it. In the semidarkness, in the absolute quietude of anticipation, we stared. I had forgotten about everything.

The storm, the chase, the fact that in our moment of discovery we were being hunted by a pack of jackals. That, as we stared at the last resting place of El Diablo's Chalice, Kinghorn and Burt were in great peril, perhaps even shot. My mind was vacant. All that we had endured slipped away in the moment. Excitedly, Bigwood pawed at the lock and clasp. It fell apart easily, as though rusted, rotted or already busted. My breath was taken away. My heart was palpitating. He pushed the lid up, its hinges creaked loudly, then gasped in awe. Incredulously, before us, in the chest was the vacuous glare from the sunken orbital cavity of a long forgotten skull. Nothing else I tell you. It was all a ruse.

"Shit!" Bigwood shouted. The anti-climax was a true ball buster. "I can't believe that I could have actually been so fucking numb." He was disgusted with himself. "What a fucking day! I've endangered all of us. God knows what's happened to my partner? And now we're trapped in a fucking tomb at the bottom of this God-forsaken rock on the edge of the Atlantic!"

"Ease up, Bigwood," I said. "Who could have known it would have turned out like this? We all took a chance."

"He's right, Alex," said Jackson. "It's been a hellish day, and a hell of an adventure, too. I don't know how it's going to end, but I do know that no one put a gun to my head to be here. I was following a dream."

"More like a nightmare," Bigwood responded, sullenly.

"Just because you fucked up doesn't mean you have to walk the plank," I consoled him, smiling. "We still think you're a beautiful man."

Bigwood stood up and took a deep breath. "There," he sighed. "Let's get the fuck out of this place before something else happens."

"Like what?" I asked.

"Like that, for starters," he responded, pointing to the floor. A minor gush of water had spilled onto the base of the cave. "Just in case you were wondering where all these piss clams came from, or why this place smells like crab shit. The tide's coming in, and I really don't want to be around to see how high it goes."

It's not like we were going to stay hiding there forever. But in the past thirty minutes or so, it was kind of nice not to have angry, wild men with pistols racing after us. The momentary thought of finding actual pirate booty and the cursed chalice had let our attention drift. It added to the false security of the moment. That said, I assure you the mood shift back to self-preservation mode was swift. About as swift as the next tidal surge that poured in and sucked out in an instant. That one made some of the bones rattle, and put us on the move. Honestly, I was all too happy to leave the chamber of horrors. We had to slouch under a low, narrow fissure, and step over chunk of granite, which may have sealed off the chamber at one time, but now lay in pieces. Once out of the tomb, the air quality substantially improved. The passage was slightly broader and higher, too, and the footing had leveled off to a mixture of crushed shells, gravel, and coarse sand.

"How the hell could this place go undetected for three-hundred years?" I asked, plodding forward. "I mean, it seems inconceivable that no one has ever stumbled on this place."

"Who's to say that no one's ever been here?" Bigwood asked.

"I can't believe it, really," Jackson replied. "It just doesn't make sense, no one ever seeing this cave."

"Maybe, maybe not," Bigwood said. We had only taken a few steps when he stopped abruptly, just short of a turn. "Suppose the entrance way is blocked or so obscured that the only way anyone could find this place is *fall* into it, if you know what I mean. That tomb back there was shut up at one time for sure. And really? Who ever comes here? When's the last time you were out here, Jackson?"

"Actually, I have to admit," he answered. "I've gone by many times lobstering or sailing, fished a few times from the old dock Bergmeister dropped us off on, but I've never wandered around the island."

"Because it was supposedly haunted?" I asked.

"Give me a break! Will you? It's not like the place is that accessible, and I had no particular interest to come here. And if I may note, this will probably be the last time I come here, in case you guys are thinking about a reunion in the future."

"That's what I mean," Bigwood countered. "Yes, all the locals may know of the island's lore, but take it for what it is—legend. Tales spin around these islands."

"If you mean chasing buried treasure, when all the silver bars were found after the hurricane of 1938, those stories died off," Jackson added. "I remember that because Grandpa Jeff and Uncle Porter used to come out to Goat Island and Frenchman's Island treasure hunting. My grandfather talked about those days with Uncle Porter quite a lot. Funny, now that I think of it, they never once mentioned coming here to look."

"See, that doesn't surprise me," Bigwood said. "This island's uninhabited and uninhabitable, near inaccessible and impassable. It's a tough hike, and long perceived to be spooked. It's kept people away. I've been here a few times birding. Our bird group came out here once, we froze our asses off and got shit on by a bunch of seagulls. Then, recently, as you know. That was exciting news. Lizard had told me one afternoon in the diner. Said that one of his crews had spotted a colony of puffins here while lobstering. I couldn't wait to come out here and check it out," Bigwood gushed. "Such a rare sighting this far south, let alone a colony, I wanted to be the first to document it."

"The way you're talking," Jackson said. "I swear it makes you hard."

"This isn't a sexual thing for you, is it?" I added.

"You're daft, each of you," said Bigwood. "I'm not going to go into a whole dissertation defending the fact that I enjoy nature."

"Which includes watching puffins mate?" I responded. "They're fucking puffins! ...Get it!?" For the first time in a while we actually laughed.

"All I'm getting at is why we're the first ones in centuries to have discovered this hideous stink hole of a cave, not the *ins and out* of ornithology," said Bigwood. "I never bumped into anyone while I was here. I saw no boats within a hundred yards of the shoreline, either. Saw no signs of anyone having been here, no cigarette butts, trash, or that telltale sign of a true hangout, a fire pit with broken beer bottles and used condoms tossed about."

"Well that's great!" said Jackson dejectedly. "Cause I was really counting on being rescued by a bunch of drunken, horny teenagers."

"Strangers things have happened," said Bigwood.

"How much fucking stranger can this day get?" I retorted. "We're trapped on an island, nearly quick-fried by lightning, being hunted by maniacs, fall into a pit, and find the remnants of a grisly murder. If I do make it out of here alive I'm going to need therapy for the next twenty years."

"You've got a microbrewery at your beck and call," Bigwood replied. "That's all the therapy anyone could ever ask for."

"Depends on the booze-to-trauma ratio," Jackson added. "There may not be enough vats."

"Look, we're going to get out of here alive, okay?" Bigwood said confidently. "And no one's going to need therapy, short of a hearty bender."

"You mean some day we'll all look back on this and laugh?" I asked.

"Or scream," Bigwood snapped. "Besides, though the treasure was for naught, think of it this way—we did make an amazing, though gruesome, archeological discovery!"

"Still, it just makes you wonder why," Jackson said, ignoring Bigwood. "You'd have thought that someone would have found this cave over time."

"I'm not disagreeing with you Jackson," Bigwood answered. "But no one apparently ever has. To begin with those poor bastards back there would have had a proper burial. It would have been the talk of the town. A tourist Mecca would have blossomed in the wilderness. A huckster's wet dream—island tours, t-shirts, and coffee mugs with Red Beard's face on them. Sleazy dives with rancid urinal cakes in the head, cluttering the waterfront."

"Like 'Pirate's Cove' or the 'Bouncing Buccaneer,'" I said.

"Exactly," Bigwood responded. "Now we'll have to confront an onslaught of developers from New York and Miami, too, who are going to show up and tell us what we've been doing wrong for the past four centuries. It's gonna be pretty hard to contain the pandemonium when word reaches the mainland about what we've discovered here."

"You mean *if* we ever get off this island," Jackson corrected him.

"Now you're starting to sound like Burt," said Bigwood.

"Enough already," Jackson interrupted. "I get the picture. We're on our way to Pottersville. But you're still missing my point. Not only are we stuck here, it doesn't seem possible that no one's ever stumbled on this cave. Even a blind squirrel will bumble on an acorn in the dark."

"Only if he's hungry, Jackson," Bigwood replied.

"You know, you can tell that you've gone to law school, Bigwood," Jackson snapped. "Because every damned attorney I've ever know has to have the last word."

"What the hell is that about?" Bigwood asked, irritated and offended.

"Can't you just agree with me that it's incredible that no one's ever found this fucking cave? What are the fucking odds of that?"

"Okay, I agree," Bigwood said. "And for the record I did say I wasn't disagreeing with you."

"See," said Jackson. "That's what I mean about the last word."

"Hey you two!" I said quietly to them. "I don't mean to interrupt a lover's quarrel, but do you hear that?" The ocean rose and fell. You could hear it, louder, just ahead, right around a bend.

"You mean the sound of the ocean?" Jackson asked as a shallow tidal rush foamed up and retreated at our feet. "'Cause if that's what you mean it's like my head has been stuck in a fucking sea shell for the past forty-five minutes." Old Jackson sounded a bit manic at this point, and on the edge. I can't blame him, though. I wasn't that far behind him.

"Not that," I answered. "Listen! Is that grunting?" I hadn't noticed that before because of Bigwood's and Jackson's bickering. The sound was distinct, now. We could all hear it. The grunting louder, more audible as we drew closer to the bend.

"It's a wild boar!" Jackson breathed excitedly. "The cave's inhabited by wild boars!"

"Ease up, will you?" Bigwood whispered. "Wild boars?" he chuckled to himself. "I doubt it." Though by the sound of his voice, there was plenty of doubt in it, and he was having second thoughts. I'll give him credit. Bigwood burst ahead without thinking twice, but stopped in his tracks when he turned at the bend. "Holy shit!" The guy nearly choked he was so flabbergasted. At the risk of being gored, we rushed up behind him. There are not enough words for me to aptly describe to you the shock I felt when I turned the corner. The front end of the cave gaped open wide. A short rise, like a natural ramp, led us out of the glorified hole we had been slithering through. As though we climbed out of the belly and into the... *jaws of a whale!* The cave arced somewhat. A keystone boulder randomly tossed up from the Atlantic eons ago jutted twelve feet above our heads. The rise settled into the center of the space, which was fairly broad and flat, relatively speaking—a good ten feet or more on either side and to the entry way. There, and throughout the space, stacked neatly along the walls outward in rows, were dozens and dozens of barrels and crates of booze—whiskey, rum, and scotch. We were standing in a veritable mini-warehouse, untouched since prohibition. The booze was stacked high and tight right to a low triangular corner slot where the light of day broke in unevenly. One case, busted open, was on the ground, near the way out.

"The Whale's Jaw," uttered Jackson, overwhelmed. "I never thought... never dreamed... This is the secret that Grandpa Jeffah went to prison for." He evinced a veneration, a reverence, as though we stood before a monument, a dedication to a long forgotten war. "He took the secret with him to the grave. I wonder if Uncle Porter knew?" he asked, a bit forlorn.

I didn't know how to respond, not sure if this was one of those times to shut up and listen or say something comforting. Even so, before Bigwood or I said anything we were startled by that grunting sound and a high-pitched squeal, somewhat muffled. We jumped in fright. The squeal went off again, right up front on the other side of a row of crates. "Wait a second!" Bigwood cried out, alarmed. "Kinghorn?" The squeal erupted urgently. We quickly found him and Burt, hog tied, blindfolded, and gagged.

"Buddy!" Bigwood mouthed excitedly. "What have they done to you?" Kinghorn had been pummeled. His face was red, welted, bloodied and swollen. Burt, on the other hand, didn't have a scratch.

"I'll make it," said Kinghorn, spitting out a mix of blood and saliva. "Good to see you guys."

"Yeah, what took you?" Burt chided us.

"My God! Where are we?" Kinghorn blurted out.

"The old-timers called this place the Whale's Jaw," said Jackson.

"I heard them talking," said Kinghorn, "like they'd made an unbelievable find."

"This place is incredible," I said. "You're not going to believe what's back there, either."

"Never mind that now," Bigwood interrupted. "We'll explain everything later. We should get out of here."

"Yes," said Jackson helping Kinghorn up. "This place give's me the creeps."

"We thought you were goners," I said. "We heard shots."

"That was to let the others know that they'd caught us," Kinghorn winced. "They showed up in a hurry."

"We're okay," Burt added.

"I wanted to get to the dock, make a phone call, but those guys were too fast," said Kinghorn. "We had to hide."

"It wasn't the greatest place," Burt added. Kinghorn rolled his eyes.

"What happened?" asked Bigwood, balancing Kinghorn against him.

"The pair of thugs chasing us had just passed," said Kinghorn. "We were all but free to sneak away, but Burt here farted loud and nasty and gave us away."

"They would have found us," Burt said, defensively.

"They tried to persuade me to tell them where you were," Kinghorn grinned, painfully.

"Yeah, they tried to persuade us," Burt quipped. "But I didn't tell them anything."

Then and there I thought Bigwood was about to level Burt. Kinghorn must have read his mind because he quickly added, as an afterthought, "Bigwood, don't waste your time. We got to move. I think the only reason we weren't eighty-six'd was to flush you out."

"Yeah, we're hostages," said Burt, eagerly.

"All of them are psychopaths," said Kinghorn, disgusted, "but that Red Beard's a fucking monster."

"Didn't your mother ever tell you," a voice from the back of the cave called out, "that it's not polite to talk about people behind their backs." We jumped. My bowels loosened. Tar and two goons were standing half way up the ramp, their pistols drawn. They'd found the nook and tracked us down. "I told Red I'd find you," said Tar, satisfied. "The stink of fear up on that crest was in the air—nothing quite like it." He sniffed deeply and grinned. "I can smell the stink on all of you now. It gets really strong when a man knows he's about to die." Tar and the rogues laughed. Too sinister for my liking. "Wolfman!" Tar snapped at the guy on his left. "Go fetch Red," he ordered him. Tar holstered his gun and pulled an exceedingly long blade from a sheaf on his calf. "Me and Lister, we're gonna carve us some turkeys." They all laughed harder then. The thought of evisceration and old fashioned bloodletting a real gas. I suppose this is the part where I write about the noble warrior in us all. In that "do or die" moment of our existence we fight the good fight to the end. Rise to the occasion. And then, in an act of kung fu madness overpower the bad guys and walk out triumphant. Truth be told, I didn't have time to think, paralyzed as I was by the terror. Also, before Tar, Wolfman, and Lister finished laughing, Burt, who was standing just behind me, screamed out insanely. I'm talking—the guy *freaked*! Stunned us, literally. In that fraction of a second he pushed me and Jackson out of his way to make a mad dash out of there. Pushed us so fucking hard that we smashed airborne into a stack of barrels and crates. The domino effect was instantaneous. The bad guys were crushed senseless under the collapsed wall of booze, but not before Wolfman got off a couple of wild shots. The next thing I knew I was seeing stars. Jackson lay crumpled up beside me. For the love of God had the man been plugged? No! He'd been knocked out cold from the force of Burt's push. I must have been, too. I was so lightheaded. Jackson had a gash in his forehead and was bleeding badly, but was coming to. All at once, I felt the warm, gooey flow of liquid dripping down my neck and back. I reached up and touched my head. The pain went through me like an electric shock. I felt my neck and the intensity of the pain made me scream out loud. *My God*, I thought to myself. *'Every bone in my body's broken*. I tried to pull myself up, but the pain was too much. Was this the end? The way of the dodo? Then I realized. *No you idiot—your left wrist's broken or something*. I'd never been so relieved by excruciating pain. Turns out I'd need a dozen stitches to close the gash on the side of my head, too. Jackson would need twice as much to close his gash and a shitload of aspirin to quell the headaches. Bigwood was fine. Kinghorn came out of that round okay, too. Burt, however, was writhing in agony, "It burns, it's burning me!" He'd taken a double ricochet in the ass—his left cheek near the o-ring. He was bleeding like he had a bad case of the 'roids. "Though I walk through the valley of death," he cried, "I fear no evil." I didn't have time at the moment to contemplate that the son of a bitch deserved it. That seconds ago, when he *was* walking through the valley of death, he was scared shitless *and* feared evil. That he pushed me and Jackson into its path to save his own ass. Days later, when the press made him out the hero for taking a bullet I wanted to kidnap him, tie him to a tree at the base of Mount Agamenticus, douse him in honey, and let the black bears eat him alive. Old Testament wrath, I know, but at the time I wasn't in a forgiving mood.

There in the Whale's Jaw we had to deal with the reality at hand—quickly. We still had Red Beard, wherever he was or lay in waiting. And there was the issue of getting off the island. Bigwood grabbed the weapons off the bad guys, tied them up tightly amidst the heap of busted barrels and broken crates. What a waste—cases of seventy-five year old Tullamore Dew Irish whisky and Johnnie Walker Scotch smashed to bits. A small fortune soaking the bones of the riff-raff. Okay, there were probably another forty cases or so untouched, but it was the principle of the loss that bothered me. I didn't dwell on it, because I knew we had to get out of there.

"You guys fit to move?" asked Bigwood when he finished tying them. My head and wrist were throbbing, and I was kind of dizzy. We'd fashioned a bandana around Jackson's head from the sleeve of his shirt and did the same for me with one of mine. He staggered slightly, but kept his balance. Kinghorn's face looked like putty and he stumbled a bit when he stood up. Somehow, he had enough strength to help Burt, who, by maneuvering his belt, was using his DIM cap as a compress. "Kinghorn, how you holding up?" Bigwood asked him.

"It feels like a sharp needle's stuck in my ass," Burt answered him.

"For the first time today Burt your ball cap's actually covering your brains," Bigwood laid into him. "For Christ's sake man, make the best of it."

"I know," he replied, deliriously, his brains bleeding out of his ass. "The pain's shooting right through every nerve ending in my body."

"Okay then big fella," said Bigwood. "Let's all stick together." We hobbled cautiously toward the exit. The moment was nerve-wracking. Red Beard had to have heard the commotion. In all likelihood he was standing outside with an axe or bazooka or something. He had to be. That was the way the day was going. At the edge of the cave, while I psyched myself out for the umpteenth time, we were rendered motionless by a terrifying scream. Not like we'd heard before back in the simian circle jerk. This one was desperate and was immediately drowned out by a deafening thunderclap that exploded outside. The cave shook with dust and debris. We were all a bit trepid about the weather, let alone the thought of human agony. But after a minute or so of silence we proceeded, stumbling into the light. The way out long overgrown and obstructed by rosebushes and dangling roots, we soon found ourselves, by the sound of waves, near the shore. Around the entrance, mounds of crushed rock, split boulders, and a canopy of heavy overgrowth, blocked our view. The bushes and stunted cedars, coarse and dense, enveloped us. Still, above, I could see the lengthening shadows of the afternoon filtered on the rocks. The sun was out. The weather had not gone bad. We crept along a narrow, gnarly path, which ran parallel with the shoreline. Gimping along, I wondered how anyone ever found the cave. The path took another hard right angle away from the shore, which led us to a row of thick bushes. Perplexed, we stopped abruptly. Stymied in part by the maze, but also the sudden, quite dramatic, intense growling and purring sound that erupted right on the other side of the bushes.

"Fucking Great!" Jackson clamored. "What a fucking day! What now? A fucking Siberian tiger!"

"What if that scream was Red Beard?" Burt panicked. "Maybe he was attacked by that thing."

"If that's the case Burt, our troubles are over," said Jackson, "or just beginning... You go first.

"Shush!" Bigwood suppressed a laugh, placing his fingers to his lips. "Just follow me," he whispered. "And don't worry," he paused, parting the bushes for us to plunge helplessly into the heart of Devil's Cove. "That sound, that's only the elusive call of mating puffins."

In the totality of the day, of all things lost or forgotten in time, this moment would forever be captured on the imaginary celluloid tape rolling in my head. We stood there, on the cove, in awe. Before us was a gathering of the puffin clans. There had to be thousands of them. On top of that, incredibly, the majority of the birds were feasting on dozens and dozens of bales of pot scattered throughout the clearing. They were devouring the weed in an orgiastic fury.

"Pa-Panama *fucking* Red!" Slocum stammered, bewildered.

We were all bewildered, except that it turned out to be one-hundred percent Colombian Gold. There was enough pot to roll five joints a piece for every freak who'd showed up at Woodstock. Off shore a forty-foot trawler, what was left of it, was smashed up and swamped in the rocks. The boat looked like it had been through a few tides. It didn't matter to me. I was dealing with glassy-eyed auks that were stumbling all over the place, passed out on the beach, or staring blankly at the horizon. Puffin orgies were taking place all around us. The little buggers had no fear or couldn't care less. They just kept munching, mating, growling, and purring, oblivious to us.

A low groan erupted amidst a stack of bales near a small boulder. There were puffins pecking away at the stack, but a nervous chatter quickly followed. "Go, go, don't take me!" Bigwood held the pistol up and snuck over, we gimps in tow. On the ground was mangled-leg guy. I'd forgotten about him. We all had. His leg was a mess. A jagged flap of flesh hung loosely on his upper right thigh. His face looked swollen and raw, too, like he'd just been punched out. His shirts and shorts were torn and tattered. There was a cell phone beside him, too, what was left of it, but the thing was smashed to shit. I guess his didn't work either. At this point, it didn't matter. The man was ranting gibberish. The poor bastard had flipped.

"Where's Big Red?" Bigwood questioned him.

"Ha!" he smiled weakly. "He's gone! Disappeared. You missed the boat. Ha! He's gone! Disappeared. Gone!"

"Okay, we get the picture," said Bigwood.

"I told him, 'No, don't do it. Don't leave. What about the others.' The boat came and he laughed. 'It's mine' he shouted at me, 'all mine!' That's when Red kissed the cup! Poured a drink and kissed it, the *goooo...old* cup!" he wailed mournfully.

Great boogily-woogily! Now *that* got our attention!

"Gold cup?" Kinghorn blurted out. "A *gold* cup?"

"Where?" Bigwood's eyes widened. "Where's the cup? Did you actually see a gold cup?"

I'm not sure if mangled-leg guy even knew we were there, in a cognizant sense. A pained, contorted look was on his face. He seemed to be staring past us, answering someone else, though we were asking the questions.

"He took the cup!" mangled-leg guy shouted, deranged. "From the cave. And the bastard was gonna leave, take it all." His eyes rolled in his sockets. He clenched his teeth, staving off the pain.

"No one's going to leave you," Kinghorn told him. "You're safe now."

"We're going to get you to a doctor," comforted Jackson. "God knows we all need one. Hang on!"

"'Go Tar. All of you. Find them. No witnesses! I'll stay with Jimmy.' Yeah! Bastard was gonna leave *me*," the guy yelled sharply. "'Hide,' he shouted. 'Hide now. There's a boat!' Ha! he laughed at me. 'It's mine!' he laughed. 'All mine!' Ha!" He jerked up, pointing. "Look! There! He's gone!

Disappeared. You missed the boat. Ha! *Look!!! There!!!*" He pointed at nothing, but it was very creepy. For what mattered, *he* saw something.

Just then, it occurred to me, how vulnerable we were, exposed. That this guy could be bait. He was expendable. Then again, we all were. Red Beard could be lurking anywhere. "Guys," I said. "Do you think we should be standing out here like this?"

"No, we shouldn't," replied Bigwood, keeping his eyes on mangled-leg guy. "But, we can't move him. I think it would be too much stress for him. He might croak."

"He's right," said Kinghorn. "He may have sustained a break in addition to the gash."

"You're a doctor of sociology, Kinghorn, not medicine," said Burt, harshly, struggling to brace himself against the boulder. "You don't know. And what the fuck? This guy tried to kill us!" Apparently, he'd returned to his sense of self.

"I know this Burt..." Kinghorn started angrily.

"Fuck him," mangled-leg guy cried. "Fuck him, I say."

"You got that right, buddy," responded Kinghorn.

"The boat!" the guy said. "The boat's coming. 'Hide!' Red told me. The engine. I heard it, too." He paused, looking around, scared. "I heard *it!!!*"

"This guy's starting to spook me out," I said. "I feel like we're being watched."

"Maybe it *would* be a good idea to stack more bales around us," said Bigwood. "Can you manage it with one hand?"

"The very thought of it makes my wrist throb," I said. "And my head hurt."

"Oh, I'll do it," said Bigwood.

"The boat!" The guy interrupted us before Bigwood moved. "The rendezvous. He took the gold cup."

"He had the cup?" Kinghorn asked urgently. "Where's the cup now? It's very important."

"Is it around here?" Bigwood implored, glancing around the clearing. Nothing but a shitload of dope and stoned auks crowded the shore.

"No! No! No!" said the guy, starting to pant. "He poured whiskey and drank and laughed. I saw him. I saw *it!*" he cried out, fitful and agitated. "The darkness came. A shadow. All around him, then me. Darkness. Everywhere. The shadow fell. Suffocating. And then Red screamed." He started to sob. Squeezed sand and stones tightly in his hands. "Don't take me," he pleaded, shaking his head right and left. "No! Not me, please. Don't let them take me!" He reached up and grabbed Bigwood, who held his arms.

"We're not letting go, fella!" Bigwood's voice rose with the intensity of the moment. "We're with you!"

"I shut my eyes," he said, tears trailing from his eyes. "Turned away from the darkness. *Red* drank from the cup—*screamed!* Thunder, lightning, shadow, darkness. So fast. Gone! Disappeared. You missed the boat. Ha! He's gone! Disappeared. Ha! I can hear the boat." He fell back. Shut his eyes. He was very pale. "He's gone!" he shuddered. "Gone."

"What do you mean he's gone?" Bigwood asked him.

"Where did he go?" Kinghorn said, mystified.

Mangled–leg guy opened his eyes. For the first time he seemed to be aware of us. With all the strength he had left in him, all that he could muster, he whispered, "To ...*hell!*" And fell unconscious.

"Is he dead?" shouted Burt. "What the heck was he blathering about? Kick him in his leg and see if he's dead!" he roared. "What does he mean Big Red disappeared? Find out where that son of a bitch went to!"

"For Christ's sake, where's your humanity?" fumed Kinghorn. "You call yourself a Christian?"

"He doesn't go to my church," said Burt. "He's a criminal."

"Stop it!" Jackson shouted. "Not now. My head's killing me."

"Please, guys," Bigwood added. "I think it's safe to say that Red Beard's bugged out. Torturing this guy isn't going to change that Burt."

I can't say how far that conversation would have gone or where it would have led to. But I didn't have that much fight left in me. My guess is neither did the rest of them. We were battered, beat up, and bleeding. We were fried and frustrated. Ill tempered yahoos. In that moment, on the brink, our collective angst faded at the sound of a distant engine. Mangled-leg guy had heard what we were too busy to not hear. The sound of salvation. I was half inclined to duck behind the rocks, not knowing what to expect, but I was too fuzzy-headed and sluggish to make a move. The boat emerged from the bend, where so many hours ago we had nearly stumbled into Red Beard and his band of cutthroats. Relief struck us all when the familiar colors of the Coast Guard came into view. There were a couple of other boats behind that one. Within minutes the cops descended on the place. Ferried in, actually. Though I'm told a helicopter arrived for mangled-leg guy, I can't recall. They flew him down to Portland. By then, once the good guys showed up, my brain stopped being functional. Not that I passed out, more like I went into a New Year's Eve-like memory deprivation mode. Minus an eight hour bender.

Everything seems dreamlike now, it happened so quickly, but I've managed to sort most of it out. Seems that after Bullethead got back from dropping us off he bumped into Lizard at the Java d' Hut. Lizard *did* want to know where we were going, but only to ask if we were heading out to the trawler washed up on Popham. Apparently in our stealth none of us was tuned into the local harbor buzz. One of Lizard's boats had spotted the wreck and radioed him. Yes, if we had simply waited and listened to Lizard, we could have avoided the whole debacle. Bullethead and Lizard contacted the Chief right away, who got in touch with the Coast Guard over in Penobscot. They were delayed by the weather, but moved on it when they could. He also called the Smokies and Feds who'd been at the moe.Republic the day before. Little did we know, sometime around stumbling into the Whale's Jaw and the puffin madness and mangled-leg guy's ranting, a convergence on the cove was impending. The bad guys were about to be trumped by the law card.

Kinghorn and Bigwood did all the talking when the cops arrived. They found Tar, Wolfman, and Lister where we left them, in the cave, senseless and in a stupor. I'm happy to report that they're well out of the picture for now. Locked up some place, somewhere, far from Downeast Way. According to the Chief, those guys were dangerous motherfuckers, ex-military, special op-types, who'd been on the lam for years. He can't believe we eluded them. Those dudes were connected with Noriega in Panama, where they escaped that fiasco and eventually surfaced in Columbia. Established themselves in the dope trade and worked the margins. Carried out their own operation. I'd like to think that they never see the light of day again. But in the back of my mind, in a corner pocket of my own delusional paranoia, I fear the worst. Someone found a use for these guys one time and there's no telling when they could find a use for them again.

As for mangled-leg guy, turns out that he's one Agent Kennard with the DEA. How these guys hooked up with him and he them is beyond me. He'd been undercover for over a year. The Chief said that he hadn't been heard from in a while. His bosses thought he was dead or had crossed over. He wouldn't have been the first. "When the cover's that deep," the Chief told me, "they recruit a certain *type* of character. Believe me. There's a fine line between the hunted and the hunter." That explains all the Feds who arrived at the moe.Republic when the dope washed ashore. "They were looking for anything, any clue," the Chief said, "that would lead them to the smugglers and Agent Kennard. They found nothing that day, mostly because of the fog."

Unbeknownst to them, Agent Kennard had penetrated the big dope smuggling operation and was reeling them in. Red Beard and the gang were on the biggest pot run they'd ever attempted. Stole the boat from somewhere up in New Brunswick. Packed it tight and headed south. The deal went all to hell when they ran into a fog bank, bad weather, and Popham, which got me thinking. There's got to be a million islands from Kittery to Calais. That's no exaggeration. If you walked the shoreline between those two points the distance is the same as New York City to Los Angeles. I shit you not. According to my estimate, the odds of them slamming into Popham were about the same as me driving cross-country and striking an albino prairie dog in Iowa. Impossible, but true.

Agent Kennard, who was in and out of consciousness for days, doesn't remember anything about what he said or what happened on the beach. The doctors say he was out of his mind—touch and go—because of the extreme pain and infection in his leg. He took the blow when a rogue wave smashed the boat into the Devil's Cove. Kinghorn and Bigwood went to visit him in the hospital and he didn't even know who they were. Apparently most of the last day on the island is a complete blank for the guy. The way we found him, from his looks and actions, it doesn't surprise me. Personally, I can't believe the guy's even alive. I heard when he got out of the hospital he ventured out to the island one last time. Went out on his own to see if he could kindle any memory to add to the investigation.

For me, what it all comes down to is simple. I was a rube. We were all rubes. Too many secrets hung over that island, more than anyone could have anticipated. They're hard to keep track of let alone believe. The island's gone from a bird sanctuary to a national enigma overnight. The tomb has blown everybody away. Who'd have thought a mass grave on Popham? A gaggle of archeologists, anthropologists, forensic examiners, and criminal investigators descended on the site to sort the dead. Talk about haunting. The grisly scene's been in my head for days. One afternoon last week I dozed off. The next thing I know I see myself working the bar. The place was busted out crowded. Then, in one sequence, one fluid motion, Porter Gibson Digit's sitting in front of me, at his usual perch. He asks for his Scotch. I reach for the top shelf. My back's to the bar. I turn around and the patrons have melded into skeletons, who're dancing, drinking, cavorting about the Liberty Ballroom. Everyone but Porter. He's still flesh and blood, grinning, giving me the finger, like he's saying welcome to the club. And that's when I notice, as I placed his drink on the bar, my hands are skeletal, too. I look up to shout, but can't. My breath is taken away like I've been punched in the stomach. My eyes fall upon the old moosehead above the fireplace, which has transformed into a fleshy human skull, its vertebrae dangling, mounted by a spike driven through its forehead. I fainted, then awoke in a cold sweat. Nearly soiled myself when the imagery flooded into my brain. The bad news was that I had the same dream that night, which had me fretting I'd cracked. The good news is, the next day, they finally finished the investigation and removed the remains from the tomb. The lost souls were committed to consecrated ground behind the Queen's Chapel. I haven't had that dream since.

I don't know if any of the other guys have had nightmares like mine. I know Jackson's still dealing with the Whale's Jaw. That find weighed on him heavy. Not so much that a generation of smugglers found the perfect warehouse during prohibition and his grandfather was a part of the action. It's not about the booze, which the state's confiscated. Sadly, we'll never see any of that vintage again unless it comes up for auction. That, or if one is lucky enough to be invited over to the Chief's for happy hour. No, for Jackson, it's personal. To gain access to the past like that, a seventy-plus year old secret, the stuff of high drama really, hit him hard. Grandpa Jeffah's going to jail nearly destroyed his family. The irony was that that's precisely why it didn't. Old man Grant didn't sing and his family lived. Porter Gibson Digit knew. Painful as it was, Jackson's mother told him how Porter had helped in those difficult times. She didn't know the full story, but she knew enough. Porter let it be known that if anything happened to Jeffah in prison, or to his family, there was a canary prepared to sing. Then he went underground and stayed there for a long, long while. The family Grant, consequently, remained healthy and prospered. Nevertheless, when Jackson got out of the hospital he hit the road, went on some "Easy Rider" sojourn in search of the inner self. Me? I've had to deal with an intense nightmare and a few bad memories. Of the latter, one in particular with hair as fiery as the setting sun.

Which leads to the question at hand. What has become of Red Beard? The man's vanished from the face of the earth. His disappearance has become the talk of the town. Despite a widespread manhunt throughout the region, one Grover 'Red' Mackenzie, modern day pirate and drug smuggler extraordinaire, remains *missing*. The consensus grows daily that the lair of Mephistopheles has claimed another victim. The authorities say he sailed off in the nick of time. Saved his own ass. They reached that conclusion based upon the eye witness account of Burt Slocum. He'd obtained the confession from Agent Kennard there on the beach when he was still mangled-leg guy. It's not that we could deny that assertion. Agent Kennard *had*, in his delusional prattle, alluded to a boat and a rendezvous. But there was so much more unsaid. What Burt didn't bother to mention was the scream we heard. The explosive thunderclap. And what of the gold cup? The darkness and shadow? Do we exclude what we cannot account for? What we cannot explain? Better left unsaid? If so, there's not much to add to this tale. Nothing but an exclamation point on one sorry-ass treasure hunt come to a merciful end! That the last person to see Red Beard alive was temporarily insane. While Tar, Wolfman, and Lister are locked away in some distant cell, people here wonder if Red Beard is, also. A cell barren and cold. Enveloped in a hoary frost in the depths and darkness of a frozen hell. Embraced by icy tentacles, at the beck and call of the ice queen. Another sacrificial victim of an ancient shaman curse. Who can blame them, really? For now, the authorities remain satisfied with Slocum's account. Why not? There's no other plausible explanation for his vanishing act. Right?

I have to admit, though not really sure what to think about this crypto-supernatural stuff, I'm leaning in that direction. That the Devil's Cove has claimed another soul. Anyone who wants to go out there can, for all I care. See for themselves what legends are made of. Walk amongst the ghosts and demons. Take their chance with fate and hope they make it out alive.

Till then, I feed. I drink. I satiate myself at the trough.

brother John

The moe.Republic Hotel
in the heart of the Lost Kingdom

Ghosts appear
Monday next, 11:16 p.m.
Still at the bar

Robbie dearest,

This would be a lot easier if it weren't so damn strange to write. I'd have called but after what Bigwood just told me you'd probably hang up. An email would have been ideal, but the computer's got a virus. Somebody's been downloading way too much porn. If Kevin were here I'd have myself a prime suspect. But we haven't heard from him and Sparky since they commenced their cosmic sleigh ride going on—what—a millennium ago? That leaves the old man, who can barely navigate the mouse without losing his balance and falling off the chair—or—wait a second—*the bride?* Never mind. I think I'll just fix the computer and leave good enough alone. Besides, when you read this you're gonna want to be where, my guess is, you probably do most of your reading, anyway. And if that's the case, you won't have to worry about shitting your pants. Because most people do when they see a ghost. Not one of those cute little orbs that dart around a room when a gypsy looks into her crystal ball. No, I'm talking a full-fledged phantom. A life-sized shadow passing before your eyes into the night. It's that real.

The queer thing, the irony, was that Bigwood should exorcise the ghosts that he conjured up and we stumbled upon. Ever the realist, he scoffed at such a notion. He only wanted the truth, he'd say, and Red Beard could find his own way to the hoary depths of hell. Less inclined to dismiss what was unsaid or conjectured, Bigwood focused on what he did know and what he had seen. For him, the foremost question was not what happened to Red Beard, but what happened to the treasure? He was convinced that it *was* there! Because if you believe that Red Beard got away, as based upon mangled-leg guy's "confession," then one has to conclude it was, at the very least, with a gold cup in hand. Thus, it doesn't matter where Red Beard went to, whether the Bahamas or straight to hell. A natural or supernatural escape or demise becomes irrelevant. The answer to the question, rational. While Kinghorn, Jackson, and myself were recovering, while Burt was basking in his new found celebrity as wounded warrior and drug buster, Bigwood was struck by a premise. Nothing profound or mind-blowing. A simple statement that helped him grasp the answer to the question that had eluded us all. *You can't find what you're not looking for!* The spark, he said, was my silly little analogy. "The odds of their slamming a boat into Popham," he told me, "*were* as likely as hitting an albino prairie dog in Iowa." This was earlier this evening. He'd been at the Huxley sisters on some business. Came by right after that. He was pretty riled up and said he really needed to talk to me.

"What if Red Beard, Tar, Wolfman, Lister, and Jimmy planned to stop at Popham rather than slam into it?" We were squirreled away in the back corner working on a pint. "Risky? Yes, but well worth it if they knew what they were looking for," said Bigwood. "A quick diversion to Popham, or perhaps, Popham *was* the rendezvous point to exchange square flounder for hard currency. It wouldn't have been the first time that island was purposely selected for such a transaction." He had a point. The island's close enough to the coast yet far enough off shore, and roughly halfway between the Cape and the Maritimes. God only knows the number of smugglers who ventured to that island over the centuries. "What if one, just one, of Red Beard's gang of cutthroats knew about or had been told of the legends of pirate gold?" he postulated. "What if that person had read a story of a body being found on the island? A near three-hundred year old victim of murder. That that one person had the brains to see that find, that *clue*, for more than it was. The person had the know how and vast knowledge to put two and two together. That would make more sense to me," said Bigwood. "The only coincidence to reconcile is the timing, which was shit luck for us."

As he told me this, expostulated his theory, my thoughts went back to a conversation. A quiet exchange between friends aboard the *Jolly Mr. Johnson* a few weeks before. How one such conversant had put "two and two together," and bluffed his way onboard. I was mortified at the thought. Cursed myself. It could not be. Where was Bigwood taking me? Where was he going with this? "There's a good chance we wouldn't have overlapped if the trawler hadn't gone aground," I reminded him, forcing the incriminating vision from my head, deciding to hear Bigwood out.

"That is if you presuppose chance," he replied. "I can reconcile the chances of us being there at the same time if we convert the element of time to a more realistic equation. Reduce it to a competition. If the certain individual or informant knew or surmised that it wasn't about finding the treasure, but who would get there first!"

The shadow of incrimination lengthened. How long would it be before Bigwood simply told me our buddy Jackson Grant had doublecrossed us?

He'd left town with the goods as soon as he could? We'd never hear from him again. Was Bigwood just being gentle with me? Taking me for a ride? Couldn't he just point the finger and be done with it?

"I've gone back to that island a couple times since that fateful day," said Bigwood. The Feds had wrapped up their investigation. No one could imagine what Bigwood was looking for. The Chief told him so when Bigwood went to talk to him about the report. They'd cleaned up the dope, cleaned out the booze, and had removed the remains by then. There was nothing else there, the Chief said. Certainly no ridiculous treasure at the end of the rainbow. Didn't it occur to him that a generation of smugglers had dibs on that cave eighty years before Red Mackenzie and his gang? And God knows how many more smugglers, spies, and parasites before that? Back to One-Eyed Red Beard and his merry band of buccaneers! You think it's possible to come in here and eclipse three-hundred years of history? "The Feds combed every inch of that cove and cave," the Chief shouted. He was adamant about that with Bigwood because he was there for the clean up. It was all in the report. "That's not the point, Mickey," he shouted back. "You can't find what you're not looking for! You can't see something when you don't know it's there!" Bigwood didn't tell me this part, the Chief had, earlier this week, over a cigar and a bottle of vintage Irish whisky.

Bigwood went out to the island the first day he could. He retraced our steps and the steps of the bad guys. He walked around and through scores of angry, irritable, edgy puffins in serious withdrawal mode. That didn't distract him. In fact he intended to walk amongst them. To search through piles of auk droppings for hours and hours until he found what he was looking for— confirmation! And he did. Not much, he didn't need much. Confirmation nonetheless, found in a dried up piece of bird shit. A small nugget. A *gold* nugget the size of a kernel of corn. The sons of bitches had found it! A treasure? The treasure? They had stashed it with the reefer, there amongst the puffins who were in a feeding frenzy, hid it. From whom? From their rendez-vous? From us? Anyone until they got off the island. That's why they freaked. Red Beard and Tar weren't talking about Colombian Gold that day when we cowered in the nook. It was the real thing! They knew they had a fortune in their hands. They were not about to share it with their rendezvous or be ID'd for all that dope by a bunch of rube do-gooders.

The treasure, Bigwood realized, *was* in the tomb. For the chamber of horrors was a tomb. A real tomb, sealed up centuries ago when One-Eyed Red Beard put at least a portion of his booty there. Buried it in blood and sealed it tight below and closed the nook above. Who's to say how or when that seal broke? That skull didn't get in that chest by itself. "Or do you think that Red Beard put it there for our sake?" he asked out loud. "To have the last laugh—even centuries later?" No, Bigwood would say. He put those men to death, cold-blooded mass murder—not beyond him—but not worth the trouble, the effort, down there. Fear was Red Beard's forte. The ultimate control method—even to this very day. Butcher the bastards in front of the crew. He would have done to them what he had done to so many others before. What better way to indoctrinate the newly impressed? No. Those poor souls in the tomb had a purpose. Ghastly sentinels left to guard a chest full of gold and gems and who knows what else. And that chest was not disturbed for three-hundred years. Despite what the Chief had blubbered on about, Bigwood knew it for certain. The seal on that tomb was newly broken. We may have accidentally found the backdoor into the tomb when I fell though the bottom of the nook, but the front door had just been opened. We stepped over the pieces. The chest may have had a stack of bones on it when we found it, Bigwood would say. But answer me this? Why were there no piss clams on the lid of that chest? There in that well, chiseled out of solid granite, on the base of that cave? A cave bottom flushed out daily by the tide and rancid with piss clams and muck? "Because somebody had been there within the past day, the last tide," he said, eager and excited. "Because they had to wipe the lid clean, clear off century's old muck before they could open the lid. Do you recall seeing any piss clams on the lid. Do you remember how easily the lock and hinges released when we lifted the chest?" Bigwood was right. The Spanish cross was clearly visible when we found it. "There was pirate treasure there," he said. "You can count on it." Everything that Kinghorn and he had deduced from his find and from Charlie Bagwell's room of lost secrets was right. Somebody beat us to it. That's what happened. "It sucks, but we were right. I feel vindicated on that front. And the pricks, for good measure, put a skull in that chest to throw us, or anyone else who chanced upon the site, off. A nice touch, I have to admit." He took a good swig of ale after he said that.

I shivered, repulsed at the thought of having fondled the skull and bones. "So you think that they found El Diablo's Chalice?" I asked him. "The find of the century?"

"I don't know if El Diablo's Chalice was in that tomb," he responded thoughtfully, "but there was a chest full of treasure there." He explained that pirates stashed their booty in many places. The problem of a single location obvious—someone else finding it and cleaning house. More so, a practical banking system evolved, as it were. They had to have access to "currency" whenever they needed. An "ATM" had to be within a day's sail at all times. "How many islands are there along the coast of Maine?" He asked rhetorically. "Or New England? The eastern seaboard?" There were many 'banks' for One-Eyed to choose from. "So we'll never know if that chalice was indeed stored in his vault on Popham," he said. "We can only conjecture. I'd like to think so, considering the price paid by those left to guard it." He fell into a moment of silence, or maybe just to gather his thoughts.

"I had spent the whole day out on Popham," he went on. "Bullethead, who'd dropped me off in the morning, had swung back and picked me up later that afternoon. I was fidgeting with the gold nugget in my pocket. Every detail was churning in my head. But I couldn't put it together. Who Knew? Red Mackenzie? Him? No. Then where was he? Who then had beaten us to the treasure? Who was it?"

Here we go, I thought to myself. You think I don't know where you're heading with this? Who took whom along for the ride? I couldn't take it anymore, being slapped around with kid gloves. "Go ahead. Say it," I snapped. "Tell me it was Jackson Grant who did us in. Get it over with. You can tell me how he did it, but quit leading me on!" I laid it on the table, angered and frustrated.

He looked at me like I was an alien. "Let me say this, first," he responded calmly. "As I stood on the deck of the *Jolly Mr. Johnson*, in search of an answer, Bullethead walked up to me. Asked me if it had been worth it. The day and all. He mentioned, in an off-handed way, something unremarkable. That if I were going to keep going back to the island I should get my own boat. To me, though, he handed me the clue, the missing link in the trail of probability I was following. It just clicked. There was another *boat!*" They had not run the trawler aground, Bigwood surmised. They had anchored it—not well enough—and used a shallow draft boat. Perhaps a dory. Probably with an inboard. To come ashore quick and easy, nice and neat—just like the rumrunners did during prohibition. The plan to find the treasure *and* make the pot rendezvous shattered when they came out of the cave. They found the trawler swamped, aground, its contents afloat. In his fury, 'Red' Mackenzie schemed how he would make his escape—alone. The key to the boat was in his pocket. When the time was right he'd leave. And that was as soon as the witnesses were eliminated. He'd sent Tar, Wolfman, and Lister to kill us. But Red had one more witness, or partner in crime, to deal with before he could make his escape."

"Agent Kennard?" I said, surprised, but relieved. "You mean Jackson didn't screw us over?"

"No!" Bigwood shouted with a laugh. "And I'll be sure to let him know, 'Dobbs,' just how much you think of him. There's a showing of *Treasure of the Sierra Madre* coming up at Bud's Bijou. Maybe you could take him there on a date when you make up."

I told him he could kiss my ass. No, I was almost willing to kiss his for exonerating Jackson. Even though I was the one who'd indicted him in my head. Merrily a fool I was. Verily a douche bag, a cad, but a happy one. "Agent Kennard is the man?" I asked, silly, needing to repeat it. "He's the culprit?"

"Agent Kennard is our man," said Bigwood. "I was pretty sure when Bullethead spoke to me. But now I'm certain of it. But a culprit?" he asked aloud. Like the Chief had said, there's a fine line between the hunted and the hunter in Agent Kennard's line of work. And really, did he doublecross *us*? "I'm not sure who he doublecrossed, if anyone," Bigwood reflected. "I believe he acted on an opportunity when it presented itself. He had to make his move or it would be forever lost. Unfortunately, he had to do it while he was undercover. He must have felt *that* compelled to share it with Red Mackenzie and the rest of them, or else at least use them to get to that island. I don't know what he had worked out, but it was falling apart until, surprisingly, we showed up."

"What?" I responded, baffled and even more confused. Bigwood stared at me. Letting me play with this one for a minute or so.

"I thought about that for a while, too," he said. "I figured that we, somehow, must have been connected to the reason why Red Beard didn't eighty-six Agent Kennard on the beach. He lay there unarmed and helpless. He needed medical attention. He was easy prey."

"But Red Beard spared him," I said, "let mangled-leg guy live. Left him, all of them, and took the money and ran."

"Now you're getting very warm," Bigwood smiled. "Red Beard didn't show mercy. He spared him because Agent Kennard had a trump card. He knew where the treasure was and Red Beard didn't."

"Huh?" I interrupted him. "You just told me a few minutes ago how they went into that tomb and found it. How could a gimp have gone in there in the time it took Red Beard, Tar, Wolfman and Lister to track us, locate the treasure and hide it, *and* return to the beach?"

"No, no!" Bigwood shook his head. "You're not following me. They had already done the dirty work. In fact, I think that's when Agent Kennard hurt himself—blowing open that seal. I don't know. But the treasure was already there, stashed in the stash, on the cove, when Burt came barreling back into the bushes like the dumb ass he is, yelling obscenities so loud that he gave our position away. The four of them may have already decided to turn the tables on their 'pal,' at least Red Beard had from what we heard him say to Tar at the nook. They may have been about to do him in on the beach, with all the moaning and screaming we heard. But then along came Burt. Panicked, startled, they left Agent Kennard and chased after us. That's when he made his move. Injured or not he had to act to save his life. He went to the cove, a short distance, and took the loot. Stowed it somewhere clever. Good enough so Red Beard couldn't find it. Good enough that the Feds and Smokies couldn't even chance upon it—you can't find what you're not looking for!" he said, smiling at me.

"I still don't know," I said. "Considering how we found agent Kennard. I can't see how he pulled it off."

"I'll get to that," said Bigwood, finishing his pint in a gulp. "By the time they returned with Kinghorn and Burt, beat the crap out of Kinghorn, and left them hog tied and blindfolded in the cave, Red Beard knew that time was against him. He had to make his move. Dispose of us. Dispose of Agent Kennard. Take the money and run. He ordered Tar and the boys off, then turned on his pal Jimmy, who lay there, ready to strike a deal as soon as Red Beard realized he'd been trumped. Maybe Agent Kennard thought he could deal with him, barter his life for a share of the treasure. "From the way we found the guy," Bigwood said, "I'd say Red Beard wasn't in the bargaining mood and decided to beat it out of him. I don't think he was in too rough a shape before the beating. He could maneuver, painfully, but enough to move the treasure and set the table."

"So when we saw him, his leg up close," I said. "You're saying that Red'd pummeled him?" Bigwood nodded yes. Somehow, the bastard held out. Long enough to convince Red Beard he'd better cut a deal—time was running out. Any boat could come along. Somebody was bound to be coming for the five of us. Then there was gun fire. The other three would be back any minute. Red Beard must have caved and agreed. Come to terms. Whatever it was, it was enough. Agent Kennard told him where it was. He'd put it on the dory. His share was already on the boat, maybe wrapped in burlap or maybe in a duffel bag. Red Beard had to laugh out loud at the thought. He pushed the dory off, hard out past the rocks. He put the key in the ignition, started her up, which was what Agent Kennard needed him to do. Red Beard could have looked back one last time, probably to take aim and fire, or perhaps Agent Kennard called out to him first.

"In either case what did Red Beard see?" Bigwood asked me like he was thinking through the answer.

"I can only presume," I said. "A gun! He shot him? No, wait. If he had a gun he would have shot him way before that. I sure as hell would have." I paused. I needed a refill. "What did he see?"

"You know it was a funny thing how those cell phones only seemed to work along the shoreline on that island. That kind of got me thinking of how Agent Kennard could have pulled it off," said Bigwood. "Then it struck me. They say all you need is a cell phone to detonate a plastic explosive. A person in the know can wire the explosive to any type of battery and trigger it with your phone. So my guess is that Agent Kennard was holding up his cell phone when Red looked back. It let Red know that the same plastic explosives he planned on blowing us up with were now wired to the boat's battery. Red realized and he screamed bloody hell. And then, ka-boom! An explosion. Big enough to shake the shit out of the cave from a couple of hundred feet away, completely obliterate the boat into fragments and Red Beard into finely minced lobster fodder. He must have thought it would work," Bigwood speculated. "When the boys came back they'd have thought that Red double-crossed them and that Jimmy boy was as much a victim as they were."

"Doublecrossed, huh?" I said.

"I Imagine that Tar, Wolfman, and Lister think of nothing in their cells but how they're going to track Red down one day and destroy him," said Bigwood.

"But it wasn't the bad guys who showed up. It was us," I said.

"Yes, worse for wear, but good guys," said Bigwood. "He must have been amazed and relieved beyond belief. He was injured, but knew what to do and say."

"Just a second," I said, "I need to think about this," and I hurriedly fetched another round. "That's a lot of conjecture," I spoke up, too loud in retrospect, walking back from the bar. "You're giving this Kennard guy a lot of credit. I mean, maybe he and Red are homosexual lovers?" That got everyone's attention within earshot. "Okay, I'm kidding everybody, just kidding," I said with a laugh, taking my seat. "But seriously," I added, when the din quieted down, "maybe there was another boat and Red Beard just left because he couldn't wait any longer. I can buy that."

"Don't you remember what Red said?" Bigwood looked at me for an answer, but didn't wait. "Up on the crest of the island? They had the explosives—Red said something about throwing us in the hole and *blowing* us to hell. I'm sure the hole was the tomb and he was planning on burying us for good. Agent Kennard obliterated the guy. It's what happened. It's the only logical explanation for the scream and the explosion. You do remember hearing a scream and an explosion don't you?" he said, a bit testy.

"Calm down, okay? It's kind of fuzzy, but yes I remember that," I replied. "But still? Murder the guy?"

"I think it's probably more like self-defense," said Bigwood, "in a game of life-and-death chess. If it ever came to it, I think Agent Kennard could make his case."

"All right. I'll give you that one," I said, "but what about the rest of it? It's quite a theory. Somewhat plausible, I'll admit. But what makes you so sure of it, the whole thing? You did an incredible amount of work, and that's why I love yah, but Agent Kennard isn't from around here. How would he be tuned into that island? And that gold nugget you found. Couldn't that really have been a remnant of a truly long, lost treasure?"

"That's just the point," he said, pounding his fist on the table. *"It was!"* He reached into his pocket and removed a flat, oblong cedar box, which was inlaid with mother-of-pearl. He placed it carefully down on the table between us. "Open it," he said.

"If I do," I responded. "What will I find?"

He stared at me for a moment. "The answer," he smiled, "that you're looking for."

Whoa! I thought. A genuine moment of truth. When I picked the box up it was weightier than I anticipated. Inches broader than my hand, I palmed it and lifted the lid. Two large Spanish gold coins lay side by side entombed in a small glass case. Solid gold doubloons, dated 1698 and 1703, each embossed with a Spanish cross, in near perfect condition. Amazing. Astonishing. This was the moment which had eluded us in the cave, I realized, or something close to it. "Wha-what? Wha-where? Ha-how?" I stammered. "Unbelievable!"

"Easy lad," Bigwood laughed. "Believe it. They're very real. These are two Royal 8-*escudo* solid gold coins. Authentic doubloons, valued, my estimate, at over $100k."

"But it can't be," I said, staring at the case. "How can it be?"

"They belong to the Huxley sisters," he said. "They've given them to me for safe keeping, at least until they've sorted this out."

"The Huxleys?" I shouted. "No way! But how?"

"They came by courier today," he answered me. "Quite anonymously, I might add, which was why they asked me to come by. I figured it was important when they called. In all the years Kinghorn and I have represented them we'd never stepped foot in their house."

"You haven't missed much," I said, my eyes still on the doubloons. "The place is a mausoleum." I replaced the lid cautiously and placed the box down.

"They asked me what they were," he said. "I recognized them right away. Knew their value. I had done substantial research on colonial Spanish coins in preparation for 'the hunt.' I was just as shocked as you were."

"Well, they're incredible," I said. Then thought about it for a second. "But this is the answer? The key to everything you've told me? This doesn't make sense. This is crazy! Who'd have sent that to the Huxley sisters? *Who...*," I pondered, "but someone to torment me?"

"To torment us all," Bigwood answered, "but especially them, in an ironic way. I was sitting there in the parlor. Handling the coins, asking them questions and answering theirs, when I glanced over at this portrait, off on a side table. I walked over, picked it up. The guy was younger. In military uniform. 'Who is he?' I asked and Emma told me in a fuss. Meanwhile, Edith's in a tizzy, kept asking me over and over who could have possibly sent them the doubloons. You'd have thought they would have been happy, but they were frantic, agitated, like the sky was falling. I studied the picture. The were no bumps and bruises on his face, nor was it bloodied. 'Who sent it?' One of 'em shouted at me in tears. I had to smile at the irony, placing the portrait down, turning to face them. 'James Huxley Kennard,' I told them. 'Your great-nephew is alive.'"

Honestly, I may have had an out of body experience when he told me. I can't remember exactly. I could have turned into a lycanthrope or something for all I know. They say shock can do that to you. Shut your brain down and all, block out reality to prevent you from hurting yourself. Anyway, the next thing I recall is me laid out on the floor, beside the chair I'd been in. Bigwood said I went purple and turned to stone. Didn't move for a minute or two before I keeled over. When he said that James Huxley was alive my first thought was he'd return and claim the house, the moe.Republic, as his. When the rush hit me, I went to a far away place. "If you're fucking with me," I told Bigwood, laying there flat out on my back. "I'm actually gonna *give* you your bar tab." He wasn't kidding and he assured me that the property was legally ours.

Blown away that I was, "It's nothing compared to Edith and Emma," he said. More than just seeing a ghost, it was like seeing the ghost of the man they'd watched drown from a boat while they rowed away silently. "They both fell apart. Literally. I had to go around with a shovel and collect them.

Put them back together. Really. I'm not that good at it either, believe me. They're both a mess. Feet where their mouths are. Elbows where their asses are. Terrible."

Bigwood hadn't gone there for a confession, but he got one anyway. For the first time in their lives Edith and Emma Huxley had to confront not only reality, but the truth. All the years everyone thought James Huxley had croaked, it was just the opposite. Not only alive and disinherited by the family, but marginalized. Denied his birthright, Huxley Manor, by his own grandmother, Enid, who, instead bequeathed it to her younger sisters. Enid's problem was that James was the bastard offspring of her only child, Ann. Ann never married the guy who begot James late in her last semester of college. Lust, not love gave James his shot at this world. Besides, the sisters told Bigwood, before she even knew she was pregnant, the father had been drafted and shipped to Vietnam. He never returned. Enid demanded that Ann give the child up. Spare the family the embarrassment. Ann refused. As an affront or peace offering, the sisters were not sure, Ann named the child for her father, her mother's family, and the boy's father. Enid disinherited her. At least as much as she could. Ann's late father, James P. Harrington, a merchant banker, had left her a good sum. Not much, but enough to start a life for her and her son. For thirteen years they lived down in Boston where she established herself as an artist. Tired of city life, and wanting to introduce and enlighten her son to the ways of the Lost Kingdom, she moved back. Raised her teenage boy the next town over, Bean's Point, out on the other side of the harbor, past Saint Mary's Lighthouse, where he was surely exposed to the tall-tales and legends under the Old Mountain by the Sea. Ann, whose work in landscapes was gaining recognition, died tragically in the summer of 1989 when a moose slammed into her car up off Mountain Road, near Uriel's Ledge. She was forty-seven. James Kennard, an honors graduate from the University of Maine, and a lieutenant in the army by then, met his grandmother and two great-aunts for the first time at his mother's funeral. Of what Edith and Emma recall, he was a gentleman, but few words were exchanged. The sisters claim they tried to make their peace then and there, but Enid would have none of it and neither would he. "Maybe they did," Bigwood reflected. "It might explain the picture of him on their table or the package they received today."

"They couldn't have tried that hard," I said. "I remember the day I went over there to discuss Colonel Huxley. They didn't even really know what happened to him. Now, I think they simply made it up."

"Who knows? Enid controlled the purse strings, which in turn controlled her sisters," said Bigwood. "They said and did whatever she told them to say and do right up till the day she died a year to the day—strangely—on the anniversary of Ann's death. Besides, after all those years, James Kennard was a non-entity to them. He and his mom had been pariahs his whole life. It was all moot. He was in the army and out of the picture anyway. Becoming an operative and *dying,* as it were, must not have been that difficult for him, or them, to accept."

"This is a heck of a piece of property to turn your back on, to walk away from," I said.

"I know," said Bigwood. "But he did. He'd been on his own for so long, when his mother died, I guess he reasoned that *he* could, too, professionally speaking, and disappeared, living his life on the edge until weeks ago. Put another way, I suppose it's easy to wipe the slate clean when there's not that much writing on it to begin with."

"Yeah. I'll have to remember that one." I noted. "So what's gonna happen now? What's to become of all this? Where did you leave it?"

"They want me and Kinghorn to find him," said Bigwood. "They want to ask his forgiveness."

"Forgiveness?" I said incredulously. "Preposterous!"

"It might be," he replied. "But I have to say, they're pretty shaken by all this. It's a queer thing watching old ladies ball. Often times they're mistaken for shriveled up flakes of humanity to begin with. Old witches, drifting like snow in and out of your consciousness."

"Oh, don't go soft on me, man," I said. "Those two would have been burned as witches. They'd have rather let the place sit there abandoned and fall into ruin after Enid croaked than have the rightful heir inherit the property. They were an accessory to a travesty, a crime really, which there're finally shamed into admitting. To me, the irony is, that James Huxley Kennard was the one who did it!"

"I'm not going soft," he replied. "But why be a hard ass? Edith and Emma are repenting. They're giving him everything, bequeathing the house, property, and trust to him. I'm drawing up the papers tomorrow. Better late than never!" He paused, contemplating thoughtfully. "Now? Can we find him? Realistically, who's to say he hasn't left town, anyway. Christ, if those two doubloons are an indication of what he beat us to, he's a very wealthy man who's probably gone far, far from here—with no forwarding address."

"Ah!" I sighed painfully. "Do you have to remind me?"

"It's the little things," he said, as he stood up, "that build a lasting relationship."

"Hey?" I shouted. "Where are you going?"

"Off to meet Kinghorn," he replied. "In all the excitement I forgot. He's on his way back from Augusta."

"What's in Augusta?"

"Oh, nothing too much. He did mention something about the need to assassinate Burt Slocum before he left, and that's where his office is."

"When you put a mad dog down, Alex, they call it euthanasia," I said.

"That would be too kind, too good, for Burt. Don't you think?"

"Well, Kinghorn always says, 'people end up where they should.'"

"So you've heard the news about Slocum?" asked Bigwood.

"Only what I've seen on TV or read in the paper," I answered. "I know he's taken all the credit for the work you and Kinghorn did. Passed us off as a bunch of amateurs who nearly got *him* killed. Despite his mendacity he's met the governor—she gave him a commendation. Interior gave him a promotion, too. Made him a deputy director. I mean—the guy isn't qualified to clean an out-house at Baxter State Park. He may just be the first bureaucrat on record to get a promotion for taking it in the ass rather than sticking it up someone else's!"

"So you haven't heard *the* news?" Bigwood smiled deviously.

"There's more?" I asked. "What else could that man possibly do to add to this memorable experience?"

"Like I said—Kinghorn went to Augusta. He was going to meet Slocum, which he did."

"Don't tell me that Kinghorn got arrested," I said, flabbergasted. "That he really didn't attack the guy?"

"No!" Bigwood burst out laughing. "Old Burt's the one who got arrested—DUI and reckless driving! Drove out of the lot of the Calvary Baptist Church and into the side of a parked cop car. Apparently, the officer to whom the car belonged was there directing traffic for, ironically, another banquet in Burt's honor. This one was at his own church. Kinghorn said that when Burt failed to yield the cop dove out of the way, nearly missed getting run down. I'd say the parade's about over for Burt Slocum."

"I'll be..."

"Kinghorn was giggling like a school boy when he called earlier. 'What'd I tell you, Alex,' he gushed. 'Don't ever forget that...'"

"...people end up where they should," we both said in unison. I had to grin. Thank the Universal God for showing me his hand once again. Not that I'm a malicious guy. I'd never wish ill on anyone. Never have or will. I grinned at fate and how it works. How true it is that where we end up is always where we should be. I know. I've got one sordid tale to prove it.

I watched Bigwood scoot off whistling happily. Left me at the table thinking about it all. My thoughts drifted wildly. Too much to absorb in one sitting. All those ghastly images, murderous souls, and broken lives. When you think about the demise of the House of Huxley, in some ways, I guess, Huxley Manor *was* haunted when we moved in. When you think about this affair, this adventure, it all makes sense now. I feel vindicated, though I don't know why. It's like I passed through another dimension and back again. Those who were once lost have been found. An immense fortune had slipped through our hands. Red Beard's Ghost has finally been put to rest and James Huxley Kennard's has risen. The great pot smuggling caper solved. Much like Red Mackenzie *and* his gold, it all went up in smoke.

For me, like I told the Chief earlier, one foggy day on the bucolic shores of the moe.Republic, back when all of this was a dream, you'll never catch me puffin'…

You know where to find me,
brother John

Act VIII

Spaced Out!

The moe.Republic Hotel
in the heart of the Lost Kingdom

moe.Microbrewery
*In*cognito
Tuesday, 10:13 p.m.

Dear Rob,

You're probably wondering why you've received this via carrier pigeon. Let's just say it's been quite hectic here over the past few days. I don't know what you've heard bandied about, but I wanted to let you know that we're okay. I hope the same for you and the boys. When I heard there was a new studio album in the offing it was like a breath of fresh air. Maybe you can have the release party here? Believe me, it would be a nice diversion. A welcome distraction from the current mayhem. Besides, the more you guys keep pumping out the music, the more buses keep rolling up to the hotel. People come as pilgrims of sorts, to wallow in the aura of the very essence of celebrity. They quaff our liquid amber by the gallons. Stumble into the same john where Chuck was afflicted with the green skitters once upon a Saint Patrick's Day ago. Talk about wallowing in the aura of celebrity. Man, you can't get a better seat than that! Those were heady days, the early years of the moe.Republic Hotel, dabbling in the ancient recipes. Thanks to McBain, we've long since concocted a Shamrock Ale as tasty and potent as it is emerald, and as sanctified as the patron saint himself. This year's batch has been a big hit since it went on tap a few weeks ago, particularly among the lab-coated geeks who've invaded the hotel, which brings me to the whole point of this wayward missive.

It's been a long journey into the dusk and beyond. Many moons have waned. The stars have fallen. A new day has arrived. The fat lady can finally sing, punch the clock, and go home. Kevin and Sparky have returned!

They were found, actually. And it didn't take long for those notorious G-men and the full bird colonel to return, either. I'm being watched now by a gray suit as I write this. They've invaded the hotel and our privacy, and are asking a lot of stupid questions, that lead to inane answers, all of which seem to point to distancing any semblance of the truth from the fiction they're creating. What else is new? The first thing they did when they arrived was run the guests off with some flimsy gas leak story, and then they imposed another communication blackout. If it hadn't been for those crazy Huxley sisters, who actually *have* the pigeons, you wouldn't be reading this letter now.

On April Fool's Day, Chief Mickey McO'Fayle found Kevin and the dog wandering around on the other side of the hill above the hotel, near where they disappeared. They were still wearing those matching pointy knit hats from that Saint Patrick's Day! According to the Chief, he responded to reports of an explosion of some kind in the vicinity just after dawn. Later he would say that he almost didn't go, it being the day of the jester. Already he'd been goofed by his son, the little prat. Done in and drenched once again by the old rubber band around the sprinkler head of the kitchen faucet. An ice cold geyser shot straight into his face and neck and down his shirt when he went to get water for his coffee. But then he heard a call-in on WMOE reporting they had seen bright flashes of light in the same area as the reported explosion. So off he went. Found the two of them wandering. They looked disoriented. The Chief swears he heard Sparky *talking* to Kevin, too, when he arrived, while Kevin just stood there drooling with a puppy-eyed look on his face! The Chief has since postulated a theory that the aliens switched their brains or something. I don't know. Could be or not. I'd say stranger things have happened but that notion's being trumped on a daily basis.

I've only seen Kevin briefly. The G-men have sequestered him in a room where he's hooked up to a bunch of monitors. They say he's not uttered a word since his return. I swear I heard barking coming from his room the other night. Could have been one of the geeks pranking me. They tend to bop around the hotel feigning a disoriented, detached intensity. Deflecting inquiries in carefully plotted evasive tactics—walk rapidly, avoid eye contact, jabber effusively into an unplugged headset on approach. Though they're rude as hell, fortunately, it hasn't deterred them from suckling the fount of the Shamrock Ale. Those guys have been on one heck of a bender. The cash register is overflowing and is greener than their teeth. Alas, the gig is nearly over. The full bird told me that the investigation into "your brother's disappearance in the woods" is just about complete. They should be gone in few days. Thankfully, if anything, so will the Shamrock.

Meanwhile, father is working on completing his latest invention, a bipolar electrolyte phase blaster. He plans to wire the boy and his dog to it, and see what happens. In theory he says it should snap Kevin "out of it." For now, the boy just sits there in his room and doesn't respond to much. He does like it when you rub his belly. And when you scratch behind his ear it makes his right leg wiggle. Sparky, on the other hand, tends to sit with the G-men in front of the TV all day watching those Bloussant breast enhancement infomercials. Ah! So many questions, so little time, and hey, this flying chicken could only carry so much info. I'll get the full story to you when the geeks leave.

Till then, no time to dither,

brother John

From: brother.john@moe.republic.org
To: rob@moe.org
Date: *May Day, May Day, 1:15 p.m.*
Subject: spaced out

dear Rob: Such a lazy day at the hotel. I have the old portable notebook out, I'm sipping coffee, and snacking on one of mother's world famous whoopee pies. A good time as any to bring you up to speed this side of the chaos. I'm as calm as Moose Harbor today. A good thing, because father borrowed your old Econoline van again to take some guests out on a scenic harbor cruise aboard the *Jolly Mr. Johnson.* Fred the Bullethead's busier than ever. Just like Bigwood predicted, everyone wants to see where Red Beard buried his treasure. They're building a shrine out there on Popham. The turistas are lining up daily at Hancock's Wharf to sally out to the island and back. All we can do is oblige our guests and feed the monkey. We're a part of it now. Especially since we started bottling Red Beard's Ale. Captain Bergmeister stocks about ten cases every other day. On the first twilight cruise he sold out. Can't say if it was the beer or the band which induced an unquenchable thirst that evening. Bwana Dick and the Hooded Dakotas were on board. When they were jamming, the ship would list left, and then right, depending on which way the conga line was snaking across the top deck. Maybe it was a little of both. The brew's been a big success since that first night. Which makes me ponder—the plan to stock the planet's refrigerators with moe.Ale is at hand. I can tell you this: the people on board all wanted more. They wanted to bring it home. They wanted to know when we're going public! I know. I was there. That night marked the historic first trip out for Kevin in the wake of the G-men's departure.

Talk about a trip. It's really funny how everything turned out after all these years. How can you make sense of it? The day after the full bird and his gang of merry men cleared out all I was praying for was a return to normality. That morning, when I woke up, I stumbled out on the back porch, a cup of java warming my hands. There was Kevin, sitting in an Adirondack chair, smoking a cigar, sipping coffee, and looking out on the islands of Moose Harbor. Verily I stood, stung and speechless.

"Good morning," said Kevin with a smile. "It's a beautiful day!" There was an air of triumph about him. A contentment I had never seen. I didn't understand anything. "I can't tell you how long I've been waiting to do this again," he ruminated with satisfaction. The late April air was light. Carried on a mild breeze from the sea. "Sit down," he said, pulling up another chair.

Truthfully, I couldn't take my eyes off of him. "Kevin? Is that really you?" I asked, stunned. He gave me a queer look.

"Who the fuck do you think it is? Sparky?" he scoffed. "You didn't actually think that we'd switched brains did you?"

"Nah," I lied. "I knew you were faking it."

"You did!" he burst out laughing. "You actually thought I'd lost my marbles. Thanks an ef-fing lot! That's a nice way to treat your brother."

"But I... you were... gone," I mumbled, staring at him.

"What does that have to do with here and now?" he said. "Sit down will you. Quit lurking over me. You're giving me the creeps."

"Okay." I sat down obediently. "Maybe I thought something was wrong considering you were missing all that time," I rambled in my defense. "And you just showed up out of the blue, or should I say, the darkness, on the other side of the hill in the middle of the night dressed the same as the day you were lost or abducted."

"Lost? Abducted?" he marveled at the thought. "Sounds like some kind of caper to me? You been reading Raymond Chandler? Dashiell Hammett?" He sipped on his coffee, drew on the cigar.

"Hey? I saw you disappear in a ball of light right up on that hill!" I said with authority. "Swallowed up by a phallic space ship!"

"If you saw me disappear," he replied, stating the obvious, "then you certainly knew I wasn't lost."

"Why are you doing this to me?" I asked humbly. "Why?"

"I'm not doing anything," he answered, "except enjoying the day."

"Kevin! Where have you... you were gone?" I stammered.

"Ah! Sort of, for a little while." He paused, gauging my reaction, which, I'm sure was even more baffled than when I walked out on the porch and found him there. "The important thing is that I never lost touch."

"What? In spirit? In another dimension? Outside looking in on us from time to time?"

"Another dimension? That's science fiction," he chided me. "This is the *real* world."

"Okay, Karnac, then how *did* you manage to stay in touch?"

"It's not that complicated. Think it through. I'll give you a hint. It was pretty entertaining when you nearly got busted for all that dope when it washed up on the beach."

"What? Now you're messing with my mind, which is already very fragile. That was a while ago, and if you were here where the fuck have you been?" I was all agitated. "You had to know that everyone was worried sick about what happened to you?"

"Calm down. I wasn't *here*, here!" he replied. "Hey, that Slocum guy really was something—saved the day!"

"Oh, he was *something* all right. He nearly got us killed."

"That's not what I heard."

"Christ! I feel like I'm in a lost episode of the Twilight Zone—bugs crawling on my flesh."

"You're so dramatic," he taunted me.

"Don't make me peel the onion," I pleaded, "to get the story out of you."

"You really need a vacation. The stress will do you in."

"It isn't stress that's going to do me in," I said. "It's the insanity, I think."

"Confusion's a sure sign, and there are other names for it."

"Call it what you will."

"Okay. Dementia. Neurosis. Paranoia. Severe Anxiety. Hey, accept the given reality for what it is and deal with it," he pronounced, satisfied. "You're a freak."

I sighed deeply, frustrated. Maybe I *was* on the edge of veg. I mean, who wouldn't be? I hated it when he did this to me—feed my monkey bananas. "Okay," I said calmly. "I am a freak. I will never change my ways. That said, if you weren't *here*, here, where the heck were you?"

"Hey relax. It's a beautiful day," he said, avoiding the question. "Man, look at that view!"

"Ugh!" I snapped. "Quit changing the subject."

"Ease up! Here, have a cigar." He pulled one from his shirt pocket. "They're fantastic. I think they're real Cubans!"

"They are. They're mine."

"Ah, so you're well connected." He pulled out a lighter for me. "I know *I* am," he added, raising a brow.

"Please." I took his lighter, stoking madly. "What happened to you?"

"Questions, questions, questions. Can't you simply enjoy my company? The moment at hand?"

Leaning back in the Adirondack, puffing hard, I sat there flummoxed and exasperated, pretending to be at one with the universe.

"Center yourself, man," he said. "We've got all day. There's not a cloud in the sky."

"Fine," I said. We sat in silence. A few guests were playing a round of Frisbee golf across the way. A few others strolled along the beach. Sparky traipsed up to us on the lawn and relieved himself like it was the first time in five years. "Might need a backhoe for that one," Kevin mumbled, chuckling. A few minutes later mother appeared and refilled our coffees. "I am so happy you're back," she said to Kevin. "Relieved, actually, especially after everything you told us." I jolted slightly. She turned and went back into the house. *Told us,* I thought to myself, staring ahead. Father came out with a plate of Danish, gave a furtive look into the house, then stuffed one into his jowls. "Eddie! The pastries are for the boys," mother yelled from some recess within, her radar activated. "Your cholesterol!" He grabbed another, garbled a hearty good morning to us, and shuttled off quickly, towards one of the out buildings.

"'Till death do us part,'" said Kevin. "Makes you wonder what the committee had in mind when they wrote that one up in the manual. Why not, 'Till the last one stands,' instead? Gives it that competitive zing, that sense of endurance you're gonna need to make it out alive."

I smiled weakly. Yeah it was funny and I could have laughed. But I was still wound up. Good thing, too, that I didn't laugh. At that moment the bride walked out the screen door with a coffee in her hands and said hello. "It's good to have you back," she said to Kevin. "We really missed you." She leaned over and pecked his cheek and squeezed his shoulder. "That was the most incredible story I ever heard this morning. Simply remarkable. I still have goose bumps. I'm spellbound to tell you the truth. You've taken my world, turned it out and shown me the universe!" She kind of choked when she said the last part. I know I did—bore a hole right through me. "And you!" she snapped at me. "You could be more sensitive about what you brother's gone through."

"I am still trying to find out *what* he's gone through!" I stated my case, looking intently at her, then Kevin.

"Have either of you seen your father?" she asked, ignoring me, scanning the yard looking for him. "Your mother wants him to take her to the store."

"He went in the direction of the carriage house," Kevin volunteered. "Right after he left the Danish."

"Thank you, Kevin," she said politely, then looked at me, muttering under her breath, "'Till death do us part!' *Honestly!*" She placed her cup on the arm of my chair in a huff, then went to track the old man down. As soon as she was out of sight Kevin began to laugh.

"Touché," I said, staring at him. "Very well executed." My demeanor had not changed. Though squirming in my chair, I was coolly collected, even while he continued to laugh spasmodically. I caught sight of an osprey over the water. The bird glided in an updraft, then nosed dived about fifty feet straight to the surf. At the last possible second it came out of the dive, skimmed through the crest of a wave and elevated with a big fish. Secured in its talons, the mackerel or pollock or whatever it was squirmed to free itself to no end. Mesmerized, I saw myself as that fish. Sort of. I wasn't being crushed to death by razor sharp talons, lungs pierced, gasping for my last breath. I can't say I'd soon be fodder for a brood of osprey chicks, eventual fertilizer for a maple sapling or something, but you get the picture. A deep curiosity. An urgent need to know Kevin's whole cosmic sojourn. I wanted closure. I had to avoid the path to the couch at all costs to get there. But I was trapped within the moment. He had me firmly within *his* grip.

When his laughter receded, the last wave of triumph passed, he looked at me, grinning, and said, "Okay, because I love you, I'll tell you what happened, even though you never said 'good morning' to me because you thought my brain had been swapped with Sparky's."

"But I…"

"No buts or interference," he cut me off. "I really *don't* have all day. I have to meet with my agent. I'm thinking of taking my story to Hollywood first thing. Maybe doing a treatment. I think the time is ripe. We're on the verge of something big, this planet. People need to know. We don't need to live in fear. So just let me tell the story and you can give all the feedback you want later." This new Kevin was quite emphatic, if not resolute, as he spoke.

"All right. You have my *full* attention," I said. "No interruptions."

"Very well then… Let me see," he thought momentarily. "The reality is that I just had to get away for a while," he began. "I had to drop out of sight. Laboring as a professional mannequin was getting the best of me. I felt paralyzed eight hours a day, five days a week. The repetition was driving me crazy."

"What!" I interrupted him. "You're hosing me!"

"Aha!" he clamored. "I knew you couldn't keep your mouth shut. You never can or never could. Everyone else did, but not you. You failed the test. Now you're going to have to wait till the movie!" I was harpooned. He wasn't supposed to say that.

"Okay, okay, okay," I cackled. "I will not speak unless spoken to, until you tell me to. I say no more." I zipped my mouth shut with my finger and sat like a gormless toad on a log.

"If only it could have been this easy when we were kids." He smiled sinisterly, then sighed. "All right then, where were we? Yes... if I recall... the wind was howling savagely that night my friend. It seemed that father time stood still..." I growled lowly and slumped in despair. Kevin, making up for lost time in the make-my-life-miserable department, laughed once again. But I did not speak. It would only prolong the agony. "...And then," he said, regaining his composure, "came that fateful Saint Paddy's when the pooch and I went out that night and ended up on that hill." He pointed to the spot where they vanished.

"I saw the ship rising behind me—this monster of an obelisk—nearly shit my pants! I waved frantically to you and anyone else who was standing on the veranda. I remember that because I was shaking at first. Then, quite impulsively—to this day I don't know why I did it—I stuck my thumb out and they picked me and Sparky up. They don't usually pick up hitchhikers, particularly ones without signs, let alone dogs. Too dangerous. But they liked my spunk. In retrospect it may be the smartest move I ever made. Shocking for everybody else, yes, but at the time, caught up in the moment, that was my last concern."

Stopping, he sampled a Danish. "Not bad," he munched. "Taste reminds of the nebular wafers I had in a small starway café in Zeta Reticuli."

"Huh?" I mumbled, and received a quick glare.

"Zeta Reticuli," he explained like it was common knowledge, "is a star system in the constellation Reticulum."

"Reticulum?" I couldn't help myself. "Sounds like a probing device for proctologists."

"No interruptions!" Kevin scolded me, then laughed a little. I shrugged apologetically, but I ask you—if Reticulum doesn't sound like a pile driver what does? Not that it matters. I zipped my mouth shut with my fingers again and resumed my toad-like gawk.

"Very well," he said, and took a quick puff on his cigar. "Let's see... It happened in a flash. Sparky and I were plucked from the hilltop. Instantaneously I'm standing in this small cylindrical terminal, my thumb still stuck out. The lighting's dim and blue. The air's heavy, damp, and incredibly, I swear the aroma's like the vat room in the moe.Microbrewery. That fragrant smell of percolating hops and malts. There's a dark, glass paneled wall in front of me. I can make out a room, like an engineering booth in a recording studio. The lights come on and several 'people' are in there.

"*Holy shit!* I'm thinking to myself." Kevin looked at me like he was about to! Then, quite animated, he bellowed, "I think, *this is real! I've been picked up by fucking aliens! And they're right in fucking front of me!*

"At that point an archway materialized out of the wall in the far left side of the terminal and the welcoming committee waddled in. There I was, standing in a bluish haze, face-to-face with a half-dozen alien beings. In that instant I knew that everything had ceased to exist. Everything I had ever learned in the realm of heaven and earth, living and loving, death and dying, was forever altered." He looked away and puffed on his cigar, thinking.

"I wanted to speak," he continued, "but my mouth was bone dry and my ass was quivering. All I could do was gape in awe. The aliens were very much humanoid. A grayish-green color, about our height." He gestured with his hand. "With a kind of balding, turtle-shaped head topped with a tuft of hair. Their necks were slightly elongated and rested on rounded shoulders. Noticeably, they had droopy, doe-like eyes that gave a permanent look of idle contentment to their faces. The one in front bowed and stepped aside. Behind him another stood holding an oval tray with a tall pint-sized drink on it. Bowing, he presented it to me and said what I understood to be 'Welcome.' I took the drink and bowed back. The one who had initially bowed looked at me and seemed to say, 'Follow me, please. You're just in time for the reception.'

"*Reception?* I thought to myself. That got my attention. *What kind of reception?* But we were on the move. Sparky and I followed him down a narrow corridor while the rest of the committee fell in behind us.

"We entered a lift similar to a capsule, and elevated, I don't know, maybe a hundred levels. We shot up like a bullet train. He kept talking to me, the lead alien, but I was too preoccupied by what to do with the drink. Naturally, I was a bit trepid—I mean who wouldn't be? Xenophobia is part and parcel of the American experience these days. Nay, it's part and parcel of the human condition. But I wasn't in Kansas any more, if you follow me, and I didn't want to insult my hosts. I was in a quandary. Did these guys sail across the universe to poison me? Drug me? Rape me? Or pray tell—harvest little old me? Had I fallen into a race of conquistadors, Puritans, fascists, or investment banksters? Nah, I reasoned. Especially when the lift came to rest and I was ushered into this fabulous topside lounge. It was the *most...*" But Kevin stopped abruptly, distracted by the sudden appearance of father. The man came from no where with a shovel in one hand and plastic bag in another.

"Just doing my duty," said father. "Just like Sparky did his," he chuckled to himself.

"I was just about to do that," said Kevin. "Or at least put a pylon next to it."

Following the rules of protocol I quickly gave Kevin the timeout sign. "Hey dad, the bride's looking for you," I said as he bent down scooping up the doo.

"What for?" he asked in a nasal pitch.

"Mom wants you to take her to the store," Kevin replied. "She went that way," he pointed.

"Okay, thanks," father said. "I'll find her," he added, and made a bee-line for the opposite direction.

"Thanks for picking up after Sparky," Kevin shouted, but father was already out of sight. "Want some more coffee," said Kevin. "I'm feeling parched." Almost immediately mother stepped onto the veranda with a pot.

"Refill boys?" She was pouring before we nodded. "Have you seen your father?" she asked, scanning the yard.

"He was just here looking for you," Kevin answered. "He was about to go to the hardware store. Wanted to know if you needed a lift into town."

"What!" Mother perked up. "*Damn* that man!" she fumed, and spun off a quick two-step into the house. "Wait'll I get a hold of him." She cursed under her breath. Slammed the screen door in her wake.

"In many ways I believe my travels prepared me for my true calling," Kevin laughed.

"And that is?" I asked him.

"Entertainment!" he proclaimed.

"You were an actor when you left," I said.

"As a mannequin? Because, if you're counting that, my career was really going no where!" He cracked a Cheshire cat-like grin.

"Very good one," I said smiling. "Inside I'm bursting with laughter. Maybe you should consider branching into low comedy."

"I'm going to do it all," the new Kevin replied. We took a few puffs on our cigars, sipped at the coffee, reflected on the moment.

"Turned out," he piped up a few seconds later, "that the 'aliens' were from the planet Breowan. Mind you," he digressed. "I'm using the place names we here on earth have ascribed to the universe. Our friends up there," he pointed skyward, "have their own names and classifications. Breowan is one such name."

'Breowan,' I mouthed silently several times over.

"Yes, Breowan," he continued. "It's located in the 47 Ursae Majoris star system." I must have looked perplexed because he quickly added, "that's in the Big Dipper, Ursa Major."

Though admittedly, perplexed I was not. Envisioning listening to myself listen to the conversation I would describe the moment as surreal and fantastic. Akin to desperate comprehension. Then again, everything about the ordeal was a matter of desperate comprehension wasn't it? The long shadow of doubt lingering. From a by-gone Saint Patrick's Day to this April Fool's; a cosmic sleigh ride on an obscenely phallic space ship; hyper-serious G-men and their chug-a-lugging geek lackeys. If I weren't so deep *in* it there would be no way I could believe any *of* it.

"I know it sounds daft, if not mad," said Kevin like he was reading my vibe. "How many people stick out their thumb and get picked up by a flying dildo the size of the John Hancock Tower? What are the odds of that happening?" He stopped, thought about it for a second, and nodded to himself. "It was pretty cool, though. The Breowans are great people. Easy going, curious, hard workers, and very friendly—their hospitality is second to none. Like I said, the moment I came on board they handed me a drink and ushered me into the ship's lounge." He gave a thumb's up. "The sight was staggering—nay, breathtaking. The lounge was about the size of a ballroom, kind of oblong and oval. On the forward side, right across from me, was an hundred-eighty degree wall, floor to ceiling plateglass exposure. It was a genuine stardeck and I was flabbergasted, awed, and overwhelmed. It wouldn't be the first time. When I entered that room I truly felt as though I were part of the universe, rather than a mere spectator. If that was as far as I went, if they had turned around and dropped me in the Mojave Desert, that moment would have carried me through until my end of days... Seriously!" he added with an emphasis.

"The lounge was crowded with other worldly beings," Kevin continued. "Their energy bubbly and effervescent. Talk about another rush. As I gawked around lounge the International Space Station suddenly came into view. Our captain glided the star ship towards it, which dwarfed the station. I remember to this day the pop-eyed, slack-jawed look on the half-dozen or so astronauts and cosmonauts." He hesitated slightly. "Those terms seem so antiquated now," he said, in a momentary digression. "Especially when a couple of hundred aliens and I were waving and toasting them as we coasted by. They caught the whole thing on film, too. I could see the cameras mounted along the side of the space station, the arms moving to capture every angle and image of the space craft. They had to be broadcasting the thing back to earth in real time. Funny how our government has denied its own people the information and knowledge they've obtained on the people's dime—and it's immense—of UFO's, contacts, and other close encounters. Whereas say, the French or the Russians have made just about everything they've ever recorded or investigated available to their public. Ironic don't you think? Whose society is really closed and whose is really open these days? I can't imagine that the footage NASA captured of me and the motley crew of interstellar travelers cruising by the space station will ever see the light of day. And I still wonder if they picked me and Sparky out of the crowd." He seemed to think about it. I already knew the answer was yes. That he was positively identified the first time the Feds came here. It would explain the post-contact vigil, the disinformation campaign, the dotty phone calls, the quiet surveillance, the spontaneous arrival upon his return. They knew all along what happened and the SOBs left us hanging in despair.

"We passed the space station," he picked up the pace of the conversation, "and I tried to get my bearings. I had to tell myself, 'Boy, this is real. You're actually on a fucking space ship.'" He looked at me intently. "I really was, you know, but I wouldn't tell those asshole Feds who showed up here anything. They were too damn rude. I was content to play the merry catatonic till they left." I have to say that I almost broke my vow of silence then. I wanted to say you only know the half of it. That his prolonged silence was a spectacular diversion. We made a bundle off those guys—equaled a quarter of our year's profits in the short time they stayed here. Okay. I was proud of him, too. That he had the balls to carry on the way he did knowing fully that the Feds could have carted him off in an instant. I'm surprised they didn't, and were so willing to let us accept their reality for what it was. That Kevin had been lost in the woods all this time and had finally found his way home. I suppose that they will probably come back to "check" on him. That the Kevin Report will only go up so high through the funnels of bureaucracy before someone shouts out, "What the fuck! This was the kid at the space station. Bring him in." But remembering my vow, I chuckled quietly and nodded my approval. It was true, yes indeed, how well he played the merry catatonic.

"So anyway," said Kevin. "The space station has faded away and we're passing the moon. I look down on the lunar surface; the peaks and valleys are magnificent. I'm completely in awe of the moment. I pick up the space buggies and other equipment and debris left by the Apollo missions decades ago—do you think its human nature to trash every place you don't call your own? Is that the American way? A legacy of Western civilization? Or simply one of the more mystifying of human traits?" Hear, hear—there's a case to made for that, I thought. All you have to do is check out the head in the lounge at around ten or eleven o'clock any given night, ladies or gents. "Then, talk about freaky," Kevin resumed, "just as we passed all this space junk, from nowhere, there was some kind of installation, an actual base. At least one in the making. A pretty good sized geodesic dome was completed, and there were several others being constructed near it. And there were big gun placements, too, in the works. Massive turrets, the size you'd see on a battleship. At the sight of the Breowan cruiser, moon buggies scurried all over the place. People in space suits bounced around on the lunar surface. But what caught my eye, there against the backdrop of earth, on top of the dome, ol' Glory stood erect on a pole. Stiff and frozen like a sheet of plywood." Kevin shook his head a little. The very notion struck me, well, as out of this world.

"Guess Osama won't be able to get them there," I cracked. "Not that it would take that much to convince the American public that he's hiding in a cave on the moon."

"It made me wonder," Kevin replied with a smile. "I always thought the space exploration thing was about, well, space exploration. But I didn't dwell on it because we were about to channel out of the solar system at mega-light speed. Besides, my attention was drawn to the room. A bar arced along the wall to my left, which was crowded and busy, but low key. Maybe, because on my right, on a small platform-stage a quartet were jamming intently in melodic syncopation. The band, I found out, was from some quadrant in the Chara system. You know how Robert always said he wished he'd had six fingers to play the bass. Well these guys all did, and man could they play—whatever kind of instruments they were. The equivalent was some kind of percussion, keyboard, horn, and bass. At least the instruments made those types of sounds." He hesitated, reflecting on that moment. The music played in his head. You could see it in his eyes. Then, he spoke softly. "Listening to that band play made me realize from the get go that music truly is a universal language. The lounge was filled with all sorts of characters. Some stood, others sat at small round tables, or on couches, sofas, or chairs. All were engrossed in the performance at hand." I smiled at the thought. Somewhat envious, but in a nice way. I could have, after all, experienced it for myself if I'd gone out skiing with him. But then I'd have missed out on all the fun here.

"When the music broke, the crowd loosened up. A full-bore party erupted, or so it seemed. Later, I found out it was a conference relating to the interstellar hospitality industry, in which the Breowans are at the forefront. My attention was drawn to the crowd. Strange *alien*-looking types from all over the universe. I'm happy to report that amidst an assortment of enlarged, elongated, and angular craniums; bulbous, exophthalmos, and attenuated eyes; beings tall and short, wide and thin; skin tones smooth and coarse, dark and light and shades between; body's haired and hairless; and hands multi-digited, my new friends were all bipedal humanoids who were chattering away oblivious to my presence. I was right at home. More so because they were quaffing and pounding down drinks similar to what I held in my hand. The Breowan who was escorting me and Sparky led us to the bar. He, or the reproductive gender equivalent, signaled a bartender, a tall, tawny fellow with prehensile-like arms who drew a pint for him from a spout on the bar wall. There had to have been dozens of spouts running along the wall, and all the barkeeps were working them in a seamless, fluid motion. Filling the glasses and unfurling their arms effortlessly, laying drink after drink down on the bar. My Breowan host grabbed his glass, turned and raised it—toasted me I guess—and quaffed it in one gulp. It was the moment of truth for me. I followed in suit. I live to tell you it was a brew. The most heavenly amber ale I ever tasted. A melody erupted in my palate. A gusto, a zest, stimulated and excited the taste buds on my tongue. The brew was frothy, rich, mellifluous, ice cold and flavorful. And it wasn't filling. I had one more. Then another, and one after that, and on and on. The experience was staggering in more ways than one. My new Breowan amigo, his name was Wyrt, matched me glass for glass. Soon enough I relaxed—maybe it was the beer, the band, and the interstellar camaraderie of the lounge. Wyrt and I fell into conversation. We spoke in our own languages. Even though I couldn't utter a word of Breow-anese, I seemed to understand everything he said and vice-versa.

"Wyrt turned out to be a good guy and a great storyteller. He put me at ease right away, told me joke after joke. His stories were funny and he laughed harder at his own jokes than I did. Kind of sounded like an excited bullfrog when he got rolling. He laughed so hard once I thought he was going to heave a lung. And he probably would have except this hot-looking Karpe-zian temptress walked into the lounge. We nearly keeled. Let it be known— the feminine mystique is alive and well throughout the universe. She was tall and lanky, close to seven feet. Conical ridges, short and rounded, protruded across the crest of her forehead. Her skin was teak-hued. Top to bottom, we stared lycanthropic, a vivacious mammalian blond-haired muse in our presence. Clad in a strappy, golden textureless swathe of material, it clung precariously from her overly abundant amplitude to every nook and gland down to her muscular Karpezian thighs. She turned out to be the torch singer for the band. Her name was Vox. Halfway through her first song she noticed me.

Kept eye contact throughout the set. Later, she would say she thought I was a related Karpezian specie because of my pointy headed knit hat, which I still had on. Funny how things work out." Kevin leaned forward and looked over his shoulder, spoke to me in a hushed tone. "We became lovers, carried on a sordid affair for months, maybe years for all I know—the space-time continuum proved a constant source of disorientation for me. She'd never been with an earthling, I, never with a Karpezian. I liked her. It was fun. We tore into each other with a primordial intensity beyond the pale." My ears perked up in anticipation, at the thought of randy alien debauchery. I pressed closer, hanging on each word. "What a great time to be alive!" Kevin sighed. "In the end, it was strictly physical, I guess. She had this ability to clench her vaginal orifice when climaxing. I would strap a board to my ass to brace myself for the grip."

Satisfied, Kevin stoked up his cigar. The embers flared brightly. Smoke twirled in eddies around his head, and drifted down the veranda. I, having nearly slipped off my seat, grasped the arms of the chair and steadied myself. "And?" I gasped.

Kevin shrugged nonchalantly. "What do you think this is—sixth grade? How much more do you want to know?"

"I want it all and I want it now!"

"There's nothing else, really. One day she tired of me. Left me for a Pleiadian, an amorphous being named Omnia. Vox suggested a three-way—talk about gender confused—to ease the transition. I decided to pass. I wasn't mentally tough enough for a *ménage à trois* with a Karpezian goddess and a non-physical hermaphrodite. It was all about the wood. Mine to be precise. And I knew it wasn't going to happen. I knew my limitations, and more importantly, my expectations.

"Besides," Kevin continued, "by then I had started to really get into the ways of the Breowans. Their customs, culture, and commerce. Turns out they're a race of master brewers. They love beer. For eons they've traveled the universe in search of the ultimate beer recipe. The quest is unending. In the process they've collected tens of thousands of samples over the ages. There's vats the size of water towers on their space ships. Kegrunners they call them. That's what picked me up, that's what you saw, and that's why the holding dock smelled like a brewery, because it was. It's part cargo ship, part cruise ship. The kegrunners go from star system to star system on beer runs while transporting holiday and business travelers to and from Breowan. Kind of a spin off, their planet has emerged as a destination point for weary travelers and vacationers from all over the civilized universe. The resorts are... *cosmic!*

Whatever you seek—a bit of bacchanalian revelry, a dash of Wally World, a quaint Irish pub, a tropical oasis, monastic solitude in an Andean-esque villa—they have it all. Because they're a civilization of veritable publicans I say, and are making a fortune doing it. It's a amazing how far you can go in the universe with a little bit of hospitality." That made me grin. That was a keeper. Whether he knew it or not, Kevin had just announced the new motto for the moe.Republic Hotel. "Breowans are a happy-go-lucky people, gently stewed, who don't really understand all this propensity for violence, fear, and rage among the earthlings. Then again, no civilization in the universe does."

"What?" I said, not sure where he was going.

"I'm serious. We're considered savage brutes, easily manipulated, prone to idol worship, self-absorption, and bureaucracy. The first time I became tuned into this notion was over a few pints up in the stardeck with Libatois, the Breowan who captained the kegrunner that picked me up. 'Doing business with your kind is risky,' he told me. 'Reports from the field are not that good. It's too bad, really. Because earth is right off one of the main interstellar trade routes. 'Reports from the field?' I was puzzled. 'What field? What interstellar trade route?'

"Libatois smiled, and when he did, with those droopy eyes, first glance made him look like he'd just walked out of an Amsterdam hash parlor. But, on a higher plane, it was the face of contentment, too, born from infinite wisdom that you and I could only hope to possess in five lifetimes. 'We do have a few people there on your planet, everyone does. Visitors come and go all the time from all over the universe. They may stay for a few days or a few decades, quietly living and observing. We Breowans have a substantial colony who reside along the I-95 corridor of your greater Miami. I have a cousin Bendhir there. He and many Breowans have successfully integrated into the landscape, irrigation, household, and hotel service sectors with relative ease and without question of their nationality or legal status… Only in America!' And Libatois laughed that Breowan croaking laugh, and the other Breowans who were crowding around us listening to their captain speak to me began to croak, too. A cacophony of bullfrogs in heat echoed throughout the stardeck. 'There's hope that, someday, with a little guidance, civility may come to the fore on your planet. There is a matter of trust, also, one of the Three Primes to obtain intergalactic abundance.' The Three Primes I would find out—open trust, open trade, open travel—drive the system of commerce in the civilized universe. 'Unfortunately, you haven't managed the first yet. You don't even trust yourselves. The Intergalactic Council has just to look at the way you treat your own kind, let alone the planet's resources. So for now, all parties agree, it's best that earth's kept from interstellar commerce.'

"I probably could have asked a couple of thousand questions right then and there. But we were entering the Mizarrh System, in crisis mode, coming up on a small planet, Xenofon, home to a race of a near flat-headed humanoids. Libatois had been ordered to evacuate the last of the Breowan observers there. As on earth, they lived incognito, merely reported from the field, and all reports were that they needed to bail in a hurry. Apparently an oligarchy of scientists and technocrats on the Xenofonian landmass of Insatiabilis had developed an electromagnetic refractor pulsar to extract and extort a blissful communion with the lesser developed, resource rich, land masses on Xenofon. The oligarchy saw themselves as benevolent and just, arbitrating the perpetual discord they themselves created on the planet. They controlled the discord through a class of ministers known as Scheferds. The Scheferds contorted the Universal God and divided Him up among the tribes. They preached high values, self-sacrifice, and conformity to the masses and practiced an ethos of outright crime, vengeance, righteousness, avarice, and betrayal. But the largest landmass, Diluvium, was not under the spell of the Insatiabilis and the doctrine of the Scheferds. Socially repressive and somewhat barren, Diluvium was controlled by a junta of anarchists, who knew of no God but the god of power and physics. They also had the largest deposits of lodestone and lodestone extract, which fueled the planet's energy plants. The Diluviumites took great umbrage with the Insatiabilitine horde bent on plundering theirs and the planet's resources unfettered and unregulated. So, they too developed electromagnetic refractor pulsar technology, except by then it was simply known as ERP-Tech. The Insatiabilis and the Diliviums went head to head to produce bigger, better, more menacing ERP-Techs—V 1.1, 2.5, 4.9 6.0, and on and on and on until one version eventually fell into the hands of a radical sect of Scheferds, one of whom actually believed he spoke for God and blasted the pulse from a stall in a market, obliterated himself and the equivalent of five city blocks, and consequently breached the time-space continuum. They, the Xenofons, were about to cast the entire universe into a multi-dimensional vibration of alternating realities. Space would drift through time and time would have no beginning nor end. Imagine living your life spending everyday doing the same thing over and over again without end or accomplishment. We were on the brink of catastrophe. Libatois evacuated the Breowans, and then, on behalf of the Intergalactic Council, he sealed the breach and left the morons to their hubris and doom. Libatois wanted to throw the oligarchy and junta through the breach before it was sealed. But the laws of civility bound him, prevented him from acting in kind. There's a genuine problem, say, when a bunch of wasps in their hive think they're the center of the universe without thinking for one second how big the universe truly is and how insignificantly small they really are. Still, even the smallest wasp can pack a sting before it dies. That's why the Intergalactic Council quietly observes pre-contact systems, not to interfere as much as to monitor and prevent them from irreparable harm or catastrophe to the civilized universe. To contemplate invoking the DOC—the day of open contact—before a planet's obtained a degree of civility usually has socially regressive results for them. But sometimes, as a matter of course, when the alert goes off from the observers somewhere, you have to remove the stinger from the wasp while you can for the betterment of us all.

"That stop was an education for me. Any dolt could see the analogy. A clique of power-hungry, ahistorical parvenus, scrofulous and obsessive, scattered about the planet, wreaking mayhem, confusion, and hatred with competing religious mythos? Fleecing the plebes dry in an orgy of consumption? In a universe of possibilities how could the torch of illumination be so dim? I wondered how many planets were like Xenofon? Like Earth?" Kevin stared at me as though waiting for a response. Like it was possible for me to comprehend the totality of that and all he had said in one breath. Deep down, I think I was still waiting for the punch line. That this story, this grand treatise, was yet, a story.

"I could have gone into a deep philosophical trench," he exhaled as he spoke, "but what saved me was arriving at the wonderful intergalactic oasis of Breowan. Instead, I proceeded to dive head first into some old fashioned hedonistic revelry. After seeing that space-time continuum breach, a slippery, swollen labia, its center a fluorescent, rainbow colored, three-dimensional membrane, on the verge of sucking all matter into infinite paralysis, I decided it was time to live it up a little. Vox and I spent a week or so exploring the inner sanctums of the nether self in the ancient pyramids along the famed Jahabhee Ridge. We were holed up there in a cliff top resort, which was carved precariously out of the mountain. The pyramids, ruins actually, were temples from a long ago Breowan civilization. Time being what it was for me there, where I thought it was but a few days must have been months. Even then, I could have stayed there for a long, long time, but Vox had an extended gig at the Club Phellatrix in the enchanted city of Meisterbrue. She seemed reluctant to leave Jahabhee, though. Later I found out that that's when she had first encountered the amorphous hermaphrodite, Omnia, who was lecturing there by channeling her being through a Bungolian diplomat in the Temple of Enlightenment. That she or he or it was channeling more than enlightenment in that temple was lost on me for some time. Not that it mattered in the overall scheme of things. I had a rendezvous with my old buddy Wyrt. We hooked up for an extended pub crawl through the enchanted city's brew district. It was the most ferocious bender I'd been on in my life. Again, befuddled with time disorientation, I can only imagine what days were nights and nights were days, or weeks or whatever. After this time of spiritual liberation I forced myself to check into the Center for Cultural Asylum on the Breowan moon of Mount Barrington. A place of eternal natural vistas dedicated to seeking inner contemplation. I'm not sure what it was I needed to contemplate other than being 46 million light years from home, a mind-numbing hangover, and the lingering glow of lust lost at the Club Phellatrix, where the being of light had made the final conquest of the Karpezian goddess of love. Life went on, and so did the many adventures I encountered in and around the 47 Ursae Majoris star system, for I took to the stars in Captain Libatois's kegrunner. Worked my way across the universe, until we made the gradual loop back toward the Milky Way, back toward home, me and the pooch." Kevin stopped for a moment—drained the last of his coffee and stoked his cigar. For my part I was absolutely stunned by his story. I don't know how much was real or not, in his grand treatise. It didn't matter for it was brilliant.

"I think back on it all and it blows me away," he said. "They pulled up to the moe.Republic Hotel that fateful Saint Patrick's Day to collect a sample for their inventory—and you thought that those short green men in bowler hats that day were leprechauns. Nope, simply Breowans in disguise. They liked what they sampled, too. You should know that moe.Ale has become quite the interstellar rage, which kind of helped my cause. Me and Sparky happened to be in the right place at the wrong time. They plucked us from the top of the hill so we wouldn't get scorched in the ship's ascension. They took us on board with open arms. It wasn't lost on me that Sparky never barked once out of fear or warning from the time we went on board. Always trust a dog," Kevin nodded assuredly. "I knew I was fortunate. They didn't have to tell me that, until that moment they picked me up, like most earthlings, I was missing out on the whole universal experience. Interstellar travel is not generally shared with our kind, being too dangerous a species by universal standards. Once, there was hope, after we mastered flight, that we were on our way. That perhaps we had evolved enough to see the grand metaphor of how close we really are to each other.

"'But your way of thinking does not change,' Libatois would say to me. 'Only the application for your technology does.' We were channeling at mega-light speed along the interstellar trade route that would take us to earth. They were bringing me and Sparky back. 'There's something about your kind, stuck in a way. When the first primitive gained consciousness on your planet, what you'd call a caveman, and picked up a stick for the very first time, he did not see in his hands fuel to keep him warm, a means to keep back the night; nor did he see its prospect for shelter, for putting a roof over his head. The first thing he did was walk over to his neighbor and crack his head open with it. Only when he discovered its lethal application for himself did it occur to him that there might be a practical application for all. Then he thought—how can I manipulate this discovery to my advantage? How can I use it to control the tribe?' Pausing, Libatois seemed to collect his thoughts, but simply said, 'Nothing has changed...Do you know why?' I shook my head in wonder. 'Because we were there observing, as we and others have through the ages. We've come to call this phenomenon in your species the detrimental constant. One continuous cycle, with each advancement in technology, acted out again and again and again to your own detriment.' The kegrunner materialized on the front side of the moon and Libatois pointed to the lunar surface. Timing *is* everything. The installation there had progressed. Five geodesic domes, interconnected in a pentagon, were nearly completed, with many more gun turrets in place."

"'Interesting,' Libatois mentioned to me.

"'Incredible!'" was all I said, all I could muster at first. "'When I was a kid, I remember watching the drama of man going to the moon and back. A giant leap for mankind it was called.' And my thoughts drifted off. I sensed the boondoggle on the lunar surface was of no threat or consequence to Libatois, the Breowans, or anyone in the civilized universe. What were they planning to do? Set up a tollbooth?

"'Mankind's leap... yes,' Libatois responded, unencumbered by emotion, 'but to your own constant detriment, you've stumbled once again.' Libatois blinked. 'On a lighter note, if you ever get down to Miami," he said cheerfully, 'be sure to stop in and see my cousin Bendhir. He knows all about you.' I smiled at the thought. I would go to Miami. Bendhir had kept me apprised of what was happening here. Through him, anyway, I received word of the happenings in the Lost Kingdom and the moe.Republic. 'For now I bid you well,' Libatois added. 'And remember—an act of civility is the measure of the universe.'"

"Like I said, for whatever reason, they trusted me. I trusted them, too. They left me where they found me, up on the hill. Left me to ponder, and ponder I did. Because the end all of this whole trip, in the grand scheme of it all, I came to know one thing, the kind of thing that everyone should experience. For the first time in my life I felt like I belonged to something bigger than myself—free of guilt, without indoctrination, or being compelled. I saw the big picture and it was beautiful. That was and is a wonderful feeling."

Kevin fell into silence. We both stared at the harbor. He was right. It was a beautiful day.

Today's a beautiful day, too. This missive's cleared my head. Consider it my first act of unrequited civility. My second is taking mother into town. She's frantically working with sister Liza to complete her cookbook for publication. I'm taking her to meet Jackson Grant, who's offered to help. Word on the street is that she's gone as far as finally revealing her secret recipe for whoopee pies! It's funny how forty-five minutes after you eat one your mouth becomes bone dry, you get an uncontrollable craving to eat about a dozen more of the tasty morsels, and confusion and indecision muddles the ability to think clearly in your brain function thought process clearly. I am parched now. Okay?

brother John

From: brother.john@moe.republic.org
To: rob@moe.org
Date: *May Day, May Day, 9:08 p.m.*
Subject: Re: spaced out

Rob—What do you mean Kevin already emailed you with the full scoop? And you and he already decided to go with the new motto? Must I always be the last one to find out anything around here?

Don't answer that... john

Act IX

The End of the Day

The moe.Republic Hotel
in the heart of the Lost Kingdom

Under the mountain,
Beneath the stars,
On the gazebo,
Near the dawn...

Dear Rob,

A big hello and many salutations to you and the boys! Things are winding down here after moe.'s grand performance last week. A raging success. No glitches, no pyrotechnics, no overly seasoned recipes, not a thing to slow the train down. The buzz has never been louder around town. A perfect ending to another enchanting season at the moe.Republic Hotel. People had begun to wonder if their favorite son had gone into exile forever. No, I told the town folk over many a tall tale and frothy ale. You'd be back—moe. would be back. One day they'd return. That the band opened the tour and kicked off the new CD here in the Lost Kingdom, well, it's enough to make a man's cockleberries warm and fuzzy. I hope the rest of the tour goes as well and the new music platinum.

You'll be happy to know that sales of the Red Beard Ale have eclipsed the moe.Ale. Both the Silent Woman Tavern and Goatlips Saloon are ordering it by the pallet load—and that's just for weekends. Tomorrow we sign the contracts with those two big grocery store chains. There's a woman from Madison Avenue here on vacation. Big time suit. She says she can take the brew national. Think about that. Guess we found gold on Popham Island after all.

Speaking of which, Bigwood and Kinghorn have located Agent Kennard. He'd quit the agency the day he'd returned from Popham with the booty. Went down to Costa Rica to live the good life. Kinghorn said they found him by following auctions, the big houses in New York, London, and Paris. "Where the elite meet," Kinghorn told me. "Knew those coins would surface eventually, and we tracked down our man." The Huxley sisters gave them their doubloons for a fee and paid for their expenses. I'm not sure if we'll ever meet old Jimbo, but I understand the negotiations are progressing warmly between him and his great-aunts. Mother mentioned that Edith and Emma are even planning a trip to meet him.

It's all part of the new book Jackson Grant's working on, *Skeletons in the Whale's Jaw*. I told him he might reconsider the title. Every time I hear the word skeleton I think of that bizarre nightmare and get the willies. He laughed. Said he'd thought about the title *Puffins, Pirates, and the Pilgrims of Popham*, but after a few beers the cadence gave him palsy and caused his mouth to wrench up. Besides, he said he owed it to the family to find out everything he could about his grandfather and Porter Gibson Digit and what really happened out on that island.

That reminds me. The statue of Porter Gibson Digit was unveiled today, or should I say yesterday. Porter now stands tall over Market Square. After much debate and contention over the design and dedication, the ceremony went rather well. The committee wanted something to represent Porter as social activist, intellectual, author, and athlete. Things got dicey when the committee recommended incorporating Porter's greatest claim to fame, his invention of the "finger," into the statue. They argued that it was important to visibly recognize his contribution—that abstract act of singular dissent and civil disobedience against a corrupt establishment and controlling authority.

The town council, though they did not dispute the significance of Mr. Digit's contribution to the planet, thought it prudent that the good people of the Lost Kingdom and beyond need not be greeted by such a salute each time they pass through town. I proposed to have him sitting on his bar stool, holding a baseball between his middle finger and thumb in one hand, raising a glass in the other, with that mischievous smile on his face. I received some applause, but no votes. The council overruled the committee and went with the scholar-athlete theme.

Porter stands proudly, larger than life, a baseball cap on his head. He's holding an open book in one hand while leaning against a baseball bat with the other, gazing placidly out on Moose Harbor. It's very nice, well done. The sculptor managed to capture the essence of Porter's famous appendage quite subtly. If you look close enough at the hand that's holding the book up, allow yourself to see it, there's just enough part between the index and ring finger for one to realize your being seriously told to fuck off. Pretty cool.

After the ceremony, we had a nice reception here at the hotel. Everyone was upbeat and telling Porter tales. Everyone but Casey McNugent, who was sitting at the bar bailing the Red Beard Ale like he was trying to drain the vat.

I wondered what was up? It looked like he'd had a rough day up at Farkleber-ry Farm. A thousand kids running around chasing llamas, goats, and wild boars could do that to you. I knew he was bumming of late. He had invested heavily in a natural exhibit for a woodchuck colony, but somehow they'd all escaped. Why so glum? I asked him. Turns out that Rafiki, the plentiful pachyderm, came up impotent. No more buck left in his shot. The veterinarian told him not to worry though. The big fella had been under too much pressure over the past couple of years. The beast needed time to reload, that's all. That and a hot bath, a bottle of brandy, and a fine cigar. My days in animal husbandry were short lived and I make no claims of expertise, but I told Casey that even the best of us need to retool from time to time.

"Just look what Kevin's done," I said to McNugent. "He retooled and went Hollywood." I showed him the postcard we got the other day of the Hollywood Hills. His agent's been peddling his screen treatment around and it looks like he's got a big fish on the line. The postcard read that a major studio's negotiating for the rights. They promised him that there would be no minors in the production of the film and no animals would be abused, which we thought queer, but they *are* professionals. We're all happy and excited for him. Come what, come may, I sense it's only a matter of time before his odyssey makes it to the silver screen.

Well, time to end this missive. I promised the bride I'd be in bed hours ago, but once again Porter Gibson Digit's kept me up till the cock crows. I'm not complaining. It's kind of nice. I see the stars recede. The coming dawn. The new day arriving. The old mountain rising above me out of the shadows. There's a slight breeze in the air. The rush of waves on the shore let me know I'm not dreaming.

Now that I think about it—father always said it would come to this.

And I have to admit, I believe the old man got it right.

For now and always, 'feedin' at the trough,'

brother John

Acknowledgments

This book stems from the old 'feedin' at the trough' column I wrote for the moe.newsletter. I would like to thank my brother Rob for inviting me to write that column, and all the members of moe.—Al Schnier, Chuck Garvey, Vinnie Amico, and Jim Loughlin—for giving me the opportunity. I was always grateful to them for allowing me to write the column, but I am eternally grateful for granting me the privilege of incorporating moe., and the spirit of moe., into this book.

I owe Rob, and my sister-in-law, Becca Childs Derhak, a special thanks. It was their suggestion I write the book. Though at first I wasn't too sure how to transform a dozen or so letters into a novel, they insisted that it would be well received by all the moe. fans and beyond.

When Chuck Garvey offered to do the artwork for the cover I was in. I can't thank Chuck enough for his superb work and the boost it gave to the book and my confidence. And thanks again to Becca, whose impressive design of the cover brought the whole package together.

I owe a great debt to my editor, Joan McCabe, whose brilliant work and guidance truly made this work complete and a much better read. Many thanks to Matthew Altruda and Melissa Rosenberg for helping me with marketing and promoting. To the good people at Back Channel Press, John and Nancy Grossman, many thanks for your assistance and for accommodating me.

Special thanks to Mary Pompeo, Elsa Cook, Ernest Letiziano, Alistair Green, Fergus Garvey, and Patrick Harrington for being there. Thanks to my family—especially my mother, father, and real-life brother Kevin (whose dog is a yellow lab mix named Molly)—for being good sports, and my bride, Wendy, who endured it all, and my boys, Alex and Casey (yes, Mr. Bigwood and Farmer McNugent are named for them). Along the way I've met many people and made many friends, who in their own right, have encouraged me, inspired me, invested in me, and supported me through the entire process. Thank you all.

About the Author

JOHN DERHAK is an historian and writer who spends his time between Maine and Florida. This is his first novel.